"The stakes couldn't be higher in this page-turning crime thriller. And Alex Stockton is the perfect heroine—a courageous and sharp-witted lawyer who is tested not only by the system, but by her own past. *Crosstown Park* is a must read for anyone who's ever been fascinated by real courtroom drama."
—ALAN JACKSON, former L.A. DA, lead prosecutor on the People v Phil Spector case, Partner, Palmer, Lombardi & Donohue, LLP

"This one is a real page turner–and a great debut novel from Melanie Bragg."
—KATHLEEN WELTON, award-winning editor and publisher

"When I picked up *Crosstown Park* I was expecting a leisurely read, but before I knew it I was intensely engaged with the characters, the legal backdrop and the story. I was struck by the fact that such an exciting page turner of a book could also be quietly insightful and express such deep spiritual truth.
I love this book and eagerly await the sequel."
—JUSTINA R. PAGE, award-winning author of *The Circle of Fire*

"*Crosstown Park* kept my attention throughout with an accurate depiction of real life lawyer drama."
—PAT CANTRELL, tax attorney and author of *Tax Procedure for Attorneys*, published by the American Bar Association

"Melanie Bragg has written a page turner. I read this book in a day. *Crosstown Park* will hold your interest on the beach or during a stormy day lying on the couch."
—JOAN BURDA, award-winning author of *Estate Planning for Same Sex Couples*, and *Family Law for Gay, Lesbian, Transgender Couples*, published by the American Bar Association

"*Crosstown Park* is an amazing debut in the legal thriller genre. Melanie Bragg combines a riveting plot with compelling characters!"
—RICHARD G. PASZKIET, Director ABA Entity Book Content Publishing, American Bar Association

"A fast-paced page turner with a spiritual twist. Kept me reading until the wee hours of the morning."
—PAT CHAUDOIR, Attorney

"Melanie delivers a very quick and comfortable read that offers an insider's look at the legal system and local's tour of the back roads and complexities of society. Pages turn as the plot develops and the reader stays ever hungry for what comes next. Gripping. Inspiring. Hopeful. The kind of story that makes you want to slow down, so it won't end. In other words, I found it to be a very easy and enjoyable read. It was fun to delve into the deepest corners of some characters' lives and minds while rolling through the kind of gritty realities that simmer below the surface of society."
—DANE SCHILLER, journalist, *Houston Chronicle*

"As a crime novel aficionado, I am impressed with *Crosstown Park* and its lively cast of characters. The novel weaves "Houstonian" lifestyles into its entertaining and suspenseful storyline. As an attorney for Child Welfare Services in Philadelphia for over 15 years, I can affirm that the legal analysis is straightforward and accurate. Most importantly, in this legal thriller, Melanie Bragg eloquently intertwines romance and drama with basic values to which we can all relate. A solid debut....an author worth watching....a great read...."
RITA BORZILLO SPARGO, Lawyer and Professor

"Compelling! Moved at a fast pace. All the excitement of a trial. Romance!"
—PATRICK MARES

"*Crosstown Park* is brilliantly executed. Through the main character, Alex Stockton, Melanie took the reader's hand and walked us through the whole story. It allowed the reader to experience the frustrations, the anger, the betrayal, the regrets, the expectations, and the highs and lows of each of the characters. I started it on Friday night, picked it up Saturday morning and did not stop reading until I finished it late Saturday evening."

—LEE VILLARREAL

Crosstown Park is incredibly well written and was engaging from the start. Because it's a great story, the book is a "page turner". When I finished, I was sorry to be through because the characters had come to life! I identified very closely with the main character on many levels and rooted for her all the way. The story's spiritual message left me feeling warm and happy. I recommend this book very highly.

—CYNTHIA SHARP, Esquire, author of *The Lawyers' Guide to Attaining Financial Security*

"Bragg hit a home run on *Crosstown Park*. I loved the fast-paced story line that kept me turning the pages to the end to see what happened next. The comfortable but descriptive conversations of characters and the familiar Houston landmarks had me hooked. The touching ending had me grabbing a tissue to wipe away my tears. I hope we hear more from these characters.!"

—ANNE RICHARDSON, Carlisle Collection

Crosstown Park is well written, entertaining, and kept my interest throughout. The characters are well defined and the plot, predicated on the work of small charities and their struggles against many odds, maintained the suspense of a good whodunit. Bragg writes with panache and creates great scenes and action. Her sense of mystery keeps the reader anxiously following the story and the relationships between the main characters, intriguing as they are. I fully recommend this book as an addition to anyone's "must read" list.

—CAPT. LL VEITCH, ATP, ATR

Crosstown Park
by Melanie Bragg

© Copyright 2013 by Melanie Bragg

ISBN 9781938467622

All rights reserved. No part of this publication may be reproduced, stored in a
retrieval system, or transmitted in any form or by any means – electronic,
mechanical, photocopy, recording, or any other – except for brief quotations in printed
reviews, without the prior written permission of the author.

This is a work of fiction. All the characters in this book are fictitious,
and any resemblance to actual persons, living or dead, is purely coincidental.
The names, incidents, dialogue, and opinions expressed are products of the
author's imagination and are not to be construed as real.

Published by

köehlerbooks™
an imprint of Morgan James Publishing

5 Penn Plaza, 23rd floor
c/o Morgan James Publishing
New York, NY 10001
212-574-7939
www.koehlerbooks.com

Publisher
John Köehler

Executive Editor
Joe Coccaro

Cover design by Dalitopia Media

Habitat for Humanity®
Peninsula and
Greater Williamsburg
Building Partner

In an effort to support local communities, raise awareness and
funds, Morgan James Publishing donates a percentage of all
book sales for the life of each book to Habitat for Humanity
Peninsula and Greater Williamsburg.
Get involved today, visit www.MorganJamesBuilds.com

This book is dedicated to my three angels.

To my mother, Lee Mayfield, who, with her gift of writing and creative soul, encouraged me to follow my passions.

To Rita Gallagher, author and co-founder of Romance Writers of America, who taught me the craft of writing.

And to Marge Caldwell, author and teacher, who inspired me to persist in faith and to never, ever give up.

CROSS TOWN PARK

9/29/13

Dearest Jan, To one of my dear friend
Dot's special friends — if she loves
you so much I know I would!
Hope to meet you some day! Hope this
book blesses you immensely! Enjoy!
Melanie

MELANIE BRAGG

NEW YORK
VIRGINIA

CHAPTER 1

Only two things scared Alexandra Stockton: turbulence and falling in love.

With her usual sense of dread, she boarded the plane from New York's La Guardia Airport to Houston and took her window seat near the back of the plane. As the other passengers boarded, she dashed out a few quick e-mails on her iPhone before she hit the off button. She needed the next three hours to think.

An African-American man with gray hair and thick glasses squeezed himself into the middle seat next to her. He leaned down and pulled a book out of his briefcase—a Bible.

Alex gave him a polite smile and turned to gaze out the window. Just as the plane pushed back she saw a white bird outside that vanished as quickly as it appeared. She closed her eyes and tried to forget TV reports of thunderstorms and rainfall. Flights weren't delayed, she thought, so how bad could it be? The plane climbed through the stormy clouds. Alex's hands tightened on the seat arms and she took a deep breath, fighting the rising panic that always came when she flew. No matter how calm the flight attendants were, Alex felt a little terrorized. The pilot's voice was soft on the overhead speakers when he told them to buckle up, that it would be a bumpy flight. She listened carefully for any signs of strain in his voice. Hearing none, she told herself that there was nothing to fear and plugged in her earphones. Music would soothe her.

Alex's thoughts turned to the weeklong seminar she attended in New York. A team of Broadway actors taught lawyers dramatic techniques they could use in trials. She especially liked learning new ways to bond with juries. The drama coach had them take off their shoes and dance around like crazy people, which had been easy for Alex but much harder for other members of her class. Some of them would still be three sheets to the wind after heavy drinking at a bar last night. Alex barely got out of there herself after one. But as much fun as it was, parts of the seminar were unsettling. It was too close for comfort. She had to reveal secrets, disclosures that left her feeling vulnerable.

The flight crew came by with the drink cart. The man next to her ordered a ginger ale. Alex noted his distinctive Southern drawl. He sounded like a man comfortable in his own skin.

"I'll have one too," she told the flight attendant.

Just as the drinks were delivered, the plane lurched again. The cart rolled with the servers holding it tight.

Alex gave the man next to her a look of abject fear. "White-knuckle flyer," she said through clenched teeth.

"Now, now," he said, patting her hand that gripped the armrest between them. "It's just turbulence. You don't strike me as someone who scares too easily."

Alex couldn't help but smile. It was true. There were few times she would admit to being afraid. "Alex Stockton. Houston home?"

He nodded. "You?"

"Yes. I'm coming back from a weeklong trial seminar."

He gave a wide grin. "You don't look like a lawyer."

"I hear that a lot." With her leggings, boots that made her

over six feet tall, and an oversized sweater, he was probably right.

"I'm Reverend C.O. Morse," he said. "I'm on my way back from a pastors' conference."

Alex thought about plugging her earphones back in, but the conversation distracted her from the bumpy ride. Something about the man's calm demeanor drew Alex to him.

"I haven't had call to need a lawyer 'til just a few days ago," he continued.

"Why do you need a lawyer?" she asked.

The pastor's Old Spice cologne smelled nice, further relaxing Alex as she listened to Reverend Morse's story. She learned that less than a year ago, he and members of his congregation bought some abandoned crack houses in Houston's crime-ridden and impoverished Fifth Ward, renovated them and opened Shepherd's Cottages, a foster home for neglected, abused and abandoned children. In her legal practice and *pro bono* work, Alex represented children. She was captivated by the Reverend's insight into problems she grappled with daily at the courthouse.

The Reverend explained how Jose Gonzales, one of his house parents responsible for caring for the children, was accused of molesting Chris Jackson, a teenage boy living at the home.

"Chris's uncle, Voodoo, who has always been like a son to me, got the boy to tell those lies on Jose about what happened in Crosstown Park," he said, then grew quiet. "Voodoo is a drug dealer and he's mad that we took his base of operations and slowed down his drug trade. We are slowly turning the community around and he feels threatened."

He leaned over and pulled a small photo album out of the computer case at his feet.

Alex looked on while the Reverend turned the pages and showed her Shepherd's Cottages. The buildings were enclosed by a tall barbed wire fence. Inside were small homes that looked freshly painted. The Reverend stood outside the modest home, next to a heavyset woman and several other people. They all looked happy. A young Hispanic man in a T-shirt and jeans stood by the Reverend with a big smile and a group of small children around him. They also grinned from ear to ear.

"That's Jose," the Reverend said, pointing to the young man.

The photo made Alex think about Tony, a security guard at a foster home where Alex once lived as a child. Tony had been accused of raping Elaine, the bipolar girl who had a reputation for thinking everyone was after her. Alex knew Tony was innocent, but she feared no one would believe her. So she said nothing. Alex felt a dull thump in the base of her stomach from the memory.

"Another ginger ale, please," she asked the attendant. Those thoughts were long since in her past and it was best to keep them there.

"Reverend, how do you know Jose is innocent?"

The Reverend pulled his glasses down on his nose and his deep dark eyes looked directly into hers. "I just know."

The rhythm of his voice and his conviction stuck a cord. Alex knew that Tony was innocent then too, but was too young to help him prove it.

"OK, let me think about this," Alex said. "For some reason, I have a feeling you are right."

"Why don't you come over to services tomorrow and I can introduce you around and you can see for yourself?" he asked.

What am I getting myself into?

"Good idea," she heard herself say. "I would like to see you preach." It would be her first time at a black church.

"By the way, Jose's arraignment is Monday."

"Don't worry, Reverend Morse." Alex gave him a pat on his arm. "You've helped me on this flight. We'll get to the bottom of it."

★

Now, two days later, sitting in the crowded criminal courtroom at Jose's arraignment, Alex wondered about her impulsive decision to take the case.

"Aggravated assault. The charge is serious." Judge Dyan Villareal's voice boomed. "Bail denied. Trial is set for December 18, ten a.m."

Alex Stockton didn't flinch.

Marilyn Rivera, the young number two assistant district attorney, gave a smug smile.

The arraignment was over. Round one for the prosecution.

Alex stuffed her file into her briefcase and stood to leave. The ruling was a setback, but it bolstered her determination to vindicate her new client, Jose Gonzales. She had six weeks to discover the truth about what happened in Crosstown Park between Jose and his accuser, Chris Jackson.

I need a witness. And fast.

As the clerk called the next case, the bailiff led Jose, handcuffed and shackled, from the courtroom.

"I'll be over to the jail in a little while," she called to him.

The forlorn glance he shot Alex tugged at the trial lawyer's heart. Today, in the dimly lit courtroom, she questioned her acceptance of the Reverend's story. She realized how little she knew about him and her new client. Swallowing self-doubt like castor oil, Alex passed a group of lawyers on her way out of the courtroom.

"Dang, Alex, you keep gettin' prettier while I'm losing my hair," Mike Turlington called out.

"What brings you to this side of the street?" attorney Bill Haley asked.

"I'm defending good against evil, what else?" she said with a grin.

Her colleagues' comments reminded Alex of her three-year absence from the criminal courthouse. She missed the camaraderie between the lawyers and court staff. Although close in proximity, the civil and criminal courthouses were separate worlds. Few lawyers successfully worked both sides of the street.

"I hear you're going for a judgeship this term," Chris Gilman said. "I'm all for it. Just don't wait until December 31st to file your petition," he warned.

"Thanks for the vote of confidence," she said as she headed for the door. Alex turned back and gave them a friendly smile. "And I'm not on the bench yet either, guys, so no need to brown-nose me."

Their comments made Alex think. After a two-year clerkship with a federal judge, Alex went into practice on her own. Her long-term goal was the judiciary, but in the meantime she busied herself with an active case docket, *pro bono* work, bar association activities, and work for the reigning political party. Now, after ten years, she had her sights set on a newly created juvenile court judgeship. Her goal was to get the governor to appoint her before the election.

Heading toward the elevator, she caught the scorching stare of a well-dressed, handsome black man.

The look in his eyes caught Alex off guard. They were filled with hate.

He was at Jose's arraignment. I wonder why ...

Alex drove to her office, a nearby small building across from Memorial Park, Houston's favorite jogging trail. She took the elevator to the top floor and stepped in the modern reception area. Alex had spent time and money creating an office she enjoyed because, like most lawyers, she worked long hours. Her office was an extension of her home, comfortable and organized.

Her longtime assistant, Ruth Stiles, greeted her with a wry smile and a quizzical look.

"Where were you this morning? Your calendar was clear."

"Arraignment on a new case," Alex answered without making eye contact as she nonchalantly thumbed through a stack of mail. "Picked it up this weekend."

"Criminal case?"

Alex nodded. "Aggravated sexual abuse," she said, heading

quickly down the hall toward the kitchen.

"Now wait a minute," Ruth called, following right on her heels. "You need to tell me about this."

In the cozy kitchen, decorated in mauve and orange hues, Alex took a Dr. Pepper and some saltines from the fridge. She sat down at the table in the middle of the room and told Ruth about Jose's case.

"The accuser is Chris Jackson, a teenage foster child. He alleges that our client molested him in the park across the street from Shepherd's Cottages, his foster home. But the Reverend doesn't believe Chris."

Ruth shook her head. "Something's not right. Why would a kid lie?"

"I'm not sure yet," Alex said with a shrug. "The Reverend thinks Chris's drug dealer uncle, Voodoo, is mad because he lost his crack houses when the Reverend turned them into the foster home. Says Voodoo is so mad he won't give up until Shepherd's Cottages is closed."

"Sounds like a ghetto turf war. But Alex, you're out of criminal law. Why help this preacher? You haven't been to church in years."

"I went Sunday," Alex said with a devilish grin.

Ruth grabbed the cabinet as if to steady herself.

"I know," Alex sighed, staring at the tall pine trees beyond the window. "Saturday's flight was strange. Just as the plane pulled back from the gate, a white bird fluttered outside my window and something weird came over me. Then I struck up a conversation with the Reverend. Before I knew it, I offered to take Jose's case."

"What did you charge?"

Alex didn't answer.

Ruth's eyes widened. "Not *pro bono*! We just finished that snarly guardianship for Judge Ross. I want to close out this year with creamy cash cows, like the Crane case."

Alex recalled the Reverend's startled look when she told him not to worry about money. "I'm not sure why, but my gut tells me to help him," she said.

"What about the judicial appointment? Juvenile judges work with Children's Protective Services to *protect* kids. Defending a perpetrator might not go over well for you. Have you thought about that?"

"It crossed my mind," Alex admitted, tucking a strand of long blond hair behind her ear.

Truth is, at the courthouse after the hearing, the realization that she may be in over her head with Jose's case had seized her entire body. Now her stomach felt like a toxic chemical plant gone haywire. She hoped the soda and crackers would help.

The phone rang. Ruth answered in the kitchen and put the caller on hold.

"Mike Delany," she said.

Alex caught her breath and headed down the hall to her office.

Mike Delany was the governor's chief of staff. She and Mike were longtime friends and met when he was an Austin lobbyist and she served on a young lawyer board. Mike insisted Alex was a natural politician. No decision of significance was made in the governor's office without Mike's input. He was a powerful ally.

Alex picked up the phone. "Hi, Mike. What's up?"

"Congratulations! You made the governor's short list for the appointment to the new juvenile bench."

She was one of two, maybe three candidates in the running. Now she just had to ensure she made it to the top of the list. If the governor appointed her to the bench in January, she'd have nearly a year under her belt before next November's election. Alex knew incumbents were hard to beat.

"When will he decide?"

"Before Christmas."

Alex swallowed hard.

Right about the time Jose's case goes to trial.

"When can I talk to him?"

"Tonight. There is a fund-raiser at the River Oaks Country Club. Be there at seven."

Alex was so excited she could barely put the phone back into the cradle. Her years of hard work on cases and networking had finally provided the opportunity of a lifetime. She thought about Jose's case. Maybe the D.A. would offer him a good plea bargain, like deferred adjudication. If he successfully lived out probation, he'd have no conviction. That was probably wishful thinking. Prosecutors go for the jugular in aggravated sexual abuse cases. So, if Jose was really innocent, she couldn't play the "bleed 'em and plead 'em" game for her own selfish reasons. Court-appointed lawyers were notorious for copping a plea as a way to move the Court's docket. That kept judges happy. The thought of a young court-appointed criminal lawyer counseling Jose through the bars of the crowded holdover cell didn't sit well with her. She didn't know Jose enough to care that much yet, but something about the Reverend's commitment to him had instilled in her a belief that justice was at stake.

Alex had to wonder if Reverend Morse was just too trusting. Her deeper senses said no. As far as she could tell, there was no graceful way out of Jose's case.

Leaning back in her chair, she propped her feet on her desk and visualized how incredible it would feel to be with family, friends, and scores of colleagues as she was being sworn in as presiding judge of the new juvenile court.

CHAPTER 2

Later that afternoon, Alex walked into the new state-of-the-art county jail. The sight of criminals eating and sleeping better than millions of needy children struck a deep chord. She told herself that politicians should allocate more tax dollars on education and family planning than they did on jails.

After an extensive security check, she sat in a sparkly chrome attorney-client cubicle, staring through a mesh grill. Like the new jail, memories of her days as a court-appointed criminal lawyer were stark. Massaging a knot in her neck with her hand, she pondered how best to approach her new client.

A guard appeared and shoved Jose inside. "Ten minutes 'til dinner," he growled, then slammed the door behind him.

Alex glanced at her watch, leaned forward, and looked intently at Jose in his orange jumpsuit. Small, well-built, with smooth olive skin, his jet-black hair and faint mustache offset intense dark eyes. She pictured Jose on the stand and wondered whether jurors would like him.

"Sorry we weren't able to talk much before the hearing," she began.

"It's OK. The Reverend, he trusts you." He gave a half-hearted smile. "Do I have to stay in here until trial?"

"I'm afraid so," she answered. "But we have a quick trial setting."

Alex understood her words didn't console her client. Six weeks was a long time to spend behind bars. "The police report is sketchy. Tell me about Cottage Five."

Jose swallowed hard. "It's where the older boys live. Chris Jackson rooms with Jaime Soliz. They's troublemakers."

"What do you mean?"

"Don't follow rules. They smoke, skip school, ignore curfew. They used to sneak out at night until we put bars on their windows."

"Tell me what happened that night."

"Chris came home late from school and wanted to go trick-or-treating with the other kids, but he was grounded. When I told him to do his homework, he ran out of the house. I followed him into the park across the street."

"Crosstown Park?"

Jose nodded. "The park is off-limits to our kids."

"Why?"

"Reverend's rules. Voodoo operates there now that Shepherd's Cottages is up and running. There's crime, drugs, hookers—"

"Where was Chris headed?"

Jose shrugged. "Maybe to the corner where his uncle's thugs sell drugs."

"What happened when you caught up with him?"

"I came up from behind and grabbed his jacket collar. He whipped around and pulled a knife on me." Jose took a deep breath. "When I saw his face, I knew he was high. I can't forget his eyes." Jose drew in a deep breath. "Snake eyes."

Alex noticed bright blue veins on Jose's tightly clenched hands.

"Drugs are all over the Fifth Ward," Jose continued.

Questions flooded Alex's mind and there was little time left. "Tell me about Chris's knife wound."

"He cut himself on the neck, just deep enough to draw blood. I let go. He ran off, cussing and yelling."

"Did anyone see?"

Jose was silent.

"It's important," Alex urged. "Were there witnesses?"

"There are eyes all over the park, but no one tells." Jose wrung his hands. "And CPS, well, they don't want to know the truth."

Alex knew he was right, but she knew that proving it would be next to impossible. "What happened then?"

"I ran back home. Then, a cop car pulled up. The CPS social worker was right behind it."

"Camilla Roe?"

Jose nodded.

Alex frowned. This morning, on the police report, she'd seen the name of one of the most difficult CPS social workers she had ever worked with. She was a woman with an attitude. And an agenda.

"Chris was in the backseat of the police car. He pointed at me," Jose continued. "Miss Roe put him in her car and they drove off. They handcuffed me and brought me here."

"Tell me about Voodoo."

Jose shook his head and looked up at the ceiling. "The boy worships him. He'll do anything Voodoo asks."

Alex put the top back on her pen and slid her legal pad into her briefcase. "I believe you, Jose. But I have to be honest. The maximum sentence is life in prison. Chris says you forced him, at knifepoint, to have oral sex in the park. He says you threatened to kill him. When he tried to escape, you stabbed him."

"It's not true. I swear it," Jose said, staring straight at Alex.

When the guard entered, Jose rose and scuttled toward the

door, his shackles clanging against his pants leg.

Alex stood. "One more question, Jose. Have you ever been in trouble with the law?"

When Jose turned back, his eyes met hers. Before the heavy steel door closed behind him, he answered, "Statutory rape. Two years ago."

★

Driving home, Alex gripped the steering wheel. Statutory rape? Did the Reverend forget to mention it or did he not know? Regulations governing foster homes required Shepherd's Cottages to run background checks on all potential employees. Surely the Reverend followed the law. If he didn't, she would withdraw from Jose's case. She had to get to the bottom of it, and quick. The Reverend said the next board meeting was Wednesday evening. She would show up, but for now Alex needed to focus on tonight and her meeting with the governor.

She entered her three-story townhome from the garage and was greeted by Siva, her trusty Labrador. She poured a glass of Chardonnay and fed the dog before going upstairs to her master bathroom. She pulled her iPhone from her purse and stuck it in a player and set it to shuffle. Then she leaned over the marble tub and turned on the hot water, doused it with foaming essential oils, then lit the scented candles on the ledge. Tossing her watch and jewelry into a crystal bowl, she peeled off her black gabardine pantsuit before she stepped into her oversized Jacuzzi tub. She sank back onto a comfortable pillow and took a deep breath.

While she relaxed, she saw the beautiful white crystal and a pink quartz on the tub's ledge and held one in each hand. Her best friend, Candy, owned a metaphysical shop and told her rocks vibrated positive energy. The white crystal would balance her masculine and feminine sides; the pink quartz would calm her nerves. Instead of celebrating today's exciting political news, she agonized over her new case. Managing her time would be a challenge since she needed to bill enough to keep the office running while she worked on the case. The judgeship was important. Somehow it would all work out. It always did.

Alex slipped into a black cocktail dress, pulled her hair up and fastened it with a barrette, and donned her favorite diamond earrings. A glance at her watch told her to leave now or be late for the reception.

On the way, she picked up her on-again/off-again lover, Assistant District Attorney Bryce Armstrong. He was handsome and ambitious, a dynamic combination. Half an hour later, Alex entered the elegant ballroom of the River Oaks Country Club. Bryce immediately spotted an old college buddy, now a city councilman, and the two men walked ahead of her, deep in conversation.

As she approached the receiving line, Alex smiled. Bryce was the perfect political function escort. They arrived together, pursued individual business and political interests, then enjoyed each other afterward.

At the ballroom entrance, honored guests formed a receiving line. Alex entered the grand room, filled with smartly dressed city dignitaries, judges, and lawyers, all gathered to raise money for Governor Paul Hastings's second-term election bid. Amid imposing columns, ornate crystal chandeliers, and lush draperies, lines were drawn and deals were cut. Fragrant rose centerpieces adorned round tables but didn't overpower the distinct aroma of old money.

Alex headed toward the bar and a short, balding man with a dark mustache and oversized smudged glasses sidled up to her.

"Mike!" Alex planted a big kiss on his cheek. She noted his crooked tie and unpressed suit. Even now as the governor's chief of staff, Mike Delany would never change.

"Alex! You look great! Excited?"

"You know I am. I want that appointment. Bad."

"That's my girl. No guts, no glory." Tipping his glass of Scotch her way, he said, "Here comes your chance to tell the old man himself."

Alex turned and saw Governor Paul Hastings approach. Tan and fit, with penetrating hazel eyes, he exuded power—an appealing aphrodisiac.

"Governor, you remember Alexandra Stockton," Mike said.

"Why sure. I couldn't forget your favorite rising star," he said. His eyes devoured her. "You look ravishing."

Alex grew flushed in his presence. She gave a demure smile.

"Looks like you need a drink, Alex. And you need a fresh one, Governor," Mike said. "I'll be right back."

With his gaze fastened somewhere below her chin, Governor Hastings took Alex's elbow and led her to a nearby secluded table. "Mike said you wanted to talk."

Once seated, Alex looked at the powerful man beside her. "I'm your choice for the new juvenile court bench, Governor," she stated.

"I like your confidence," he said with a boyish grin. "For a young lawyer, you've already accomplished a lot. Mike sings your praises and I trust his judgment. Unfortunately, I have other political interests to consider."

Alex lowered her eyes. "If there's anything I can do to make your decision easier ...," she began.

"Don't say that," he said with a chuckle. "You never know what an old man like me might want."

"I'm speaking politically, Governor." Alex knew his reputation as a ladies' man and in this room, right now, she didn't care whether her legal abilities or his predilection toward tall, shapely blondes persuaded him to choose her. "I hear next term you plan to overhaul the Department of Protective and Family Services."

His expression grew serious. "Nothing short of an atom bomb will change any dammed bureaucracy, especially one entrenched in its own power like CPS. But I think the public shares my view that, in some areas, the agency has gone too far. Parents should have the right to discipline their children. Taxpayers are tired of paying millions of dollars for inefficient programs that don't work."

"I worry about the thirty-five thousand children stuck in the foster care system," Alex said, pushing away childhood memories. "I shudder to think of how they will parent." She caught herself wringing her hands and stopped, clasping them tightly in her lap.

"The agency needs to refocus on education and family reunification," the governor said with a gentle elbow in her side.

"You're right. The system needs change. I want to help," Alex said. She couldn't help but think of the children at Shepherd's Cottages.

The governor had a twinkle in his eye when he took her hand and squeezed it. "Don't worry, Alex, you are on my short list."

When Mike sauntered up and handed them both a fresh Scotch, several people crowded around the governor, vying for his attention. As quick as he appeared, he was gone.

"Did he tell you?" Mike asked with a quizzical grin.

"Yes!" Alex answered. Her excitement was irrepressible. She grabbed Delany and gave him a big hug.

"I told you the time was right," Mike said. "Glad you listened?"

Alex nodded. "You won't regret helping me."

He glanced over his shoulder at his surrounded charge. "I need to keep tabs on him. I'll get the three of us together again soon."

Watching him leave, Alex was grateful for his friendship. She surveyed the room for Bryce and spied him carrying three drinks between both hands, making a beeline toward two attractive females, one a federal judge. Watching him, Alex wasn't jealous. She appreciated the fact that Bryce had everything most girls wanted: a brilliant career; wealthy family; good looks. None of that mattered since she'd vowed to herself no man would derail her career.

Keeping her conversation with the governor to herself, Alex mingled with lawyers and judges for over an hour before she caught Bryce's eye. She tilted her head and arched an eyebrow toward the entrance, then ducked into the ladies' lounge.

While Alex stood at the sink and washed her hands, she thought about how quickly her life would change if appointed. Once everyone knew who was on the governor's "short list" and until the appointment was announced, her life would be a fishbowl. Her choice of cases and clients would have to be carefully analyzed. She thought of Jose. The governor planned to propose sweeping foster care reforms. His agenda needed popular support and his judicial appointee should promote his interests. If she exposed flaws in the current system during Jose's trial, a solid victory would increase her chances of the appointment. Win-win deals were her specialty; somehow she would turn the situation to her advantage.

While she applied lipstick, a friendly judge entered. "Any truth to the rumor you're running for the new juvenile bench? Hal Winslow is already campaigning hard."

Before she could reply, a woman already in a stall jumped into the conversation. "I heard the governor will appoint him."

The two women must have seen her with the governor. She knew better than to take their bait. Politics was a nasty business, not for the weak or fainthearted. "I trust the governor's good taste. He'll appoint the best man, *or woman*, for the job. Ladies, in the meantime, I have a handsome man to attend to," she said as she ducked out the door.

Alex found Bryce in the foyer.

"Let's go," he said.

She took his arm and they walked toward the exit. "Productive evening?"

He grinned. "You bet. Lined up a golf game Sunday with a

couple of the governor's biggest contributors. I'll persuade them to share their generosity with me next election." Like his father before him, Bryce planned to become Harris County District Attorney.

Alex gave him an admiring gaze. Bryce's race was more than two years off, but he had already begun laying the groundwork for his campaign.

Alex and Bryce had met a few months earlier at a University of Texas alumni party. Before the night ended, they had generated enough electricity to light up downtown Houston. Despite common interests in law and politics, both agreed that building their careers took priority over a full-time relationship.

The valet pulled up with her Mercedes and Alex let Bryce take the wheel.

"Did the neckline on your little black dress give the old geezers a heart attack?" he asked.

"I hope so," she murmured. "You look handsome in Armani, darlin'. 'Til now, I didn't realize how much I missed you this evening."

His right hand stroked her hair and neck. At the first red light, he gave her a passionate kiss. "I've waited for that all night," he said, then pulled her closer.

Gently, she pulled away. "We're almost there. I know it'll be hard, but—"

"You're right about that," he interrupted. "I can't wait to get you home."

The rest of the way, Bryce discussed his most recent capital punishment verdict and plotted his political future aloud. "This death sentence will seal my status as top prosecutor in the office," he said with a proud grin. "Capital cases are great campaign copy."

"As usual, you're right on target," Alex said. She didn't tell Bryce about making the governor's short list. Whether or not there was a silent rivalry between them, Alex knew Bryce would be envious if she beat him to political office.

When they passed the security gate and entered her townhome complex, Alex placed a hand on his arm. "I need to check my mail. Drop me off here and I'll meet you at the house in a minute."

"I'll open the Dom."

The taillights quickly disappeared toward the back of the property and Alex opened her mailbox.

CHAPTER 3

Each week Alex received a letter from Lila Henderson, her maternal grandmother who lived in West Texas. Born to a teenage mother with no means of support, Alex had quickly been adopted by a young couple. Soon thereafter, her adoptive parents divorced and when her adoptive mother could not take care of her, she gave Alex back to the agency. Alex remained in foster care from age eight until high school graduation. Determined and always at the top of her class, she won a college scholarship and never looked back until she was twenty-five.

Alex traced her roots and found her maternal grandmother, Lila, her only lifeline to family. They were similar in both appearance and personality and felt like they had known each other all their lives. They vowed to make up for lost time. Now in her seventies, the woman's heart was weakening and Alex was anxious to learn results of her recent medical tests.

She thumbed through a stack of mail and found the letter. Opening and scanning it long enough to be assured of Lila's good health, Alex headed home with a mischievous grin on her face. Tonight was her celebration. Champagne, along with fresh berries and whipped cream, would be a great way to start dessert.

Car headlights blinded her as she turned onto the path to her townhome. Tires screeched around the corner as the car sped toward the exit. Something did not feel right. She had seen that car before.

Was it the same one I saw outside the Reverend's church on Sunday?

She quickened her pace.

Close to home, Alex heard Siva barking from the outside patio, where she stayed when Alex was gone. Entering the front door, she walked through the living room to the back sliding glass door where she saw Siva jump wildly against the door to the garage. Alex's heart rate quickened as an eerie foreboding descended. Bryce should be inside the house, sipping champagne by now.

She crossed the patio and entered the garage. The overhead light was on and her car, engine running, was halfway inside. Bryce was nowhere in sight. Then she heard a loud moan. She ran around the car to look.

On the cold concrete, Bryce lay crumpled in a ball, blood pooling beside his head.

Alex's heart raced. "Bryce! What happened?!" she screamed as she knelt, grabbed his arm and turned him toward her. His face was covered in blood, his lips and eyelids were already puffy and he was unconscious.

Alex reached into his pocket, grabbed his cell phone, then dialed 911. Luckily, the fire station was right around the corner. Alex knew it wouldn't be long before they arrived, but the few minutes she waited felt like hours.

Alex held Bryce. It was frightening to see such a strong man so vulnerable. He might be in a coma, or have a debilitating head injury. Watching his blood pool, she hoped he would make it to the hospital alive.

If only she could talk to him, find out what happened, but that would have to wait. Then she remembered the dark car that, minutes before, sped around the corner. Whoever attacked Bryce must have been inside.

The cops arrived first. Paramedics were close behind. They checked Bryce's vital signs, placed him on a stretcher, then motioned Alex to follow.

Distraught, Alex drove to the hospital. The incident sobered her up and any trace of alcohol from the party was gone. She wondered how Bryce's attackers got by the usually tight security. She didn't see how, unless they followed another car in while the night guard was on rounds.

She ruled out a random burglary-in-progress. The perpetrators did not enter her townhome. She had to consider that Bryce might have been the target. He was a formidable prosecutor and known to be ruthless toward defendants. He surely had enemies, but in his case, they usually ended up on death row. Besides, why attack him at *her* home rather than *his*?

At St. Luke's Hospital, she stood outside the glass window of the treatment room quietly watching busy ER doctors work on Bryce.

After a few minutes, the doctor stepped out. "His nose is broken; the cut on his cheek needs stitches; he could have internal bleeding, skull or rib fractures," he told Alex. "We'll keep him here a couple of days just to make sure. You can see him now."

Alex stepped inside and went to a now semiconscious Bryce. "Thank God you are alright," Alex put her hand over his hand.

He pulled his hand away. "They were looking for you," he sputtered through swollen, bloody lips.

Alex's eyes widened. "Who?"

"They said to tell you to mind your own business," he said.

Bryce coughed and his face wrenched with pain. "This is about your new case, isn't it?"

"New case?"

"Come on, Alex. Your first criminal case in three years and you think I wouldn't know?"

Alex was busted.

"What kind of mess have you gotten into?"

This was no time to explain. "You need to rest."

"Call my father."

A pretty, doe-eyed nurse entered the room. "I have to take him to radiology," she announced and wheeled Bryce out of the room.

"Get off the case," he said through gritted teeth.

Nerves rattled, Alex ducked into the nearby restroom where the strong smell of cleaning fluid made her retch. Courthouse gossip spreads like wildfire. The minute she left Judge Villareal's courtroom in the morning, Bryce must have gotten word. She wiped her brow with a paper towel and assessed herself in the mirror: What had been an artful makeup job was now raccoon eyes, her couture cocktail dress looked like a wrinkled hand-me-down, and her black hose had a fresh run down one leg.

She walked back into the waiting room where no one seemed to notice and poured a cup of stale coffee, then called Bryce's father on her cell phone.

While Alex waited, she watched worried mothers holding sick babies, fathers consoling tired children, and a lost-looking elderly man sitting in a corner. One after another, ambulances arrived with car accident victims; an injured man suffering stab wounds from a barroom brawl. Alex tried to focus on her surroundings, but couldn't keep her mind off the vicious attack on Bryce and the connection to her new case—and the possibility that the attackers were after her.

Her thoughts turned to Jose's arraignment hearing earlier and she relived every moment. It seemed like a lifetime ago. She remembered the scorching stare of the well-dressed black man by the elevator. In the sterile hospital, it occurred to her he might have something to do with Jose's case. He could be Bryce's attacker.

Alex thought about Bryce. He had a right to be angry; he was hurt. She wondered how unforgiving he could be, especially if the deep gash on his cheek left a scar. He and his father were notorious for their tempers. If she didn't succumb to his demand to withdraw from the Jose Gonzales case, it wasn't farfetched to think he might ask his father to make phone calls to the right people and hurt her politically.

"Alex, what happened?" Ronald Armstrong's gruff voice broke into her thoughts. The ex-D.A., in tan slacks and polo shirt, stood before her and ran a hand through his uncombed, steel-gray hair. His penetrating eyes riveted Alex to her seat. She gave him the facts. Bryce could tell him the rest.

"Who did this?" he demanded.

She shook her head.

He gave her a look of disgust, then strode to the main reception desk and demanded the best private room for his son.

She had been dismissed.

Alex left the hospital. On the ride home she stewed over what had happened—and why. Was championing some alleged sex offender really worth all of this? Was it worth securing the judgeship? She knew winning the case was a long shot and that her spotless trial record was at stake. Tonight, a new element presented itself: her personal safety. Withdrawing from the case would guarantee her well-being, or would it? She was conflicted. From what she'd learned, Voodoo was capable of anything. Her pride wouldn't allow him to run her off that easily and to let Bryce or his father do it was out of the question. She wasn't married to Bryce. He didn't pay her bills and had no right to tell her what to do. Bailing out on the Reverend and Shepherd's Cottages went against her moral grain. Her independence as a woman was on the line.

Alex focused on her promise to the Reverend. A stubborn streak, most likely inherited from her grandmother, inclined her to keep her word no matter what the cost. Her deeper instincts told her Shepherd's Cottages was worth it. Though she did not know him well yet, she liked Jose and, so far, believed him. She also believed in Shepherd's Cottages, which was a rescue line for abandoned children. It was late and her mind was a maze of competing thoughts and emotions. She needed to discuss Bryce's attack with the Reverend. He would surely be able to make sense of things.

★

Wednesday evening came quickly. After a long day in the office, Alex headed for Shepherd's Cottages to confront the Reverend and his board about Jose's prior conviction. If she wanted an out, this would surely give her one. It was almost dark at half-past five and the overcast sky threatened rain. She navigated rush hour traffic to the Fifth Ward, birthplace of many county jail inhabitants, turned off the main road, and drove toward the Shepherd's Cottages compound.

The streets had no sidewalks, only dirty ditches filled with branches and leaves. Every few feet there was another large pothole. No wonder Shepherd's Cottages was surrounded with a barbed wire topped fence.

Alex recognized the place from the photos on the plane. Floodlights lit the perimeters of the property, consisting of six small cottages, an activity center and playground with a blacktop basketball court.

Alex parked and was immediately surrounded by a group of pre-adolescent boys who gawked at her new car. Several little girls peered shyly around the corner of a building.

She stepped from the car and looked for someone to direct her to the board meeting. Moments later, a teenage girl with shiny black hair and brown skin emerged from a cottage.

"Hello, Rosemary," she called to the girl she met at the Reverend's church Sunday. "Where's the meeting?"

When the girl motioned toward a small house with "Administration Building" in bold letters over the front door, Alex fell into step beside her.

Even with a row of small children clamoring behind her, Rosemary was poised and graceful. "Go on over to supper now," she told them gently.

Inside the main cottage, Alex saw a computer atop an old secretary desk. A worn black sweater hung on the back of a rickety wooden chair behind it.

"That's where I do my homework," Rosemary said.

"Good," Alex said. "Keep up your grades."

"I'd like to be a lawyer." Rosemary lifted her chin proudly.

"Great! Let me know if I can help."

Alex wondered how often the girl had been told she'd never amount to anything. Suddenly, she sensed a presence behind her and turned.

"This is Miss May," Rosemary said politely.

Hands on hips, feet shoulder-width apart, the administrator looked formidable. The hem of her royal blue polyester dress didn't quite cover knee-highs. Her intense stare was meant to intimidate, but unperturbed, Alex just met her gaze.

"So, you're Lawyer Stockton," she said.

Detecting a hint of disapproval in her voice, Alex nodded. "I need your help with Jose's case."

"I do whatever the Reverend tells me," she answered. "Come into the boardroom. We're waiting on the Reverend and Mr. Wright."

Alex followed Miss May down the short hall. She glanced inside a half-open door marked "Administrator" where mounds of paper covered the desk and boxes lined the walls. Children's toys covered an old lime-green vinyl couch and a TV with aluminum-tipped rabbit ears sat on a metal stand.

When Alex entered the boardroom, the flurry of activity came to a halt. Six adults, munching sandwiches and snacks, sat at a scuffed and scarred conference table. All eyes riveted on her. Alex straightened her jacket, squared her shoulders, and gave them her trial smile.

The best defense is a good offense.

She plopped her leather briefcase on the table. "I'm Alex Stockton," she began. "I represent Jose Gonzales. I only have a few weeks to prepare for his trial and will need your cooperation."

Miss May walked in, carrying an overloaded plate and put it down in the middle of the table along with the rest of the feast. She settled in her big chair at the head of the table.

One by one, the board members introduced themselves. There was Mrs. King, whose husband was a deacon in the church. Mr. Samples, a deacon and recent widower, worked as a handyman and looked the part in overalls and red plaid shirt. Dr. Hope, a retired psychologist in a tight red sweater and skirt, wore her hair in a French twist just shy of a beehive.

Next was Virginia Murphy, a retired schoolteacher. "I'm the secretary," she announced.

Mr. Washington proudly proclaimed his boss at Best Buy recently donated a printer to Shepherd's Cottages. Bertha Jackson sat next to Miss May. Equal in size, Alex guessed they were sisters. Bertha cooked at the nearby high school and prepared the board's snacks. It was obvious she enjoyed the fruits of her culinary skills.

Intrigued by their stories and colorful personalities, Alex looked into their eyes and gave each a firm handshake. In last week's trial seminar in New York, she'd learned to take time to make a personal connection. The technique worked here. She felt them warm to her.

Moments later, dressed in a windbreaker, khaki Dockers and a jaunty beret, the Reverend entered. A tall, lanky young man followed and immediately went for the sandwich tray. "Aw, Bertha, my favorite," he said, stuffing one into his mouth. When his sea-blue eyes met Alex's dark gaze, his expression changed. He looked like a child caught with his hand in the cookie jar.

"Excuse me," he said, then swallowed hard and wiped his mouth with a napkin. "I'm Nick Wright, the token white guy on this board."

The others giggled and grinned. The blue-eyed man's charisma filled the room.

"Nick, meet Alex Stockton," the Reverend said, "Jose's lawyer."

The others grew quiet.

Alex gave him a nod, then wasted no time getting into the subject of the meeting. "The Reverend believes Jose is innocent and I agree," Alex said, then looked directly at the Reverend. "But I am concerned about what I found out Monday when I met with Jose at the jail. He told me he has a prior for statutory rape. I assume you knew there was a law against hiring sex offenders as house parents in certified foster homes?"

An uncomfortable silence fell over the room.

The Reverend began slowly, measuring his words. "I should have told you about that." He took a deep breath then continued. "Jose told us what happened with his high school sweetheart and her father. The day I went to the police station to do Jose's background check, Nick was still on the police force and he helped me. When we looked, the incident didn't appear on the report. I can assure you we were aware of the hiring procedures. We thought we followed them."

Alex shot Nick a fierce look. "Not disclosing Jose's prior sexual offense is 'proper procedure'? You should know better."

"We followed CPS rules," Nick responded in an even tone. "When Jose was hired, his case was on appeal. That's why it didn't show up. We thought he might win his appeal. Since it wasn't on his report, we didn't mention it."

Alex turned to Miss May. "I need a copy of Jose's file, please."

Miss May looked at the Reverend. He nodded.

The woman got up and left the room. Moments later she returned and handed over a slim file. She scanned it quickly. Sure enough, the background check showed no prior convictions.

"This report may clear Shepherd's Cottages from civil

negligence claims," she said with an arched eyebrow toward the Reverend. "But, if Jose takes the stand, the D.A. can impeach him about his prior offense."

"Jose deserved a second chance," Nick said. "Until this whole mess with Chris, everything was fine." Leaning back in his chair, he crossed one leg over the other, then folded his hands behind his head.

Alex recognized Nick's aggressive body language. Loaded with testosterone, she realized he could be dangerous—in more ways than one. She scanned his lightly starched cotton shirt and Wrangler jeans, then noted the bulge in his brown Roper boots.

A pistol. Texas cowboys.

Alex wasn't happy, but what she heard at least made her less angry.

"Jose thinks Chris lied for his uncle, Voodoo. Tell me about him."

The Reverend shook his head. "Voodoo is an angry man. Been knowin' his family clear back to his great grandfather. His mother died when he was two. His grandmother raised him. Until she died, he came to church. That same year, when he was twelve, his father died of a stab wound. Barroom brawl. Although I'd hoped he'd take a different path, he hardened his heart against God, and me. It seems he wants the same for Chris."

Alex repeated Jose's version of what happened in the park that evening. "Does anyone have anything to add?" she asked.

Miss May spoke up. "Jose's right. I was the only one here that evening."

"What about the CPS investigation?" Alex asked.

Tension in the room rose. The board members shifted in their seats. Alex's gaze locked with the Reverend's. "Is there something I should know?"

"We've had some problems with CPS," he answered. "Camilla Roe, our caseworker, doesn't like me. She'd like to see the home shut down."

"She'd like to burn our church down too," Dr. Hope muttered angrily.

"Now, Evelyn, let's not scare Alex off with all this," the Reverend said in a calm tone. "By the time we get the children, they've already been through a lot. We're patient with them. We know we don't have much time to make a difference in their lives. The state can send them home anytime." He paused, carefully choosing each word. "The problems between Miss Roe and me began with a Cottage Five discipline problem. Chris and his roommate, Jaime, refused to follow rules. Jose and I had concerns about how their behavior affected the other children. So we set stricter rules. Told them they'd get a paddling if they broke the house rules. The next day, Jose caught Jaime smoking and as promised, he got a spanking. Jaime called CPS and now they're investigating me for it."

Alex shot Nick a fierce glance. "If you are a cop, you know corporal punishment in foster homes is strictly forbidden!"

Overwhelmed by the enormity of the board's blunders, Alex pushed back her chair and stood.

"Sorry, Reverend," she said. "In light of this new information, I have to think about handling Jose's case." Turning abruptly, she left the boardroom.

Alex was livid as she headed into the cool night air.

She reached for the front door when Nick came up behind her and grabbed her arm. "Alex," he said, "please, listen. I'm no longer on the force, but this whole thing is my fault. I advised the Reverend to hire Jose when I saw Jose's case was on appeal. I banked on his conviction being reversed. Jose needs a good lawyer and we can't afford anyone else. If you walk out now, we're sunk."

"I said I need to think," Alex answered.

Nick abruptly released his grip and gazed deeply into her eyes. "Please let me help you investigate the case."

"I don't need your help," she said as she stepped outside.

CHAPTER 4

The breeze cooled Alex's cheeks. Nick's touch had sent a charge through her body, but she could not think about that. Mixing business with pleasure was off-limits now.

Children's laughter rang through the night air, still heavy with impending rain. She had promised the children Sunday she would come see them. As she walked toward the lights of the activity center, a tension headache formed at the base of her neck. Her thoughts went back to last Sunday and her first visit to the Reverend's church:

As she had entered the Fifth Ward she'd seen dirty, neglected children playing in the streets. Scraggly dogs picked through trash on the street. Men and women sat listlessly on sagging front porches.

The Fifth Ward is more like a Third World country than the U.S.

She parked amidst several old, dented cars in the parking lot and walked toward the church. Just then, a black Lincoln with darkened windows slowed as it passed her.

Something about the car and the unknown occupants gave her the creeps. She quickly entered the clean, modest church and was greeted by a lovely Hispanic girl who introduced herself as Rosemary. When she'd signed the guest register, Rosemary pinned a red visitor ribbon on her lapel, then led her to a second row seat in a well-worn pew.

The first row was filled with happy children in their Sunday best. The choir, in red-trimmed white robes, sang a gospel hymn which ended when a side door opened and the Reverend appeared. The room grew quiet. Excitement, like a powerful electrical charge, was in the air. After climbing the few stairs to the podium, Reverend Morse began in a low, soft voice, "Good Morning. Today we'll talk about how God allows us to go through tough times for our own good. Think about Peter, the impetuous, overly self-confident Apostle. He had to fail in his area of greatest confidence in order to see his weaknesses and then change for the better."

Alex had never heard someone preach with such passion. He told the story as if he was there. Alex looked around and saw love and admiration in the beaming faces of his congregation.

The Reverend's voice grew stronger with each word. "Let's remember the day Peter told Jesus he would go with him ... even to death. Jesus predicted, 'When the cock crows three times, you will have denied me three times.' Peter didn't believe it then, but picture him later on that day when Jesus's words came true."

The congregation heated up. Women cooled themselves with paper fans, saying "Amen" and "Praise God" when the urge came over them.

In rhythmic cadence, the Reverend's voice rose and fell. He grew more animated and his right hand clutched the Bible. "And, in that very moment, Jesus walked through the garden courtyard and looked directly into Peter's eyes." With a handkerchief, the Reverend wiped sweat from his brow. "We know Peter wept bitterly, but we can only imagine his inner torment. It took an instant for Peter to see himself for who he really was."

Alex never thought church could be interesting, but something about the Reverend's delivery fascinated her.

"After God sifts us, He *always* restores us. God ended up using Peter in a powerful and mighty way. He was the rock the church was built on; people were healed by his shadow; he preached a sermon one day and three thousand people were saved."

Like the day she met him, Alex was enthralled by the Reverend.

Alex snapped out of her reverie and bolted the last fifty feet to the activity center. She entered and saw thirty-five children between the ages of three and sixteen eating dinner in a crowded dining hall. The room was plain except for paneled walls covered with children's drawings on colored construction paper. Tables and chairs were government-issue. Sloppy Joes with Fritos served on paper plates barely passed for a healthy meal.

Several little children screamed and pointed in her direction, "That's Jose's lawyer." They ran over and hugged her knees. Clearly less trusting of a stranger, the older children were more subdued.

Alex picked up a little girl and held her in her arms. The precious thing, in a pink jogging suit over a white T-shirt, was hungry for love and affection. "Honey, what's your name?" she asked.

"Nikita." She pointed to a boy sitting alone in the back of the room. "That's my brother."

With Nikita still in her arms, Alex walked over and sat down next to him. "Hi. What's your name?"

"Thomas."

"How old are you?"

He held up a hand, extending his fingers broadly. "Five."

His too-long jeans were cuffed at the bottom, and a faded red windbreaker almost hid the yellow cotton shirt beneath.

An awkward adolescent girl tugged on Alex's blazer. "Miss Lawyer, will you get Jose back for us?"

Alex was at a loss for words, too confused about the case to give her an answer. The children needed honesty. Knowing they had often been lied to, Alex searched for the right response. "I hope so."

"Chris and Jaime is liars," a young girl blurted out angrily.

The rest of the children nodded agreement.

"That's Christina," Rosemary said.

Alex looked at her, who with three children in her lap looked more like a woman than a frightened young girl.

"Christina, I promise I'll do my best."

Looking pleased, Christina nodded.

The others clamored for Alex's attention.

"Miss Stockton has to go," Rosemary interrupted. "It is bedtime. Don't worry about Jose. Just remember to include him in your prayers tonight."

"Yes, ma'am," they chimed in unison.

Heading for her car, Alex thought of how the old computer monitors on the floor and the half-assembled bookshelves in the main room echoed the children's incomplete existence. Alex wanted to see order restored in their lives.

Just after Alex entered her car and locked her doors, the skies opened up and it started raining hard.

Alex decided to drive past the Reverend's church on her way out of the neighborhood. Turning the corner she saw the steeple, a beacon in a dark world. Soft light inside the church outlined the image of a white bird in the round stained-glass sanctuary window. It looked like the white bird outside her plane window the day she met the Reverend. A strange wave of warmth washed over her and she felt at peace. Something was going on inside her and she did not understand why. Everything was changing and it was hard to stay angry at the Reverend for long.

★

Saturday morning, after three hours of fitful sleep, Alex woke up and called the Reverend.

"Hello, Alex," he greeted. "I'm going fishin'. Want to come along?"

"Sure," she answered. They needed to talk.

"Meet me in an hour at Denny's on the Gulf Freeway at Nasa One. It's just a short piece to where I fish."

"Can I bring my dog?"

"Sure."

Alex paused. "Rev, I don't do worms."

"No problem," he said with a chuckle. "See you there."

Alex washed her face, pulled her hair into a ponytail, then she threw on jeans and a sweater. The thought of going fishing with the Reverend made her smile. Normally about this time she'd be making love to Bryce, but instead, she thought with a pang of guilt, he was still recovering from a brutal attack.

It was an overcast, chilly November day. After a quick stop at Starbucks for a cafe latte, she was on her way. Twenty minutes later, Alex pulled into Denny's parking lot. Her heart skipped a beat. She saw the Reverend and Nick, busy organizing their fishing gear. The Reverend hadn't mentioned Nick would be there. A quick glance in her visor mirror drew a sigh. She hadn't worn makeup, but it was too late.

She looked at Nick. He was dressed in jeans, a UT sweatshirt, and baseball cap turned backward. He looked like an overgrown kid, but a handsome one.

When he saw her, Nick's face lit up. He approached and said hello, then greeted Siva like an old friend. The dog responded by offering her right paw. "She smells my dog," he said. "What's her name?"

"Siva."

"Meaning?"

"Blessed one. What about him?" she asked, pointing at his Golden Retriever.

"Just Sam. He's my best friend."

Alex looked at Siva, who was sniffing around Sam like there was no tomorrow. "She's mine too. Where are we going?"

"The Rev likes a little place on the bay a few miles down the road. Let's hop in the truck. Siva can ride in the back with Sam."

Alex gave him a concerned look.

"You ride up front with the Rev," he offered. "I'll stay back here with the dogs."

Once in the truck, she marveled at the Reverend's outfit. He looked like a career fisherman in his rubber boots, thick green pants, fisherman's vest with dangling lures and a funky old cap covered with tournament pins. He started the truck, looked back at Nick's thumbs-up sign, then backed out of the parking lot and pulled onto the feeder road.

"I almost didn't recognize you," Alex said. "Pretty serious hobby, huh?"

The Reverend nodded. "I love to fish."

"You need a T-shirt that says, 'Fishing is my life'," Alex offered.

They turned off of the main thoroughfare and took a gravel road toward the bay.

Seagulls hovered near the water and the moist air smelled salty. Alex was relaxed and hesitated to spoil the moment by talking about Voodoo.

"Reverend, I've been thinking about what happened to my friend Monday night. Could Voodoo be behind it?"

"It is possible," the Reverend said sadly. "I'm afraid it's my fault for getting you into this."

"No, I volunteered," Alex assured him. "One of my problems

is that both Bryce and his father, our former D.A., ordered me off the case."

"They may be right. Your safety is the most important thing."

"I'm no quitter, but I'm not sure what to do next." Alex wanted to tell him more.

"Let's fish," the Reverend suggested. "Maybe you'll get some direction. I usually do." He turned into a small graveled area on the bay.

While Nick and the Rev assembled the fishing gear, Alex took Siva off her leash to investigate the area. She observed the comfortable silence between the Reverend and Nick. What an odd pair they were: a tall, handsome white man and a short elderly black man. Their warm camaraderie made her feel safe and secure.

When she approached, she heard the Reverend telling Nick about the attack on Bryce.

"I'm glad you weren't hurt too," Nick told her.

"I guess I'm lucky I checked my mail," she said. "Bryce's father is Ronald Armstrong."

"The D.A.?"

"Ex-D.A. They both ordered me to withdraw from Jose's case. I think they are chauvinists."

"They may be, but they're probably worried about you too," Nick said gently.

The Reverend held up a thermos. "Hot coffee anyone?"

Both Alex and Nick accepted and the Reverend poured them a cup. A cold wind blew in from the bay and the mugs warmed their hands.

Being so close to Nick did strange things to Alex. Her voice skipped a couple of octaves higher; her pulse quickened.

Nick set up three chairs, placing poles and a bucket of lures between them.

"Someone needs to show me how to do this," Alex said, then sat in the middle chair.

"Are you teachable?" Nick asked.

"I don't know," she answered.

"You seem pretty hardheaded to me," Nick teased.

"I am. So watch it."

Nick approached and helped her cast the rod. She was aware of how the touch of his arms and chest made her heart race.

"Now, just wait," he said. "That's what fishin's all about—waiting. When you get a tug, I'll help you. Just don't try to reel him in too fast. You'll lose him that way." He gave her a slow grin.

"I'll remember that," she laughed.

The men cast their lines and waited patiently.

They sat quiet for what, to Alex, seemed an eternity. Solitude wasn't her strong point. When she couldn't stand it any longer, she broke the silence. "Reverend, Jesus was a fisherman, wasn't he?"

He nodded. "He was a fisher of *men*. By trade, some of his disciples were fishermen."

"Tell me about them."

"Here's a good one: Jesus's Apostles had been fishing all day and hadn't caught a thing. When they came in, Jesus told Peter to go back and put out into deep water for a big catch. Peter complained, but did what he was told. After a short time in deep water, they caught so many fish their nets broke and the boat began to sink."

"What made the difference?" Alex asked.

"The first time, they fished in shallow water," the Reverend announced with obvious delight. "When they went into deep water, they caught a haul."

"I don't get it," Alex said.

"They didn't get what they wanted because they were in the wrong place. Maybe, in order for us to find answers, God means for us to go deeper spiritually."

"I need an answer," Alex said. "I need to make Bryce

understand why I can't just drop Jose's case."

"Can you change your boyfriend's mind?" Nick asked.

Alex bristled at the word *boyfriend*, but didn't correct him. "He was hurt and angry. Surely he doesn't think he can dictate my life. Last time I checked, I was a grown woman."

Alex saw a smile form at the corners of the Reverend's lips as she talked to Nick. Moments later, when his line began to pull, the Reverend jumped up to reel it in. From the way he acted, you would think he had a killer whale on his line. Then Alex and Nick's lines started to pull. All three were preoccupied with activity at the end of their wires.

"Steady," Nick shouted.

When both men's lines came up empty, they looked at Alex. To their obvious surprise, Alex reeled hers in after a brief, but fierce struggle.

"A twelve-pound redfish!" Nick exclaimed. "I'll be darned."

"You know the old saying," the Reverend said with a twinkle in his eye. "Lucy got the fish."

Alex returned home in late afternoon with a new surge of confidence and some fresh fish filets. She jumped into the shower to wash away the fish smell. The fishing trip had energized her.

When she caught the big redfish, she took it as a sign she could reason with Bryce. Common sense told her he would listen and, after hearing the whole story, would understand the importance of her commitment to Jose and Shepherd's Cottages. A silent alarm went off inside when she realized she didn't know anything about Bryce's values. Something deep down in her gut told her it was time to find out whether there was more to their relationship than great sex.

Alex jumped into her car and headed the short distance to Bryce's condo. Just before turning onto his street, she called him from her cell phone.

"Hello," he said in a gruff voice.

"I'm around the corner," she said.

"Did you withdraw from the case?" he asked.

When she said no and started to explain, the phone went dead.

Alex dismissed his attitude. He was still angry. Once he saw her, she'd get him to listen.

She parked behind his Porsche and walked up the drive. His front door was ajar. She entered, walked into his spacious den, and found him propped up on the couch in front of the big screen TV watching a noisy college football game.

Bryce took a swig of beer and stared at her through lifeless eyes. His face was puffy, bruised, and the gash across his cheek still had stitches. His mood was as sour as his looks and Alex wondered if, for the first time, she saw the real Bryce.

"I told you not to contact me until you withdrew," he said, not hiding his anger.

Like a sandcastle hit by a sudden wave, her rehearsed speech vanished. Eyes lowered, she searched for the right words.

Before she found them, Bryce slammed the remote control down on the ottoman. "That's great, Alex. Because of you, I'm attacked by a couple of thugs and you don't think it's important. Your priorities are screwed up!"

His harsh words deflated her resolve to explain. She lost the desire and momentum to work things out with him. He'd seized the offensive edge and she knew he wouldn't quit until he bullied her into submission. "You won't give me a chance to—," she began.

"There's nothing to explain!" he interrupted. "Why defend some sleazy Mexican who molested a foster child?"

Alex kicked the ottoman so hard the remote control and big bowl of chips and salsa hit the floor, splattering all over Bryce's bare leg. "Don't you dare call my client names!" she screamed, then stormed toward the door. "My client is innocent. I'll prove it!"

"You'll regret it," he warned.

"Don't threaten me, Bryce," she shot back. Alex opened the door, stepped outside, then slammed it behind her with as much force as she could muster.

On her way down the drive, blinded by tears of frustration and disappointment, Alex nearly bumped into a girl she recognized as the pretty nurse from the hospital.

Noting the pharmacy sack in her one hand and a six-pack of beer in the other, Alex said, "He's all yours, honey. All yours!"

Backing out of the driveway, she headed for home. She was angry, not at Bryce, but at herself. Bryce wasn't capable of understanding or supporting her decision on Jose's case. A few minutes earlier, in his condo, she realized how shallow their relationship was. They didn't really know each other. With startling clarity, she realized how much alike she and Bryce were: emotionally unavailable career slaves. Like an icy gale on a hot summer day, it hit her that, like predators, she and Bryce had feasted off each other with reckless abandon.

This morning at the bay, she wasted time and emotional energy trying to figure things out. Now, she felt foolish for thinking of him in such intimate terms. What upset her was not ending it with Bryce, but her own lack of character. For the first time, she saw something inside herself she didn't like or understand. Her outer shell, the fortress she'd built around her heart, was breached.

At the first red light, she flipped down the visor mirror and took a long, hard look at herself. There was renewed strength in her brown eyes. She thought about Jose's case. It was time to get down to business and find out the truth about what had happened in Crosstown Park. Then, a smile formed on her lips. Surely Nick's offer to help her on the case was still open.

CHAPTER 5

A sunrise jog Monday at Memorial Park kick-started Alex's workweek. Energized by the crisp air, she marveled at the barely brown leaves on the trees. Texas didn't have seasons. She showered in her office building's locker room, thinking about the day ahead as the hot water ran down her neck and back. Then she headed upstairs to work.

"Morning," Alex called when she heard the door open around eight-thirty a.m.

"You're here early!" Ruth said on her way to the kitchen to pour a cup of coffee.

"New hours 'til after Jose's trial."

"This may be your last ... Your Honor," Ruth said with a smile.

"And you'll be out of law school and practice in my court," Alex quipped. "But right now, I have to take one thing at a time." Over piles of paperwork, Alex looked out her windows to the park across the street. A young mother pushed her little girl in a swing, while an infant slept in a nearby stroller. Alex wondered what her life was like.

Choices—life choices determine our fate.

Ruth reappeared, coffee cup in hand. "How was the governor's reception?" she asked.

"He leered longer at my chest than he talked to me."

"Sounds like him."

"After the reception, Bryce was attacked outside my condo. It might be related to Jose's case." Alex detailed the events of the past two days.

"Are we safe here?" Ruth asked, looking worried.

"We'll be extra careful. During the day we'll lock the doors and Ray can walk us out evenings. Call him to give a heads-up. We'll be safe," Alex said, hoping she sounded more assured than she felt.

A few minutes later the phone rang. "Nick Wright," Ruth called over the intercom. "Says he's your private investigator on the Gonzales case."

"Since I haven't hired him yet, he must have mental telepathy," Alex told Ruth, then picked up the line. "This is Alex."

"I want to help with Jose's case," he said, his voice deep with conviction.

Before she answered, Alex took a deep breath. "I'm glad you called. After what happened Friday night, I have to say yes. Since I'm doing the case *pro bono*, I hope you'll accept alternative forms of payment, like say, banana bread."

"No problem. I'd like to take my world famous fisherman to lunch. We can discuss it."

Alex felt a slight tingle in her stomach when she glanced at her calendar. "How about eleven-thirty, Patrenella's on Jackson Hill?"

"See you there," Nick answered before hanging up.

A moment later, Ruth walked into Alex's office with a broad smile on her face. "Our new investigator sure has a sexy voice."

Alex felt her cheeks flush when she told Ruth about Nick's connection to the Reverend. She hoped Ruth didn't notice, but little escaped her.

"Can't disagree with you there."

"We're having lunch. He's still amazed I caught a twelve pound redfish Saturday."

"You what?" Ruth said.

Alex laughed and held her hand as if to stop Ruth. "Saturday morning, I went fishing with the Reverend. Nick came along. I ended up catching the only fish."

Ruth shook her head.

"This Reverend has already done wonders for you. First, you volunteer for a *pro bono* case with impossible facts. Then, your boyfriend gets beat up and you go fishing. Is this a cartoon?"

"No, it's a carnival. Buckle up for a ride on the big rollercoaster," Alex said as she opened one of many files on her desk. "And he isn't my boyfriend."

"Yeah, right," Ruth muttered as she headed back to her desk.

The morning flew by. Alex returned calls, scheduled meetings, and began preparing Jose's trial notebook.

She usually represented children like Chris Jackson in family court. Now she was defending an alleged attacker. She wondered if CPS would cooperate with discovery. They were typically reluctant to divulge much to the other side. Alex thought about Bryce and wondered whether his ego was bruised, but she decided he was too self-involved and preoccupied with politics to give her or her case any consideration.

Just before leaving for lunch, Alex called the local party chairman, Grady Frears. He answered on the first ring.

"This is Alex Stockton," she said. "What's up?"

"Politics as usual. Don't have your petition yet."

"I'm working on it," she assured him. "Any truth to a rumor that Hal is on the short list for my bench?"

"Where'd you hear it?"

"Ladies' lounge, River Oaks Country Club. Judge Palmer saw me talking to Governor Hastings and, while we touched up our lipstick, went on a fishing expedition."

"Sounds like her. But she had the wrong bait. You're better looking than Hal and the governor isn't stupid," he said with a hearty laugh.

"Keep me posted." His comment made Alex cringe.

Patronizing men.

If men like Grady Frears only knew how hard she'd worked to put herself through college and law school, they'd think twice. Or maybe not.

"Next week is the candidates' signing party. Bring your petition and we'll fix you up."

"Will do," Alex said.

Before Alex left for lunch, Ruth called Ray, the security guard. When Alex left the office, he was by the elevator. The seasoned professional walked her to her car. "I won't let my favorite girls get hurt."

The old man's concern was touching. "Don't worry about me, Ray," she said, then patted his shoulder before entering her car. "Just make sure Ruth is OK, please." In her rearview mirror, she saw him wait for her to enter the busy street before returning to the building.

Noon hour at Patrenella's was busy. She spotted Nick outside the restaurant, wearing dark sunglasses and casual work clothes. As he watched her approach, she felt his admiring gaze sweep over her form-fitted tailored suit and purple silk blouse.

"Nice," he murmured, then took her elbow and led her to a window table where they could enjoy the sights and sounds of the lively neighborhood.

The trendy Italian restaurant was comfortable. Color-washed terracotta walls were covered with modern art, complementing clay jars of multi-colored flowers on waxed pine tables. Though it was Thanksgiving week, the mild temperature allowed the restaurant doors and windows to be open wide.

When Nick offered the breadbasket, Alex wasted no time taking a thick slab and dipping it into herb-laden olive oil. "I always get the Sammy's Eggplant."

"Creature of habit? Sounds good to me."

When Nick ordered for them both, Alex noted his kindness toward the waiter. "I used to wait tables," she said. "Started at Dairy Queen when I was fifteen. I make a mean banana split."

"I figured you were a self-made woman. I tended bar in college."

"Really? The restaurant business is crazy. I served cocktails my second year in law school. Great money, but I got tired of drunks pinching my rear end."

"I can see where they were coming from," he teased.

When the food arrived, Nick asked questions about her background and they took turns exchanging basic information. Alex learned he was a Houston native, oldest of five. Unlike her, he came from a stable and loving family.

As Alex listened, the sound of calming jazz music played in the background. Their conversation was easygoing and Alex almost forgot why they were there. When he talked, the look in his eyes made her feel like the most beautiful woman in the world. It didn't take long to realize Nick was a man at home with himself, truly comfortable in his own skin.

Handsome, eligible and dedicated to helping the Reverend with Shepherd's Cottages, he could be a woman's dream man. She kept reminding herself she wasn't looking for a relationship; they were just working on Jose's case together; this was professional.

Nick caught her gaze. "A penny for your thoughts."

She wished she had the nerve to tell him what was on her mind. "You were still on the force when you met the Reverend?"

Nick nodded. "When he came in to do Jose's criminal background check, I was at the desk up front and I helped him. I liked him instantly."

"When he learned about Jose's conviction, what did he do?"

"He believed Jose. Because he was doing such a good job with the kids, he didn't fire him. The board agreed Jose's past was behind him and we felt he deserved a second chance."

Alex sighed. "I understand the board's thinking, but I'm realistic. If Shepherd's Cottages was negligent in their hiring practices, there could be a civil suit."

"Let's cross that river when we get to the bridge," Nick said firmly. "I assure you the Reverend was right about Jose."

Alex shook her head. "I can't disagree. The Reverend convinced me of that on the plane the day I met him."

"He had the same effect on me. I met him that day and before I knew it, I was on the board. Since then, he's taught me so much about life."

"Like what?"

"Like, how, in the midst of my problems, to trust God. I was going through a divorce. I had twenty years at the force and wanted to leave to start my own business, but didn't know how to take the next step. I kept thinking that everything in my life was shattered, like a broken plate. I thought I had to somehow glue all the little pieces back together and was overwhelmed by the thought. The Reverend gave me some spiritual insight that instantly gave me hope and changed my perspective."

"What did he say?"

"He told me that I did not need to glue all the pieces of my life back together. He said that God has as many new plates as I need."

"Did he mean that God gives you second chances?"

Nick nodded. "And third and fourth chances. It was such a comfort to me to know I could have a fresh start. We began to fish together and I took his advice about getting my act together with God before I did anything else. With his help and wise counsel, I found confidence to leave the force and start my own security company."

"Was it a good move?"

"Without a doubt. Almost immediately, I landed several city and federal surveillance contracts. Bread and butter. And I also sell and install business security systems."

"You don't trail cheating husbands with a zoom lens?"

Nick shook his head and chuckled.

Alex was intrigued when Nick discussed his spiritual life. His deep voice filled with excitement; his hands grew expressive; his charm became more appealing. As she listened, her insides quivered. "The Rev's been a good influence on you," she said. "Maybe that's why I met him."

"He thinks you're special."

"Let's talk about Jose," Alex said.

"You sure change subjects quick. Don't take compliments well?"

Alex squirmed in her seat. He had read her mind. Again.

The waitress appeared and Nick ordered coffee. "First, I'll tell you about the alleged statutory rape. Jose's high school sweetheart is named Angelina. Her father was an abusive alcoholic. Jose and Angelina dated secretly for three years and prom night was the first time they ever had sex. Angelina was terrified her father would find out, so they decided to elope. Since her dad was usually passed out drunk, Angelina snuck into the house to pack her suitcase, then attempted to sneak back out. Unfortunately, her enraged father waited for her at the foot of the stairs. He beat her, then called 911 and said Jose raped her. While they waited for the police, he threatened to sexually abuse Angelina's baby sister if she didn't go along with his story."

"That is terrible," Alex said with a dismayed look on her face.

"The poor girl didn't have a choice; she wouldn't let her sister suffer like she did. The rape kit was positive and Jose was arrested for statutory rape. He knew Angelina's father would carry out his threats and didn't blame her for protecting her sister. His love for Angelina kept him from defending himself in court."

"You are right, he could have defended himself by saying the sex was consensual," Alex said. "What did Jose do?"

"He thought he'd been offered deferred adjudication. But he had an inexperienced court-appointed lawyer who didn't check the papers. His probation officer later told him his conviction was final. When he met the Reverend and applied for a job at Shepherd's Cottages, he'd just appealed his case alleging ineffective assistance of counsel."

"What happened on his appeal?"

"The appellate court agreed his attorney screwed up and sent the case back down to trial court. A new D.A. gave him the deferred adjudication he'd been promised."

"Jose was lucky. Penalties for sexual offenses, even statutory rape, are stiffer. Unfortunately, since he's still on deferred adjudication, it will come into evidence at trial."

"And when it's all said and done, you'll get him acquitted, and he'll successfully live out his probation and end up with a clean record."

Alex smiled at Nick's confident assessment.

"That is the best-case scenario. But the State has already moved to revoke his probation. They want to use the statutory rape to enhance punishment."

Nick shrugged his shoulders. "He's in a tough position. Jose will just have to tell his side of things and hope the jury appreciates him for caring more about Angelina than himself."

Alex frowned. "We've got more than enough lemons for lemonade, but, at least he was on appeal when the Reverend hired him. That should clear the home."

"My turn to change subjects," Nick said, looking deep into Alex's eyes. "My first priority, besides protecting you, is to find Angelina. Let's hope she's still in the Valley." He grew sober. "Any more trouble since Friday night?"

Alex shook her head. "I'm still not sure how they got past my security guard. Everyone's looking out for me now."

"You can't be too careful," Nick warned. "To make sure you're safe, I'm going to stick close. Do you have a security system?"

"Yes. She weighs seventy-five pounds and has a ferocious bark."

"Good protection, but this week I'll install a system monitored twenty-four-seven."

Alex couldn't believe her ears. This gorgeous man was serious about protecting her.

"Don't go out to Shepherd's Cottages alone," he continued, setting ground rules. "Call me and I'll go with you. Deal?"

"Deal." His concern endeared him to Alex. It was the first time she remembered needing a man for protection and was comforted by his strength.

When the waitress appeared with the check, she handed Alex a Styrofoam container of tri-colored biscottis. "From Sammy."

"Thanks." Alex smiled and took a bite of one.

Nick picked up one. "Sammy read my mind."

"Sammy is the owner and a former client. We share a sweet tooth and trade baking tips."

Nick's eyes widened. "You were serious about alternate forms of payment. Fancy lawyers don't usually have time to bake."

"There's a lot you don't know, Sherlock. In fact, on Thanksgiving I'll take some of my homemade banana bread and chocolate chip cookies to Shepherd's Cottages. Will you be there?"

Nick nodded. "I'll pick you up and we'll go together."

They stood and walked outside. "Where are you parked?" he asked.

With a wave of her hand, she indicated her car a few feet down from the restaurant.

Reaching for her keys, Alex heard a woman's voice: "Nick!"

They both turned and saw two smartly dressed women approach. The pretty one, whose body could stop a fire truck, rushed up and threw her arms around Nick. "I didn't see you at the Longhorn Saturday night. I had to polka with another cowboy," she said with a pout of her full lips.

Alex stepped inside her car.

"Alex," Nick called.

When she pulled out too fast, her tires squealed.

CHAPTER 6

Alex felt unaccustomed emotions. Jealous? No way. There wasn't a green-eyed bone in her body.

Lost in her thoughts, she passed her office building and didn't stop until she pulled in and greeted her familiar valet parking attendant at Saks Fifth Avenue. Shopping would soothe her.

Could I really be jealous?

Once inside, she went straight to the designer sports department, where Gina, her regular saleslady, enthusiastically greeted her. "You're just in time! The trunk show is about to start. I'll get you a glass of wine."

Ensconced in a comfortable couch, Alex sipped wine and watched models displaying the latest fashions. She tried tamping down visions of Nick dancing at the Longhorn Saloon. An alarm inside said *beware* but something deeper cried *this feels good, keep going.* Her self-made rules about relationships were harsh and paralyzing. *Where did they come from? Were they necessary?* Part of her wanted to confront and explore them; another part said, *forget it, keep moving.*

Since leaving Bryce's condo Saturday, she'd felt no sense

of loss, just an undefinable emptiness. She'd known from the beginning there was no commitment between them; it was sex, pure and simple.

She compared Bryce and Nick. In the restaurant, Nick's attitude was sincere. Unlike Bryce, who always looked for people he knew, or needed to know, Nick gave her his undivided attention. Bryce never asked about her background or seemed interested in getting to really know her. Bryce was history.

Alex closed her eyes to conjure images of Nick. Fishing Saturday was great; he was so easy to be with. She remembered the delight in his eyes when she caught the big fish; his apprehensive voice telling her not to go alone to Shepherd's Cottages; his grin outside the restaurant when the pretty girl rushed up to him. She gave a mental shrug, opened her eyes and sat upright. With a sinking feeling, she told herself Nick was friendly to everyone. Falling for him would complicate things. Jose had to come first; her client's freedom had to be the priority. Being distracted by a man, no matter how handsome or seductive, was not an option.

Tuesday afternoon, Miss May phoned. As promised, she'd set aside time for Alex. Before leaving the office, Alex paged Nick and convinced him to let her drive alone to Shepherd's Cottages. Although concerned for her safety, she wasn't used to being shadowed. On the way, Alex formulated questions for Miss May. She needed complete information on Jose's employment and the boys in Cottage Five.

Turning into the compound, she saw Nick unloading a truck with Mr. Samples, the newly widowed board member. As she exited her car, he stopped and headed toward her.

"Hi. Glad you still have rubber on your tires," he said with a mischievous grin.

Alex replied, "Sometimes my sex-goddess-mafia-machine

gets away from me."

"The what?" Nick asked.

Alex pointed to her car. "'Dark windows, gold trim, chrome wheels ...'"

Nick pointed to his truck. "Just a regular ol' Joe in my pick-up truck."

"You don't fool me. I saw girls oohing and aahing over you yesterday. You must be a good dancer."

"You might just find out one day," he said with a shrug, then turned back to help Mr. Samples unload the truck.

Just then, Miss May stepped outside the administration building. "I'm ready," she barked.

Alex winked at Nick, then said goodbye to Mr. Samples. Entering the building, she asked, "Did you pull the files I requested at the board meeting last week?"

"No," she hedged. "Haven't had a chance."

Alex kept her cool. After her response at the board meeting, she'd anticipated a rocky start. But there was no time for power struggles; she needed to prepare Jose's defense.

Alex followed Miss May to her office. Once inside, she made no attempt to seat Alex. Her desk was covered with message slips and loose papers. Alex wondered whether, despite strict CPS regulations, the files she needed even existed. Paperwork obviously wasn't Miss May's forte.

"May I move these?" Alex asked, motioning to old newspapers stacked on a chair in front of her desk.

"Just put them here." She pointed to the floor by the bookshelves. "'Want some coffee?"

"No thanks. Do you have bottled water?"

"No, just tap water," Miss May said with a snort. "Might be some left over Hawaiian Punch."

While Miss May got drinks, Alex looked closely at diplomas and certificates on the wall. In college, she was a member of the Honor Society and earned a master's degree in social work from Texas Southern University. By the date on the diploma, Alex figured she was at least seventy years old. Framed class photographs revealed a younger, slimmer Miss May.

When she returned with drinks, her phone rang as she plopped down in her chair. Someone volunteered to bring the children Christmas gifts. Alex reassessed the woman. At least to her caller, Miss May was friendly, cooperative and genuinely interested in the children's welfare.

Shortly, the call ended. "Thank heavens for that donation!" she exclaimed. "We're on a shoestring budget and I don't know how much longer we can hold on. We get a meager subsidy per child, per diem, but our expenses are the same regardless of the number of children. But until Jose's trouble is resolved, CPS won't send us more. We're supposed to spend all our time doing paperwork when children need food, clothing and shelter. Not to mention love, something CPS can't regulate."

Alex was sympathetic. The home had only been open a year and already faced overwhelming financial pressure and serious problems with CPS. "If Jose wins his trial, it might help," she offered. "And I'll get you a Bar Foundation grant request form. Maybe the homeless committee can provide some assistance."

Miss May's smile told Alex she'd won some points.

"Let's focus on Jose," Alex continued. "I need to know everything about the night he was arrested."

Miss May retold the story while Alex took notes.

"And what can you tell me about Chris Jackson's history."

"He didn't know his father and his mother was a junkie. She overdosed five years ago. He's been in foster care since." A sigh escaped Miss May's lips. She picked up a framed photograph from her desk and showed it to Alex. "I've been knowing the family for years. Chris's grandmother Odelia was my best friend. You never met a more godly woman."

"Voodoo's mother?" Alex asked.

Miss May nodded, then pointed to a framed photo of a cute

little boy in his Sunday best. "That's Voodoo. He inherited his mother's brain and personality, but ain't puttin' them to no good use. He lived with Odelia and loved her more than the air he breathed. Used to be real close to the Reverend. Came to church every Sunday. When he was a teenager, Odelia died of a heart attack. He began livin' on the streets, quit coming to church and turned to crime. Now, because the Reverend bought up his crack houses and opened Shepherd's Cottages, he's hellbent on destroying us. Odelia always feared there was a family curse, and maybe she was right."

Alex frowned. "But why does the Reverend still believe in Voodoo's good side?"

"Because he has faith in God's ability to change even the hardest hearts."

"His faith's sure stronger than mine," Alex murmured. "What's Chris like?"

"He's like Voodoo, a real rebel. Wants to be just like his uncle."

"Has Chris been in trouble with the law?"

Miss May snorted. "His juvenile record is long. We think he pushes drugs for Voodoo."

Although it was evidence favorable to Jose, Alex knew the jury would never hear about Chris's record. The law didn't allow the defense to impeach a minor about his prior juvenile offenses. The hard truth was, unless the State brought it up, Chris's criminal background wouldn't help Jose.

Deeply troubled by what she'd learned, Alex thanked Miss May, then left Shepherd's Cottages. During trial, she had to find a way to lead Chris into opening the door to his criminal past. She needed the jury to hear about his background.

The Reverend's church was a few blocks away. She swung into the church parking lot a few minutes later and killed the engine.

Alex knew the prosecutor would prepare Chris and it would

be hard to trip him up. She was used to using the rule in her favor at trial; now it worked against her. She gritted her teeth at the irony. Even if she had independent evidence Chris ran drugs for Voodoo, it still wouldn't come in. Her theories were pure speculation. Chris would be cleaned up and coached. The jury would see him as a victimized foster child and believe his story.

The squeal of brakes broke her concentration. Nick pulled into the parking lot and stopped beside her car. She watched him leave his truck, slam his door, and come to her open window.

"Did you forget our agreement?" he asked.

His angry expression startled her, but she knew he wouldn't stay upset long. "Sorry, I forgot. I need to talk to the Reverend. Jose's defense is weak. Voodoo may be the key and I need to know more about him."

Nick leaned his arms on her window, bringing his face inches from hers. "Good idea," he said. "Voodoo is dangerous. Promise you won't run off again, counselor?"

Alex didn't respond.

He reached out, gently tilted her chin, and forced her to look straight into his eyes. "Deal?"

"Yes," she answered, feeling a warm flush on her cheeks.

The sound of a car engine roared past and they turned to see the now familiar black car.

Alex froze in terror. "That's Voodoo. I just know it."

Before the car sped around the corner, Nick grabbed a pen and paper from his shirt pocket to jot down the license plate number. Too late, the car was gone.

Alex noticed the bulge at the bottom of Nick's right pant leg. "Is that a gun?" she asked when he returned.

Nick nodded.

"Let's go talk to the Rev," Alex suggested.

Inside the church, the corridors were empty and the halls were dark. The sanctuary smelled of gardenias and the majestic white bird in the stained-glass window seemed to soar overhead.

There was an orderly security about the room, with the large wooden cross, organ, mahogany pulpit and pews with hymnals, Bibles and fans neatly tucked in each row. Alex saw why people in crisis came to church. It was a refuge, a shelter from life's storms.

At the back of the room, Nick knocked lightly at a closed door.

"Come in," said the Reverend in a faint voice.

When they entered, he was seated in an armchair reading the Bible. A shaft of sunlight pouring through the window gave him an ethereal glow. Removing his reading glasses, he put his book aside and began to rise.

"No, sit." Alex leaned over and kissed his cheek and smelled his familiar Old Spice cologne. For a moment, he looked his age and Alex felt a touch of concern for him. He had no son. Who would take his place?

Alex surveyed the small, stuffy room. Overflowing bookshelves lined the wall. A large painting of Jesus covered one wall, and the other was covered by photographs, plaques and various certificates. The Reverend's face beamed in a framed picture of him beside a happy little boy holding a pole with a big fish on the end of his line. He wore what looked like last Saturday's fishing hat, less a few tournament pins. The boy was about ten and had the handsome face of the man she'd seen at Jose's arraignment. "Voodoo?" she asked, pointing to the picture.

"Yes," he said, pain etching his face.

Nick went to the photograph and stared.

Alex glanced at a needlepoint pillow on the Reverend's side chair that read: THERE IS A GOD, BUT YOU'RE NOT HIM.

"Who's work?" she asked with a giggle.

"My wife's," he said with a loving smile on his face, "before she died. She did it back when I personally took on my congregation's problems, instead of turning them over to God. It was her way of telling me to 'stop playing Holy Ghost, Junior.' "

"Sounds like a wise woman," Alex said.

The Reverend grew wistful. "She was my one and only. I sure miss her. Now, what can I do for you?"

"I just met with Miss May," Alex began. "She was helpful. Jose's trial isn't your only problem with CPS. Tell me about the spanking incident with Chris's roommate, Jaime."

The Reverend gathered his thoughts. "First, I want to give you some background. The Fifth Ward is a close-knit community. In the early days, the streets weren't paved and there were no sidewalks. We were lucky if the city supplied water and electricity. You see, colored folks weren't too important then.

"We grew up in a different time," he continued. "At school we were led in morning prayer and taught about Bible heroes. There was a moral standard. Through trial and error, we learned the difference between right and wrong. When we misbehaved, we knew the consequences. My momma would grab a switch off the tree in our backyard and I'd get a whippin'. At school, teachers paddled us when we needed it."

"We're a long way from that today," Alex remarked.

"To see how far they can go, children will test adults. But deep down, they all crave the consistency discipline with love provides." He shook his head and gazed out the window facing a bleak city street. For just a moment, he went to another place and time. "Today's kids are bombarded by violent images and sex. Then we ask ourselves why teenage crime is so bad."

"I agree," Alex said. "But a reckless beating isn't discipline with love. Most troubled kids don't know the difference."

The Reverend nodded. "Discipline and abuse are two different things. The fact CPS can't define the distinction troubles me."

"Parents don't take time to discipline their kids anymore. If you're a minority, or poor, or both, you'll go to jail if you spank your child and he or she fights back," Nick said.

"It's gotten out of hand and, unfortunately, the law isn't

applied fairly," Alex added. "When Jaime reported the paddling to CPS, it probably gave Chris the idea to make a false report against Jose. But, at trial, it won't come into evidence. It's pure speculation. I need some direct evidence. Tell me about your history with Voodoo and Chris."

"All of our families are connected. Voodoo's mother and Miss May were best friends. Odelia had a hard life, but always remained strong by keeping her faith. She believed in family curses," the Reverend said. "Maybe she was right. Her mother died giving birth to her younger sister. Then her husband died of lung cancer, leaving her to raise her family alone. No matter what she did, her two children stayed in trouble. She buried her oldest son, Voodoo's brother, when he was thirty. He'd been in prison for manslaughter while Voodoo was a kid. When he got out he drank himself to death. When Voodoo was young, I spent time with him. He hated his brother's actions."

"Why did he change?"

"When Odelia died, I think he lost hope."

"Do you believe he has a family curse?"

The Reverend shrugged. "Maybe it's in the genes. Deep down, I think he knows he's wrong."

Alex looked intently at the Reverend. "Do you honestly think Voodoo knows he's wrong?"

The Reverend nodded. "But the action is in the streets. To my knowledge, he's never been arrested. The cops have been after him for years, but he's been too clever. His thugs do his dirty work. He didn't beat up your friend Friday night, Alex. He probably sent two or three of his boys to do the job and the police won't be able to pin it on him."

"The children at Shepherd's Cottages might lose their home," Alex said. "Why aren't you mad at Voodoo?"

"I don't like his actions, but I love him," the Reverend stated, his eyes fixed on the faded photograph.

Alex was dismayed by the depth of the Reverend's feelings

for the evil man who made sport of destroying lives.

Closing the door behind them, Alex and Nick tiptoed out of the church.

"Let's sit here on the stairs a minute," Alex said, watching the expansive blue sky turn several shades of pink, orange and purple. The sunset camouflaged the fact that they were smack dab in the middle of the ghetto, where barefoot children went hungry while mothers sold their bodies for ten dollars; where men shot each other in the street over a rock of crack. Even trash on the street wasn't noticeable now.

If only I can make Jose's case look this good. The Reverend could paint the picture for the jury.

"You pouting or thinking?" Nick asked.

"I don't understand how, at the same time, the Rev can be angry and forgive."

"Maybe it's his way of dealing with disappointment. He won't give up on Voodoo and prays constantly he'll fulfill his destiny."

"Destiny?" Alex queried with knitted eyebrows. "That two-bit criminal has one?"

Nick nodded. "The Reverend has seen miracles and believes with God, anything is possible. He believes God's plan for Voodoo's life is for good, not evil. He sees how Voodoo could be an important influence in this community."

"He's a dreamer too."

"Rest assured, he's not happy with Voodoo. But, to him, forgiveness is not an option. It's scriptural, black and white. He believes unless we forgive others, our prayers won't be answered."

"That's what he taught you?" Alex asked.

Nick nodded. "You just got the equivalent of a month of sermons. Private tutoring has its advantages." The sun finally slipped out of view and darkness overcame them. "Texas skies," he observed. "Can't beat 'em."

Alex jumped up and headed for her car. "Let's get the heck out of here before I get religion."

CHAPTER 7

With the help of an old friend at the jail, Nick ran a background check on Voodoo. The Reverend was right: Voodoo was clean. Although he was suspected of running drugs and pimping, undercover investigations had never produced probable cause for an arrest. So far, Voodoo had been smart enough to insulate himself—or he paid off the right people.

Concern for Alex's safety fueled Nick's desire to see Voodoo go down. Despite a threat to her safety, she kept the case. He admired her courageous spirit. He smiled to himself at the thought of last week's abrupt boardroom exit and her shocked expression when he grabbed her hand at the door. She had a habit of making quick exits. Did she ever look back? Did she leave out of anger or fear? Nick thought he saw through her.

She acts tough, but her little girl quality gives her away.

Recently, Nick had decided to back off relationships. He chose to follow the Reverend's advice to spend more time with God and focus on himself for a while. The Reverend did not know he still spent time at the Longhorn Saloon. Nick told himself he just went to dance, and so far, no one in the bar had tempted him beyond his ability to resist.

Still, since they'd met, he couldn't get Alex off his mind. Nick wondered if she'd be happy with a simple man like him, one without a fancy job title and sports car. She was special and he knew the chemistry between them was rare. Until after the trial, it was important to take it slow with her. As a man, Nick knew his job was to be strong. He hoped the Reverend was right about God always making a way from temptation because he would need help around Alex.

Nick left the jail and instead of heading home, he turned onto the freeway toward the Fifth Ward. It was time to pay Voodoo a visit.

Just minutes from Shepherd's Cottages, there was a small section of the Fifth Ward populated with dilapidated old mansions with paint-chipped siding and sagging upstairs porches, boarded windows, and graffiti-covered buildings.

This neighborhood is a landscaper's dream.

Nick turned onto a two-lane boulevard separated by a grassless medium.

He searched for Voodoo's street. Tax records showed the sprawling house still in Odelia's name, but property taxes were addressed to and paid by Voodoo.

Then he saw the familiar black car in the driveway. A new Toyota Camry was parked at the curb and an old TransAm was on cinder blocks in the front yard. Drapes drawn, the house looked quiet. Nick glanced at his watch. It was nearly eleven a.m.

Nick exited his car and walked up the front sidewalk. Finding the doorbell out of order, he knocked and was overwhelmed by the smell of bacon and eggs when a pretty young girl answered in a revealing red tube top that covered artfully enhanced breasts. Her toned limbs were accentuated by short-shorts and high heels. With a spatula in one hand and a cigarette in the other, she waved him in like an expected guest.

"Honey, who's there?" a cheerful male voice called from

inside.

"Who are you?" she asked Nick. "You's so cute. It don't matter to me long as I get's to look atcha."

"Nick Wright. I'm here to see Voodoo. We have mutual friends."

Her heavily lashed eyes lit up. "Says he's a friend," she called. Then, leaning her perfumed body close, she whispered, "We'll have ourselves a party. Follow me."

The provocative swish of her hips made Nick wonder which high-dollar strip club she worked. Years ago, for extra cash, he'd been a bouncer at the Red Door. But, while his ex-wife loved to spend the money, she was insanely jealous when he worked after hours as a bouncer. Looking back, he saw it may have contributed to the downfall of their marriage.

The interior of Voodoo's house was not the devil's den he'd envisioned. There was no doubt the man of the house had plenty of cash. Nick entered a huge kitchen adjacent to a comfortable den that looked out onto a landscaped swimming pool and yard. Tall tropical plants were everywhere.

"Hey, man." Voodoo smiled, then stretched out a hand. "What can I do for you?"

Returning the handshake, Nick introduced himself. "I'm on Shepherd's Cottages Board of Directors. Seems you're hellbent on making trouble for us."

"That so?" Voodoo's tone changed. His coal black eyes danced with curiosity.

"It bothers me you want to shut the place down."

Voodoo was silent and the two men stared. They were both at least six-three and weighed around two hundred pounds. Voodoo's muscles rippled in a black T-shirt and jeans. The man was strong and just crazy enough to be dangerous. Nick didn't want to start a fight.

The girl's sigh broke an uncomfortable silence. "You stayin' for breakfast, cowboy?"

"No, thanks," Nick answered.

Voodoo shot her a look that said, "Keep quiet."

"Follow me," he told Nick. Then squeezing her rear-end, said to the girl, "Keep those biscuits warm, honey."

He walked toward a closed door on the far side of the room and took a key from his jean pocket. They entered what was obviously his mission control center. The walls were deep crimson, tubular black lights around the perimeter illuminated fluorescent posters of sixties heroes—Jimi Hendrix, Peter Fonda as Easy Rider, and Janis Joplin. The only thing missing was a butt-filled ashtray and a bong. A huge vase of red roses emitted a fragrant aroma that permeated the room.

Voodoo sat behind a massive chrome and glass desk in an expensive leather chair. He waved Nick toward a similar chair opposite him.

An enormous TV screen, several regular screens, and a cluster of small surveillance screens covered one wall. Nick wondered how many cameras were aimed at Shepherd's Cottages or Alex's townhome. As a knot formed in his stomach, he made a mental note to install Alex's security system immediately.

A stereo and computer system sat on a credenza behind Voodoo. Along with some books, Nick spied the same photograph he'd seen in the Reverend's office. He wondered why. Voodoo clicked a button on the stereo remote control and Janis Joplin's voice filled the room. The crystal-clear sound emanated from strategically placed speaker cubes. A mantled fireplace was in the middle of the far wall and Nick guessed it might disguise a hidden vault. Voodoo was organized and smart, a fact which made him more dangerous.

Leaning back in his chair, Voodoo steepled his hands and leveled a penetrating gaze at Nick. "What do you want?"

"Tell me why you want to hurt the only man who's ever been a father to you."

A scalding flash of anger blazed in Voodoo's eyes. "What do

you mean?"

"We both know you put your nephew up to making the false charge against his house parent, Jose Gonzales. I'm likewise sure you know if Jose is convicted, the Reverend will lose Shepherd's Cottages."

"What happens at the Reverend's foster home has nothing to do with me."

"You've talked to CPS."

Voodoo yawned. "A lady named Camilla did come out and talk to me. Let's just say her and I got along fine."

Nick felt his blood pressure rising and knew he had to maintain self-control or he'd throttle the guy. Although he didn't agree with the Reverend, he respected him enough not to do something he'd regret. Nick resolved to be slow to anger and quick to forgive. "You've followed in your brother's footsteps. Big mistake."

"I may be going straight to Hell," Voodoo taunted. "But, on the way, I'll have a good time."

"In the meantime, you ignore those affected by your poor choices. The Fifth Ward is your home too, and innocent children will lose if you shut us down."

Voodoo shook his head. "They can go other places. He didn't need to put them there."

"So far, you've escaped the consequences of your actions. But count on it, your days are numbered."

"Maybe so." Voodoo lit a cigarette and filled the air between them with smoke. "Tell the Reverend if he wants to play with fire, he's going to get burned."

★

Alex's phone rang early Thanksgiving Day. Already baking banana bread and cookies, she grabbed the cordless in the kitchen. "Hello?"

"Morning. Anyone need a security system?" he said cheerfully.

"Give me a minute. I'll open the garage door." Alex slammed down the phone and dashed upstairs, two steps a stride. After washing flour-caked hands, she splashed water on her face, smoothed blush on her checks, then hastily applied lipgloss. "I'm a mess," she shrieked, pulling a headband over uncombed hair.

She tore off her flannel pajamas and drew on a pair of jeans and a shirt. Bolting down the stairs, she smelled something burning. Grabbing a potholder, she whisked a tray of cookies out of the oven just in time.

Siva barked and jumped against the sliding glass door until Alex opened it. She stepped into the garage and flipped the outer door switch. When the door opened, she found Nick unloading gear in the driveway.

Alex's heart skipped a beat. In his usual casual garb, Nick's long, wet hair had a natural wave.

"Hello, gorgeous." Nick grabbed his tool kit and a spool of wire.

She looked at the materials he held. "What's this going to run me?"

"We'll put it on your tab," he said. Then, sniffing the air, he said, "Or ... do I smell cookies?"

After closing the garage door they walked through the patio toward the house.

"Alex, look! Between the fence and the bricks just above the hose holder, a mama dove sitting on her nest."

They stood a moment staring at the bird, who looked placidly back at them.

"Unusual she would be here now," Nick said.

"When will the eggs hatch?"

"Probably in three or four weeks."

"I wonder why they picked my patio. This should be interesting." Alex disappeared into the kitchen. "Want to try the first batch of the day?"

With a big grin on his face, Nick followed her inside.

When Alex handed him a warm cookie, he took his first bite. Nick's expression was blank, then he closed his eyes for a second.

He ate the cookie in only a couple of bites.

"Um, um good!" he said with a coy smile.

"Get busy," she said. "I have lots more to do before we go."

While Nick wired windows, installed motion detectors and a panic button beside her bed, Alex baked. Then it was time to head to Shepherd's Cottages. "The dispatch service will start Monday," he said, rolling wire back onto the spool.

Nick helped her load her baked goods inside the truck.

When they arrived, Shepherd's Cottages was in high gear. Guests prepared tables of food while young children darted around. Rosemary hugged Alex, then helped carry treats to the activity center.

The children clamored around Alex. Once inside the dining hall, she viewed their latest drawings and played games until the cook announced dinner. Everyone flocked to the dining room. Alex's mouth watered at the delicious smells of home-cooked food arranged on folding tables, decorated with baskets of miniature pumpkins, dried corn ears and artificial fall leaves.

Board members, their families and members of the Reverend's church gathered before an array of traditional holiday dishes: three kinds of dressings, several homemade cranberry sauces, mouth-watering gravies, yams done every-which-way-but-loose, casseroles, several hams, turkeys, chicken, homemade breads and plenty of sugared ice tea and coffee.

Nick and the older boys from Cottage Five finished playing tag football. "Save me a place," he muttered, then disappeared to the men's room.

When everyone was seated, they all held hands while the Reverend said grace. Alex was moved by his sincere praise and thanksgiving to the Lord. She wasn't sure she'd ever felt like that about anyone, much less a God she couldn't see or feel. But a warm current passed between them—the same tingly sensation she felt on the plane the day she met the Reverend.

When the prayer ended, Alex felt light and woozy.

For a moment, she felt as if she'd floated on a cotton candy blanket without a care in the world.

An instant later, the children were their rambunctious selves again and everyone lined up to devour the feast. Thanks to Alex's contribution, the dessert table was loaded and there was plenty for everyone.

The joyful atmosphere was shattered when an older boy, eyes filled with fear, burst into the room and let out a chilling scream, "Fire! Cottage Five is in flames. Thomas is missing."

Alex froze. She remembered the shy little boy she'd met the first day. The Reverend's faith couldn't overcome the dark cloud over the home. Her lawyer's mind sought the reason for the fire—and the source.

Voodoo?

A chilling thought struck and she swallowed hard. *Voodoo!* Despite all she'd heard about him, he was still an enigma. She'd trusted the Reverend, even put her judicial career on the line to help him, yet he insisted Voodoo was like his son.

Would Voodoo harm an innocent child to destroy Shepherd's Cottages? If so, would it make a difference in Jose's case?

Again, she thought of the foster home's vulnerability to civil liability.

If a child was harmed in the fire, CPS could accuse Shepherd's Cottages of negligence.

Her legal mind was spinning.

As though in slow motion, she saw Miss May run to the phone to call 911 while the Reverend ordered everyone out onto the lawn. Outside, she wasn't prepared for what she saw. The front of the small cottage was ablaze with shooting flames. Heavy smoke swiftly cast a pall over the late afternoon sky. Mr.

Samples grabbed the garden hose and doused piles of burning leaves sparked by a sudden wind. The acrid smell made the children cough. Screaming, they backed away toward the drive.

Alex's heart sank when she saw Nick pull a handkerchief from his pocket, wrap it around his face, then run into the building.

Please let the cottage be empty.

How could a child survive those flames? Was Nick too late? She pictured little Thomas huddled in a ball in a closet, or under a bed, crying in fear as the angry blaze overcame him.

A tug on her arm made her look down. Thomas's big sister, Nikita, stared at her through tear-filled eyes. As the sound of fire engines drew closer, she folded the child in her arms. "He'll be alright, baby. Nick will take care of him."

The words had no sooner left her lips when she heard an explosion from inside the building. "Nick!" she screamed, as the unmistakable smell of gas permeated the area and merciless flames raged toward the skies. Fearful the blast had ended Nick's life, she realized how deeply she felt for a man she'd only known a short time. As she watched the house burn, moments seemed an eternity.

The Reverend ordered everyone back to the activity center, out of harm's way. Just then, fire trucks arrived and quickly showered the fire with high-powered blasts of water. Two men in flame-retardant suits prepared to enter what was left of the building. Moments later, an ambulance pulled up and prepared to receive survivors.

Like a bad dream she couldn't awaken from, the fire held her captive.

Suddenly, Nick, with little Thomas in his arms, burst through the already shattered front window one step ahead of a second blast that leveled the building.

Alex put Nikita down and began to run toward Nick and Thomas, both of whom were knocked unconscious.

"No, Alex," the Reverend ordered, then restrained her by

grabbing her arm and pulling her toward him.

Wild with emotion, Alex leaned against the Reverend for support as they watched paramedics load Nick and Thomas, still clutching a blackened teddy bear, into the ambulance. As it pulled away, tears flowed down her checks. "This is Voodoo's Thanksgiving present, isn't it?"

Eyes on the dying blaze, the Reverend nodded.

CHAPTER 8

On the way to the hospital, Nick fought for air. The oxygen mask helped, but the putrid smell of Thomas's burned flesh remained in his nostrils.

Nick's injuries were minor, and ER doctors told him that Thomas was worse off.

"He's in shock," the doctor said. "Second-degree burns cover eighty percent of his body and he may have lung damage. I'll give you something to treat those superficial burns and pain medicine in case you need it. You're both lucky to be alive."

While waiting to be released, Nick recalled Voodoo's words from the previous day, "Tell the Reverend if he wants to play with fire, he's going to get burned." Had Voodoo deliberately set the fire? If so, was it planned before or after yesterday's visit? He thought of Thomas. Was Voodoo's rage so deep he'd burn down a house with a child inside? Nick was certain the message was a warning and the fire was planned. Part of Voodoo's game.

The Reverend didn't know about his visit. He'd tell him later, but now he wanted to get to the investigation before it was botched. He'd already attributed Voodoo's ability to elude the law to sloppy police work. He regretted not installing surveillance cameras at Shepherd's Cottages. Until now, he wasn't aware how far Voodoo would go. Nick had to stop him before he hurt Alex.

While Miss May and the Reverend sat calmly, Alex paced in the patient waiting room. The Shepherd's Cottages fire was the lead story on the evening TV newscasts. Alex could barely watch the coverage. While paramedics loaded Nick and Thomas into the ambulance, Alex saw herself sobbing on the Reverend's shoulder in front of what was left of Cottage Five.

"Thanksgiving dinner for thirty-five abused children ended tragically when fire broke out at Shepherd's Cottages, a foster home under investigation by Children's Protective Services," veteran reporter Christy Malone began. "Former police officer Nicholas Wright risked his life to save a small boy trapped in the burning building, one of five cottages on the property. The boy and his sister are in CPS custody pending permanent placement. Although the man escaped serious injury, the boy has been seriously burned and will take Life Flight to Shriners Burns Hospital in Galveston. Investigators say the blaze may have been caused by a gas stove leak. In other news involving the foster home, trial of a house parent at the facility begins next month. The defendant, Jose Gonzales, has been accused of sexually molesting a teenage boy in his custody. His lawyer, Alex Stockton, was at the home during the fire. CPS social worker for the home, Camilla Roe, told Channel Two the facility will close. More on the fire and the burned boy's condition at ten. Back to you, John."

Viewing the image of the day's events stunned Alex. She didn't remember seeing a TV reporter earlier, but she now saw the fire in living color. Alex's hopes of being discreet about her involvement in Jose's case vanished nearly as quickly as the cottage succumbed to flames. If Mike Delany didn't see the TV report, he'd soon hear about it. Mike was a friend, but his political interests came first. The governor wanted a winning candidate, not a crusading lawyer who could fall flat on her face. Alex would have to find a way to explain why it was a good political move for herself and Governor Hastings. It would be tricky since she wasn't entirely convinced herself, but she'd use a technique she'd been trained to master right out of law school. She'd wing it.

The smell of smoke and a hand on her shoulder interrupted her thoughts. It was Nick. His face and arms were cut and bruised, but he was there and she was glad to see him.

Grabbing his shoulders, she gave him a big hug. "I'm so glad you're safe."

"Ouch," he said.

"Sorry, cowboy." Alex ran a hand through his singed hair. "While saving Thomas's life, you got a cheap haircut. I'm impressed."

Nick gave a half-smile, looking at her through pained eyes. "Thank God he was under the bed in the back bedroom. Voodoo warned me yesterday. I wish I'd taken him literally."

"Voodoo?"

"Yes. Last thing he said to me was, 'Tell the Reverend if he plays with fire, he's going to get burned.' "

"Is he capable of murder?"

Nick shrugged. "After today, I don't know." He then told Alex about his meeting with Voodoo. "Since we were all in the activity center, I doubt he thought anyone would be inside the cottage. I need to talk to the arson investigator."

"Channel Two beat you to it. They attributed the fire to a stove gas leak, not arson, which makes Shepherd's Cottages look bad."

Nick frowned. "Only a sloppy fire investigator would attribute that fire to a gas leak." He paused for a long moment. "Let's go see Thomas before he goes to Shriners Hospital."

When they entered Thomas's room, a nurse was treating his burns. Alex wondered if his biological parents knew about the fire. Her heart went out to the innocent boy caught in a turf war between Shepherd's Cottages and Voodoo.

The rapid click of high heels in the hospital corridor grew louder, then entered the room. Alex turned and faced Camilla Roe.

"Move over," the woman snapped, pushing Alex aside.

Alex was too stunned to speak.

"What have you done to this child?" Camilla shrieked.

"The fire was an accident," Alex answered. "No one knew he was in the house."

"Always an accident when it comes to Shepherd's Cottages." Camilla bit out her words. Then turning to the nurse, she said, "This child is in my care. Note his file that there are to be no visitor's from Shepherd's Cottages under any circumstances."

Alex gasped. "What about Nikita?"

"She's already in my custody."

"Camilla, this is wrong," Alex said. "The fire wasn't an accident."

Camilla rolled her eyes.

Alex knew it wasn't the right time or place to bring up Jose's case, but she couldn't resist the opportunity to discuss it. "You know I represent Jose Gonzales. Unless you'll turn them over voluntarily, I'll ask the Court to make you produce your investigative and psychological reports on Chris Jackson."

"You'll get nothing from me without a court order."

Alex expected her answer. Camilla would never turn over reports without a fight. True cooperation occurred only when you agreed with her. It dawned on her that CPS wouldn't take kindly to her actions on behalf of Jose. Her image with the powerful agency was at stake. If she rocked the boat now, she'd only create future problems for herself. As judge of the juvenile court, the last thing she wanted was CPS to buck her every step of the way. But it was professional misconduct if she didn't fight CPS to get the reports. She'd file the discovery motion Monday morning and set a hearing.

When the nurse asked her and Nick to leave Thomas's room, they joined the others in the waiting room. While Nick talked to the Reverend and Miss May, Alex tried to listen, but her chest was tight and pent up with tears. She slipped into the nearby women's room where her grief was insuppressible. She cried at the sink and didn't hear the door open. Miss May took her in her arms.

Moments passed before Alex raised her head from Miss May's shoulder and stared at their image in the mirror. When handed a paper towel to dry her eyes, Alex stared at the woman's serene face. "How can you stay so cool?"

"Once in a while I have a cry like that, hon, but I just keeps going," she answered. "Do your best, that's all you can do. There's lots of things in this world we don't have control of. Just put them in God's hands and he'll carry your load."

Alex wanted to take Miss May's advice to heart, but she'd never embraced religion. She wondered if there was a God who could really take care of things. Just to be safe, she'd file that discovery motion next week.

Saturday afternoon Alex prepared to entertain her good friends, Derek and Candy. When they arrived at seven, a cozy fire burned, assorted candles flickered, and a tray of sumptuous appetizers was on the coffee table: pâté, baked Brie, boiled shrimp, smoked trout, and plenty of French bread.

Candy wore a short, tight skirt and skin-tight bodysuit to accentuate her tan, ripped body. Friends since girlhood, loyalty bridged the gap between Candy's free spirit and Alex's studious nature. But Alex was always ready to walk on the wild side with her best friend.

"Where have you been?" Candy asked, planting a big kiss on her cheek.

"'Working on a new case, and thinking about becoming a judge," Alex answered on her way to the kitchen.

Derek hugged Alex, then plopped down on the couch and fired up his laptop computer. "Before you file your petition, let's look at your chart."

Moments later, Alex returned with an open wine bottle and three glasses.

"How's that handsome stud of yours?" Candy asked.

"Last week, he wasn't so handsome," Alex said. Then she filled them in on Bryce's attack, their subsequent breakup, and the possible connection to Jose's case.

"The violence worries me," Candy said when she finished.

"Me too," Alex said. "But I'm fairly secure since I have a new security system and my own personal bodyguard."

"Bodyguard?" Candy followed Alex back into the kitchen. As Alex pulled a tray of artichoke squares from the oven, she told her about Nick.

"Alex," Derek called from the living room, "Come see this."

For the past three years, Derek's knowledge of astrology had guided her through the alligator-infested swamps of Houston's legal scene. He'd given her advice on all aspects of her career: from hiring employees to choosing and handling cases. She'd also consulted him on personal matters, including men in her life. Before a date, Alex would log onto the Internet, retrieve his birthday from driver's license records, then call Derek to run his astrological chart. How often the information turned out to be accurate was amazing.

Derek peered at his computer screen. "When did you take the case?"

"Mid-November."

"Lots going on here," he mused.

"I knew something weird was happening," Alex remarked.

"You were on the news Thanksgiving," Derek said. "Was it about your new case?"

Alex nodded. "My new client worked at the foster home where the fire took place. We were there for lunch and then realized the little boy was in the burning home. We suspect arson by the same person who beat Bryce up."

"I'm sorry I missed it." Candy tossed her mane of tight, dark curls. "I fasted all day, to balance my energies, you know."

The friends talked while they drank wine and munched appetizers.

Derek intently studied his computer screen. "Expect drastic life changes in the near future," he said at last.

"I'm feeling them now," Alex giggled.

"Be careful, girl," Candy warned. "Don't let this case spoil your chance at the judgeship. You love the law almost as much as you love men."

"Must not have loved Bryce. She let him go easy," Derek told Candy.

"That's a woman's prerogative," Candy said in Alex's defense. "Tell us about this cop. What's his sign?"

Alex shook her head. She hadn't thought about Nick's birthday. "He's not a policeman anymore; he's a businessman. And his sign, I don't know," she answered. "We're just working together."

"Tell it to someone else, Alex," he laughed.

Candy pulled a cigarette from her purse. "Want to share one?"

Alex shook her head. "No, thanks."

Candy's eyes widened. The girls had shared cigarettes since junior high.

Suddenly, the room was stuffy and Alex longed for fresh air. "Come outside, I want you to see something."

They followed her to the back patio where she pointed to the mysterious dove's nest. The mama bird zealously guarded her eggs.

"Cool." Candy lit her cigarette and the women talked a few

minutes before she put it out in the clay pot.

The timer signaled dinner and the close friends dined with the sounds of John Legend on Alex's iPod. Then Alex served tiramisu and coffee with Frangelico.

Shortly thereafter, Candy and Derek stood to leave. They invited Alex to go dancing with them, but she begged off saying she needed to prepare for trial. Truth was, she didn't want to go.

"I know that everything is going to go alright with your trial," Candy said as she hugged her goodbye.

Later, after she finished cleaning up, Alex thought about her friends and their lifestyle. Metaphysical hobbies had always been a part of her life, but tonight for some reason, she felt uncomfortable. It crossed her mind that she was outgrowing her old lifestyle. If it wasn't the cards or the planets, who would she turn to? Maybe the Reverend could help. Tomorrow was Sunday. She'd attend morning services, then talk to the Reverend afterward.

The next morning, Miss May greeted Alex warmly at the church door. The only white face at the church, Alex was more at home there than any other church she ever attended. Moments before the service began she took a seat next to Rosemary and the children.

She looked at the front pews. Today was different. Looking like nurses clad in pristine white, a group of elder women filled them.

Rosemary must have seen the look of confusion on Alex's face. "Communion," she whispered.

Moments later, Nick slid into the aisle seat beside Alex. He wasn't his usual self. His pale face was still bruised and his slicked-back hair lacked its usual luster. His presence comforted Alex. The congregation was somber; Thursday's fire stirred a need for togetherness.

The organist's soulful hymn lightened Alex's heart. An elderly choir member led them. "Praise the Lord," he sang. "I thank Him in the morning ... I thank Him in the evening ..." The audience began to echo his praises and before long, the room's dark mood lifted.

Soon, the Reverend appeared, Bible in hand, and climbed the pulpit. During the opening prayer, Alex felt a strong breeze blow through the congregation. She looked for air conditioning vents, but saw none. They were surrounded by an unmistakable supernatural presence.

The Reverend welcomed the crowd, then brought up the fire. "Thanks go to Mr. Wright for risking his life to save Thomas."

As Nick humbly acknowledged a standing ovation, tears formed in Alex's eyes. Then, she felt an inner glow when the Reverend singled her out with a special greeting. None of her career accolades had ever made her feel this good.

"People, we've got to be strong," the Reverend preached fervently. "Since we began Shepherd's Cottages, opposition to our efforts to rid our community of drugs and violence has intensified. But God gave us the authority and power to fight and win!"

The congregation responded with cheers and shouts of "Amen."

"Let's don't see these setbacks as stumbling blocks," he continued. "Let's view them as opportunities to grow! In these dark times, we must increase our faith."

The Reverend entreated them to pray for Jose and his upcoming trial. In closing, he directed Mr. Samples to lead communion: "Let's share the Lord's supper."

With a nod, Mr. Samples motioned for the women in white to serve everyone a small plastic cup of grape juice and a fresh piece of bread. Then, he read the communion prayer. " 'Do this in remembrance of me,' " he quoted.

After the service, Alex waited for the Reverend to finish

greeting parishioners. "Can we talk a minute?"

He waved a hand toward his office.

Once inside, Alex began, "Do you have an opinion about psychics?"

"My opinion isn't important. God's thoughts are what matters," he answered. "Do you read the Bible?"

"No."

He scribbled some notes on a Post-it pad, then handed it to her. "Study these and pray about it. You might find some answers."

Strangely lightheaded, Alex left the Reverend's office and walked through the sanctuary to the front door. A quick glance at his note revealed he had written down scripture references. Gazing up at the white bird in the stained-glass window, she was thankful he didn't hit her over the head with a sermon.

Alex thought about following through on the Reverend's advice.

What if it changes my life?

She liked things the way they were now. Success came easy and since graduating from law school at twenty-three, she'd climbed the career ladder faster than she had ever dreamed. She was fortunate to have the energy, drive and motivation to achieve status in life. Her relationships with friends and coworkers were good. Thinking about marriage was a different story. Her childhood dreams involved business and achievement, not white dresses and honeymoons. She cherished her independence and marrying young was never her goal. Although past thirty, she knew she still had time. Someday having children and buying a home with a white picket fence would move to the front burner. But right now, she was where she wanted to be. Comfortable. Like her best friend, Candy, always said, "If it ain't broke, why fix it?"

The thought of reading the Bible for the first time in her life was intimidating. Was it her inner rebel or did she fear change?

Curiosity fueled a hunger for knowledge. Once in a probate case, while disposing of an elderly woman's property, she came across an old leather-bound Bible containing records of the woman's family history. For some reason, Alex couldn't throw it away.

One of these days, I'll look up those verses from the Reverend.

CHAPTER 9

Tuesday morning, just before the hearing on her discovery motion, Alex met Jose in the holdover cell behind the courtroom.

"How are you?" she asked.

Head down, Jose shrugged.

He looked fatigued in his rumpled orange jail suit and with his sandaled feet shackled to the chair. Alex winced at the poor inmate treatment.

Plastic sandals in the middle of winter?

"I know you're nervous. Our appearance in court this morning is just a discovery hearing, and I think we have a good chance of getting what we want."

Her words seemed to ease him, and he began talking.

"Nick came by on his way to Laredo to find Angelina," he said. "I loved her. But her father was evil."

"I hope he finds her. Angelina could explain your statutory rape charge. But I need an eyewitness from the park to corroborate your story."

Jose shrugged. "I didn't see nobody there."

Alex updated Jose about the Cottage Five fire, Thomas's condition, and Nick's recent visit to Voodoo's house.

"Voodoo's anger—I don't understand."

Alex shook her head. "I've racked my brain to find a way to prove Voodoo orchestrated Chris's charges."

"Me too."

"Nick thinks he's intimidated everyone in the neighborhood. I wouldn't be surprised if Camilla Roe, the social worker, was in his pocket."

"I'm sure it's true."

"Why?"

"Because, since I know him, whenever the Reverend has trouble with Voodoo, she gives us trouble."

Alex grew interested. "Tell me about it."

"One night last summer, around ten, I went 'round the corner for breakfast milk. On the way, when I passed Billy's Pool Hall, I saw her playing pool with Voodoo."

"You saw them from the street?"

Jose nodded. "There's big windows in front. I was curious, so I parked across the street and watched them. When they left, Camilla was so drunk she couldn't walk straight. Voodoo carried her to her car. I couldn't see what they was doing but they were there for awhile."

"Guess she sobered up," Alex said. Her heart raced. Her fears about Camilla's true interests in Shepherd's Cottages' downfall were confirmed. But unless she could tie it to other damaging evidence, none of it would be admissible. Marilyn's objection that it was irrelevant and mere speculation would surely be granted. The law doesn't prohibit Camilla and Voodoo from being friends.

"I hope I can get that information in at trial, but there may be problems," Alex said, then glanced at her watch. "We need to get into the courtroom."

Minutes later, Alex sat at counsel table, reviewing her notes.

Marilyn Rivera, the number two prosecutor, approached her table. "Good morning," she said.

"Mornin'," Alex returned. "You sure we can't compromise on this motion?"

The pretty young woman shook her head. "Not this case. I'm just the messenger. CPS wants your man."

Marilyn's words sounded cold, but Alex knew they were true. Normally, she worked well with adversaries. But this case was different. Marilyn's tone had an uncharacteristic iciness. Alex's hunch was she didn't control the case; she just took orders from her chief.

The back door opened and Alex turned and saw Camilla Roe, clutching a huge file, strut into the courtroom. Wearing a too-tight suit, her high heels clicked on the linoleum, and her perfume filled the air. Her frown toward Marilyn showed contempt for the legal process. Prosecutors knew she was notoriously difficult to work with at trial.

Judge Villareal entered the courtroom. "Counsel, ready to proceed?"

As usual Alex was awed by her grace and beauty. Alex stood. "Thanks for hearing us today, judge. We are here on a defense motion to compel the State to turn over the complainant's CPS and juvenile file, including any and all investigative and psychological reports."

It was Marilyn's turn. "Judge, before ruling, the State requests you to review the file *in camera*. Under the Brady case, information to which the Defendant is entitled is limited."

Judge Villareal nodded. "I'm aware of the case, counselor."

"Chris Jackson, the victim of this crime, has been in CPS custody for years," Marilyn continued. "We contend that the bulk of his CPS file is irrelevant to the present case. By reviewing the documents *in camera* and selecting only items the defendant is legally entitled to, you'll protect the child's constitutional right to privacy."

"The Brady case also supports my motion, judge," Alex responded. "Chris Jackson's entire record is crucial to my client's defense. He has both extensive juvenile and CPS history. To deny Jose Gonzales access to information about the complaining witness denies him a fair trial."

"Let me see the file," Judge Villareal said, holding her hand out toward the prosecutor.

Marilyn turned to Camilla Roe, whose lips were pencil-thin as she handed over the file.

"I'll review it during lunch," the judge ordered. "Court is recessed until one-thirty."

Lunch break flew by and Alex returned to the courtroom a few minutes early and found the judge still at her desk, reviewing Chris's CPS file. She quietly slipped into her seat at counsel table and while she waited, thought about the woman in front of her.

Judge Dyan Villareal was a pioneer for women in the legal field and the first female district court judge in Texas. With over thirty years of judicial experience, she was still beautiful and highly regarded. Soft lines on her face imparted wisdom, strength and boosted juror's confidence in the legal process. Alex trusted her to do the right thing. She only hoped that when she became a member of the judiciary, she would be like Judge Villareal.

At one-thirty sharp, Marilyn Rivera and Camilla Roe entered the courtroom through a side door.

When everyone was seated, Judge Villareal looked up. "I've reviewed the child's protective services file," she began. "Arguments, counsel?"

Marilyn Rivera stood. "For the record, the State objects to the production of any CPS reports prior to and unrelated to the incident."

"Your Honor," Alex responded, "since this case is a swearing match between my client and the complaining witness, it's crucial for the defense to determine whether Chris Jackson has a pattern of lying.

"I agree," Judge Villareal said. "For purposes of discovery only, you can see his file." She looked at Marilyn. "As to what portions the defense can use at trial, we'll take it up then."

"Thank you, judge," Alex said when the clerk handed her a copy of Chris's file.

After the judge left the courtroom, Camilla Roe glared at Alex, slammed her file shut, then turned on her heel and stormed off.

Marilyn rolled her eyes and shrugged.

Alex quickly reviewed the file. "Part of page three of the incident report is missing!" she exclaimed.

Marilyn located the original in her file, then nodded. "Mine too."

"Grab Camilla," Alex told Marilyn. "I'll get the judge."

Alex knocked on the judge's chamber door.

"Come in," she called.

"Excuse me, Your Honor. There's a problem with the investigative report," Alex said. "Miss Rivera went to get Ms. Roe."

The judge frowned. "I have a jury coming in at two."

Marilyn entered chambers. "I couldn't catch her."

"Part of page three of the CPS investigative report is missing. It looks like it was torn off to me," Alex said.

"Same with the original," Marilyn added.

"What do you two suggest?" Judge Villareal asked.

Alex and Marilyn looked at one another.

"The report is crucial to my client's defense," Alex answered.

The judge opened her black desk calendar. "We could put the trial off until late spring."

Alex's heart raced. "My client needs to get this trial behind him."

Not to mention Shepherd's Cottages.

"The third page only contains blanks for witness information," Marilyn Rivera said. "The social worker assured me there were no witnesses, so it's questionable whether page three will even help the defense."

Judge Villareal tapped the desktop with her pencil eraser, poised to change the trial entry in her calendar. With a deep sigh and a purposeful look from over her reading glasses, she told Alex to make a snap decision and hope it was correct.

Alex's deeper senses screamed Camilla Roe tampered with the report. But how could she prove it? It was an uphill battle because proving CPS wrong was nearly impossible. Besides, the jury was only allowed to consider solid evidence.

Alex had to think fast. Judge Villareal forced her into a corner. If she put off the trial, there was no guarantee she'd ever learn what entry the page originally contained. Jose would remain in jail and Shepherd's Cottages would probably close. If she kept the early trial setting and won, everyone could again focus on the children.

Before she decided, she wanted to make sure self-interest didn't motivate her to move forward with the trial. Television coverage had opened Jose's case up to public scrutiny and a victory might seal her appointment. On the other hand, a loss could dampen her chances. Besides, if the trial was put off and she got the appointment, she wouldn't get to see the case through as planned. Under the circumstances, it was clearly best to keep the original trial setting.

"Let's move forward," she announced. "But I'll preserve my appellate record before we bring in the jury."

"I'll argue the report is privileged anyway," Marilyn said.

"Very well." Judge Villareal glanced at her watch. "See you two Monday morning at ten."

The two attorneys left chambers and, while they quickly gathered their things at counsel table, a jury panel filled the courtroom.

"How long will this week's case last?" Alex asked, motioning toward jurors.

"Couple of days," Marilyn answered. "Because of his priors, the defendant won't take the stand. "Will your man testify?"

Good question.

"I'm not sure."

"He better think twice," Marilyn warned before leaving the courtroom.

★

Back at the office, Alex pulled the file from her briefcase. "Ruth?" Alex called. "I want to pick your brain. Judge Villareal let me review the entire file, but an important page was missing. The judge would have allowed me to postpone the trial, but we decided to move forward."

"That sounds right."

"Now, I need to decide whether Jose will take the stand."

"Have you made your list?" Ruth asked.

"Good idea." Alex pulled out a legal pad and drew a line down the middle of the page and wrote "pro" on one side and "con" on the other. "Pro," she thought out loud, "Jose gets to tell his side. Con: They don't believe him. Either way, his prior offense comes in."

Elbow on her desk, Alex rubbed her chin a moment. "Safest route for the defense is to rest right behind the State, then argue reasonable doubt based on insufficient evidence. My fear is if we don't present defensive testimony, the jury will think we're hiding something."

"Tough call."

"The State's burden of proof is steep. Chris's word alone shouldn't cut it. There's no scientific evidence a sexual crime took place."

"Won't the jury believe Chris?"

"Probably," Alex reluctantly acknowledged. "Unless Jose convinces them otherwise."

"They charged Jose with lesser-included offenses?"

Alex nodded. "They can try for aggravated sexual assault, which carries up to life; sexual assault which can also carry up to life; and simple assault, which could get him up to twenty years."

"So, unless you get an acquittal, Jose faces up to twenty years."

"That's the minimum if he's convicted of the least offense. You're ready for your criminal law final," Alex said with a grin. "I'll wait until trial to decide if Jose will testify. First, we need to find Angelina."

"What kind of plea bargain did the State offer?"

Alex stopped reviewing her file. "Plea bargain? Funny you should ask."

Picking up the phone, she called Marilyn Rivera. "Can we meet to discuss a plea? We should at least explore it."

"No deals, this case," Marilyn answered.

"What?"

"You heard me."

"That's against office policy," Alex blurted, nearly losing her temper. "Besides, Judge Villareal will expect it."

"I just follow orders," Marilyn stated before hanging up.

CHAPTER 10

Nick left for Laredo that morning long before dawn. During the quick flight from Hobby Airport, he thought about his mission. He had to find Angelina. She could corroborate Jose's story, proving that the previous rape charges against him were trumped up by Angelina's abusive father. She had been Jose's high school sweetheart, and he still loved her. If only she had not been caught by her father the night she and Jose planned to elope.

Jose knew nothing about Angelina's whereabouts, only her old address. It would be a start for Nick. Unaccustomed to driving a rented Toyota Camry, he entered Laredo's narrow streets where children played. They scattered before his slow moving car. Overweight women pushed baby strollers past small shops and liquor stores. Like Houston's Fifth Ward, poverty and oppression placed its heavy hand here.

Sounds of salsa music kindled memories of Nick's youth. During spring break, it was tradition for him and his friends to cross the border, buy cheap tequila, then head straight to Boys Town, Matamoros's infamous red light district. Then, to prove their manhood, some of them entered sleazy rooms and paid twenty dollars to bed a prostitute. Nick felt sure some of his friends didn't sincerely want to go through with the ritual but, like him, wouldn't admit it.

As Nick drove deeper into the residential section of Laredo, the neighborhoods worsened. Nick studied Mapquest on his iPad. When he came to where Jose's old neighborhood should be, he faced the entrance to a new highway. Plan A was out. Now he had to formulate Plan B.

Nick found a small diner and ordered lunch before calling information. There was no listing for Angelina Ramirez or her father. His only option was to search courthouse records. If Angelina was still in Laredo, he'd surely locate her. He wolfed down a cheeseburger and fries.

What would he do when he found her? His hunch was Angelina would testify for Jose, but things might not go that smoothly.

The waitress was attentive and talkative when, because of the new highway, Nick shared his disappointment over not finding Angelina's old house. She said some homeless victims of the city's condemnation proceedings had filed suit against the city. Nick thanked her for the information, then left her a twenty dollar tip.

Nick found himself amidst construction in Laredo's old courthouse. The smell of old books and floor wax mingled with the scent of new plywood.

At the information desk in the clerk's office, a friendly employee pointed him to a computer at the end of the counter. "Punch in names, then press enter," she said. "If you get stuck, I'll help."

Nick started with lawsuits. He found nothing under Angelina's name, but when he entered her father, there were dozens of lawsuits with his common name. It was impossible to tell which might have involved him.

Unfortunately, he didn't know Pedro's middle name. When he searched vital statistics records, he found a death certificate for Pedro Ricardo Ramirez. His address was the same one Jose gave him for Angelina. It had to be her father. The cause of death was listed as cerebral hemorrhage from a gunshot wound. Date of death was four months after Jose's rape conviction.

As the focus of his search narrowed, Nick's adrenaline flowed. When Nick did a lawsuit search under Pedro Ricardo Ramirez, a case number flashed across the screen. He was a respondent in a lawsuit filed by Angelina's mother shortly after Jose's case, and a month before his death.

Jotting down the case number, Nick couldn't contain his excitement. With a big smile, he approached the information clerk. "Can you pull this file, please?"

She entered the case number into her computer and frowned at the information appearing on her screen. She continued to punch keys, muttering under her breath.

Nick waited.

"It's a family court case," she said. "But I can't tell what kind. The record is sealed. You need a court order to look at it. Unfortunately, Judge Gomez is on vacation until the end of the month."

Nick gritted his teeth. "Can another judge give me permission?" he asked in an even voice.

"Not this week," she said. "They're all in Dallas at the Advanced Family Law Conference."

"Thanks for your help," he said, then strode out the door.

The courthouse was old. There was still a row of phone booths where you could sit down and make a call.

Ducking into one of them, Nick ran a hand through his hair and tried to remain calm.

Just a temporary setback.

Nick speculated about the file contents. Would they impact Jose's case? Had Angelina's mother filed for divorce because she learned the truth about her husband? Nick knew court-sealed records contained confidential information involving children's privacy or criminal conduct.

There must be a way to get the file.

Desperation can lead to absurdity. He thought about impersonating a police officer and asking to see the file, or sneaking into the courtroom after hours to find it himself. Nick shrugged. As a last resort, Alex could file a motion to open the records.

Out in the hall, Nick stepped directly into the path of the information clerk who had helped him earlier.

"I don't know why you need to see that file," she said, "but my gut tells me you have a good reason."

"It might save an innocent man's life."

"After you left, I remembered why the case sounded familiar. A friend of mine used to work in the county attorney's office. She knows about that family." She handed him a slip of paper. "Here's her name and number. Tell her I sent you."

Before he could thank her, she abruptly headed back to her desk.

He glanced at the note, then, walking outside, dialed the number on his cell phone.

A woman answered.

"Sylvia Moore?" Nick asked.

"Yes. Who's calling?"

"My name is Nick Wright. Helen, your friend at the courthouse, gave me your name and number. I'm a private investigator from Houston, ma'am. I need to find Angelina Ramirez. Helen said you might be able tell me about her family's case."

"What do you want to know?" she asked in a suspicious tone.

"Anything you tell me will be helpful. Can we meet?"

"Where are you?" the woman asked.

"I'm just outside the courthouse."

"Can you see Joe's Taqueria from there?"

"Yes. It's across the street."

"I'll meet you there in ten minutes."

At the restaurant, he ordered coffee and sat facing the window. His heart pounded when he saw an ancient white Chevrolet park in front. A middle-aged woman in a gray sweat suit left the car and walked into the restaurant.

Sylvia Moore wanted to know about Nick's quest. She listened with interest when he told her about Jose's case and why he needed Angelina's testimony.

She agreed to talk to Nick after he convinced her he would protect her confidentiality.

"Angelina's mother filed for divorce. Her husband beat her youngest daughter to death and called it an accident. Two days later, she killed her husband, then herself," Sylvia sighed.

"Why is the case sealed?"

"Because she was eight months pregnant and doctors were able to save the baby. Apparently she already had mental problems. Police believe she went off her medication."

The story stunned Nick. "Where was Angelina?" he asked.

"She was gone when it happened. After the funerals, she petitioned the Court for custody of her infant brother, but lost. She was still a minor herself. The Court placed her in a foster home. I don't know what happened to the brother."

"Where did they place her?"

"There's only one in Laredo: St. Agnes Center. She's probably gone now, but they may know where she is."

Nick drove into another depressed neighborhood. St. Agnes Center was a two-story building surrounded by boarded-up apartment complexes. He entered a weathered door and waited. No one was around, but he heard noises in a nearby room. He walked over and peeked inside the door. Several teenage girls sat together in front of the TV watching a Spanish soap opera. Nick tapped lightly. "Hello. Is the manager here?"

The girls looked up at him. One stood, walked to the door

and looked toward the stairs. "Maria." She sat back down and took her place in front of the TV. The other girls followed suit.

"What?" a woman yelled back.

Moments later, a thin woman with black eyeliner who looked to be in her early twenties, descended the stairs two at a time. "What can I do for you?" she asked, smoothing her hair.

"I'm looking for Angelina Ramirez."

The woman stopped. "Who are you?"

"Nick Wright. Private investigator from Houston. An old friend needs her help."

She motioned him to follow her. They sat at the kitchen table and Nick began his story.

"I don't have much time," he ended. "Trial is coming up quick."

The woman eyed Nick, then began to talk. "Angelina and I were placed here by the agency at the same time. We became friends," she offered. "Her heart was broken. She lost her whole family. She lived for winning custody of her baby brother."

"Where is she now?"

"Don't know. When she turned eighteen she left with a guy old enough to be her father. Don't know where she met him. He was mean. I didn't like him."

"What's his name?"

"Rudolfo Martinez. He wasn't from here."

"Are they in Laredo?"

She shook her head. "I don't think so. If you find her, say hello for me."

Nick thanked the kind woman, then left. Back in his car, he dialed information for Rudolfo Martinez. He tried each number he obtained, but none matched the one Angelina left the shelter with.

Before heading to the airport, Nick pulled up to the courthouse to do a last-minute records search on Rudolfo. He browsed through computer files and found no leads.

The bizarre story about Angelina's family fascinated and repulsed him. Though he'd learned a lot about her family, he was disappointed he didn't find her. He must have overlooked something.

The trip was over. He did all he could do in Laredo. As the sun set on his way to the airport for the short flight home, all he could think of was how he dreaded facing Alex empty-handed.

CHAPTER 11

Alex left the office and, paralyzed with fear and dread, made a beeline home. Marilyn's voice on the phone and harsh words told the story.

Bryce must be involved.

The State's case was weak, but evidently, Bryce saw the Thanksgiving day TV news. He must have seen an opportunity to boost his political clout by exposing what he thought was a crooked foster home. The fringe benefit would be retaliation against her. Or was it the other way around? Alex considered calling and confronting him but knew he would deny any involvement. She could play his game and anyway, Jose didn't want a deal. Now was no time to look weak.

She entered her townhome, poured herself a glass of Chardonnay, then went upstairs and drew a hot bath. Half an hour later, after she relaxed, she remembered the signing party!

The signing party!

Alex jumped out of the bath, startling Siva, who was asleep on the bathroom rug. Tonight she wasn't up to politics, but she promised Grady she would come. Besides, it was a fast, easy way to get petition signatures and a positive step toward becoming a judge. Her petition would be ready to file by five p.m. on December 31.

Rummaging through her closet, she reminded herself judges had a duty to avoid the appearance of impropriety. No more low-cut tops and leather miniskirts. She selected a conservative red crepe dress and diamond stud earrings, then styled her hair with a roller brush and dryer.

When her thoughts turned to the evening ahead, she frowned.

Surely Mike Delany saw, or heard about, the Thanksgiving newscast. Should she tell him about Jose's case and stretch his loyalty to the limit?

On her way out the door, she paused briefly to check on the bird's nest on her patio, wondering when the baby birds would hatch.

At the luxurious Four Seasons hotel, she handed her keys to a valet and then entered the crowded ballroom, where the signing party was in full swing. There was a lavish buffet and open bar. Candidates sat behind tables, supplied with blank petitions and pens.

Ruth waved from her row with a big smile.

All she had to do was acquire signatures from loyal registered party voters. Once she settled in at the long table, she noticed several candidates distributed printed literature. She wanted to be more prepared, but as of late, her political interests took backseat to Jose's case. She hid her apprehension behind an engaging political smile.

Within minutes, she was into her element. Friendly registered voters signed her petition and questioned her about the new judgeship. She hoped her enthusiasm for children's rights would win their support.

"Hello, Alex." Grady Frears's handshake turned into a bear hug. "Don't pay attention to Hal," he whispered. "Just keep doing what you're doing."

Alex looked across the room and, for the first time, saw Hal's campaign booth, complete with blown-up advertisements placed on easels. She couldn't read the fine print, but the headline on one read, "WE CAN'T AFFORD TO ELECT JUDGES SYMPATHETIC TO CHILD ABUSERS." Below it was her most recent bar association picture alongside a photocopy of Jose's mugshot.

Hal's posters stunned Alex. Although politics were typically brutal, the race hadn't officially begun. She was unprepared for the malicious attack. An inner voice told her Hal was threatened; another screamed she was dead meat. Alex went to law school with Hal and though not close friends, she never dreamed he'd become an adversary. Confronting him was tempting, but her common sense prevailed.

Hal was baiting her. He wanted an altercation—all the attention he could get. Alex decided her best defense was to treat Hal like the nit on a gnat he was. Alex held her head high.

"We need to talk."

Delany's voice startled her. Alex turned and looked into his face.

"How 'bout a beer at Griff's Sports Bar when this is over?" she asked with a breezy smile. She knew the comfy bar filled with lawyers and the best comfort food in town was his favorite watering hole.

Mike glanced at his watch. "Nine-thirty." He meandered off into the crowd.

When her petition was complete and Alex began to pack her things, Grady Frears appeared. "Want me to mail it for you?"

"No, thanks," she answered. She wanted to see it go directly in the mailbox. "Don't those posters of Hal's violate a party regulation?"

Grady shook his head. "You should thank me for letting him leave them up. He's shown his true colors. Besides, he knows Delany's on your side."

"Thanks, Grady."

Alex found Delany and tapped his shoulder. "See you there."

She entered the sports bar lined with televisions set to different sports events and Irish memorabilia. A few minutes later, Mike appeared and ordered two dark beers.

"Why do you think Hal decided to play so dirty?" she asked.

Delany shrugged. "He knows we're good friends. He must worry you'll get the appointment."

"Is he right?"

Delany smiled, pulled a package of cigarettes from his shirt pocket, then offered one to Alex, who shook her head no.

"What's up with the posters?" he asked.

"Hal wants to use a new client against me," she answered and took a deep breath. It was time to come clean. "I have a new case: defending a man falsely accused of sexual assault. He worked as a foster home parent helping to take care of foster kids. This case illustrates the wisdom of Governor Hastings's proposed reforms."

"I'm all ears."

"I'm on the right side of this one, Delany," she began. Painting it as a classic battle between good and evil in the Fifth Ward, she told an abbreviated, politically correct version of Jose's story. "The Fifth Ward is a breeding ground for cases involving neglected and abused children. It's easy for a misguided social worker to push her own agenda ... to the community's detriment." She outlined her theories about Camilla and Voodoo.

His eyes narrowed. "You have proof?"

"Sure." She took a big gulp of her beer.

If he only knew how scared I am.

"I admire your guts," he said.

"This won't jeopardize my appointment?"

"Just keep doing what you're doing," he said.

Alex sighed. "Trial starts next week."

"I'll keep my fingers crossed."

Alex kissed him on the cheek, then left.

At home, she faced herself in her full-length mirror and decided to rethink her priorities and future. Jose's case would be over soon, but the rest of her life was still ahead. There was no use beating herself up about her decision to take Jose's case. If she really wanted the judgeship, she'd better get busy playing the political game.

Nick entered Alex's building and took the elevator to her office. "You don't look happy," Ruth said when he entered, then showed him to Alex's office.

When he saw a mosaic of degrees, plaques, and professional accolades on her trophy wall, he whistled. "This explains why you aren't married."

Alex looked up from her files and smiled. "Law is a jealous mistress." She shot him a questioning look. "Did you find Angelina?"

Nick shook his head. "No, but I learned some interesting things." He sat down in one of her side chairs and gave her a blow-by-blow account of his scavenger hunt in the valley. "Lots of clues, but no prize."

When Alex's eyes darkened, he added, "I'm disappointed too."

Alex sat at her desk and motioned Nick to pull up his chair around the desk to sit beside her. "What's the man's name? Martinez?"

"Rudolfo Martinez."

Alex Googled Rudolpho Martinez, then looked him up in the Accurint public data website she used in her law practice. "There are six in Houston. It's worth a try." She hit speakerphone and dialed each number. The first three were disconnected; two were home, but not the person they wanted. On the last call, they heard a young woman's voice on an answering machine: "You've reached the Martinez residence. We're not home, but leave your message at the beep."

Alex hung up. "What do you think?"

"She sounds about the right age. What's the address?"

"2217 Oxford," she answered. "In the Heights. Let's go. I've got a hunch it's worth a try."

Fifteen minutes later they stopped before an old two-story framed house badly in need of paint. The unkept yard led to a crooked front porch.

"Wait here." Alex stepped from the truck.

All the way to the front door, her heart pounded. She took a deep breath and knocked.

The door opened a crack. "Who is it?" a soft voice inquired.

"Alex Stockton. I'm looking for Angelina Ramirez."

The door opened wider. "That's me. My last name is Martinez now." The young woman's sad, dark eyes stared fearfully at her.

Alex was taken aback by the girl's thick raven hair and smooth olive skin. "I'm a lawyer," Alex said, handing her a business card. "My client, Jose Gonzales, is on trial for a crime he didn't commit. He needs you to be a character witness."

Color drained from the young woman's face and she clutched the doorknob.

Sensing her panic, Alex touched her hand.

When Angelina stepped onto the porch into bright sunlight, Alex saw ugly purple bruises on her neck and arms. She looked up and down the street. Realizing Angelina was a battered wife, Alex's heart sank. Childhood patterns too often repeat themselves.

"You're the only one who can help Jose."

"Please go," Angelina begged. "My husband is at work, but he will be home soon."

"Jose really needs your help," Alex insisted.

A baby's cries reached their ears. Angelina backed into the

house and slammed the door.

Stunned, Alex stared at the wooden portal blocking communication with her crucial witness. Jose needed her and she had to take the stand. There was no other option.

She walked down the sidewalk and entered Nick's truck. He started the engine and they drove down the street.

An old blue station wagon passed them.

"Slow down!" Alex turned and watched the car pull into Angelina's driveway.

Nick pulled to the curb. They saw a Hispanic man with long stringy hair in baggy jeans step out of the car.

"That SOB must be her husband!" Alex glanced at her watch. It was five minutes past five p.m. "Guess he's home to beat her again!"

Nick's brows rose questioningly. "That's her?"

Alex nodded. "She married a man just like her father. I saw the bruises. She's so afraid she slammed the door in my face."

Nick's fears were confirmed. "That's what crossed my mind when I heard she left the shelter in Laredo." Nick's voice had an angry edge.

"The mention of Jose's name terrified her."

"Will she help him?"

"We didn't get that far. We'll come back after he goes to work first thing tomorrow morning. If she stays, the child will eventually get in the way. I'll convince her to go to the women's shelter."

Nick dropped Alex back at her office. "I'm on my way to see Jose."

On the drive to the jail, Nick worried about what to tell Jose about Angelina. The news was mixed. They had found her, but Nick didn't want to tell him about her abusive marriage.

"Hey, buddy!" Nick said when Jose entered the cubicle.

"Did you find her?" Jose's expression was both hopeful and anxious.

Nick nodded. "She's in Houston."

Jose's expression brightened. "Will she see me?"

"It's not that simple. She's married; has a baby."

Jose's face lost hope.

"The bad news is we learned her husband is like her father. She's afraid of him."

Jose's eyes lost their light.

"There's more."

"Go ahead."

Nick recounted what he learned in Laredo about Angelina's family.

"Her father deserved to die. But her sister, and mother ..." Jose choked back tears.

"We'll go back in the morning. Alex wants to convince her to go to the Gulfway Women's Shelter. Then we will talk to her about testifying at your trial."

"I don't want to cause her any problems." Jose's tone was sad. "Tell Lawyer Stockton to leave her alone. I can tell my story."

Nick shook his head. "Alex will make the call. She's a good lawyer. We want to help Angelina, but her trial testimony is important."

Nick looked at the thin young man in the soiled jumpsuit. Jose was depressed. He didn't need to hear how prejudiced juries can be against minorities or how easily the State could paint Chris Jackson as a morality poster child.

★

The next morning, Alex and Nick drove through the fog to Angelina's house. Nick parked the truck around the corner. When sure her husband was gone, Alex walked to the door and knocked lightly. She saw a front window curtain lift, then drop.

In a few long moments, Alex saw a crack in the door.

"Angelina, we have to talk," she pled. "I want to help you."

Angelina pulled the door open and motioned for Alex to enter.

Inside, Alex surveyed the gloomy house. Mismatched furniture with torn upholstery covered old hardwood floors. The walls were bare, except for a crucifix and a warped, unframed print of Mother Mary thumb tacked over the mantel.

From another room, a child cried.

Angelina hurried into the kitchen and Alex followed. She saw an infant, his face smeared with oatmeal, sitting in a rickety highchair.

When Angelina soothed him with soft Spanish words, Alex felt an odd pang of envy. "He's precious. What's his name?"

"Antonio Jose."

Alex smiled. "You're a good mother, Angelina."

The woman's dark eyes lit up and tension in her features eased. She wiped Antonio's face, lifted him from his highchair, then placed him in Alex's arms.

The child relaxed and his eyes grew heavy.

"You are a mother?" Angelina asked.

Alex shook her head. "Not yet."

"But someday?"

"I hope so," Alex answered.

The baby burped, then fell asleep in her arms.

A few minutes later, Angelina took him and left the room. When she returned, she sat opposite Alex at the kitchen table.

"We have to talk," Alex said.

Angelina's face tensed and she began to wring her hands in her lap. "I can do nothing for Jose," she said. "My husband ..."

Alex reached out and ran a finger across her neck. "Those bruises look better today. You should leave before he hurts you again, or the child."

Angelina lowered her eyes. "If he ever hurt Antonio ..."

Alex took her hand. "I help women like you build a better life. You'd both be better off at the Gulfway Women's Center. Let's go there now."

Angelina started to cry.

Alex scooted her chair closer and placed her arm around the woman's small shoulders. "Do you love your husband?"

Angelina shook her head. "I had no place to go. He promised to take care of me."

While Alex held her, Angelina sobbed.

Suddenly, the front door opened then slammed shut.

Angelina jumped. Her eyes filled with terror.

"Angelina?" a gruff voice called.

"Rudolfo?"

CHAPTER 12

Alex's heart raced. When he saw her what would he do? She had almost talked Angelina into leaving. Rudolfo's presence would change her mind. Alex thought of Nick outside. No doubt he still had a bulge in his boots.

Rudolfo burst into the kitchen. "Who are you?" he demanded.

Before Alex answered, Angelina blurted, "She's the social worker from the food stamp office."

"She don't look like any social worker," he muttered angrily. "Where's my lunch?"

Angelina went to the refrigerator and pulled out a dish. "I'll heat it up. It will only take a minute."

"Leftovers is all you have?"

Angelina's face was etched with fear.

Alex picked up her purse, put it on her shoulder and stood to leave. "Your application should be approved. You'll get a letter in the next thirty days."

"Thank you," Angelina answered politely.

Before Alex reached the front door, she heard Rudolfo chastise Angelina. "We don't need any handouts. What did you do without my permission?"

As she pulled the door to leave, Alex shuddered. She walked briskly to Nick's truck.

"How did it go?" he asked when she opened the passenger door.

"I tried to convince her to come with us, but Rudolfo came home for lunch."

"I saw."

"He must have sensed something going on."

"I doubt he's that intuitive. What happened inside?"

"Angelina told him I was a food stamp social worker," she answered. "He probably didn't believe her."

Nick looked at Alex's slim-fitting pantsuit. "Social worker doesn't come to mind. What now?"

"When he leaves, I'll go back."

As sprinkles turned into a full-fledged rainstorm, they waited in silence. Twenty minutes later, they heard Angelina's front door slam and watched Rudolfo storm to his car. He quickly backed out of the driveway, pulled out onto the street, and with a screech of tires drove away.

Alex's pulse raced. "Pull into the driveway. I have a bad feeling."

As Nick and Alex approached the front door, they heard tortured sobs. They entered without knocking and found Angelina, Antonio in her arms, on the living room floor. Her nose bled and fresh wounds covered her face and neck.

Alex grabbed a tissue from her purse, took the crying child from Angelina and wiped his face. Thankfully, he was not cut. "Angelina, let's go," Alex commanded. "Now."

Nick helped her up from the floor.

Angelina's mood approached hysteria. "He hit me! With Antonio in my arms!"

"Get your things," Alex said calmly. "Hurry before he decides to return."

Angelina disappeared into the next room, then returned a few minutes later with an old suitcase, diaper bag and stroller.

She sobbed all the way to the Gulfway Women's Center.

"He'll find me," she said. "What will I do?"

"He won't," Alex responded. "You'll be safe."

★

They approached a large, beautifully landscaped two-story brick building located in a quiet residential area close to River Oaks, the city's wealthy neighborhood. They entered and were greeted by the administrator and her assistant.

"Call the nurse," the administrator said to her assistant. She touched Angelina's cheek. "We need to call the police."

Angelina shook her head. "My husband is on probation. He'll kill me!"

Alex took Angelina's hand. Alex knew strong resolve would keep her here. "You've done the right thing. We'll come back and check on you later."

The nurse approached and took Antonio in her arms. Angelina followed her down to the hall toward the infirmary.

Leaving the shelter, Alex glanced at her watch. "I need to read briefs for my three p.m. conference call on my civil case. I still have to make a living," she said with a playful smile at Nick.

Nick dropped her off at her office and Alex rode the elevator up to her floor. The front door was unlocked and Ruth wasn't at her desk. A strange sense of foreboding overcame her.

"Ruth?"

There was no answer.

As she walked through the reception area, her heels on the parquet wood floor sounded eerily loud. She told herself the morning's events made her edgy.

"Ruth?"

She walked down the hall toward her office and noticed her

door slightly ajar. Pausing a moment, she pushed it open wide and froze in her tracks. With a switchblade knife at Ruth's throat, Rudolfo stood behind her desk. Ruth was in her executive chair, arms tied behind her back. What could not be said, because of the duct tape on her mouth, was evident in her eyes. They blazed with fear and anger.

"Where's my wife?" Rudolfo demanded. His long stringy hair was drenched in sweat and the purple vein in his forehead stood out.

Alex snapped out of her momentary stupor. From the irrational behavior she'd witnessed earlier at his home, she knew Rudolfo would follow through with his threat.

"Where is she?" He inched the knife closer to Ruth's neck.

Sensing a forceful presence behind her, Alex heard a click and a shot.

With a shocked look on his face, Rudolfo dropped the knife. A red stain drenched his shirt and he crumpled to the floor.

Alex turned and saw Nick clicking the safety on his pistol.

He walked over to Rudolfo and felt his wrist pulse.

"Dead?" Alex asked.

Nick nodded. "Clean shot through his heart."

Alex watched numbly as Nick gently pulled tape from Ruth's mouth and released her feet and arms.

Ruth gasped air and tears flooded her eyes. Alex went to her and held her tight.

Alex looked up at Nick. "How did you know?"

"When I pulled out, I noticed his blue station wagon in the parking lot. I told Ray to call the police and rushed up here. How did this creep find you?"

Alex shrugged. "I gave Angelina my card yesterday."

Moments later, Ray rushed into the office with two HPD officers in tow.

The next hour was a blur. While they waited for the medical examiner, they answered questions. Luckily, Nick knew the veteran policemen. They didn't question Nick further after he explained that he had to shoot Rudolfo to prevent him from slitting Ruth's throat.

Alex was relieved Nick didn't have to worry about charges being filed. One less problem. A shooting in her office was enough. The bright red stain by her desk chair would be a constant reminder.

The medical examiner arrived and pronounced Rudolfo dead. He filled out the necessary paperwork while paramedics removed the body. "County morgue," he told them.

Ruth was too shaken to drive. Nick and Alex took her home. On the short drive to her apartment, Ruth told them how Rudolfo burst into the office and attacked her. "He was out of his mind." She touched Nick's shoulder. "Thanks for saving my life."

"You're welcome," he said.

Once inside Ruth's apartment, Alex fixed her a cup of chamomile tea. She replayed the scene in her office, remembering Rudolfo's surprised expression as he fell lifeless onto her new office carpet. Without Nick's brave intervention, both she and Ruth would be dead. Again, Nick was a hero.

While Ruth prepared for bed, Alex rummaged through her medicine cabinet and found some Tylenol PM. "Take this. It will help you sleep."

Nick waited in the living room while Alex made sure Ruth was fast asleep.

Alex entered the living room and sat by Nick on the couch. "I need to thank you for saving my life too."

Nick took her in his arms and held her close. "We need to tell Angelina."

She nestled her chin closer on his shoulder and relaxed in his embrace. Alex's heart sank. She felt no personal remorse at Rudolfo's death, but he was Angelina's husband and the father of her child. She dreaded breaking the news, but knew it was inevitable. "The sooner, the better."

When they were a few blocks from the shelter, Nick asked, "You sure you can handle this?"

"I'll break it to her gently," Alex answered. She ignored the sinking feeling in the pit of her stomach.

"I don't want her to hate me for what I did."

"Once she hears the truth, she'll know you had no choice."

It was sunset when Alex and Nick entered the women's shelter. A friendly receptionist led them down a short hall, then knocked lightly at the door to a small room. Alex and Nick stood in the doorway and saw Angelina seated in a rocker holding her sleeping baby. The room was tastefully decorated with a twin bed, bassinet and dresser.

Angelina's face was peaceful. When she saw Alex and Nick, her eyes lit up. They were now her only friends.

Angelina must have sensed their mood because her smile faded. "Is something wrong?"

"Angelina, please put Antonio down. We have some bad news."

Angelina stood and placed her sleeping baby in his bassinet. Then she turned toward them.

Alex took Angelina's hand. "Rudolfo is dead."

Her face registered shock and disbelief. "What happened?"

Nick stepped forward and gave her the complete story. "I'm sorry, Angelina," he said at the end.

Angelina began to cry. "I shouldn't have come here."

Nick shook his head. "You had to."

"He was cruel, I know," she sobbed.

Alex took Angelina in her arms. She stroked her hair with one hand. "You have to be strong now. For Antonio. You can count on my help."

"We have to go to the morgue," Nick said. "You need to identify his body."

"Oh no," Angelina cried. "I can't."

"We'll be there right beside you," Nick said.

Alex stood and led Angelina out of the room, holding the grief-stricken woman tight. Leaving Antonio in the care of the nurse, they headed downtown.

When they entered the dismal county morgue, Angelina burst into tears. The frigid building smelled of formaldehyde. An efficient, white-clad attendant appeared with a clipboard. They walked down a long hall, then entered the dank room containing rows of dead bodies. He located Rudolfo's vault and opened it.

When he flipped back the sheet, Angelina stared at Rudolfo's contorted face. "It's him," she gasped.

The man shoved a form under her nose. "Sign here."

Angelina quickly signed her name.

They walked out of the building as fast as possible. Once outside and back in Alex's car, they rode in silence for a few minutes.

Alex turned to Angelina. "Jose's trial starts Monday. He needs your help."

She shook her head. "I can't think about that now."

Saturday morning came early. Alex stood alone in the doorway of her office. Six months ago, she'd done a complete renovation, including new carpet. Tall ceilings, large windows with park views, mahogany desk and credenza didn't dispel the dark-red blot on her pale rose carpet. The sight nauseated her and she decided to prepare for Jose's trial in the kitchen.

She gathered her files, notes and research books and carried them down the hall. Arranging her things on the antique table, within a short time she was engrossed in Jose's case.

Later she heard the sound of the front door chime, then footsteps on the entrance hall floor startled her.

Clad in jeans and sweatshirt, Ruth entered the kitchen.

"You spooked me," Alex said.

"Sorry. I'm jumpy too." Ruth's pale face held dark circles under her eyes.

"Did you sleep last night?" Alex asked.

"A little." Ruth poured herself a cup of coffee. "How did Angelina take the news?"

"She's upset."

Ruth gave a tired smile. "Will she testify?"

"I hope so. She needs time to pull herself together. I won't need her 'til midweek."

"Will she stay at the shelter?"

Alex nodded. "I doubt she can afford to keep the house. I'm sure she'll need a job. When she's ready, maybe she can help out with the phones and filing."

"That would be good since I have to study for the bar exam starting in January ... " Ruth paused. "Any word on the judgeship?"

Alex dropped her pen and stared out the window. "Unless I win Jose's trial, I can pretty much forget it."

"You'll win. I have confidence in you," Ruth said. "I'll copy those cases you wanted."

Once alone, Alex picked up where she left off. These past few weeks, Jose's case consumed most of her waking thoughts. Her lifelong dream was pushed so far down her list of priorities, she wondered if there was still hope. She didn't have her logo, her list of potential supporters, and hadn't begun to make her list of who she would ask for campaign money.

Ruth entered the kitchen with a strained look on her face. "We forgot yesterday's conference call!"

Alex froze. "Oh, no!"

"I checked voice mail," Ruth said. "Lead counsel is furious. He threatened to have you removed as discovery master."

Alex shrugged. "I'll straighten it out before trial Monday morning. A dead man in my office should be a good enough excuse, even for him."

When Ruth went back to her desk, Alex panicked. For the last six months, she billed more than ten thousand dollars a month on the Crane Chemical Company case. The position as discovery master was a crucial stepping-stone in her career. It involved big money and powerful lawyers. Word travels fast in the close-knit legal community and could affect her ability to raise campaign funds. Since drifting deeply into the Fifth Ward world these past few weeks, her cash flow was down. For more than one reason, she had to salvage the Crane case.

Deep in thought, she stared out the window. Since she'd gotten the case, Alex worked extra hard because lead counsel, Pat Stewart, was opposed to a woman discovery master. Alex knew because it was such a lucrative position he wanted an excuse to put his man in the job. She couldn't be sure he'd understand when she told him about Rudolfo. It crossed her mind to go ahead and resign, rather than deal with him, but she decided against it. She hoped a quick phone call Monday morning to reschedule the conference call would do the trick.

The phone rang and Ruth sent the call to the kitchen.

"How are you doing today?" Nick's voice was deep and resonant.

Alex's mood softened. "OK. You?"

"I just saw Jose. How long will you be there?"

"Most of the day."

"How about I pick you up at five? We can go see Angelina, then grab a bite to eat."

Alex paused. "I thought Saturday nights were reserved for the Longhorn."

CHAPTER 13

Nick showed up at five and they drove to the women's shelter.

When they entered, they found Angelina in the dining room talking to another Hispanic woman. Her face was drawn and colorless, but when she saw them, her eyes brightened.

Alex gave her a hug.

"The funeral is tomorrow at Garza Funeral Home," she said sadly. "Will you come?"

"Of course," Alex said. "Does he have family?"

"No. They are in Mexico. The county will pay for the funeral. My church is helping too."

"I'm so sorry, Angelina."

The woman just retreated inside herself and was silent.

Nick patted her shoulder. "Things will improve," he consoled. "I promise."

Alex was somber as they left Angelina.

"Where to?" Nick asked when they got into his truck.

"How about Carrabba's? It's loud enough to drown out my thoughts. A couple of glasses of Chianti will help."

Inside the restaurant, clusters of fashionably dressed professionals sipped wine and engaged in animated conversations. Waiters, trays laden with sumptuous Italian dishes, scuttled busily between tables. Delicious aromas filled the air and Alex realized how hungry she was. The hostess told Nick the wait would be an hour, but Alex knew better. When she caught the manager's eye, his startled face broke into a wide grin. He rushed over to Alex, gave her a big hug, then led them to a quiet corner table.

"It pays to be with a celebrity," Nick said once they were seated.

"I'm a regular," she said. She left out "with Bryce."

After the waiter brought wine and appetizers, Nick raised his glass in a toast. "Here's to a big win."

Fighting a sinking feeling in her stomach, Alex clinked her glass with his. Could she win this one? Memories flooded her mind. From spelling bee victories to law school mock trial team championships, her life was a string of good choices and favorable outcomes. Now, the odds against winning Jose's case filled her with doubt.

"Have you ever lost something you really wanted?" she asked.

Running a hand through his hair, he grinned broadly. "Like when I didn't make varsity team quarterback?"

Alex smiled and took a sip of her wine. "I can't imagine you not being number one, whatever you do. For some reason, this trial scares me."

"Why?"

"Because I've never failed and don't want to start now. Back when I did criminal law, the State begged me to take their lenient plea offers, but I always held out for an acquittal. Now I feel like a beggar at a ball."

"Cinderella?"

"No. I'm used to that role," she said with a wistful smile. "This time I'm not sure who I am."

Nick studied her face. Sadness filled her eyes. "Oh, Alex. I hate to see you so down."

"I'm not usually like this, but this case has done a number on me. Then there's Rudolfo's funeral tomorrow. How will I be ready?"

"Whatever I can do to help," Nick said softly. "Just let me know."

"Thanks. Just talking helps." She sighed and looked away. "Everyone has to lose sometime. Maybe it's my turn."

"Don't say that. You can win. I feel good about it."

"I forgot. God's on your side."

He touched her hand. "Yours too."

They left the restaurant and Nick drove the short distance to Alex's office for her car.

"See you tomorrow," Alex said.

"I'll follow you home and make sure you get in safe."

"Then head to the Longhorn?"

Sunday morning, the Reverend was somber. After a prayer for Jose, he began:

"God 'sifted' Peter, the Apostle. His self-illusions had to be shattered before he could become the man God wanted him to be."

As usual, the Reverend grew animated and the congregation responded with enthusiasm. "After his resurrection, Jesus asked Peter if he loved him. Three times. When Peter answered 'Yes,' Jesus told him he would be the rock his church was built on. People, in spite of our faults and weaknesses, God loves each and every one of us." He wiped sweat from his brow and lowered his head. "God bless you."

Alex followed the Reverend into his office. He took a seat behind his big desk. "Are you ready for tomorrow?"

"I'm nervous," she confessed.

"I have confidence in you."

Alex smiled. "Reverend, let's go over the spanking incident with Jaime."

He leaned back in his chair. "You see Chris and Jaime roomed together. While most kids follow the rules, Jaime breaks them. CPS and I have different views about disciplining children."

"But, Reverend, you are a kind man. You know those children have already been hurt by someone, physically or mentally."

"That's right. Most of them's never had anybody love them enough to give them rules and make them stick. The Book of Proverbs tells us to discipline children with love. Jaime knew what would happen when he broke house rules for the third time."

"How hard did you hit him?" Alex asked.

"I didn't hit him, Alex," the Reverend said firmly. "There's a difference between a spanking and hitting someone. But what I did to him was nothin' like the whippins my momma gave me when I was his age." The Reverend pulled a wooden paddle out from under his desk. "Jaime got three whacks on the butt and he knew it hurt me worse than it did him."

"What about CPS foster home regulations?"

"By their rules, the kids is in control. We're supposed to just babysit, not teach or parent them. I'm worried they aren't gettin' what they need. Those boys crave discipline with love."

"The jury might not understand. I don't want them to hear about your problems with the agency. If the prosecutor baits you, keep your opinions to yourself."

"Alright."

Something about the way he said it made Alex think he didn't mean it.

"Before trial, I'll ask the judge to keep out evidence of the Jaime incident because it's not relevant. If she agrees, the State can't question you about it. Unless you bring it up and open the door."

"Alex, you need to know. After the trial, I'll resign from Shepherd's Cottages. I won't do things the CPS way. It's not good for the children."

"Does the Board know?"

"Not yet. Please don't mention it to anyone."

Alex left the Reverend's office with a deeper insight into how much was at stake. She doubted the Reverend could keep his strong convictions to himself in court and wondered whether to call him as a witness. Right now she needed him to stand up for Jose. So far, he was her only witness.

She walked out to Nick's truck and joined him.

"To the funeral?" he asked.

Alex nodded.

★

They drove through the Fifth Ward. Alex saw a rare string of colored lights framing a dirty window with an occasional frosted Christmas tree inside. In a meager way, the Christmas spirit was evident in this needy community.

"How did it go with the Reverend?" Nick asked.

"Just wondering if his testimony will help Jose."

"Will it?"

"Depends on my jury."

When they arrived at the county funeral home, a middle-aged woman greeted them at the door. They followed her into a small chapel where Angelina sat in the front row holding a rosary. Wearing a black dress and sweater, tears streaked her face. "Thanks for coming," she said.

Alex glanced around. "Where's the casket?"

"Outside. The service is there."

Dark clouds filled the sky as they followed the funeral director to the cemetery. Beneath a well-worn green striped awning, a half a dozen chairs were arranged at the gravesite. The spray of red carnations covering the casket was the only bright spot on this gloomy day.

"You ordered the flowers?" Nick whispered.

Head down, Alex nodded.

While the priest prayed in Latin, Angelina wept. Then, he led them in the Lord's Prayer.

It was over.

Angelina tugged Alex's sleeve. "Can we talk?"

"I'll wait in the car," Nick said.

After workers lowered Rudolfo's casket into the grave, Alex and Angelina walked a short distance to a bench beneath a big oak tree.

Angelina's voice was clear and calm. "Jose's trial, if I testify, will he be free?"

"I can't guarantee it, but it should help."

"I can do it. I should have told the truth the first time."

Alex placed her arm around Angelina's shoulders. "Don't look back. We can't change the past. I'm glad you decided to help Jose. He needs you."

"When can I see him?"

"We can go now. Are you sure you are ready?"

Angelina nodded.

Half an hour later, they entered the jail and approached the information desk.

"Attorney visit. Jose Gonzales," Alex told the clerk. She tried to enter with both Nick and Angelina.

"Visiting hours ended at five," the sour-faced attendant said.

Alex didn't insist. If she pushed too hard, Jose might face the guard's wrath. "I'm sorry, Angelina," she said. "You'll see him soon."

Nick pointed toward a small area with vending machines and chairs. "We'll wait there."

After clearing security, Alex was shown to a small cubicle.

A few minutes later, Jose entered.

"Nick and Angelina are downstairs. She wanted to see you, but visiting hours are over."

"How is she?"

"Strong. We just left Rudolfo's funeral. She wants to testify for you." She leaned back and sighed.

Jose's face held a look of relief and joy.

"Let's talk about tomorrow. Where do you keep your knife?"

"In my nightstand drawer."

"Did you know it was missing?"

Jose shook his head. "I'm not surprised Chris took it. He would do anything to get me in trouble."

"I know and we need to make sure the jury knows it." Alex thought for a moment. "Get some rest. I'll see you in the morning."

They dropped Angelina off, then drove to Alex's townhome. "I've still got work to do," Alex told him when she got out of the truck.

"You should follow the advice you gave Jose and get some sleep."

The first day of trial was an unusually cold, overcast day. At dawn, Alex blow-dried her hair, applied makeup, with special attention to the dark circles under her eyes, then put on her most conservative black trial suit.

The weather matched Alex's mood. Ignoring the friendly greetings of fellow colleagues, she entered the courthouse and took the elevator to Judge Villareal's courtroom. She found Nick, Ruth, and the Reverend waiting outside.

Nick's eyes took in her tailored suit. "You look great," he said.

"Thanks."

"Jose is dressed and ready to go."

The Reverend gave her a confident smile. "We're here to cheer you on."

The elevator doors opened and Camilla Roe, with a well-groomed Chris in tow, approached the entrance.

"Hello, Chris," the Reverend said.

Before he could answer, Camilla grabbed his arm and pulled him into the courtroom.

Nick shook his head. "That is one angry woman."

"Her goal is to destroy us," Alex said. "And who knows? Maybe snag Voodoo too."

She glanced at her watch and remembered the call to Pat Stewart on the Crane case. "Docket call is in a few minutes, but there's time for you to get coffee downstairs before the jury panel comes in. I need to make a call."

Alex walked over to the window and dialed Mr. Stewart.

His secretary put the call through. "Stewart here."

"Alex Stockton. Please allow me to apologize for Friday. A psychopath entered my office and held my secretary hostage. We were lucky because he was shot before he killed her. We both forgot to cancel the conference call. Can we reschedule it for later this week?"

"I read about the shooting in today's paper." The cranky old man's voice softened. "Since you're in trial, will you be able to do it this week?"

"Sure."

"Won't your mind be on the trial?"

Alex's frustration level rose. "Mr. Stewart, please! The trial will be over Thursday or Friday. Please show me the same professional courtesy I would show you."

"OK," he relented. "I won't file the removal motion. My secretary will call everyone and reschedule. The holidays have slowed things down a bit. We'll let you know."

Alex heaved a sigh of relief. "Thanks," she said, then hung up the phone. At this point she did not have time to worry about the Crane case.

As usual the courtroom was bustling. Lawyers scurried around negotiating plea bargains with prosecutors in an effort to finalize as many cases as possible before trial began. Alex arranged her file on the defense counsel table, while Marilyn Rivera conferred with Camilla at the prosecution's table.

Moments later, Judge Villareal entered the courtroom's side door.

Bryce was right behind her.

Shocked, Alex remained outwardly calm.

What's he doing here?

Alex kept her head down and pretended not to notice Bryce join Marilyn Rivera at the prosecution table. "Piece of cake," she overheard him say.

Alex slammed her trial notebook shut and strode over to prosecution counsel table. Her face betrayed no emotion, but her eyes blazed with anger. "What the hell are you doing here?" she muttered between clenched teeth.

"I'm Marilyn's co-chair on The State of Texas versus Jose Gonzales."

The young attorney gave Alex a smug smile and tugged at the hem of her short skirt.

"You don't try cases in this court," Alex stated, struggling to keep her voice low. "Especially not number two sexual assault cases!"

"You remembered," Bryce said with a feral grin. "But I have a special interest in this one. Your man's going down."

Alex stared into cold, dark eyes that once evoked her passion. In a split second, she relived long nights in bed, drinking champagne and talking shop in between passionate lovemaking. At this moment, she couldn't see what she ever saw in him.

"Jose's innocent and I'll prove it." Her firm voice belied her rising panic. Beating Marilyn Rivera would have been easy, but Bryce was a formidable opponent. He was a more experienced criminal trial lawyer with capital cases under his belt. She knew he intended to keep his unblemished trial record. One day soon, it would undoubtedly earn him the position of Harris County District Attorney.

She realized how naive she'd been to think he wouldn't avenge his brutal beating and her for choosing Jose's case over him. That the State had refused to talk plea bargain should have been a tip-off, but she didn't see it coming.

What will I do?

She had few options. What she felt right now wasn't anger; it was a dangerous fury. Alex swore not to let Bryce sense weakness. He'd attack like a shark on bloodied prey. He thrived on the fear he incited in his opponents.

"Alex!" Ruth's voice rang through the courtroom.

Turning from Bryce in time to hide a scarlet flush, with head held high Alex walked toward her. She thought of her many trial victories and how hard she'd fought to gain a place in the male-dominated legal profession. Whatever her past with Bryce, it no longer existed or mattered. A lapse in judgment in her personal life wouldn't send Jose to jail for life, nor would it destroy the Reverend's vision for Shepherd's Cottages.

When she left the courtroom, Alex nearly knocked Nick down.

"Ouch!" he teased.

Alex was relieved he didn't see the interchange between her and Bryce. "Be right back," she muttered. Continuing briskly toward the ladies' room, she entered and ducked into a stall.

Moments later a familiar voice called: "Alex?"

"I'm here, Ruth."

"What's Bryce doing here? What a snake! Don't worry, you'll show him."

Alex didn't answer.

"Alex? You're always telling me not to let things get me down, remember? Saying problems aren't problems, they're opportunities."

"You're right," Alex admitted, opening the stall door and stepping out. "Bryce wants to intimidate me. He knows how weak their case is."

"We'll pick a great jury who will acquit Jose."

Alex smiled. "I'll practice what I preach to young lawyers. Whenever I look at Bryce, I'll see a clown."

Ruth laughed. "You'll drive him mad. He's only getting back at you for breaking up with him. And for standing up for your beliefs."

"Why would he care?"

"Don't underestimate yourself. No man would want to lose you. Especially not to a Fifth Ward foster home."

"I'm not sure whether he hated to lose me or he just plain hated to lose." The old fighter spirit had returned.

Alex and Ruth headed to the door.

In the hall outside the courtroom, Nick approached Alex. "Everything okay?"

"Just pre-trial jitters." She decided to keep quiet about Bryce. He'd find out soon enough.

Alex entered the courtroom. Bryce and Marilyn conferred with Camilla at their table. Jose waited at defense counsel table. She joined him. "Good morning. Your suit and tie look great. How are you?"

"Nervous."

"Stay calm."

"How's Angelina?"

"She's fine. We won't need her until at least Wednesday."

The bailiff appeared. "All rise," he bellowed. "The Judicial District Court is now in session. The Honorable Dyan Villareal presiding."

"Be seated," Judge Villareal addressed the crowded courtroom. "Counsel, before we begin, have you discussed a plea bargain?"

Bryce jumped to his feet. "No, Your Honor."

Over her reading glasses, the judge frowned.

Alex stood. "Judge, the State has refused to entertain plea negotiations."

Judge Villareal raised an eyebrow, glanced at her watch, then slammed her gavel. "You've got fifteen minutes to discuss one and, if there's no agreement, we'll call the jury panel. While we are waiting for them to come over, we will take up pre-trial motions."

Neither Alex nor Bryce looked at one another.

Marilyn Rivera remained seated, her eyes locked on Bryce.

Bryce pushed back his chair, touched his co-counsel's arm, and headed toward the jury room. "I'll be in there," he said.

Alex's heart went into her feet, again. Every nerve was frazzled, but for Jose's sake, she kept her face impassive. She couldn't let the fact that Bryce was her opponent affect her ability to try this case.

She knew Jose didn't want a plea bargain, but since he was looking at life in prison if convicted, she had to ask: "Do you want to accept *any* kind of plea bargain?"

He shook his head.

As she started toward the jury room, Alex knew it didn't matter one way or the other. Bryce would try the case. They simply had to have the discussion for the Court. She took a deep breath and geared herself to face him. Her mission was to prove Jose's innocence at any cost.

Alex entered the jury room and went to stand at the window, her back to Bryce.

"How about some coffee?" he asked.

"No, thanks," she answered. "You're behind the no offer stance on this case."

"Is that a question or a fact?"

"I think we both know the answer. You're holding what Chris's uncle did to you against my innocent client."

"If he's innocent, then he wants a trial."

"Your confidence will fade when this case is over, Bryce."

His laugh sent a cold chill down Alex's spine.

What did I ever see in him?

Seconds passed as they stared, neither willing to break eye contact. There was nothing to discuss.

Alex glanced at her watch. "Time's up." She turned on her heel and left the room.

Alex approached the court clerk. "No-go," she said, then sat down with Jose.

"What happened?" he asked.

"Nothing. It's time to get serious."

The bailiff announced the judge, who took her seat on the bench. "Cause number 706,342, the State of Texas versus Jose Gonzales. Shall I call for the jury panel, counselors?"

Both Bryce and Alex answered, "Yes, Your Honor."

"Very well." She frowned. "Let's proceed with pretrial motions. Counsel, please approach."

Knowing it was a long shot, but in order to preserve her appellate record, Alex asked the Court to exclude evidence of Jose's prior conviction. After a lengthy discussion, the Court quickly denied her motion. Alex wasn't surprised. Judge Villareal merely followed the law.

Next, the State moved to exclude Chris's juvenile record and CPS history.

Alex swallowed hard and began, "Your Honor, Chris Jackson's juvenile criminal record is relevant to my client's defense because we think he was high at the time of the alleged incident."

"Counsel," Judge Villareal interrupted. "It's not what you think, it's what you can prove."

"Right, Your Honor," Alex answered. "We intend to prove Chris Jackson was high on October 31. His prior marijuana possession charge is relevant."

Bryce rolled his eyes at Alex. "Miss Stockton knows it's black letter law. It's reversible error to admit Mr. Jackson's prior record."

"I'll determine reversible error, counselor," Judge Villareal said. "I have a duty to balance the defendant's right to a fair trial against constitutional protections afforded a minor victim witness. But letting in a minor's prior juvenile record in a sexual abuse trial would be wrong."

"Thanks," Alex said. Even though Judge Villareal obviously understood her predicament, she couldn't disagree with case law. The judge knew about Chris's record, including his misdemeanor possession, petty thefts, and truancy violations. Maybe that insight would help her down the road.

The bailiff indicated to the Court that the jury panel was in the hall. "Anything further?" she asked.

Bryce opened his briefcase, pulled out a large, shiny knife with a wooden handle, and placed it on the table in front of him.

Alex leaned over to Jose. "Is that yours?"

"No!" he whispered. "Mine's much smaller."

"Does it have any identifying marks?"

He nodded. "My initials."

Alex drew in a breath. Where was Jose's knife? She turned around and whispered to Nick, who sat with the Reverend directly behind her, "Could Jose's knife still be in the park?"

"I doubt it. The cops didn't find it and neither did I the day we looked," Nick replied. "I'll run over there right now."

Alex wasn't happy. No doubt Bryce would leave it on his counsel table, smack dab in front of the jury. It was a familiar ploy the prosecution used when there was no actual weapon.

"Your Honor," Bryce began. "Because the knife used to threaten and cut the complaining witness wasn't recovered, I would ask to use this one as a reasonable facsimile."

"That knife is bigger and more threatening than my client's pocket knife," Alex objected. "To allow Mr. Armstrong to brandish that knife around in front of the jury will be highly prejudicial to my client."

The judge looked at the knife, then at Bryce.

"The victim said it was similar to the one the defendant used in the park," he said.

"I won't allow it during voir dire, but if a witness testifies about a knife, you can use it during trial."

Judge Villareal motioned for the bailiff to bring in the jury panel. By excluding the knife during voir dire, Judge Villareal gave Alex the chance to win the jury over before they saw it during the trial. Jurors often form lasting impressions before they hear evidence. Successful trial lawyers knew case facts weren't as important as the jury's perception of them.

"All rise," the bailiff announced. Everyone stood as the jury panel filed into the courtroom.

Alex faced sixty strangers, twelve of whom would be Jose's jury. Seated numerically, Alex knew the first thirty were most likely to be chosen. Bryce and Alex had just a few minutes to hurriedly review the jurors' questionnaires, which revealed marital status, employment, religion, and prior jury service. Alex knew Bryce wanted conservative white jurors. She needed minority churchgoers.

After the jury panel settled in, Alex did what she had done with the Shepherd's Cottages board: She made eye contact with each potential juror. She needed them to like her. And Jose.

"Judge," Bryce's resonant voice interrupted her thoughts. "May we approach?"

The Court nodded.

Out of earshot of the panel, Alex and Bryce went before the bench.

"The State moves for a jury shuffle," he announced.

CHAPTER 14

Stunned, Alex kept her poker face. Bryce must have seen what she saw in the first few rows of the panel—potential jurors likely to be sympathetic to Jose. By switching their order, his picks could potentially move closer to the front and her good picks move to the back. He had the right to pull every trick in the book. And he knew them all.

"One shuffle is allowed. State motion granted." Judge Villareal glanced at the clock on the wall across from the jury box. "This is a good stopping point. Bailiff, show the jury panel out. We will resume at one."

While the court clerk processed Bryce's request, Alex sat with Jose. She knew he was stressed, but had remained calm.

Jose leaned into her. "What's happening?"

"The prosecution has the right to change the order of the jury panel," she answered. "The judge simply followed the law. She's fair. Don't worry."

Jose lifted his chin and nodded.

A few minutes later the clerk returned with a new jury list. A quick glance told her she wouldn't like what she saw.

At one o'clock sharp, the bailiff re-seated the jury panel.

In the new order, out of the first thirty there were only four African Americans and one Hispanic. Most of the jurors she had planned on picking were seated at the back. It was no time to fret; trial had begun and Alex needed all her faculties. She pushed her emotions back and called forth her trial mode. She'd never had to try so hard before. She'd never been in a trial that meant so much to her, both in terms of the person she represented and her future. While the judge explained the process of voir dire, Alex studied the demeanor of the jury panel, paying close attention to nonverbal clues. Ruth studied the juror information sheets and made notes in the margins.

"Our legislature has determined that criminal offenses are kind of like snowflakes. From a distance, they may all appear to be the same, but when examined closely, each is unique," Judge Villareal admonished. "If your knowledge of criminal prosecutions comes from television, movies, or newspapers, do a brain scrub because little of what you've seen or read occurs in a real court. And it will not occur in this court. Everyone still with me?"

The members of the panel nodded.

She continued. "Is there anyone present who has selective hearing like my husband? Twenty-two years, he has yet to hear, 'Honey, please take out the garbage.' "

The jury laughed along with the attorneys. Judge Villareal was an expert at building rapport with jurors and that's what made her such a good jurist.

"Now, I'll turn it over to the attorneys. Each side has forty-five minutes."

Trial had begun.

Bryce straightened his tie and stood. Being the consummate gentleman, he introduced Marilyn Rivera as his "capable" co-

counsel. "Judge Villareal was right about the defendant being entitled to a fair trial. Does everybody also agree that the State is entitled to a fair trial?"

The jury panel nodded agreement.

Bryce looked and sounded just like the boy next door: honest, trustworthy, and just. She couldn't deny his incredible good looks. Alex had always admired his trial skills. And, in her wildest dreams, she never envisioned sitting across counsel table from him. It was next to impossible to wear her cheery trial smile, the one that said, 'I'm OK, you're OK,' but Alex managed to swallow her disgust.

Fortunately, years of eating nails for breakfast had given her an iron stomach and an uncanny ability to hide her emotions.

Alex looked down and saw that Ruth had passed her a juror information sheet with the word "preacher" highlighted.

Alex fixed her gaze on juror number eleven. He was white, overweight, and probably in his late sixties. His lips were pursed tight and his stern gaze met Alex's. She was hesitant to assume just because he was a preacher, he would be a good juror for Jose. Whether loyalty or antipathy existed between religious denominations was a question she could not answer. She would question him thoroughly before deciding to strike or keep him.

Alex kept her eye on two young professional women, who, before the shuffle, had been in the rear of the panel. She hated to use two strikes on them, but it was obvious by the tone of their giggles when Bryce even approached humor that he'd already won them over.

Bryce's forty-five minutes flew by. He was a silver-tongued devil and, like a snake charmer, had already hypnotized the jury panel. His questions were carefully peppered with innocent metaphors designed to plant seeds inferring Jose's guilt. True to his reputation, by the looks on their faces, he ended with the jury panel in the palm of his hand.

Alex remembered his victories in capital murder trials.

Focus!

She hadn't come this far being a wilted vine. It was time to stand up, walk over to the podium, and give it her all.

"Ladies and gentlemen, thank you for being here today. I've only got forty-five minutes to get to know you. And this time is crucial for my client, Jose Gonzales, because his life will be in your hands if you end up on this jury."

Alex took a deep breath, then stepped out and walked over within a couple of feet of the panel. "I want to illustrate the State's burden of proof beyond a reasonable doubt." She held her arms out by her side, using her body as a scale. Tipping them slightly to one side, she said, "This demonstrates the civil burden of proof, preponderance of the evidence." Then she moved one arm down close to her side and the other up toward the ceiling. "This is what beyond a reasonable doubt looks like. Does anyone have any questions?"

Suddenly she felt foolish.

I haven't done that since law school mock trials!

She saw the jury panel's polite stares, but felt no connection. She either sensed or imagined Bryce's inner smirk. Her confidence level dropped another notch.

Moving back behind the podium, her voice sounded tinny in her ears as she rambled on about what the evidence would and wouldn't show during the trial. She was relieved when the Court told her she had three minutes left. "Can I get a commitment from each of you that if you are chosen to serve on this jury, you will listen and decide this case only after hearing all of the evidence?"

They nodded like school children waiting for the bell to ring.

Alex's vision of herself as a polished trial lawyer evaporated. She was thankful that Nick was not here to see her flail so miserably before the jury panel.

"Thank you for your time," she said, smiling, then returned to her seat.

The Court excused the panel to the jury room while both sides decided who they would eliminate according to their right to strike jurors without cause.

"That was the worst forty-five minutes of my life," Alex muttered under her breath to Ruth.

Jose gave her a weak smile.

She was all he had.

Bryce and Marilyn moved from counsel table to the jury box while Alex, Ruth, and Jose stayed put. Both sides began working on their peremptory challenges: the ten prospective jurors they were allowed to eliminate for no reason other than personal choice.

"That Hispanic woman," Jose said, "she don't like me. I can feel it."

"We need Hispanics on the jury, Jose. She'll like Angelina for sure."

Jose shrugged.

"Strike that preacher," Ruth advised, referring to Juror Number 11.

"Why?"

"He pastors a small charismatic church on the North side."

"What's a charismatic church?"

"Holy rollers. They talk in tongues. A far cry from the conservative doctrine your Reverend teaches."

"If you say so, we'll strike him," Alex said. "For some reason, I don't trust him either. My gut tells me he would end up as foreman."

"When Bryce spoke, he listened," Ruth added. "But when you talked, he didn't."

Alex scratched his name off the list. "And those cute professionals with the short skirts? They go." Alex crossed two more names off. When she reached ten, she realized they were all white. She couldn't afford to strike any of the blacks or Hispanics, because she felt they would be naturally sympathetic to her client.

Both sides handed their list to the clerk.

Judge Villareal announced the State's strikes. Alex noticed Bryce left one Hispanic on his panel: the one Jose thought didn't like him. She wasn't surprised. The woman wasn't a threat to the prosecution; she would most likely follow the leader.

When the Court read Alex's list, Bryce's objection came quick. "Batson challenge, Judge! The defense struck ten Caucasians. The State alleges the defense based their decision to strike jurors solely on the basis of race, thereby showing prejudice on the basis of color."

Alex's face turned bright red. Bryce's motion was clever and unique.

A reverse Batson challenge.

Now she understood why he'd kept one Hispanic on his jury.

The judge frowned at Alex. "Counsel?"

Alex frantically fumbled through her trial notebook, looking for case law.

"It's not there," Ruth whispered. "I forgot to copy the Batson case."

Alex groaned. Bryce had gotten away with the jury shuffle this morning for the very same reasons, but she couldn't bring it up now. It wasn't a defense to a Batson challenge and there was no way she could prove it. She had to think fast. The Supreme Court in the Batson case decided that peremptory strikes couldn't be made solely on the basis of race. She remembered a blurb in a recent case digest about a federal appellate case that held that disqualification due to mere involvement in a religion violated the equal protection clause of the 14th Amendment, but that striking jurors with a "heightened religious involvement" didn't violate the Constitution.

She quickly formulated an argument. Everyone she had struck, including the preacher and the two young professionals, were involved in church work. "Your Honor, as far back as the 1700s and William Blackstone, peremptory challenges are allowed without giving a reason for the decision. Batson did change the common law and now lawyers can be forced to explain decisions that were previously protected. Under a recent federal appellate court ruling, I'm prepared to take each juror I struck, one by one, to demonstrate how my decision was not based upon the protected province of sex or race, but was based on the juror's 'heightened religious involvement.' "

Bryce looked dumbfounded.

The judge held a wry smile. "Counsel, I'm familiar with *United States v. De Jesus*. Isn't it from the Third Circuit Court of Appeals?"

Alex knew she meant "that Yankee court" and decided the less said the better. "Yes, Your Honor."

The judge looked at the bailiff, then at her watch. "This will take some time ..."

Bryce leapt to his feet. "Judge, in order to save time and keep the process moving, would you allow me a minute with opposing counsel?"

"I have a couple of calls to make. Court will take a ten-minute recess." She rose and went into her chambers.

Bryce strode to Alex's counsel table and looked her squarely in the eye. "I'll withdraw my Batson challenge if you withdraw your strike against Mr. Smith."

Juror Number 11.

Alex clenched her teeth. Logic told her that the preacher would identify with Jose's side through the Reverend. But Ruth felt strongly that the preacher was the last person she wanted on Jose's jury. And Ruth knew more about religion than she did. She couldn't fathom why Bryce wanted to keep him over the two young women. But it didn't matter. She wasn't prepared for a Batson hearing and didn't want to hold up the process and risk ticking off the judge.

Alex turned to Jose. His face was ashen. "I think we should

move forward," she whispered before turning back to Bryce.

"OK. In the interest of saving time, Mr. Smith is back on the panel." She'd never give him the satisfaction of knowing how she felt about her choice.

Judge Villareal returned and the parties announced their agreement. "Good, then we have our jury."

She called the panel back in, announced who was free to leave, then admonished the others to return at ten the next morning.

On her way out of the courtroom, reporters surrounded both Alex and Bryce.

"Get the jury you wanted?" a familiar newsman quizzed.

Television cameras were the last thing she needed right now. "No comment," she said and kept going toward the elevator.

Nick walked out of the elevator and grabbed her elbow.

Alex was too numb to object. She followed his lead into Judge Stovall's deserted courtroom, where they burst into the startled senior judge's chambers.

"I'll explain later," Nick called to the judge as he and Alex headed out his back door exit into a fire escape stairwell.

"Pretty clever," Alex said, marveling at how Nick always showed up at the right place at the right time.

"I worked his court in several trials years ago."

Alone in the stairwell, Nick turned to her. "Sorry I missed voir dire. You look like you need a hug."

Alex nodded and allowed him to take her in his strong embrace. She felt like letting her day, full of frustration and disappointment, wash out onto his white shirt, but held back. She couldn't risk letting the press see her outside looking like she'd lost it. But she did savor the moments in his arms. He was a refuge in a time of need.

When Nick released her, they continued down the stairs to the ground floor. Outside, she spotted his truck nearby.

"I knew the press would be here. I doubt you heard this,

but this morning, Governor Hastings announced sweeping CPS reforms. The agency responded by blaming their troubles on foster homes like Shepherd's Cottages."

"Oh no. That's all we need."

Alex knew she would eventually have to deal with the press, and she hoped the jurors would follow court orders not to listen to, or read, the news during trial.

"Leave your car in the garage tonight," Nick suggested. "I'll drive you home and pick you up in the morning."

Alex looked at her overstuffed briefcase. "Alright."

He helped her into his truck.

After a moment, she asked, "How did it go at the park?"

"All I found were empty syringes, used condoms and worthless trash."

"Figures." Alex shut her eyes and leaned her head against the rear window. "We need a witness ... bad."

CHAPTER 15

The first thing Alex did was heat up some of Siva's homemade food. Then, worn-out and exhausted, she plopped down in a patio chair while her hungry dog ate. She glanced up at the dove's nest and saw how the mama zealously guarded her eggs. Alex wondered when the baby birds would appear. Knowing not to get too close, she poured some birdseed Nick dropped off into the plastic bowl near the nest.

Alex relaxed and, for a moment, her mind left the trial. She stretched with a couple of neck rolls. It felt good. Exercise would invigorate her before beginning work on tomorrow's opening argument.

She went upstairs, slipped on jogging clothes, then headed out the front door for a quick run. It crossed her mind to grab the dog and her cell phone, but she needed time alone and a neighbor had already taken Siva on a long walk.

The cool, crisp air felt invigorating. She waved at her security guard and headed out of the complex toward the jogging trail. It was dark, but the track was on the median of a well-lit street. Pushing apprehension to the back of her mind, she concentrated on her run.

Clouds covered the full moon when Alex entered the unusually deserted jogging path and ran to the end of the trail. Just as she began the curve home, a car slowed and pulled up beside her.

Alex turned her head and saw the familiar black Lincoln. In a split second, a man in a ski mask jumped out and ran toward her. She sprinted faster, but he quickly overcame her. Then, with one hand grasping both of hers behind her back and the other around her neck and mouth, he pulled her over to a cluster of nearby shrubs and trees. Alex struggled, but was overpowered by the man's size and strength. He thrust himself against her and pinned her back and hands against the bark of the tree so forcefully that she felt her skin tear.

"We're watching you." The man's breath smelled of tobacco and alcohol. "You're in over your head."

With his free hand, he pulled the mask up over his nose and licked and bit her neck, while with his other hand he tugged downward on the elastic band of her pants.

"Stop!" a sharp voice called.

The command startled Alex's attacker. He turned and looked back.

Instinct, reflexes, and adrenaline all came together and Alex jumped at the chance to break free. With all her strength, she thrust her knee into the man's groin. The attacker groaned and released his grip momentarily, but then landed a sharp punch to her right eye as she pulled free.

Alex ran for her life.

She knew the voice had come from the back of the car. When the car door slammed, the car came after her.

Fear provided her speed as she mentally plotted the best way home. During long walks with Siva, she'd learned the nooks and crannies of her neighborhood. She headed up the street, turned into the alley and ran the short distance to the deserted back parking lot of the high-rise condos whose rear fence faced her garage.

The Lincoln was close behind.

Alex looked at the tall fence. There was only one way. She had to climb it.

She heard the squeal of brakes. A car door opened; footsteps approached. She surged forward and grabbed the metal above her head and propelled her body upward. Barbed wire topped the fence, but it didn't matter. Alex had no choice but to hoist her body over the top. A hand grabbed her foot. One of her tennis shoes came off but she pulled herself free and over, landing hard on her back, safe on the other side.

Quickly rolling over to get up, she was relieved to see that the man did not follow. She watched him enter the dark car parked a few feet away, but could not see inside. She heard an ominous voice: "It's not over."

Alex punched the automatic garage door opener on her key ring as the car wheeled around and sped down the alley. Wiping blood from her face and hands with her T-shirt, Alex entered her back patio and collapsed on the same chair as earlier, with both Siva and the mama bird staring at her.

Alex swore under her breath. Stupidly and stubbornly, she broke her promise to Nick again. She paid a dear price for leaving without her cell phone. Her stomach knotted at the thought of calling him now. He would be furious! He would insist on coming over; would make her go to the doctor; make her call the police. She didn't want to have to explain why she was too proud to go; too embarrassed to admit her mistake.

Voodoo had evaded arrest for years. Other than to notify the press, what purpose would making a police report serve? Anyway, she couldn't identify her attacker out of a photo I.D. Today's news story would shift focus from Jose to herself and the trial would become more of a three-ring circus. And Bryce would find a way to capitalize on it.

No. Alex didn't need doctors, policemen, or press—she needed time to prepare her opening statement.

Nick would just have to understand.

She grabbed an ice pack out of the freezer and made her way up to her bathroom. Washing blood off her face and hands, she saw her reflection in the mirror and was startled. A dark-blue circle was forming under her right eye and there were several deep cuts and scrapes on her hands and wrists. While her tub filled with hot water, she took two over-the-counter pain pills and held the ice pack to her rapidly swelling eye.

Slowly, she entered the bath and let the water caress her skin. It soothed her screaming nerves and restored clarity to her thinking.

Why had the voice in the back of the car stopped her attacker from molesting, possibly raping her? It didn't make sense, but he'd given her the opportunity to get away.

Was it Voodoo? It had to be.

Half an hour later, she left the tub and towel dried her body. The scrapes and cuts on her hands were deep. How would she hide them from Nick? Or the jury? Alex rifled through her medicine cabinet and found antibacterial cream, gauze and tape, and while administering to her injuries, hoped they'd improve overnight.

She crawled in bed with the ice pack on her eye, a heating pad on her aching back, and opened her briefcase beside her. When she put down the pages of her opening statement, it was three-thirty a.m.

★

Nick's cheerful knock awakened her.

Sore and not ready to face the day, she went downstairs. "You're early," she called from inside. "I'm not ready yet. I'll unlock the door, but wait a couple of seconds before you come in." She turned the deadbolt and headed upstairs.

She heard Nick enter and go into the kitchen. "I'll make the coffee," she heard him yell.

A quick glance in the mirror brought relief. The swelling on her eye had gone down and she could cover the bruises with expensive concealer.

After she dressed, she studied her image in the mirror. "It's the best I can do," she muttered.

When she came downstairs, Nick was on the couch reading the morning paper. She sailed past him toward the kitchen.

"We better hurry," he warned.

"The judge calls docket first," she said as she filled her to-go cup, hoping to stay out of eyeshot for as long as possible. "We'll make it."

Nick walked out the front door ahead of her and she lingered behind to lock up. It wasn't until he opened the truck door for her that he saw her face in full sunlight. "What happened?" he exclaimed.

Alex jumped into the truck and pulled her oversize Prada sunglasses from her purse.

Nick slammed her car door, then quickly entered the driver's side of the truck. "Cut it out! What happened?"

"I don't want to talk about it."

"Don't give me that! We made a deal. You better tell me quick, or you won't see the inside of the courtroom today."

Nick was irate. She'd never seen this side of him.

"Nothing. I just got in a hurry and bumped into the wall."

Nick saw through her story and stopped the truck in the middle of the complex exit. Cars were behind them.

"OK. I did something stupid and I regret it." She told him what happened. "I didn't call you because I didn't want police or press involved."

Nick shook his head. "The worst part is that I can't trust you." He was silent for a few moments. Then his voice softened.

"I'm staying with you until trial is over."

"Sounds like house arrest."

"Call it what you want."

Alex's heart quickened and she felt a funny tingle in her lower stomach. She looked at him and realized she'd probably gotten the better end of the bargain. She wondered whether she could concentrate on the trial with him around. But he was determined to protect her. After last night, it was hard to deny his concern was comforting.

Nick dropped Alex off at the courthouse's back entrance.

When she entered the courtroom, she was greeted by her whole team: Ruth, the Reverend, Miss May, Rosemary, Mr. Samples, and all of the board members. She stayed in motion and concentrated on preparing her counsel table. Alex was grateful no one mentioned her black eye, or the Band-Aids on her hands.

When she saw Bryce and Marilyn conferring with Camilla and a woman who appeared to be her supervisor, Alex wondered what surprises they had in store for her today.

"Want to tell me what happened?" Ruth said quietly when they sat down together.

Alex shrugged and kept her eyes on her notes.

"I'm worried about you. What gives?"

"I did something stupid last night, but I'm OK," Alex assured her. "Nick is going to stay with me until the trial is over. By this time next week, everything will be back to normal."

Ruth didn't look convinced. "I hope so because the bills are due."

"We've been behind before. If necessary, I'll break into my savings to catch up."

The bailiff entered the courtroom with Jose, who took his seat beside Alex. Then the jury panel filed in and took their seats. Judge Villareal entered with a regal flair of her black robe, and day two began.

Alex couldn't help but admit that Bryce's opening statement was brilliant. He depicted Jose as a deranged repeat sexual offender hired by a negligent foster home with sloppy hiring practices. Painting a bleak picture of Shepherd's Cottages, he hinted at trouble with the agency and mentioned a boy caught inside a blazing building while others enjoyed Thanksgiving dinner. By carefully prefacing his allegations with the magic words "the evidence will show," Bryce prevented Alex's objections. Besides, she didn't want to alienate the jury by objecting too much this early.

Anticipating one of Alex's lines of defense, Bryce openly discussed how teenage complainants who allege sexual abuse can often have credibility problems. The jury looked as if they understood. His insinuations about the legitimacy of Chris Jackson's story began to sound like the gospel. When he finished, he gave them a confident smile, then sat down.

Alex took one last deep breath then stood to address the jury. "The evidence will show that Mr. Gonzales works as a house parent at a CPS foster home. Shepherd's Cottages is owned and operated by a church in the Fifth Ward. Though you were admonished by the Court to refrain from reading newspapers or watching TV news during this trial, I'm sure you noticed TV cameras outside the courtroom. You may wonder why this case has attracted so much attention. Yesterday, the governor announced sweeping foster home reforms which include increased dependence on community resources, such as churches."

Alex felt them slipping away and knew she had to stay on track with her argument. "My client is entitled to a fair trial. Jose Gonzales is a victim of politics at its finest. And we can't let what is going on out there affect what goes on in here. Politics is not a part of this trial."

"Objection!" Bryce was angry. "This isn't final argument. She's trying to distract the jury from the real problem at hand— sexual abuse of an innocent child."

"We'll see how innocent he is," Alex shot back under her breath, just loud enough for the jurors to hear.

"Sustained." The judge frowned at Alex. "Counsel, please keep your comments to the evidence in this case."

"Of course, Your Honor." Alex was respectful, but she'd planted a seed. "My client's future depends on your ability to assess the credibility of the testimony. Each witness who comes before you is metaphorically naked. No matter how exalted or humble their stage in life is, until you hear what they have to say, the judge admonished you not to prejudge their testimony. Once you listen, then it's up to you to decide the weight and value you put on their testimony."

Alex paused.

Jesus, did that just sound like a lecture?

"On October 31, Mr. Gonzales followed the complainant, Chris Jackson, into Crosstown Park," she continued. "The evidence will show that the child made this allegation against my client because he was angry at him for making him stay at home and finish his homework. You will learn that Chris Jackson made up this story in an effort to cause Shepherd's Cottages problems."

She took a deep breath. "I trust when you hear the evidence, you will make the right decision and acquit Jose Gonzales. Thank you."

When Alex sat back down, a sense of discomfort stole over her. The hair on the back of her neck stood up. Instinctively, she turned and looked past Nick, who was sitting behind her, into the dark eyes of a handsome black man seated in the back row. He was at Jose's arraignment.

"Voodoo," Nick whispered.

CHAPTER 16

Judge Villareal directed her attention to Bryce. "Begin the State's evidence, counselor."

Bryce stood. "Thanks, Your Honor. The State calls its first witness, arresting officer Peavy."

Bryce artfully conducted direct examination of the stocky middle-aged policeman.

Officer Peavy was arrogant and Alex hoped the jury would pick up on his attitude. His stomach flopped over his belt by a few inches and he kept slicking what was left of his hair back with one hand.

"When the boy waved your patrol car down, what did he say?" Bryce asked.

"He told me he lived at Shepherd's Cottages and that his house parent just forced him to perform oral sex on him in the park."

"What happened then?"

"I asked him to get into the patrol car and took him home."

"Did you see blood on the child?"

"Yes, there was a cut on his neck."

"Did he tell you how he was cut?"

"Yes. He said the man had the knife and when he tried to run, cut him on his neck."

When Bryce dramatically pulled the big knife out of his briefcase and laid it on counsel table before the jury, Alex jumped up. "Objection!"

"Overruled."

Alex's blood pressure shot up. Judge Villareal had kept the knife out during voir dire, but now allowed it at trial. It was her court, her trial. Nothing to do but move on.

"Is this the knife you recovered from the park?"

"No. We didn't find one, but it's the kind of knife the child described that evening."

Alex fumed and contained her emotions as best she could.

"Did Chris Jackson identify his assailant?"

Officer Peavy nodded. "When we pulled into Shepherd's Cottages driveway, he was outside."

"Is he in the courtroom?" Bryce asked.

"Yes." He pointed at Jose.

"Let the record reflect Officer Peavy just pointed to the defendant, Jose Gonzales," Bryce said. "What happened next?"

"We took him down to the station and charged him with aggravated sexual assault of a child."

It was Alex's turn.

"Officer Peavy, you told the jury you were in charge of the investigation; but, in fact, you never went to the scene of the alleged crime, did you?"

The witness shook his head. "No, the rain would have washed any tangible evidence away."

"So, you don't conduct investigations unless the weather is perfectly clear, right?

"Well, no," he answered.

Alex went to Bryce's counsel table and picked up the "reasonable facsimile." "In fact, you didn't even try to find the alleged weapon did you?"

"No. The boy said the defendant had it."

Alex raised a brow at him, then looked at the jury. "And what a child says negates police procedure?" With knife in hand, Alex approached the witness. "This is quite a big knife for a foster parent to carry, would you agree?"

"Crosstown Park is dangerous."

"Officer Peavy, doesn't the child's story about the knife sound a bit exaggerated?"

"No."

Alex looked at the jury members; they were all attentive.

"And where was the knife when you arrested my client?"

"I don't know."

"And when you searched his room, was it there?"

"We didn't search his room."

Alex rolled her eyes in frustration and returned to her counsel table to glance at her notes. "On your way to Shepherd's Cottages that evening, did you call the CPS social worker, Camilla Roe?"

"No."

"Who did?" Alex asked with a surprised look.

"I don't know."

Alex rubbed the back of her neck with one hand. Quizzing him further would be risky. She didn't want to break a cardinal rule of trial law: Never ask a question you don't know the answer to.

She looked at the judge. "Your Honor, I'm finished with this witness now, but will reserve the right to recall him later."

During the two-hour lunch break, Alex walked Ruth, Nick and the Reverend to the nearby Courthouse Club, an exclusive restaurant for lawyers. When they entered the dimly lit facility, a crowd of fellow lawyers standing in line to be seated greeted her. Not having undergone a renovation in some years, the walls were dark-wood-paneled and the windows were covered in heavy crimson drapes. A thin haze of blue cigar smoke hung in the air. Life-or-death deals were made here by mostly male judges and lawyers in conservative suits and ties.

When they were escorted to a table in the far corner of the room, Nick didn't hesitate to pull out Alex's chair. "Nice place," he observed.

The Reverend examined the menu. "Food here is probably richer than Bertha's tuna sandwiches," he said with a chuckle.

Edgy and tired, Alex glanced across the room and was stunned when she saw Mike Delany seated with Hal, her political opponent.

Her stomach did a somersault and landed in her throat. She remembered the signing party and how Mike had ignored him all night. What was going on? Had Mike switched horses in the middle of the stream?

An overwhelming sense of dread swept over her. It dawned on her that for the first time in her life, she wasn't on the winning team. It was time for a quick bathroom break. She told Nick what she wanted and excused herself.

On the way to the restroom she avoided eye contact with Mike. She knew she had to consider Mike's interests too. The governor's political agenda was paramount. If his candidate didn't deliver results, his job would be on the line.

Alex entered the foyer next to the ladies' lounge and was stopped by an old friend. She was polite, but tried to hurry up and get out of the conversation.

A moment later, Mike Delany appeared.

As if nothing was amiss, he gave her a quick kiss and hug, then narrowed his eyes intently on hers. "How's the trial going, Alex?"

She didn't blink. "Too soon to tell."

"Alex, I ...," Mike began.

Anger welled and she didn't give him time to finish. "Listen, Mike, I'm going to win this one. My client is innocent. When it's over, the press will validate the governor's proposed reforms."

She touched his lapel. "Don't give up on me. Please."

He looked at the bruise over her eye and started to say something, then stopped.

Inside the restroom, she leaned against the counter and wished she'd had that same kind of confidence and determination in the courtroom earlier.

Somehow I'll get it back.

Alex returned to the table where the food had been served. She wasn't hungry, but she knew she had to eat. On his way out, Mike stopped by the table. When he left, she saw Nick's quizzical gaze.

"He's an old political friend," she stated. "The governor's chief of staff. Seems I'm in line for a newly created juvenile bench."

Nick's eyes widened. "You want to be a judge?"

"I always thought I did."

"You'd be a good one," the Reverend offered.

Nick nodded agreement.

"Thanks for your support," Alex smiled, then glanced at her watch. "I have to get back."

Nick watched her leave the restaurant and marveled at her ability to withstand pressure.

Ruth broke into his thoughts. "Alex has a heart of gold, but sometimes takes better care of others than she does herself."

"I've seen that already," he said. "Tell me about this judgeship."

"Her friend is helping her get appointed to a new bench. Being the incumbent will help her win the election next fall."

"Is there anything we can do?" the Reverend asked. "We are all very grateful to her."

Ruth shook her head. "The jury is still out. No pun intended. Unless she wins Jose's trial, she doesn't stand a chance."

★

"Call your next witness," the judge told Bryce after the jury was seated.

"Camilla Roe," he announced.

In a navy suit, low-cut camisole and tight skirt, Camilla climbed the steps to the witness box.

Alex noted the jury's keen attention to the State's primary witness and hoped they saw what she did: a woman who could not quite put herself together.

After his questions about her education and her five years experience as a caseworker, he asked, "On October 31st did you receive a referral of aggravated sexual assault of a child?"

"Yes."

"Did the allegation involve Jose Gonzales and Shepherd's Cottages?"

"Yes," Camilla answered.

"Was it the home's first referral?"

Camilla looked straight at the jury. "No, there have been many others."

With clenched fists, Alex stood. "Objection. May we approach?"

The judge nodded and switched off her podium microphone.

Trying to maintain her composure, Alex began, "Because it doesn't directly pertain to my client, I object to any testimony involving prior CPS referrals to Shepherd's Cottages. If you allow it, I'll be forced to move for a mistrial."

Bryce shook his head. "Judge, the home's credibility is relevant because we intend to show they knew the defendant was a sexual offender when they hired him. The home could be guilty of conspiracy."

Alex fought to keep her voice low. "What?" she gasped. "Your transparent attempt to build a civil case for some gutless lawyer is obvious, but criminal charges against the home?"

Beneath his movie star smile, Bryce gritted his teeth. "I will not rule it out."

Perspiration formed on Alex's upper lip. For a moment, time stood still. If the judge allowed the damaging testimony, she would have to call the Reverend to counter. If his testimony exposed his strong religious convictions, the trial's focus would shift from Jose to Shepherd's Cottages. Bryce would benefit from a nasty inter-community battle being waged on the state political arena. She took a couple of deep breaths and waited for the ruling.

Judge Villareal looked thoughtfully at TV cameras pointing through the courtroom windows. "This courtroom will not be the venue for a political debate between the governor and CPS. Mr. Gonzales is on trial, not Shepherd's Cottages." She turned the microphone on. "Objection sustained. Mr. Armstrong, you are warned to refrain from testimony relating to Shepherd's Cottages and CPS."

Alex swallowed the lump in her throat and silently thanked Judge Villareal. It was an important victory. For the first time in weeks, she saw a dim light at the end of a dark, dark tunnel.

Her glory was brief.

Bryce smiled as they returned to their counsel tables. "No worries. The defense will open the door."

CHAPTER 17

Bryce had read Alex's mind. If she called the Reverend as a character witness, Bryce knew how to push a man's buttons. Even after careful wood shedding, before he knew it, the Reverend would open the door and the testimony would come in after all.

Her decision was made. She wouldn't call the Reverend. In an instant, Angelina's character testimony became her only hope.

Bryce questioned Camilla without further objection. When she pulled out her handkerchief to wipe away tears, Alex felt nauseated. "The precious child did nothing to deserve what happened to him," she said, sobbing.

Alex glanced at the jury to see if they saw through Camilla's act, but they looked convinced of her sincerity.

"Your witness," Bryce said.

Camilla's tears dried up quick.

"Hello, Miss Roe. We know each other, don't we?"

"Professionally," she admitted.

"We've worked together on family cases."

Bryce jumped to his feet. "Objection. My witness and defense counsel's prior dealings are as irrelevant to this case as mine and opposing counsel's relationship, in or out of court."

A hot red flush rose inside her. "Your Honor," she urged in an even tone, "I would ask that you strike Mr. Armstrong's remark and ask the jury to disregard it."

The judge nodded. "Mr. Armstrong's comments are stricken and disregarded. Go ahead, counselor."

Alex continued. "Miss Roe, how did you know to arrive at Shepherd's Cottages almost simultaneously with the police?"

"I received a call," she answered curtly.

"And you just happened to be in the neighborhood?"

Camilla stared at the jury as if for confirmation. "I suppose so."

"Who called you?"

Bryce jumped out of his seat. "Irrelevant. Miss Roe can't compromise the agency's ability to protect informants."

"Objection sustained."

Alex continued. "You know, Camilla, I'll bet it was Chris's uncle who called."

"It was not!" Camilla cried before Bryce had a chance to object.

Alex looked straight at the jury. "So you can't tell me who it is, just who it isn't?"

"I meant it wasn't proper for you to ask that question." Camilla smoothed the wrinkles in her skirt.

"So, you don't know Chris's uncle?"

Camilla looked at Bryce.

"Objection," he said. "Irrelevant."

Alex turned to the judge. "May we approach?"

The jury gave an almost inaudible community moan as the lawyers went up to the bar. After a short discussion, Judge Villareal granted her leeway to question the witness about her relationship to Chris and his uncle.

The lawyers returned to counsel table.

"Camilla, you do know the complaining witness's uncle. A man who goes by the nickname Voodoo?"

"Well, I ...," she balked.

Alex's voice rose to a high pitch. "In fact, you recently let him carry you out of a Fifth Ward pool hall. Or were you too drunk to remember?"

"No!" Camilla shouted.

Chaos erupted in the stately courtroom.

"Objection." Bryce looked fit to be tied.

Camilla reached for her handkerchief.

Judge Villareal pounded her gavel.

"Bailiff, fifteen-minute break," Judge Villareal ordered, then rose. "Counsel, I'll see you in chambers."

Inside her office, Judge Villareal was serious. "What's going on here?"

Alex avoided eye contact with Bryce.

Both of them shrugged.

"I don't know whether it is *your* political ambitions," she said to Alex, "or *yours*," she said to Bryce. Judge Villareal pointed to the chairs in front of her desk and both lawyers sat down.

Leaning forward across her desk, her eyes intent, she said, "I did some checking. You two dated. And from the looks of it, you didn't part amicably. We'd better be searching for justice here today. A man is on trial, and my courtroom won't be a stage for personal disputes or wanton ambition."

Both lawyers nodded with sheepish looks. The judge continued, "And why all the press?"

Alex spoke up first. "The governor wants to reform foster home care and the agency is against it. I'm concerned about my client's interests getting lost in the shuffle."

"Judge, she can't have it both ways," Bryce interrupted. "On the one hand, she doesn't want the witness to talk about CPS's history with the home. But she does want to talk about the social worker's personal relationships. What Camilla Roe does after office hours has nothing to do with this case."

"Unless she's part of a setup," Alex argued.

Bryce shook his head. "Your imagination has got the better of you. I don't understand why you took this case, but I've made it my business to see it through."

"I'd like to finish this week," the Court interjected. "You *both* must stay within the parameters of the law. There will be no further grandstanding or badgering of witnesses."

★

It was cold and dark when Nick and Alex left the courthouse.

On the short drive home, Alex thought about being alone with Nick. She couldn't deny knowing he was in the guest room while she worked would be a distraction. Nick probably wouldn't make a move, but would *she*? Romance didn't come to mind when she took a quick glance at her reflection in the rearview mirror. Her makeup had long since worn off and her black eye stood out like a sore thumb.

Nice guys had never been her strong suit. Nick's devotion to the Reverend and the development of his spiritual life was genuine. But then again, Nick said he'd changed since his failed marriage. Regardless of how he used to be, now he was fun, generous and good-looking as they come. She couldn't ignore the butterflies in her stomach when she thought about him.

I can't afford these feelings now.

Chris's testimony was first thing in the morning and she had to prepare.

Her phone rang.

"Alex." Mike Delany's voice was urgent. "I forgot to tell you about the governor's town hall meeting at the Barbara Jordan Convention Center tonight."

Alex was silent.

"You don't need to be there the whole time," Mike said.

"Meet me outside his bus around nine. It's red, white and blue, with an eagle painted on the side. You can meet with him in private; shore him up on your ideas for CPS reform."

"I'll be there."

Alex's work plan was dashed. Her priority now was to put her face back on and think of something pithy to say to Governor Hastings.

She looked at Nick.

"What's up?" he asked.

"Plans have changed," she said. "Mike Delany set up a quick meeting with the governor at the convention center. Mike will meet me right outside of the bus."

There was a long silence. "OK. Call me on your way home."

Alex sensed Nick's disappointment. Did he still plan to stay with her tonight? Part of her wanted him there tonight; part of her didn't. Lighthearted relationships were familiar, but heavy emotions were a luxury she couldn't afford right now. After Nick dropped her off, she tuned into the Access Channel to listen to the town hall meeting while she showered and dressed for the governor. Under fire for his proposed reforms, he handled the crowd with silk gloves. He was smooth. Elegantly handsome in blue jeans and starched white dress shirt, he looked fit and younger than his years.

Again, Alex concealed her black eye with layers of makeup. There was no way to speed up the healing process. If she was lucky, it would be gone by final argument.

She drove downtown to the convention center, where big stadium lights lit the parking lot. As promised, Mike waited outside the governor's garishly patriotic bus.

"He's nearly finished." Mike led her to the bus. "We'll wait here."

They stepped inside into a large seating area with built-in TV screens and computer system: American pie and baseball all the way. Political paraphernalia was everywhere. The small kitchen held a full pot of fresh coffee, fruit baskets and sandwich trays. As Alex moved toward the kitchen table, she looked down the hall and saw bunk beds covered with political material and T-shirts and a small bathroom.

"The governor doesn't like to fly," Mike said. "We use it to travel around the state. When I can, I go on the road with him."

"Nice," Alex said as she took in her surroundings.

Mike put a videotape in the VCR. "These are some rough cuts of next year's endorsement strategy for upcoming political candidates."

The program's quality and professionalism was impressive. The governor had a big stake in who ran with him on the party ticket. Suddenly, Alex felt like a small piece of a big machine. She swallowed hard and thought about Jose.

The governor entered the bus in high spirits. "Open me a beer, please, Mike," he said, his voice full of confidence and testosterone.

"Gov, you remember Alex Stockton," Mike said. "She stopped by to congratulate you on the work you're doing."

The governor stared at Alex.

When his look made her flush, she wished she hadn't chosen the black, scoop neck body suit. She didn't want to mislead him, but she did want to leverage her femininity. For a powerful woman in a male-dominated profession, it was a tough line to draw. Alex had it down to an art. So far, she'd never been faced with a challenge she couldn't overcome. Her interaction with the governor was different. Her future was in his hands.

The governor held her eyes until she lowered hers. She needed to let him think he was the alpha dog.

"Would you like a beer?" he said, slapping his big hand on her shoulder as he walked past to take his seat at the kitchen table.

"No thanks. I still have work tonight."

"Well, humor me; have one," he said. "You can still work."

Mike handed her a beer.

"How is the trial going?" he asked. "From what I see on the news, not too good. But reporters twist things sometimes, don't they?"

Alex took a seat across from him at the small table. "My client's case is the litmus test for your reforms," she said.

"Tell me about it." His interest was genuine.

Carefully choosing her words, she recounted the facts of Jose's case.

"You have your work cut out for you," he said when she finished, visibly impressed. "You just may be the right candidate." He stood, grabbed her hand, and pulled her out of her seat. "Come here. I want to show you something."

When he led her down the hall toward the rear of the bus, Alex turned and gave Mike a questioning look.

He shrugged and continued to flip through the channels with the remote control.

Alex began to formulate an escape plan for whatever lay ahead.

The door opened onto a room with a king size bed, hunter green comforter and matching satin sheets. A stereo system and well-stocked wet bar completed the scene.

A real bachelor pad.

A desk and two chairs in the makeshift back office did nothing to relieve her anxiety. The room was a politician's version of the casting couch. Trapped, she knew what her next move meant. It wasn't the first time a powerful man came on to her. She was determined to fend him off without damaging his fragile male ego or her political future.

She decided to take control of the situation. "How nice," she gushed. "Your wife has good taste."

He chuckled. "She has the Capitol, a ranch, a beach house, and a ski condo to decorate. This place is mine."

Still holding her hand, he led her to the desk. Picking up

a bumper sticker with Hal's name on it, he held it out to her. "Know him?"

"We went to law school together."

"He's working hard to get on my good side. He seems very organized. Already raised eighty thousand dollars for his own campaign and another forty for mine. How much do you have in pledges?"

Alex's heart sank. She couldn't compete with Hal. Was the governor baiting her? She took a deep breath. "I'm not sure ... Jose's trial is more important than bumper stickers and slogans."

"You're passionate about this foster home. I like that," he said, moving closer. Before she knew it, his arms went around her shoulders and she was caught in a ferocious bear hug.

There was no denying Governor Hastings had incredible sex appeal. If her career future didn't hinge on what happened in the next couple of minutes, she might be tempted to give in to him. Instead, she'd scare the dickens out of him by fighting fire with fire: flirt and tease, then leave him hanging, wondering what had just happened. She raised her chin, moving her lips up his neck. It was hard to ignore the sensual smell of his aftershave as she drew a deep breath close to his ear and paused. For a moment, she forgot it was a game.

The governor groaned and moved his hands over the contours of her back. He grew bolder and, in a swift move, he cupped her rear and pulled her down onto his bed.

Before he could get comfortable, she broke away and rolled up off the bed like Catwoman in action. She stood before the full-length mirror and straightened her clothes and hair.

The governor was clearly aroused, frustrated, and alone in a big, soft bed. "Where are you going?"

Alex's hand was on the door. "I'm out of here before we do something we both regret."

CHAPTER 18

Driving home, the governor's cologne still clung to her clothes, a reminder of the dangerous game she just played. Alex wanted the judgeship fair and square; she was qualified and the best candidate for the job. But her deepest fears were confirmed: The appointment came with strings.

She smiled, remembering the stricken look on the governor's face when she bolted. Her exit left no doubt: If he chose her, it would be on her terms, not his.

On the way home, her phone rang.

"How did it go?" Nick asked.

"Great," she lied.

"I'm still coming over?" His tone was hopeful.

Alex paused. Last night's attack on the jogging trail seemed like long ago. She had a lot on her mind and Voodoo's henchman wasn't one of them. "You'll be more comfortable in your bed," she answered.

"That's not the point. Just throw me a pillow, a blanket and I'll sleep on the couch."

"OK," she agreed. "But I'm going straight to bed."

When Alex got home, Nick was there waiting outside her townhouse. As they entered the patio, the floodlight illuminated the bird's nest. The first egg had hatched and the hungry baby bird's eyes were barely open.

"I don't know where they came from or why they chose my patio, but I like them," Alex confessed.

"Maybe they're watching over you. Just like me."

"I don't need anyone to watch over me." Turning on her heel, Alex opened the back door. "I've managed on my own until now."

"Maybe this is a bigger battle."

Alex didn't answer.

As they entered the townhouse, she asked, "Sure you don't want to stay in the upstairs guestroom?"

"Right here is fine," he said, plopping his briefcase and overnight bag on the coffee table. "Mind if I make a fire?"

"Make yourself at home."

Alex watched Nick put logs in the fireplace and start the fire. He was long, lean and masculine, but at times alarmingly tender. *Had the Reverend's influence softened him?*

On her way upstairs, she wondered if perhaps he needed to soften her. Minutes later, she returned with an armload of bedding and handed him a log cabin quilt. "I made this."

"It's beautiful," he said, surprise in his voice. "How did you find the time?"

"During the three months between the bar exam and results. Quilting relaxes me, kind of like Country Western dancing."

"Quilting and the two-step? Never thought about the connection."

Nick sat on the couch and pulled out a file. Alex pulled up the ottoman and faced him. Flames cast flickering shadows on his rugged features, playing tricks with his hair. He was more appealing than ever in the warm firelight. Alex tried to ignore her feelings.

He pulled a report from his file. "I've done some checking into

Shepherd's Cottages' Thanksgiving Day fiasco. The fire captain on the scene has to determine which of three types of fires it was: accidental, incendiary, or unknown. His report states he smelled natural gas coming from the stove. He assumed it was a gas leak and ruled it accidental."

"Accidental? So should anyone pursue that angle, Shepherd's Cottages could be negligent." She grabbed the report, his legal pad and pen, and started writing.

"Counselor." Nick leaned toward her and gently took the pen and pad from her hand. "When I dance, I lead."

Alex flushed. "Sorry. Go ahead."

"The case was closed because the initial report didn't call for an arson investigator. I checked the original city inspection sheet and learned that the gas stove coupling wasn't up to par. But a later inspection shows the Reverend replaced it."

"So we're clear on negligence?"

Nick nodded.

Alex barely suppressed a yawn.

Nick noticed. "Go on upstairs. I'll work on this awhile. In the morning at nine, I'm meeting an arson investigator friend at Shepherd's Cottages to inspect Cottage Five."

"You'll miss Chris's testimony," Alex said.

"I want to see Voodoo arrested before week's end."

They fell silent. Alex noted a small leather-bound Bible on the coffee table. "You really read it?"

"Every day."

Alex was perplexed as she climbed the stairs to draw herself a hot bubble bath. She'd never been this close to a man who was at once handsome, down to earth, and spiritual. Undressing, she knew no amount of Candy's essential oils would erase the smell and feel of Governor Hastings. The political romp left her feeling hard and tough. She knew this was just the beginning. As long as he was governor and she was in politics, she'd have to fend off his advances.

She put all of Candy's energy rocks in the tub for good measure and played soothing music. Her thoughts turned to Nick. He was downstairs and she was upstairs. She would sleep better knowing he was there. After meeting so many men who had tried to crawl all over her body, it was a relief to not have to fight him off or dive into an uncertain relationship.

In the past when she met someone new, she jumped headfirst into a relationship. Then, after a few months, she would realize it was all wrong. Bryce was a good example. They quickly discovered mutual political aspirations, a love for champagne and then ended up in bed. Their deal was no commitment; it was more of a business transaction than a relationship.

She thought about the variety of excuses she'd used all her life to keep men at bay: working her way through school, her first job, traveling too much, building her career. Although she told people she wanted a life companion, she ran each time a man tried to possess, control, or tie her down. True love eluded her.

Next year, I'm thirty-five. Maybe it's time to think about relationships.

The December day was cold, but the sky was clear and blue. As Nick drove toward Shepherd's Cottages, he looked forward to working with his old friend Johnny Wharton again. When Nick phoned, he sounded eager to help find the cause of the blaze. Johnny was a fire chief for thirty years before he retired and opened his arson investigation firm. In years past, he and Nick worked tough cases, forming a solid friendship based on competence and integrity.

Turning into Shepherd's Cottages, he saw Miss May outside talking to the Reverend and Mr. Samples.

Nick parked in front of the administration building and exited his truck. "How is everyone?" he asked.

Miss May forced a smile. "I wish I could hear Chris's testimony this morning, but things needs to be done here."

Nick patted her shoulder. "Don't we have a board meeting tonight?"

She sighed. "Yes, but our spirits are so low, I don't know how much we'll get done. This trial is the only thing on our agenda."

"I can't bear to hear him tell his stories to the jury," the Reverend said.

"Surely there's other business to attend to?" Mr. Samples interjected.

"The budget, maybe," she admitted. "Since Jose's arrest, we don't have any new children. I figure, unless there's a miracle, we only have thirty days."

Johnny Wharton's oversized truck pulled into the drive and the short, stocky man hopped out. Although in his mid-sixties, he was still robust and ruggedly handsome. He greeted Nick with a big hug. "Hey, buddy, it's been too long."

"I know," Nick said.

"Cottage Five is unlocked," Miss May said. She and Mr. Samples entered the administration building.

On the way to Cottage Five, Nick and the Reverend recounted the Thanksgiving Day fire for Johnny.

"Thank God you were able to save the boy's life," he said when they finished.

"We still don't know why he was there," Nick said, "or whether the person who set the fire knew it."

"Have you talked to the boy since the fire?" Johnny asked.

Nick shook his head. "He's in Shriners Hospital. CPS won't let us see him. Besides, he's only five. I doubt he could identify the arsonist."

"Unless he knew him," the Reverend said. He opened the front door of the burned cottage and the three men entered.

"Has anyone been inside since the fire?" Johnny asked.

"No, we've kept everyone away. Since the fire chief made his finding, no one has been back," the Reverend answered.

The three men inhaled the stale air.

"I smell gasoline," Johnny stated.

"So do I," Nick said.

"My nose ain't the best anymore," the Reverend admitted.

"On the day of the fire, natural gas would cover up the gasoline smell," Johnny explained. "The natural gas is gone now, but the odor of gasoline lingers. You've got yourself an arson, alright."

He handed the Reverend a notepad and a pen. "You take notes." Then he pulled two pairs of plastic gloves from his pants pockets and handed one to Nick. "Let's carefully go through this debris starting in the back."

The cottage had been a small three-bedroom house with a kitchen, two bathrooms, den and living room. Now, it was a shell with a few singed timbers. The floor was ankle deep in soot and charred items. Nick and Johnny examined the remains for a couple of hours and found nothing recoverable.

Then Johnny inspected the stove. "See this coupling?" He showed Nick a warped piece of metal. "This is why the fire captain assumed the fire was accidental. When he smelled natural gas, he didn't think it was necessary to investigate further."

"Maybe he was on the arsonist's payroll?" Nick mused.

"I doubt it," Johnny answered. "Arson is just hard to prove."

It was eleven-thirty when Johnny looked at his watch. "I have a noon appointment. I'm sorry we didn't find anything."

Nick swallowed hard.

The Reverend's face showed disappointment. "We need to get to court."

Arson is just hard to prove.

All the way to the courthouse, Johnny Wharton's words echoed in Nick's ears. It could be Johnny's burgeoning caseload, but he was preoccupied this morning. Something told Nick they'd given up too soon. Frustrated by the morning's fruitless search, he pounded his fist on the steering wheel.

He glanced beside him at the Reverend, who was lost in his own thoughts.

Neither man spoke.

Nick wanted to pour his heart out, but felt guilty for not telling the Reverend about his pre-fire visit with Voodoo. He should have heeded Voodoo's parting words as a warning and felt responsible for the Cottage Five fire. He vowed not to rest until he uncovered evidence linking Voodoo to the fire.

When they pulled up in front of the courthouse, Nick told the Reverend to go in. "Tell Alex good luck today."

Nick re-entered Cottage Five with trepidation. He put on gloves Johnny gave him earlier and vowed not to leave again without proof of an arson. This morning, they began the search in the bedrooms and moved to the front. Now, Nick started where the fire began. First, he pulled the gas stove from the wall and searched the debris. Then, he worked his way outward.

After forty-five minutes, he overturned a big piece of linoleum tile. Underneath was the remains of a large white plastic container, whose bottom was eight inches in diameter. All but two inches of the sides were burned away.

Nick's heart raced. Was this a gas container? He placed it on top of the stove, pulled off a glove, reached for his cell phone, and dialed Johnny, who answered on the first ring.

"It's Nick. I came back to the cottage and found part of a white plastic container under some linoleum near the stove."

"Is there a label?"

With gloved hand, Nick picked up the container. "It says Gottex."

"Bingo!" Johnny's voice filled with excitement. "Don't know how we missed it this morning, but it's a gasoline container. Do you see the barcode?"

Nick looked. "On the bottom."

"Your work is cut out for you," Johnny said.

Nick was elated. "What should I do first?"

"First, the bar code will tell you which chain store sold it. That's the easy part. Unless you get lucky, it'll take several weeks and a court order to identify the purchaser."

Nick's resolve hardened. "I don't have time for red tape, so I'll count on a miracle. Thanks for your help."

Nick left the cottage and burst into the administration building. "Miss May?" he called.

She appeared in her office doorway.

With a big smile on his face, he held up the remains of the gasoline container. "Evidence of Cottage Five arson."

Miss May's usually dour face brightened.

"I need something to put it in."

Miss May went to the kitchen, pulled a plastic bag out of a drawer, then handed it to Nick.

"If Voodoo bought this container, we can pin the fire on him."

"Oh, Lordy," she gasped. "That'll be the day."

"And I'll be there with the arresting officer."

CHAPTER 19

In the courtroom, Ruth and Angelina greeted Alex, who wore a conservative red suit. The color gave her a much needed power boost. Still tender, her bruised eye was a lighter shade of blue-green and easier to conceal.

Her first day in court, Angelina looked professional too in a conservative black dress with a white collar. Her long, shiny black hair covered her shoulders. "I haven't seen Jose since that night," she told Alex. "I hope he's forgiven me."

"He has." Alex took her hand. "He's grateful for your testimony."

The bailiff entered with Jose. When he saw Angelina, his face came alive. Alex saw happiness on it for the first time. Leg shackles prevented any show of affection.

"Witnesses are not allowed to watch the trial," Alex told Jose. "But you two can talk a couple of minutes before we start."

In excited but hushed tones, they spoke to each other in Spanish. Alex sensed their strong bond.

Soon, the bailiff announced trial would resume.

As the jury entered, Angelina scooted out the back door.

"Call your next witness," Judge Villareal said to Bryce.

"Chris Jackson, the complaining witness."

The side door opened and Camilla escorted Chris Jackson to the witness stand. Wearing khaki slacks, white button-down shirt and navy windbreaker, he looked like a military school preppie instead of the "gang-member-wannabe" he was. Polished tasseled loafers, trimmed nails and clean, neat hair completed his CPS poster child look.

Alex kept her face calm. Since pretrial discovery is so limited, she wasn't allowed to talk to Chris beforehand. She could watch the five-minute video taken by the DA's intake office the day he came into custody. Bryce could have chosen to just play the video for the jury, but cleverly, he was smart to bring Chris live.

Alex turned to the back of the courtroom and stared straight into Voodoo's eyes. Chris's resemblance to his handsome uncle was uncanny. Grinning from ear to ear, his smug attitude infuriated her.

Alex knew the truth about Chris, but over the past few weeks came to grips with the fact that, because the law protected him, the jury would never know.

Bryce's body language toward Chris told Alex his star witness had been zealously coached. During his tenure at the D.A.'s office, Bryce had tried hundreds of cases. This case was a chance to spotlight his bid for district attorney and he wouldn't risk losing.

Alex knew, during Chris's testimony, the jury would watch her closely and be offended if she badgered a witness they believed to be a sexual assault victim. Her cross-examination of Chris would be a challenge and her efforts could be fruitless. She needed luck.

Bryce eased into his direct examination by asking Chris about school and sports.

"How are your grades?"

"Mostly B's," Chris answered in a deep voice. "But now it's

C's." He looked straight at the jury. "I'm trying hard to get them back up."

"What about sports?" Bryce asked.

"Straight A's," he answered with a confident smile. "Especially Tai Kwan Do. I'm a brown belt."

"Did that skill come in handy on or about the early evening of October 31 of this year, Chris?"

The boy's eyes darkened and he turned his face away from the jury.

"Chris, are you alright?" Bryce asked. "Do we need to take a break?"

He shook his head and straightened his shoulders. "No, I'm OK."

Alex seethed. She knew it was an act, rehearsed time and again in just the right rhythm to sway the jury. Alex couldn't deny Bryce's trial skills. No wonder he never lost.

"Chris, tell the jury what happened."

"I was in Crosstown Park." Chris pointed at Jose. "He followed me into an area where there's lots of trees."

"Your Honor," Bryce interrupted. "Let the record reflect the complainant pointed to and identified the defendant, Jose Gonzales."

"So noted," the judge answered. "Continue."

"What happened then?" Bryce asked.

"He grabbed me from behind, stuck his knife in my face and ordered me to give him a ..." Chris faltered. "I don't know how to say it, but he wanted me to ..."

"Perform oral sex on him?" Bryce helped him out.

Chris nodded. "Yes, he made me do it. Then he cut me."

"Your Honor, the prosecution is leading the witness," Alex objected.

"Overruled. Considering the witness's age I'll allow wide latitude on direct."

Alex knew better than to upset her and the rest of Bryce's

questions proceeded without objection.

Chris told the jury how, when he fought back, Jose cut him on his neck. He escaped and ran to find help. Then Camilla Roe, the social worker, came and took him into CPS custody. There were no surprises. Not once did Chris open the door to further questioning. He came across as a model teenager who was violently assaulted, then sexually abused by his house parent.

When Bryce finished direct examination, the Court recessed the jury for the lunch break. Numbed by the perfection of Chris's performance, Alex slipped out the courtroom door and headed to the ladies' room. As if sleepwalking, she didn't hear familiar lawyers' voices wishing her well, nor did she see television cameras queuing to interview Bryce. She'd never before taken such a bad case. It was a swearing match with one-sided odds.

Inside, she rested on an old couch in the lounge area. With an arm over her forehead, she relived the morning. Chris's testimony was flawless. The jury's faces and body language told her they sympathized with him.

Alex thought about her next move. If she tried too hard to catch Chris in a lie and failed, she would alienate the jury even more. Bryce's undeniable good-old-boy appeal made her femininity a disadvantage in this trial. If she couldn't ask Chris questions about his juvenile record and CPS history, what would she ask? Bryce had covered the incident. Unless she had new areas to explore, her cross-examination would reinforce Bryce's direct. The jury already heard it once. If, through her questions, they heard it again it would sound more credible. There was power in repetition.

She squeezed the back of her neck in a vain effort to squelch a headache. Then she made the toughest trial decision of her life. She decided not to cross-examine Chris.

★

All afternoon, Nick went from store to store in his search to find the barcode match. After three unsuccessful attempts, he rushed into the last one with high hopes. He found the auto department and quickly learned the barcode matched.

Elated, Nick approached a salesperson and pulled the container from the plastic bag. "Can you tell me which of your stores this came from?"

The elderly man studied him through his bifocals.

"You police?"

"Used to be," Nick answered. "I'm investigating a fire I suspect was arson. A little boy was badly burned."

"Let me see those numbers." The old man pulled a list from a drawer and scanned it. "It's store number 86, over on MacGregor, Fifth Ward."

"Thanks." Nick turned to leave.

"Don't bother to go over there." The man scribbled on a sheet of paper and handed it to Nick. "They can't tell you who bought it. Company policy. Headquarters is downtown, One Allen Center."

Nick thanked him and headed out of the store. He glanced at his watch. It was after three. He looked down at his soot-stained clothes. He headed home for a quick shower. Just after four, Nick arrived at One Allen Center in his best shirt, slacks, and jacket. He took the elevator to the fortieth floor, where he was greeted by a friendly receptionist.

Five minutes later, the inner office door opened and a pretty young woman motioned to him. She introduced herself as the district manager.

He shook her hand. "Nick Wright. I'm investigating an arson."

He followed her down the hall to a plush corner office. "What can I do for you?" she asked when they were both seated.

He pulled latex gloves from his pocket and took the container from the plastic bag. "I need to know who bought this."

She leaned over her desk to look at the barcode.

"Don't touch it," he said. "We hope to find fingerprints."

"It's ours—the MacGregor store," she said. "But before we'll investigate, we have to have a court order. I just have to tell you, unless they paid with a credit card, you're out of luck."

"There's not time for a court order," Nick said firmly.

"I'm sorry, but it could take three weeks."

Behind her Nick saw the downtown skyline and the new athletic stadium. He took a deep breath, then told her about Shepherd's Cottages' fire, little Thomas's burns and Jose's trial. "I need an answer before the end of the week," he concluded. "Can you work with me on this?"

The woman stared at Nick a moment and her face betrayed a look of recognition. "Was this fire on Thanksgiving?"

Nick nodded.

"I saw it on TV. You almost died trying to save that boy. I understand why you want to catch whoever set it. I've been following the trial too." Her tone softened and she glanced at her watch. I'll see what I can do and call you in the morning."

Thank you." Nick laid his card on her desk and left.

Alex left the ladies lounge and saw the Reverend approach. She greeted him with a friendly smile. "How did it go at the cottage?"

"I'll tell you about it over lunch."

The cafeteria in the courthouse basement was crowded with defense lawyers and their clients. The Reverend picked up sandwiches, chips and Cokes, then led her to a small corner table.

When handed lunch, Alex said, "Thanks, but I'm not hungry."

"I know, dear, but you have to eat."

Alex obliged him. "I was hungry after all," she stated between bites. "Thanks for taking care of me."

"We appreciate your hard work for Jose."

"Thanks," she said. "What did the arson expert say?"

"He noticed the unmistakable scent of gasoline inside."

"It wasn't there Thanksgiving day?"

The Reverend repeated Johnny Wharton's scientific explanation. "Right off the bat, he called it arson. But we didn't find any evidence to back it up." He paused a moment. "I think Nick went back to take a second look."

"Good." While they talked, Alex's tension drained. His presence calmed her. "Rev, I feel like I've known you my whole life."

The Reverend patted her hand. "Me too."

Alex glanced at her watch and gulped the last sip of her Coke. "Gotta get back before the jury returns. Thanks for lunch."

The Reverend stood and dug in his pants pocket for a couple of quarters to leave the busboy.

His humble manner, consistent consideration toward others, and his belief in a world where good triumphs over evil and justice prevails set a good example for the already jaded young lawyer.

After the short recess, Judge Villareal got right to business. "Cross-examination, counselor?"

Alex stood. "The defense has no questions of this witness."

Bryce's faint smile didn't escape Alex. He addressed the court.

Your Honor," he said. "Our final witness is Dr. Karl Ethan, a child psychologist who interviewed Chris Jackson."

The doctor's gray hair nearly touched his collar and wire-rimmed glasses gave him the air of Berkeley in the sixties. He shuffled to the witness box.

Bryce's initial questions qualified him as an expert witness.

"I worked in psychiatric hospitals to pay rent while I completed a three-year master's program. For over fifteen years I've been a licensed family therapist."

"What is your work experience?"

"Besides my private practice, I've worked with CPS in a fifteen county area for ten years. For the past five, I've been under contract with the Houston Independent School District Child Abuse Division."

"And do you meet HISD students regularly?"

"Yes, when the school calls, I go there and do therapeutic intervention."

"And in the course of your practice, do you work with sexually abused children?"

Dr. Ethan nodded. "Extensively."

Bryce's questions highlighted the doctor's training and experience in sexual abuse cases. "Doctor, on November 1st, did you receive a referral on a Chris Jackson?"

"Yes. From Miss Roe, the caseworker responsible for children at Shepherd's Cottages."

"And what was the nature of her call?"

"She indicated that Chris Jackson, a foster child, had been sexually assaulted by his house parent in a park near the foster home."

"What did you do then?"

"The next day, after I reviewed the investigative report and met with Miss Roe, I interviewed the boy."

"Did you videotape the session?"

"Yes."

"How long were you with him?"

"About an hour."

"What did you observe?"

"The child was withdrawn, insecure and quiet. Although he told me about the incident with the defendant, he never really opened up."

"Do you have an opinion as to why?"

Alex stood. "Objection. Calls for speculation."

"Overruled. He can state his opinion."

"Chris doesn't trust adults."

"Did he cry?"

"No. Male victims of child abuse often don't show their true emotions. The situations involve deep shame and guilt. Victims can't forgive themselves for not being strong or brave enough to stop the attack. Oftentimes the perpetrator is someone they know and trust, which magnifies the pain and decreases their ability to trust."

"Doctor, in your opinion, is Chris Jackson a victim of aggravated sexual assault?"

"Yes." The witness cleared his throat. "I observed a twelve-year-old boy who was sexually molested at knifepoint."

"And do you have an opinion as to the long-term effects this assault will have on Chris?"

"Yes. He's deeply scarred and emotionally wounded. He'll need ongoing psychiatric treatment and possibly medication for some time to come."

"Thank you, doctor. No further questions."

Alex took a deep breath and addressed the man warmly.

"Dr. Ethan, your qualifications are impressive."

"Thank you," he said, beaming.

"When you reviewed the investigative report did you note the absence of scientific evidence to back up the child's story?"

"Well, I ...," the doctor mumbled. "It's not my job to assess anything other than the child."

Alex gave the jury a puzzled look. "But with your extensive experience with sexual abuse cases, didn't the lack of an alleged weapon seem strange?"

"Not particularly."

"During your investigation, did the lack of scientific evidence pointing to my client affect your opinion about the truth or veracity of Chris Jackson's story?"

"No."

Bryce stood. "Objection. Miss Stockton is badgering the witness about an area outside his scope."

"Sustained. Please keep your questions on track, counselor."

"Doctor," Alex asked in a low voice. "How often do foster parents molest children in their custody?"

"Statistically, because of background checks, it's low," he answered.

"In a case against a foster parent without hard evidence to back it up, is it your testimony that a teenage boy's word is reliable?"

The doctor pulled at his shirt collar. "In this case, yes."

Alex leaned over, pulled a paper from her trial notebook and approached the court reporter with a request to mark it as Defendant's Exhibit No. 1. Then, she handed it to the witness.

"Is this a published paper you wrote during your fellowship some years back?"

The doctor's face blanched. "Yes, but this was years ago, before my experience with CPS."

"And was this paper on the resume the prosecution tendered as an exhibit earlier today?"

"No."

"Doctor, could you read the jury the title of your paper?"

Dr. Ethan swallowed hard, kept his eyes low, and mumbled, "The Inherent Unreliability of Adolescent Testimony in Sexual Abuse Cases."

"Doctor, could you repeat your answer so the jury can hear it?"

"The Inherent Unreliability of Adolescent Testimony in Sexual Abuse Cases."

Alex shot a triumphant look at Bryce. "No further questions."

CHAPTER 20

At dawn Thursday morning, Alex entered the deserted jail and flashed her security badge to a sleepy-eyed guard. A short elevator ride later, she entered a trial ready room where Jose waited.

"Good morning," he greeted.

Alex sat across from him. "This is the day we've been waiting for, Jose. Are you ready?"

"I guess so." He straightened his tie nervously.

"That suit looks great."

Jose smiled, buoyed by the compliment.

"You'll do fine. Just tell the truth. Last night we prepared Angelina. She's ready. Pretty remarkable, considering what she's been through."

Jose lowered his eyes. "I feel bad about her husband."

Alex pulled at a tendril of hair that came loose from the clip in back. "Things happen for a reason. I'm sorry about the way things turned out, but no one deserves an abusive husband." Alex opened her trial notebook. "She'll take the stand first, then I'll call you."

"You did good with that doctor yesterday."

"I hope the jury thinks twice about Chris's credibility. The best we can hope for is they read between the lines."

For the next two hours, they went over questions and discussed Bryce's anticipated cross-examination. "The prosecutor is clever."

Jose rolled his shoulders. "I know."

"Listen carefully to his questions. Make sure and give me time to object before you answer. If you respond to an improper question, even if the judge tells them to disregard your answer, they'll remember."

"I'm afraid the jury won't believe me."

Alex knew the possibility of a life sentence for a crime he didn't commit scared him. She put a hand on his. "Jose, I won't let that happen. Somehow truth will prevail."

Jose's dark eyes filled with tears. "I shouldn't have followed Chris into the park."

"Don't look back. What's important today is your testimony." Alex stood. "See you in court."

Despite her fleeting victory yesterday afternoon, Alex left the jail feeling discouraged. She saw court bailiffs herd leg-shackled defendants across the street for court appearances, visitors trickle in to see loved ones, and eager bondsmen surface to post bail. The jail was coming alive.

On the short walk to the courthouse coffee shop, Alex thought about her chosen profession.

Why couldn't I have wanted to be a housewife?

Instead, she chose a male-dominated profession that oftentimes sucked the lifeblood out of its members. No wonder many trial lawyers were alcoholics and had a hard time holding relationships together. Her mood was gloomy. Her usual trial confidence hadn't kicked in yet. Normally at this stage of a trial, she was flying high and felt like she held the jury in the palm of her hand. Today, she realized the best she could hope for was to fake it.

These past three days, every chance he got Bryce waved the big knife in the jury's face. She knew it made an impression on them. The knife was crucial because it determined the difference between finding Jose committed aggravated sexual assault or sexual assault. Possible life sentence, or up to twenty years.

How would she establish Chris stole Jose's knife and cut himself in the park? Alex wished truth was the best defense, but with Jose's future on the line, the truth would be a big gamble. Jose's word wasn't enough. Alex knew that. Would the jury believe a child made a false allegation to help his uncle get revenge? Even if his defense sounded far-fetched, it still could create reasonable doubt in a juror's mind. Alex knew her only option was to do her best for Jose.

Alex mentally prepared herself to face TV cameras and the crowded courtroom. She entered the courthouse coffee shop, a sideshow for people watchers. Men and women of all ages and economic and cultural backgrounds graced the building daily. Sad mothers, frustrated fathers, angry wives, disappointed husbands—all were represented and no one was happy to be there. At least, Alex thought, across the street on the civil side, cases dealt with one basic commodity: money. People's liberty wasn't at stake.

She spotted Nick sitting with the Reverend, Ruth and Angelina. Alex filled a cup of coffee and headed to their table.

Nick stood and pulled out a chair. Then Ruth offered her a pastry from a plate on the table.

"No!" Alex patted her stomach and pointed at Nick. "My bodyguard doubles as cook. Bacon, eggs and toast were ready when the alarm went off at five."

"How's Jose?" Nick asked.

"Nervous. But that's to be expected."

Alex looked at Angelina. Ruth's influence these past few days was evident. Her star witness was no longer a timid, cowering woman. Her skin was clear; her eyes light; her shoulders straight. She wore one of Ruth's navy suits. Her hair was cut and styled; her trimmed nails were painted a neutral shade. If you looked close enough, you could see the dark circles under her eyes and the tenseness of her jaw. It was hard to believe that her husband died less than a week ago. She'd come a long way and Alex was grateful for her strength. Justice isn't meted out in equal portions. The girl was due a share. "You look wonderful."

"Thanks," Angelina said.

"So, Nick, how was the board meeting last night?" she asked.

"It was a somber group," Nick admitted. "Miss May discussed fund-raising, but we tabled it until Shepherd's Cottages reputation is restored."

Alex frowned. "What about the on-premise school to help the kids keep up during the transition phase?"

The Reverend sighed. "We have the school district's approval. But, for now, the project is on the backburner."

"We don't want to lose momentum," Alex urged. "Foster care is a big disruption. They need a home school before they're dumped back into the system."

"I agree," the Reverend said.

"Ruth called several computer stores and education supply companies for donations and they've shown strong interest."

"We won't let the project go down the tubes," the Reverend added.

"Don't worry about it now," Nick said in a comforting voice. "Once Jose's trial is over, we'll focus on the school. Right now, we're concerned about Thomas and Nikita. Thomas is still in Shriners Hospital. To my knowledge, no one from his family has visited and CPS refuses to give us information. We don't know where Nikita is placed. My news about finding the gas container did cheer the board members up though."

A smile brightened Alex's face. "When will you know who purchased it?"

"Today, I hope. The district manager was familiar with the case. She promised to try and expedite the process. I'm heading straight to her office. Keep your fingers crossed. Sorry I'll miss trial again today."

Alex smiled. "It's better we divide and conquer. Wouldn't it be great to nab Voodoo just before or after the jury acquits Jose?"

A flash of hope crossed Alex's face. It was the first time she had looked positive all week. He stood to leave, anxious to make her dream a reality.

Nick's eyes held hers a long moment. "I like the way you think, woman."

Alex ducked into the ladies' room to steel herself before the trial. She stared into the mirror, into her own eyes, trying to conjure her game face. Glad she'd chosen a black double-breasted suit and red mock turtleneck sweater, she straightened her earrings, powdered her nose, and blotted her lipstick. Somehow, looking self-assured gave her confidence. And in mere minutes, she'd need all the composure she could muster.

Alex wished Judge Villareal had granted her motion for instructed verdict at the conclusion of the State's evidence yesterday. It would have saved her from having to go forward with the next two days of trial. Although defense attorneys routinely asked the judge to dismiss the case before presenting evidence, courts rarely acquiesced. Judge Villareal obviously didn't buy her argument that the prosecution's case lacked sufficient evidence to support a conviction. It was small consolation if worse came to worse, an appellate court would agree.

The bathroom door opened. "Alex, the court just finished docket call," Ruth stated.

Alex took a deep breath. It was showtime.

★

Nick left the courthouse and headed straight to the district manager's office. On the short drive, just in case she hadn't made her decision, he rehearsed what he'd say to convince her to bend the rules. If possible, Nick wanted to implicate Voodoo in the fire before final arguments. He had a hunch it might make a difference.

The friendly receptionist looked surprised when he appeared and asked to see the boss. Motioning him to a seat, she picked up the phone and held a brief conversation. "I'm sorry," she said sincerely. "Miss Jenson is in meetings until noon. Come back later and she'll try to have an answer for you."

No use burning bridges when I need a favor.

"Thanks, I'll see you this afternoon."

Back in his truck, Nick called Johnny Wharton.

"It's time we let the fire chief in on this," he said. "Meet me at the MacGregor station at noon."

He wanted to convince the chief to amend his report and label the fire intentional, but didn't want to lose control of the investigation. Nick didn't mention his afternoon appointment with the district manager to Johnny. Let the fire department go through normal channels. If he could get the information quicker, he would.

With time to spare before meeting Johnny, Nick dropped in on his former partner, Fred. After years on the streets in a patrol car with Nick, he'd taken a desk job as station chief. The tall, balding man slapped Nick on the back. "Good to see you, buddy," he greeted. "It's just not the same without you."

"Fred, I need a favor." Nick showed him the new evidence and recounted events leading up its discovery. "Before they ask me to turn this over, I want to do my own print check. Just in case."

His friend smiled knowingly. Both men shared the same pet

peeve while working together on the force: Too many bad guys went free because of sloppy investigations and lazy coworkers.

Fred stood and grabbed his keys. "Let's see who handled this puppy."

The two men headed down to the basement crime lab. "We'll get forensics on it, then meet with the fire chief and no one will be the wiser."

A willing technician helped Fred painstakingly check the container for fingerprints. It didn't take long to get three sets. "These could be yours, store clerks, or culprits," Fred said. "We'll run local, state, and national services for matches. It'll take most of the day, but I'll call you the minute we get results."

"Thanks. I owe you," Nick said, heading for the door.

On the short drive to the fire station, Nick was jubilant. At last he was making progress. Fred could be right: The prints might be anyone's. Voodoo had evaded arrest all these years; the chances of his prints being in a database were slim to none. Surely he'd been clever enough to have someone else do his dirty work. But if it was one of his henchmen, it might get them closer to Voodoo than ever before.

When he pulled up to the fire station, Nick saw Johnny talking to a uniformed man. Just then, alarms sounded and firemen hustled preparing the trucks for action.

Nick left his truck to walk over to Johnny. "What's up?"

"Nick, this is Chief Dunstan."

Nick nodded. "I remember you."

"They just got a call on a three-alarm fire at an apartment complex. I told him what you found out there at Cottage Five," Johnny said.

"Go ahead and leave the container here," the distracted fire chief mumbled. "I'll look at it when I get back." He walked over barking orders to drivers and motioning them to be on their way.

Nick froze.

"Just leave it inside with Matt's secretary," Johnny said.

He must have sensed Nick's distrust because he added, "It'll be alright."

Nick's throat tightened. Something told him not to leave the gasoline container. The chief's first report was hasty and Nick knew chances of him overturning his previous finding were slim. Incriminating evidence could turn up missing, especially in the Fifth Ward. Nick wasn't going to leave the container and jeopardize his chance to implicate Voodoo in the fire. "I'm not leaving it, Johnny. I'll come back when the chief has time to talk."

CHAPTER 21

When the jury panel filed into the courtroom, Alex and Jose stood. She knew Jose was praying silently. The dread she felt moments ago in the ladies' lounge was dissolved by a gut-level determination to prove her client's innocence.

"Call your first witness," Judge Villareal addressed the defense.

"Angelina Martinez," Alex answered.

The bailiff opened the courtroom door and Angelina entered. Alex watched the jury's reaction to her. Walking, shoulders straight, with the composure of a runway model, Angelina entered the witness box.

"Mrs. Martinez, are you here today to be a character witness for the defendant, Jose Gonzales?"

"Yes."

"Tell me about your relationship with him." Alex knew telling the story would be difficult for Angelina. She counted on her to endure the tough questions.

Angelina looked first at Jose, whose face held an expression of gratitude and sadness, then the jury. "We've known each other since childhood. We were best friends and became boyfriend and girlfriend when we were older."

"Did you have consensual sex during your relationship?"

"Yes. He was falsely accused of raping me when I was sixteen years old."

"Did he plead guilty to that charge and receive a ten-year deferred adjudication probation?"

Angelina nodded. "I think so."

Alex noted several jurors' surprised looks. Mr. Smith's lips were pursed and his eyes held contempt.

"How old was he?"

"Nineteen."

"How old are you now?"

"I'm twenty, almost twenty-one."

"Why was he charged with statutory rape?"

With hands folded on her lap, Angelina swallowed hard and looked at the jury. "My father was an alcoholic. For years, he beat my mother and sexually abused me."

"Did your father know about your relationship with Jose?"

"Not at first."

Through a series of questions and answers, Angelina told the story of what happened the night Jose was arrested for statutory rape.

"My father said if I didn't say Jose raped me, he would do to my sister what he did to me."

Alex saw tears forming in Angelina's eyes. She got up and walked over to the clerk's desk, pulled a Kleenex out of the box and handed it to her only witness. "Do you need a break?"

Angelina shook her head. "I couldn't let that happen to her. I went along with my father," she said, gulping back sobs. "When the police got there, I told them Jose raped me."

Alex waited a moment; she wanted the jury to absorb the full impact of Angelina's story.

"Why did he plead guilty if he was innocent?"

"To protect me."

"After that night, did your father continue to physically abuse you?"

"Yes."

"Did he leave your sister alone?"

Angelina lowered her eyes. "No."

"Tell me about it," Alex said gently.

"One night when I was gone, he beat my sister to death and my mother shot him, then shot herself."

"Did they both die?"

"Yes, but my mother was eight months pregnant and they saved my brother."

Bryce jumped to his feet. "Objection. I hate to interrupt this sad story, Judge Villareal, but I have to question its relevancy."

The judge looked at Alex. "How far do you plan to go with this?"

"One more question, Your Honor." Alex turned back to Angelina. "Did Jose Gonzales ever physically or emotionally abuse you in any way?"

"No. He is a kind and gentle man."

"That's it, judge," Alex said. "No further questions."

Alex looked at the jury and sensed some jurors had been moved by Angelina's story. If Bryce was too combative on cross-examination later, the jury might become even more sympathetic.

Bryce introduced himself to Angelina, whose facial muscles tensed at his sugary sweet tone. Alex had warned her that he'd pour on charm before going for the kill.

After a few general questions, including Angelina's sketchy work history, Bryce popped the big one. "Mrs. Martinez, why should this jury believe what you say about the defendant when minutes ago you told us you lied to police about him three years ago?"

Angelina was prepared. She sat up straight and looked at the jury. "Because I'm telling the truth."

"Were you paid for your testimony today?"

Angelina looked surprised and her answer rang with sincerity. "No."

"Were you promised anything in return for your testimony?"

"Of course not," she answered.

Bryce didn't look convinced. "I'm surprised you can testify today. After all, you just buried your husband on Sunday, isn't that right?"

"Yes."

"Isn't it true that your husband died in Miss Stockton's office?"

Alex stood. "Objection! May we approach the bench?"

The judge nodded and Bryce and Alex went to stand before her.

"Your Honor," Alex began, "the relevancy of this testimony does not outweigh possible damage to my client. The sole purpose of this witness's testimony is to show that my client didn't rape her and is not a repeat sexual offender. Period."

"Then why did you waste our time with all the gory details of her family life?" Bryce sneered.

"It was limited to why she went along with her father's story."

"I agree," Judge Villareal said, her hand covering the microphone. "I won't allow further questions about her husband's death." Then she turned on the microphone. "Objection sustained. Jury, please disregard the last question by Mr. Armstrong."

"Thanks, judge," Alex whispered on her way back to counsel table.

"You may continue," Judge Villareal addressed Bryce.

"If your former lover is acquitted, I assume you plan to get back together with him?"

Angelina's big brown eyes widened. "I have no such plans."

"You just told Miss Stockton you loved him and wanted to

marry him. Seems to me that helping him get off this time would be the best thing in the world for you. You have a young baby, no work skills. You need a man to support you. Jose would be your easy way out."

Alex tensed. All of the advance coaching in the world couldn't take the place of human emotions and Bryce knew just what buttons to push.

Angelina's face reddened. "That's not true! I don't need a man. I have a job."

Bryce gave a sly smile. "And where would that be?"

A hard knot formed in the pit of Alex's stomach. If Angelina mentioned working at her law office, it could look bad. Despite the fact Judge Villareal told them to disregard Bryce's question, they still knew Angelina's husband died there and were probably already curious. The wrong answer would raise questions and Angelina might appear selfish and dishonest, and her valuable testimony on behalf of Jose would be lost.

Alex's first instinct was to jump up and object.

But on what basis?

In fairness, Judge Villareal would give Bryce wide latitude on cross-examination. An objection now would not benefit Jose. She held her breath and her tongue and decided to let Angelina answer.

"I babysit infants at the women's shelter," the surprisingly self-assured witness answered.

★

Nick had just finished wolfing down his Goode Company barbeque sandwich when his cell phone rang.

"We've got a match," Fred reported, excitement in his voice.

"I'm on my way." Nick grabbed his jacket and headed over to the station. Fifteen minutes later he walked into Fred's office.

"One out of three ain't bad," Fred said. "We got a Mr. William

Cates, last known address: Fifth Ward. His record goes back to junior high school: possession, delivery, assault, you name it. He's done time twice for short periods and his parole is up in three months. He falls under the habitual statute and if convicted, will do a minimum of twenty-five, no exceptions." Fred laid his mugshot down in front of Nick.

Nick was disappointed; it wasn't Voodoo. "It's not who I'm looking for, although Mr. Cates is probably an associate. If I get an arrest warrant on him now, other incriminating evidence may disappear."

"Your guy's prints may be here," Fred said in an encouraging tone. "They're just not on file. Remember, we only ID'd one set."

"I know and I'm bettin' one is mine and the other's is the man I'm looking to catch. At this point, it's my own personal mission."

"I'm off at five," Fred said with a mischievous grin. "Want to check it out and see if we can come up with some new evidence?"

Nick laughed. "Sure, like old times." He glanced at his watch. It was after two. "Meet me in the downtown bus station parking lot at five-fifteen."

Nick hopped in his truck and wished he could call Alex for a trial update. All the way to the district manager's office, Nick thought about how important the next twenty-four hours was to Jose and Shepherd's Cottages. Time was running out.

Nick parked in the truck zone and hurried up to the fortieth floor. The friendly receptionist saw him and buzzed her boss. "Miss Jenson will be just a minute," she said, motioning him to sit.

Nick was keyed up. It'd been years since he was this edgy. He didn't want to blow it, but his newfound patience, what the Reverend called "fruit of the spirit," wasn't kicking in. Too much was at stake.

Five minutes later, the office door opened and Miss Jenson ushered him into her office. "I don't usually do this," the pretty young woman told him, "but this is important and I want to help you catch whoever set that fire. I pulled some strings and found a way to get your information. Just haven't had time to look it up yet."

She pulled another chair up in front of her computer monitor and motioned Nick to sit. "He wasn't happy, but my boss gave me the code to electronically canvas store receipts to learn who purchased this gas can. If he used cash, we're out of luck. But a credit card may get you your man."

Nick sat patiently while she executed a complicated series of commands and screens. He watched her handle the computer like a pro and was impressed by her intense interest in helping him. While she waited for the computer's response, she questioned him about Shepherd's Cottages, Jose, and his lawyer. Once, when Nick spoke of Alex in glowing terms, she stopped tapping computer keys and gave him a strange look. "Sounds like you really like this girl."

Nick felt his ears burn.

"I saw her on TV Thanksgiving," she continued. "And this week during trial. She's not only smart, but pretty too."

Nick shrugged and the young woman giggled.

He smiled back, but kept his mouth shut. Miss Jenson was attractive, but she was no match for Alex. In that moment, Nick came to grips with his feelings toward Jose's lawyer. His old self would have asked Miss Jenson out in a heartbeat. Not being tempted must mean he was hooked.

"Bingo!" Miss Jenson broke into his thoughts. "Credit card. Does the name Joshua Hamilton ring a bell?"

Suddenly, Nick realized he didn't know Voodoo's real name. "No, but it might." Nick picked up the phone and dialed Miss May. "It's Nick," he said when she answered. "What's Voodoo's real name?"

When he heard the answer, a broad smile crossed his lips. "We got him!"

"Hold on a second, let me print this out," Miss Jenson said.

Nick's enthusiasm was contagious. On her way to the printer, she knocked several things off her credenza.

Seconds later, written evidence spewed out, confirming Joshua Hamilton, a.k.a Voodoo, purchased the gas container that ignited Cottage Five.

Nick grabbed the paper and headed out the door. "No time to lose. Thanks for your help."

Miss Jenson yelled from her office door as he headed down the hall: "We'll still have to go through the proper channels to get this evidence admissible in court!"

CHAPTER 22

During the break, Jose became increasingly nervous. When he began to wring sweaty palms, Alex stood. "Be back in a minute."

Alex found the Reverend alone on a bench outside the courtroom, bent over his leather-bound Bible. "Jose needs you," she told him softly, not wanting to be overheard by jurors.

The Reverend looked up. "I've been praying for him."

"How do you always know what people need?" Alex asked, leading him to the holdover room where Jose waited.

He smiled. "Many years of shepherding a flock. Sometimes I wonder, seeing as we're in this kind of trouble now."

"Don't you go gettin' down too. I need positive energy now!"

The Reverend patted her forearm. "I don't worry about you. You're strong and will find your way."

"Thanks." His confidence in her was a jolt of adrenaline.

Inside, the Reverend embraced Jose and held on.

Obviously embarrassed by his show of affection, Jose said, "I'm sorry."

"Nothing to apologize about, son," the Reverend said gently.

"You've been locked up and carrying a big load these past few weeks. Seeing Angelina yesterday must have brought back a lot of memories."

Jose nodded. "I tried to do the right thing by her. She's brave to help me like she did."

"I know and I think she helped you," the Reverend agreed.

"Will my past ever be behind me?" Jose was plaintive.

"It is now, as far as God's concerned."

"Yes. But will these people believe me?"

"I hope so. Let's pray about it," the Reverend said, turning to an entry in his Bible.

"Excuse me," Alex said. "I'll come back in ten minutes." Something told her Jose would feel better after talking to the Reverend.

★

Judge Villareal's voice resonated in the courtroom. "Call your next witness."

Alex stood. "Jose Gonzales."

As he walked to the witness box, Jose looked surprisingly sophisticated. Today he'd worn a blue shirt and matching tie. Blue was his good luck color.

As Jose took his seat and adjusted the microphone, she searched juror's faces to ascertain their mood. They seemed distant and Alex hoped that they hadn't already decided Jose's fate and turned off—a defense attorney's nightmare. It was her job to keep them connected.

"Please state your name for the Court," Alex began.

"Jose Gonzales."

"Mr. Gonzales, you've been charged in this case with two felony counts: aggravated sexual assault of a minor and sexual assault of a minor. Do you understand the charges against you?"

"Yes."

"And are you guilty of either offense?"

Jose's dark eyes were fixed on the jury. "No," he said boldly and sincerely.

In this type of case, it was important to jump right in, feet first. "Mr. Gonzales, are you a heterosexual man?"

"Yes."

"It's true you are on deferred adjudication for the statutory rape of your former girlfriend, Angelina Martinez?"

"Yes," he clarified.

"That means when you successfully live out your probation, you won't have a final conviction on your record?"

"That's right."

"Did you agree with Mrs. Martinez's testimony this morning?"

"Yes."

"If you weren't guilty of the offense, why did you take the plea bargain agreement?"

"They told me deferred adjudication was the only way I could keep my record clean and still not harm Angelina. If I fought, she would have to come to court. I was worried about what her father was doing to her."

"Was there an initial mix-up with your plea bargain?"

"Yes, I thought I'd agreed to deferred, but my lawyer messed up the paperwork and it was straight probation. When my probation officer pointed it out, I appealed my case."

"Was that during the time you were hired by Shepherd's Cottages?"

"Yes."

"Did you win your appeal?"

Jose nodded. "Yes, I got to redo the sentence."

"How did you meet Reverend Morse?"

"When I came to Houston, I moved into a boarding house near his church. The lady who runs it cooks a big supper there on Wednesday nights. I went and listened to him." Jose looked fondly at the Reverend, who sat in the first row behind Alex. "He ended up taking me under his wing."

Alex glanced at the jury and couldn't miss the unmistakable look of scorn on Mr. Smith's face. She couldn't imagine why he so overtly disliked her witnesses.

Could he be jealous of another preacher, or was he simply a racist?

"Did you begin working for him?"

"Yes. I started out helping him fix up the old crack houses he was making into a foster home. Then he asked me to be a house parent for Cottage Five."

"Were you qualified to be a house parent?"

"I think so."

Alex questioned him about foster home regulations and the forms he had to fill out for Shepherd's Cottages.

"Why didn't you tell the Reverend about your trouble with Mrs. Martinez?"

"Since it was on appeal, my lawyer said it wasn't a final conviction."

"You knew there would be a background check?"

"Yes, but it came back clear."

"When did you tell Shepherd's Cottages about your legal status?"

"Right when I knew they were going to hire me. The board met again and approved me."

Alex was relieved Jose remained calm while he told his story. She glanced at the jury, which appeared to be paying close attention.

When Alex asked him about his duties at Cottage Five, Jose told the jury he had responsibility for the home's older boys, giving them a clear sense of how Shepherd's Cottages was run: All decisions were made through the Reverend.

"Was there trouble with the boys in Cottage Five?"

Bryce stood. "Objection. Outside the scope."

"Overruled. He can answer generally."

Bryce frowned and took his seat.

Jose looked at the judge, who nodded for him to continue. "Most foster kids in our neighborhood come from troubled backgrounds. We try to give them love and help them. They have to mind, do their homework and chores each day."

"Did the boys in Cottage Five follow the rules?"

"No."

Alex knew better than to get into specifics about the boys in Cottage Five. The judge had already given her some latitude.

"What kind of neighborhood is the home in?"

"The Fifth Ward is a bad part of town. People are poor and there's lots of crime, especially in Crosstown Park across the street."

"Do you have security?"

"Shepherd's Cottages has a big fence and lots of lights. Crosstown Park is off-limits to the kids."

"What happens if they go over there?"

"They lose privileges."

"What privileges?"

"Depends on their age. Younger ones lose TV; older ones lose the telephone or computer."

Alex glanced at Bryce. She could tell by the look on his face he wanted to object, but he knew she had a right to talk about the park.

"Are there drugs in the park?"

"Yes," Jose said with an emphatic nod. "Drugs are bought and sold. Junkies sleep by trees or on benches."

"What about the police?"

Jose shrugged. "We call and try to get them to clean it up, but it never changes."

Alex carefully questioned Jose about the night of October 31. He told the jury about how Chris came home from school late, refused to do his homework, got mad and ran out of the house.

"What did you do when he ran?"

"I followed him into the park."

"What happened there?"

Like Alex had instructed him, Jose looked directly at the jury while he told his side of the story. "I ran up behind him and grabbed the collar of his jacket. He turned and yelled at me. We struggled and I saw a knife in his hand. Before I knew it, he nicked his neck. Then he ran off laughing, calling me names."

"What did you do then?"

"For a second, I was in shock. Then I got scared and ran back home. A few minutes later, the police showed up with Chris. He pointed at me from the car. The social worker drove up and Chris got in her car. The policeman handcuffed me and took me downtown."

"Did he question you at the scene?"

"No."

"Did he ask to search your bedroom?"

"No."

"Did he talk to Miss May?"

"No."

Alex shook her head as in disbelief, then looked at her notes a second before she continued.

"Did Chris cut you with your own knife?"

"Yes."

"Where did you keep it?"

"In the drawer of my nightstand."

"Is the knife you've seen the prosecutor waving around during trial yours?"

"No."

Alex took the knife off the prosecution's table and showed it to Jose. "Does it even look like yours?"

Jose shook his head. "Mine is much smaller."

"Do you think if Chris Jackson had cut himself with this knife here, he would have the small scar he showed the jury?"

Before Jose could answer Bryce was out of his seat.

"Objection! Calls for speculation."

"Your witness talked about the knife," Alex shot back. "My client should be afforded the same opportunity."

"Overruled. The witness can answer."

Alex took a deep breath. One small ruling; one giant step for Jose. "Go ahead and answer," she told her witness.

"He would have a much bigger scar. I don't think he wanted to hurt himself. I think he just wanted to get me in trouble."

"How long were you in the park with Chris?"

"A couple of minutes."

"You heard him testify that you made him perform oral sex on you?"

"That isn't true."

"Did you suspect Chris was on drugs?"

Bryce jumped to his feet. "Objection. Outside the scope of pretrial order."

"Sustained."

Alex had at least planted the inference. She tried a different tack. "Did Chris exhibit strange behavior that day?"

"His eyes were glassy and he was angrier than usual."

"Angrier than usual?"

"He didn't want to live with us. He wanted to live with his Uncle Voodoo."

"Voodoo? What is Chris's uncle's real name?"

"I don't know, but he's over there." Jose pointed to Voodoo.

"Let the record reflect that Mr. Gonzales pointed to the man in the black leather jacket seated on the aisle in the back row," Alex said.

Bryce stood. "Your Honor, relevancy? Mr. Gonzales is on trial, not the victim's uncle."

"Judge, my defense theory is that Chris Jackson wanted to live with his uncle so bad he would do anything, including falsely accusing my client of sexual assault."

Judge Villareal frowned. "Objection sustained. Move along,

counselor."

Alex's cheeks burned. She wanted to crawl into a hole. She knew Chris had lied. She wanted to show the jury the truth, but Judge Villareal cut off her only source to prove Chris's motives. If she called the Reverend to the stand, the same objection would be lodged and granted. Jose's side of the story was forever hidden from the jury. She did the only thing she could do and preserved her objection for appeal.

"One last question, Mr. Gonzales. Do you believe this charge against you is false and part of a conspiracy to force Shepherd's Cottages to close?"

"Yes."

Alex wished the jury could hear what she knew, but had no choice. Returning to counsel table, she looked at Bryce and said, "Your witness."

Alex watched Bryce casually approach Jose and begin cross-examination. She seethed at his cocky trial strategy, bracing for an aggressive assault on her client. It was clear he had the jury wrapped about his finger. Their faces showed intrigue at the way he held his head and listened to an answer. She thought back to a time in the recent past when he was her lover. It was great to be with someone so skilled, but now, on the other side of counsel table, it was murder.

"Mr. Gonzales, you figured the best way to prove you aren't a sexual pervert is to find your last victim and convince her to tell us a different story today, isn't that right?"

"No, I mean yes." Confused, Jose stared at Alex. "I mean no."

"No, what? You didn't get your lawyer to find Mrs. Martinez so she could come tell this jury a different story than she told three years ago?"

"No. This time she told the truth."

"So, Mrs. Martinez is a liar?"

"Objection, Your Honor," Alex called. "Mr. Armstrong is

badgering the witness."

"Sustained. Counsel, let the man answer the question."

Wiping a bead of sweat from his upper lip, Jose gave a thoughtful look toward the judge. Then he turned back to face the jury. "Sometimes people do wrong things because they have to. Mrs. Martinez said she wasn't truthful the first time because of her sister. She didn't change her story to help me now."

"Mr. Gonzales, you testified boys in Cottage Five were bad. Isn't it true that on October 31, you'd had enough of Chris Jackson? You wanted to show him you were boss, even if it meant sexually assaulting him?"

"No."

"Do you expect this jury to believe that a teenage foster child stole your knife, made you follow him into the park, cut himself in the neck, then ran off and made a false allegation of sexual abuse?"

"Yes, that's what happened."

"Thank goodness these jurors have more sense than that," Bryce muttered.

Alex jumped up, but before she could object to his sidebar remark he said, "No further questions." Then, sitting down with a confident smile, he templed his hands on counsel table.

Judge Villareal banged her gavel. "Any more witnesses, Miss Stockton?"

Alex made a quick calculation. She thought about evidentiary rules protecting minors, the court's rulings about speculative testimony regarding Chris's motives, and the Reverend's troubles with CPS—and then made her decision. There was too much at stake. Letting Bryce make mincemeat out of the Reverend was out of the question. She would not call him as a witness. She would say the hardest words for a defense lawyer to say: "No, Your Honor, the defense rests.

Judge Villareal looked at the clock. It was nearly five. "Court will recess until tomorrow morning at ten.

CHAPTER 23

It was dusk when Nick arrived to meet Fred at the downtown bus station. Christmas lights illuminated the landscape. During the short drive to Voodoo's, Nick filled Fred in on their plan.

"What if he's home?" Fred asked.

"He's been at trial all day," Nick answered. "They may be adjourned by now, but we'll cross that bridge when we come to it."

Nick drove into the quiet, old subdivision and they rode in silence the few blocks to Voodoo's house.

"First, I'll drive by," Nick said. "Then we may want to come up from the alley on foot."

Voodoo's house was dark.

"Forget about the front door," Fred stated. "It will be impossible to distinguish his. Besides, what if he drives up?"

Nick knew evidence obtained without a search warrant is inadmissible in court. What was he thinking? He was acting like a vigilante. Didn't good guys in white hats follow rules? The problem is he didn't know who Voodoo had in his pocket down at the precinct. Nick set his jaw and thought about little Thomas at Shriner's Hospital enduring traumatic burn treatment. Inadmissible, or not, Nick wanted Voodoo's prints. "We'll park on the next block and walk up the back alley. I'll find a way to dust his back door."

Fred read his mind. "If your set matches, we'll find a way to get a legitimate one."

Nick stopped near a house where several cars were parked in front. They left the car and walked up the dark alley. Voodoo's house stood out from the others. Barbed wire topped a tall, wooden fence, delineating his property.

No longer a cop, Nick didn't want to get his former partner in trouble. But Fred's excitement was evidenced by his loud heartbeat and labored breath. Nick smiled in the darkness. Fred's desk job probably bored him to tears.

When they reached the gate, Nick wrapped a handkerchief around his hand and tried the handle. To his amazement, it was unlocked. He and Fred exchanged excited glances. "Give me the duster. You stay here," Nick said.

Fred handed him the fingerprint kit.

Slowly Nick pushed the gate open, halfway expecting the sound of an alarm. He went through the gate and looked for security cameras. Nick remembered television screens in Voodoo's office. He found only one and it was dismantled. He gauged the distance from the gate to the back sliding glass door. There was plenty of cover in between: trees, shrubs, a marble fountain and a birdbath. The house was dark inside. It looked like no one was home. He went straight to the back door. Then, adjusting his eyes to the darkness, he pulled out the duster and began fingerprinting the door handle.

Just then the porch light came on and Nick found himself staring into Voodoo's dark, angry eyes.

Caught in Voodoo's malevolent gaze, Nick's heart raced. Quickly, he slipped the print kit into his pocket. He had only a moment to stay, or flee. Voodoo knew him. If he ran, Voodoo would be within his rights to shoot him. Fatally wounding an intruder was justifiable homicide. Nick wasn't ready to die. He waited. What excuse would he have? Should he tell him the truth, confront him, beg? His options were many, but time had just run out.

An amazingly calm Voodoo opened the sliding glass door. "Something wrong with coming to the front? Want to tell me what you're doing here?"

Nick debated a moment. His gun was in his bootleg and wouldn't be hard to reach. Fred was close. "We need to talk," Nick said, then stepped inside.

Voodoo didn't stop him. He motioned Nick to a comfortable chair opposite his leather couch. He plopped down and put his feet on the coffee table.

"Why are you here?" His voice held a lurking hostility.

"The Cottage Five fire. I have serious questions about your involvement. Last time I was here, you warned me and I didn't take your threat seriously. Now an innocent little burned boy is fighting for his life at Shriners."

"Now why would I want to hurt a little boy?"

"I doubt you knew he was in the house. From what I've heard, the Reverend's been nothing but good to you. He defends you, believes in you, and for some ungodly reason, he loves you."

While Nick talked, he noticed Voodoo sinking lower into his couch. Had good memories of the man who taught him to fish, the man who was more like a father to him than his real father, surfaced? Nick hoped he was getting through, but he was also buying time.

Voodoo stood and motioned Nick to the front hall. "You're wasting your time. You can't pin anything on me. Don't come again without a search warrant." Just before he shut the door, he said, "Too bad that lady lawyer is going to lose the case. I'll bet she's a tiger in bed."

Rage rose in Nick. He recalled Alex's attack—her bruises and her trauma. Convinced that Voodoo was behind it, he fought the urge to flatten him with a hard punch to the gut. But he refused to let Voodoo see his fury. Nick walked outside and hoped he had a fingerprint in his pocket that matched the one on the gas container.

★

A few houses down the block in the cool night air, Nick breathed a sigh of relief. Once again, being with Voodoo had been surreal. A battalion of angels must have been covering his rear end tonight. For a couple of minutes, he and Voodoo had talked man-to-man.

Is God working? Are the Reverend's prayers finally being answered? Will Voodoo admit he was wrong and put the past behind him?

Nick knew every man sins and has secrets buried deep within his heart. Nick knew that facing those demons, dealing with them once and for all, was a difficult process. For some reason, the Reverend was confident if Voodoo ever had to make a choice, he would make the right one.

Jail will be a good place for him to start.

He jogged around the corner to his truck and found Fred clutching his mobile phone.

Fred looked at his watch. "Exactly eight minutes. I was going to wait ten before I came after you."

Adrenaline racing, Nick climbed into the driver's seat and started the truck. "I'm lucky he didn't shoot me. The man is an enigma. He's pure evil one minute, then a perfect gentleman the next."

"Where I come from, they call that a sociopath," Fred said.

"I hope I got the print."

On the way to Fred's car, Nick spoke of his feelings about

Alex. "The first day I met her at the Reverend's board meeting, I knew she was special. It takes a lot of guts to take on a case like Jose's. At first, I didn't think she would be interested in a man like me. We are so different. But now that we have spent time together, I think there might be something there and I want to pursue it. Am taking it slow though. I don't want to mess it up."

"Sounds like you're on the right track," Fred said. "Good luck with the girl."

Nick handed Fred the fingerprint kit as he dropped him off.

"I'll run it first thing in the morning," Fred said as he exited the truck.

★

All the way home from the courthouse, her words and "The defense rests" rang in Alex's ears. Except for one final plea, her final argument, it was over. Then it was in the jury's hands.

She opened her sunroof and cool December air refreshed her. With Christmas a week away, the temperature was back in the lower fifties. It was unlikely they'd have a white Christmas. Alex told herself it didn't matter. Her decorations were still packed. She hadn't made her Christmas list yet, much less a purchase. Her usual Christmas spirit was absent. This year, she didn't feel a thing.

Alex dialed her astrologer friend, Derek, on her cell phone. "I just finished trial, closing is in the morning, and I need some company," she told him.

"Sorry, hon. Candy and I are on our way to the Christmas party at the mansion. You coming?"

Suddenly, Alex remembered the annual bash, one of many. The functions, sometimes two and three a night, were good for business and seeing old friends. Because of her campaign for judge, socializing was particularly important this year. She knew her opponents were hitting the party circuit hard. "No. Final argument is in the morning. Give my regards to everyone."

Derek must have sensed her despair. "We'll stop by for a minute on our way. Shall I bring my laptop?"

"You're a mind reader. We'll have a quick glass of wine and see what the stars say about this mess."

"Be there in half an hour."

Alex pulled into her neighborhood liquor store. "Long time, no see," the friendly Vietnamese clerk greeted her.

Moments later she set two expensive bottles of wine on the counter.

When she got home, Siva greeted her warmly as she entered her back patio. The little doves were quiet in their nest and Alex felt safe.

Inside, she opened a bottle of white wine, poured a crystal goblet and quickly prepared a tray of cheese and crackers. After turning on music, she hurried upstairs to change. Transforming from her power suit, she donned a black sweatshirt and tights. Then she rubbed the day off her face with a splash of cold water. She took a sip of wine and caught her reflection in the mirror. No bra, no underwear, no makeup.

Just let it all hang out tonight, girl. You deserve it.

The doorbell rang and when she saw Candy, dressed to the nines, Alex felt a touch of envy. Her best friend's skimpy red satin cocktail dress and signature black feather boa were outrageous, but she carried them off. Derek headed right to the living room couch.

"Girl, you look like a whipped pup!" Candy exclaimed. "What's wrong?"

Alex didn't take offense at her honesty. "Nothing that a good man won't cure," she joked.

While Derek booted his laptop, Candy noted folded blankets and pillow on the couch by the fireplace. "He sleeps there?" she asked with a raised eyebrow.

Alex nodded.

Derek looked up from his computer. "Are you sure he's not gay?"

Alex threw back her head and laughed. "I'm sure. He's gone for the God thing and he's pure as driven snow."

"A born-again virgin?" Candy asked. "Guys like that don't exist. He hasn't hit on you, or vice versa?"

She shook her head. Candy made her realize that she'd been so focused on the trial she hadn't had time to really give it thought. She wondered what Nick would do if confronted by her sexuality.

Candy read her thoughts. "Get it over with. You'll feel better."

"Coming from the expert on successful short-term relationships, that's probably good advice," Alex joked.

Candy smiled. "I need a cigarette," she said and headed for Alex's patio.

Once on the patio, Candy immediately noticed the doves. "That's strange. They're still here."

Alex nodded. "They showed up right when you were here last, right after I met the Reverend. Don't know why they are here, or how long they will stay. Momma's tough, yet totally protective."

Candy took a deep drag. "Like we'll be when we have kids."

Her statement hung in the smoky night air.

Moments later, Derek called them inside. "Hey, Alex. Remember what I said about the planets? Major stuff is going on."

"Sounds profound," Alex said with a hint of skepticism.

"I see great sex ahead for you, my friend."

Alex told herself that holiday spirits might have enhanced his ability to read the stars. "That would be good," she said with a grin.

"Things always work out for you, girl." Derek snapped the laptop shut and looked at his watch. "Let's go. If we leave now, we'll be fashionably late. I just love it when two queens make a grand entrance."

Alex kissed them goodbye.

"Call me tomorrow and tell me how he is in bed," Candy teased as they left.

Alex started a fire and thought about Nick. Was Candy right? Was it time to move forward? She remembered how often she wanted to kiss him, but didn't.

Nick was a gentleman. He took good care of her. She decided to return the favor. What man could resist a home-cooked meal? Quickly, Alex defrosted hamburger meat, heated spaghetti sauce, and boiled pasta. It wasn't a gourmet meal, but Nick would appreciate it.

A glass of wine later, Alex was feeling no pain. The wine had successfully turned her thoughts from trial to enticement. Deciding to freshen up, she took a quick shower, leaving her hair wet and slicked back. She applied face moisturizer, shimmery, scented body lotion and a hint of blush. For a short time, the cares of the world vanished.

She called Nick. "Dinner is on the table. Where are you?"

"Fifteen minutes away. Keep it hot."

"No problem."

CHAPTER 24

Siva's bark signaled Nick's arrival.

Alex opened the door and Nick's face betrayed surprise. "Smells good," he mumbled.

Alex smiled. She knew she'd thrown him off course. He'd never seen her like this. "Spaghetti and salad OK?"

"Sure." Nick rubbed his hands. "Can I help?"

Alex handed him a glass of wine and pointed to the cheese tray on the coffee table. "Help yourself while I finish."

After setting the table with expensive placemats and napkins, she decided to bring out her grandmother's silver. "Ready," she announced.

"Royal treatment," Nick said, staring at the table and the bowl of steaming pasta.

"You deserve it." Alex poured more wine.

Nick's eyes narrowed. "You tryin' to get me drunk?"

Alex tilted her head innocently and answered, "Why would I want to do that?"

Without another word, Nick served her first, then filled his plate. He took a bite, then gave her a thumbs-up.

"Thank, Mamma Rizzo," Alex giggled, taking in the handsome man across the table. His dark-blue sweater, open at the neck, revealed a patch of light hair on his chest. As usual, he wore jeans and boots—a consummate blend of gentleman and cowboy. His azure eyes had the same hypnotic affect tonight as when they met at Shepherd's Cottages' board meeting. She remembered the electric charge between them when he grabbed her arm at the door and the urgency in his voice when he offered to help. She'd been stubborn and refused, but fate brought them together.

"How was trial?" he asked.

Without going into too many details, Alex quickly updated him. "We did our best. I decided not to call the Reverend to the stand. Bryce would eat him alive."

"I trust your judgment."

"Your turn. How was your day?"

"I learned Voodoo's real name is Joshua Hamilton. I'm going for an arrest warrant tomorrow."

Nick put down his fork and placed his napkin on the table. "I was careless today, but I don't regret it." He ran a hand through his hair. "I went to Voodoo's to get his prints and he caught me, red-handed."

Eyes wide as saucers, Alex set her wine glass down. "No!"

Nick gave her a sheepish grin. "Yes."

"You could have been shot!" Alex jumped up, rushed around the table, and put her arms around him.

When he pushed his chair back, she climbed onto his lap. In his arms for the first time, in private, she marveled that it felt so right.

Their bodies melded together, and resting her head on his shoulder, she inhaled the faint scent of his aftershave. Tingly rushes flowed through her veins. For a long moment, she reveled in his embrace.

Then she smelled something burning.

"The pie!" Alex jumped up, ran to the stove, and rescued

dessert.

"Smells like apple."

Nick sounded strangely breathless.

"It's OK. Compliments of Mrs. Smith. Vanilla ice cream on top?"

"Sure."

Moments later, Alex set a tray on the coffee table and sank into the couch beside the fireplace. Nick followed.

They ate in silence before the warm fire.

Later, when dishes were in the sink, they sat staring into dying embers, then Nick placed a new log on the fire.

Alex waited. He wasn't making a move so she decided to take things into her own hands. "I'll be right back," she said before slipping upstairs.

She re-entered the living room a few minutes later. With every step, her long, lean legs appeared from beneath a loosely belted white robe. Satin fabric slipped from one shoulder, exposing a smooth expanse of skin when she sat beside him. For a long moment, she looked into his eyes. "I want you," she whispered.

Nick was overwhelmed by her beauty. He'd never wanted a woman so much. She was sensuous, with an intriguing girlish quality about her. As longing rose, his emotions went into overdrive. He pulled her close and planted a soft kiss on her willing lips. As passion intensified, he gently caressed her curves. With a sultry moan, Alex broke the embrace and leaned back on the couch.

Nick looked deep in her eyes where passion flamed. The picture of her face was forever imprinted in his memory. He wanted her more than he could say. Was it love? He wasn't sure, but knew he wanted more than a wild night. Nick recalled the Reverend's sage advice on relationships. He'd vowed not to make the same mistakes again. Alex was vulnerable tonight; the stress of trial was staggering. Her feelings may be different tomorrow.

He wanted to make love to her the first time in the right way and in the right time. If he didn't quit now, his desire would intensify to the point of no return.

"Alex," he whispered. "We've got to stop."

Stunned by Nick's words, Alex jumped off the couch, muttered an apology, and scampered upstairs. Before she thought about it, the bedroom door slammed behind her, echoing the sting of rejection. Head spinning, she set the alarm for five and crawled into bed. Embarrassed, she covered her head with a pillow and burrowed deep into the covers.

Her history with men hadn't prepared her for tonight. In romantic situations, she'd always been in control. Declining male advances with finesse was an art she'd cultivated to perfection. Tonight, she'd miscalculated Nick's feelings for her and taken a chance. She simmered for a few minutes, trying to convince herself that Nick's actions weren't a putdown. She wondered whether her true feelings for Nick had been exposed tonight, or if she'd just been avoiding working on her final argument. She groaned at the thought of facing Nick in the morning. How would she act? She couldn't just ignore him, but giving him the cold shoulder was an option.

Had he stopped for the right reasons?

Fairytale heroes did that, but this was reality. Alex couldn't deny his kindness toward her. He was different from other men. Not intimidated, he seemed to sincerely value her abilities and brains as much as her looks. Nick stood up for what he believed tonight and as hard as it was to admit, Alex respected him for it. Alex tossed and turned until she was too tired to think, falling asleep without even looking at her trial notes. She had worked on her final argument since the first day she began work on the trial. Tomorrow was now or never.

★

Long after the CD player stopped and the fire quit crackling, the sound of Alex's slamming door rang in Nick's ears. He had upset her, but didn't regret his decision. Wine and passion had had the high hand tonight. It had been no time to communicate his feelings; he knew she wouldn't listen. He took a deep breath. The trial would be over tomorrow. There would be time to spend to get to know each other better.

Since they met at Shepherd's Cottages board meeting, most conversation was about Jose's case. Lying in darkness, he hoped that, after she cooled down, he would have a chance to explain his feelings. Maybe when she understood his reasoning, she would agree with his decision. He thought about the morning. His best bet was to choose the path of least resistance and stay out of her way. Siva's deep snore sounded beside him and Nick decided to mimic the dog and fall asleep.

Alex rose before the alarm sounded and downed a couple of Alka-Seltzers. Hoping Nick was still asleep, she quickly showered and dressed in her conservative navy trial suit with her pearl earrings. Today was final arguments and it was her last chance to persuade the jury. She headed out the door just after Nick entered the guest bath.

The law library wouldn't open for two hours so Alex stopped at One's A Meal, her favorite breakfast café.

"You're up early," a familiar waitress noted.

"Final arguments are today," Alex answered, then ordered coffee, scrambled eggs and a bagel.

"I saw you on TV this week. Isn't that your old boyfriend on the other side?"

Alex nodded. Just a few weeks ago, her handsome opposing counsel was her lover. She remembered late night snacks and early morning post-run breakfasts here with Bryce. They never hid their ambition, or their priorities.

Something profound happened that day in New York when she saw the white bird through the plane window. She'd sensed it was an omen and knew, for some strange reason, that her life would never be the same from that moment forward. Then she met the Reverend and within minutes, had impulsively agreed to represent Jose *pro bono*. If not for that crucial life decision, she realized that her Christmas tree would now be up, her judicial appointment secure, and her social life satisfying. Alex felt a tug at her heart. Was anything ever that secure, that satisfying, or that much fun?

By seven she was holed up in a small room at the county law library, rehearsing her final argument.

A mentor had taught her an adage she never forgot: The best impromptu speech is one planned well in advance. Alex had three major arguments for the jury, each an independent example of reasonable doubt. Although the jury was obligated to follow the letter of the law, she doubted it would.

When it comes to this jury, will they allow personalities and perceptions to trump legal doctrine?

Alex straightened, took a couple of deep breaths, then glanced at her watch.

Game on!

Nick's morning began at the police station.

"Coffee?" Fred asked when Nick came through the door.

Nick nodded. "Did you get a match?"

"Voodoo's prints aren't there. I'm sorry."

Nick's heart sank. Even though he had proof that Voodoo bought the gas can, he still needed to prove he was at Cottage Five the day of the fire. Disappointed and discouraged, he debated what to do next. The only way to positively place Voodoo there on Thanksgiving was to find his prints on the gasoline can or locate an eyewitness. It was a long shot, but he wondered if little Thomas saw Voodoo? Nick sighed. Even if he could identify Voodoo, he knew the child's testimony wouldn't be credible in a court. He'd run enough rabbit trails. He needed an arrest warrant today. His only option was the fire chief.

He called Johnny Wharton and arranged to meet him and the fire chief at the fire station. Once inside the small, windowless office, Johnny spoke in earnest. "Chief, your first impression about the gas stove coupling was a good one, but when we entered the cottage for the first time a couple of days ago, the natural gas smell was gone and we smelled gasoline. In my opinion the fire wasn't accidental. It was incendiary."

Nick recounted how he found the gas can with the prints of Voodoo's associate, Cates. He gave Cates's mugshot and police record to the chief, then he showed him the paper from the district manager's office. "That's my best evidence. Voodoo's real name is Joshua Hamilton. His prints aren't on the gas container, but he purchased it." Nick paused. "Think we can get an arrest warrant? Today?"

The fire chief looked over the papers, then smiled. "You've done a good job. I'll amend my report. With this evidence, we'll get a warrant immediately."

CHAPTER 25

Bryce entered the busy courtroom in an Armani suit, white dress shirt and red silk tie, and Alex remembered his trial strategy. For the main case, he had dressed in J.C. Penney suits, and lulled the jury into thinking he was one of them. But on final arguments, he went all-out to impress them with his skill and sophistication. Bryce had boasted the strategy contributed to many a guilty verdict. He claimed jurors realized how much the trial means to him when he spends more than he earns in a week on a nice suit. They didn't know that he was a scion of old money and his family's future was secure for generations to come.

Alex knew the "I'm just a poor country lawyer" routine never worked for a woman. Confident about her looks, she didn't have to think about what to wear on this most important day. Trial skirts were always knee length; short skirts didn't play well in the courtroom. Her jewelry was classic and her hair was pulled up and clasped with a handsome barrette.

When the bailiff announced Judge Villareal, the courtroom grew quiet as everyone watched her climb into the podium and seat herself at the bench. The atmosphere was tense. She donned her reading glasses and looked out over the courtroom, first at the jury, then at counsel. "Counsel, are we ready for final arguments?"

Alex gave Jose a nod and a smile.

He sat straight in his chair and his face held a look of concern. It was clear to anyone who looked that he knew his life was on the line and now was no laughing matter.

Alex pushed her chair back and stood. "We are ready, Your Honor."

"The State is ready, judge," Bryce stated.

"Then proceed," the judge said, motioning to Bryce.

Bryce took a last look at his notes, then stood and approached the jurors. With an engaging and informal style, Bryce warmed up to them before talking about the case. "I didn't get much sleep last night because of this pesky raccoon that has been plaguing my neighborhood for months." He made the jury chuckle with the punch line to the fatal tangle.

Alex groaned inwardly and wondered how many times that same raccoon had died the night before a trial.

He had broken the ice. With the jury in the palm of his hand, Bryce looked down for a moment, then got serious.

"Enough about me," he said. "Let's talk about this case. It has been a tough one to try, because it involves a child's life and his relationship with a house parent hired by a foster home charged with caring for problem children sent by the State. We have all heard the statistics in the news on the alarming increase in child abuse. Children's Protective Services is the one government agency solely committed to protecting children. When the State takes abused, abandoned, or neglected children into care, we expect them to receive maximum security and insulation from what they've already been subjected to in their homes. Sexual abuse is only one reason children come into the system. Foster children have experienced emotional and physical abuse, and neglectful supervision. We hold the State to a high degree of care and that's why the laws governing foster care are so strict. The foster home, Shepherd's Cottages, is not on trial today. But, you've heard how they willfully hired a man with a prior sexual offense and chose to ignore regulations that prevented them from hiring the defendant ... and never reported it to CPS."

He paused a moment and gave them a look of disbelief.

"Here we are a year later and I was forced to put Chris Jackson, an adolescent child, on the stand to tell his story. I didn't like to do it because I know Chris Jackson will never forget what happened to him on October 31 of this year in the park across the street from the foster home. But it was necessary because, despite CPS's best efforts to screen foster parents and foster homes, a child molester slipped through the cracks; the radar didn't pick it up and the home responsible for doing so made a unilateral decision to bend the rules. Jose Gonzales is a predator and no one caught it until it was too late."

While Bryce talked, Alex watched the jury closely. They were attentive, engaged, and their body language expressed agreement with many of Bryce's points. She winced inwardly, knowing she was the underdog. She forced herself to hold her head high. Alex realized she'd kept her commitment to help Jose and she had done the best she could do. In a few minutes it would be completely out of her hands.

Bryce looked down a moment before concluding. He insisted that, despite his age and foster child status, Chris Jackson's testimony was credible. He assured the jury that the State met its burden of proof as to every element of the crime beyond a reasonable doubt. He reminded them Jose Gonzales's conviction could be based solely on circumstantial evidence.

"This case boils down to a swearing match. Your duty is to determine the credibility of the testimony you've heard. How credible is a man on deferred adjudication probation for a sexual crime? How credible is his former victim, an obviously mixed up woman, who shows up and tells you a different story now within a week of her husband's death?"

Bryce shook his head. "Something doesn't add up. There are two counts of the indictment. If you find that Jose Gonzales threatened Chris Jackson with a knife and forced him to perform oral sex, then you must convict him of aggravated sexual abuse of a child. Chris Jackson told you Jose Gonzales cut him with a knife. The defense tried to make a big deal about the fact that we don't have the knife in court today, but the law says we don't have to. We know he was cut. When you get back there in the jury room, think about what the defendant might have done with the knife that day. There's no doubt in my mind that the defendant is guilty of aggravated sexual abuse of Chris Jackson. Thank you."

Alex took a deep breath. Bryce was a tough act to follow. She stood and addressed the jury.

"Ladies and gentlemen, Jose Gonzales and I appreciate your patience during this trial. On October 31st, my client's life changed dramatically. One minute he was acting in the course and scope of his duties as a foster parent at Shepherd's Cottages. The next minute, no questions asked, he found himself on the way to jail in the back of a patrol car. From the time he was charged with this offense until now, my client has vigorously maintained his innocence. You are the trier of fact. You determine the credibility of the testimony you've heard during trial. I know you take your job seriously and I'm confident you appreciate how important your decision is to the remainder of Jose Gonzales's life."

Alex paused a moment and looked directly at them. "Mr. Armstrong told you the State has proven each and every element of this crime beyond a reasonable doubt, but that's simply not true. Reviewing the testimony, I can point to at least three glaring examples of reasonable doubt in this case."

"First, the investigating officer admitted his investigation was flawed. He simply didn't follow routine police procedures, and, for that matter, neither did CPS. Other than reading him his rights before shoving him into the patrol car, the arresting officer didn't formally interview my client at anytime; he didn't attempt to locate any eyewitnesses, nor did he do a diligent search for the alleged weapon. If investigating sexual offenses against minors is a priority, as Mr. Armstrong stated, then why dispense with standard procedures? *That is* what doesn't add up in this case."

Alex shook her head and paused a moment, searching the jurors faces for clues.

"Second, rather than follow standard investigatory procedures and look for the alleged weapon, either in the park or in my client's bedroom at the cottage, the State chose to come here and wave a big scary knife at you all week. This evidence, or lack thereof, casts substantial reasonable doubt about the aggravated sexual abuse charge. I keep asking myself, 'Why did they not look for the knife?' "

Alex looked at the jurors, none of whom were able to maintain eye contact. One woman on the second row rubbed her eye while Alex talked; the elderly man beside her looked as if he were falling asleep; and every time she met Mr. Smith's contempt-filled eyes, Alex shuddered. What little confidence she had faded in his gaze.

Nonetheless, she continued, "And third, Dr. Ethan's published paper on the inherent lack of credibility of adolescent testimony in sexual abuse cases casts reasonable doubt on the case. Their own psychologist proved Chris Jackson's testimony is flawed."

Alex walked over to the jury and placed her hands on the rail in front of them. She shook her head and said, "There is more than enough reasonable doubt here. The State simply can't prove Jose Gonzales sexually abused Chris Jackson in the park that day. The investigation was botched; the victim's testimony lacks credibility; there were no eyewitnesses; they did not find the weapon ..."

Her voice trailed off for a moment, then she shrugged her

shoulders and raised her arms, holding her hands toward the jury. "I admit, you're probably asking yourself, 'Yes, but why would an innocent child make something like this up?' It is hard to fathom, especially when you consider the consequences of a conviction on my client's life. I regret that because of strict rules protecting minors, you didn't get to know the real Chris Jackson." Alex paused again.

She looked at the judge, who eyed her closely and knew she skated on thin ice. Alex chose her words carefully. She couldn't give Bryce grounds to object and interrupt her rhythm. "Jose Gonzales told you as much about Chris Jackson as the law would allow, even though the Fifth Amendment says he doesn't have to say anything at all. The State has failed to meet its burden of proof. I hope you agree and vote to acquit my client. Thank you."

Alex sat, looked at Jose, nodded to Judge Villareal and to Bryce and Marilyn at opposing counsel's table.

Judge Villareal reminded the jury of their duties before reading the charge. "You must answer these questions before rendering a verdict. I trust you will take your job seriously and follow the law as set out herein. Bailiff, please show them to the jury room."

As the panel filed out, Alex took a deep breath and squeezed Jose's hand. He gave her a relieved look. When the jury left, the bailiff escorted him from the courtroom to await verdict.

At a tap on her shoulder, Alex turned and found Marilyn Rivera.

"You did a good job," the young prosecutor said.

"Thanks." Alex was surprised. It was the first thing the woman said to her during the entire trial. "You too."

Bryce walked up and extended his hand. "Nice closing."

Alex wondered what was going on. Although they showed enormous professionalism, was there something behind it? Did they have a plea in lieu of an acquittal? At this stage of the game, she could afford to indulge herself in wishful thinking.

Her instincts didn't trust them, but she kept up appearances. "Thanks."

"Too bad Mr. Gonzales is probably going to prison for life. He seems like a nice guy."

Alex's eyes blazed. "Save the false sentiment, Bryce. It's not over yet. Whether this jury believes it or not, Jose is innocent and I'll prove it."

Looking smug, Bryce glanced at his watch. It was just after eleven. "You want to bet we get a verdict before lunch?"

Alex ignored him and turned to the Reverend. "Let's get a cup of coffee."

A few minutes before noon, she returned.

Bryce and Marilyn were seated at counsel table with a couple of other district attorneys. Marilyn's high-pitched giggles belied nervousness and what appeared to be a serious crush on her co-counsel. It wasn't often district attorneys so low on the totem pole got to try a case with hotshots like Bryce. Because he had the pull to try any case in the courthouse, he'd insinuated himself into this trial just to get even with Alex for choosing Shepherd's Cottages over him.

He'd gone after her instead of Voodoo.

Why would he try so hard for revenge?

Bryce was used to being pampered and adored. In Alex he had met his match. If he couldn't prevail personally, he'd show Alex up in court.

How did I miss it?

Alex checked her watch. "The jury has been out just over an hour," she told the Reverend.

Just then, the bailiff's buzzer sounded. They were either finished or had a question.

Moments later, the bailiff returned with a piece of paper. "They've got a verdict."

Alex's heart raced. She didn't expect them back this early, but Bryce always bragged about his speedy jury verdicts. The quick decision meant that before going in, they had probably already decided the case.

The bailiff brought Jose to the table. Alex stood with him as the jury filed in and the judge reviewed the verdict silently then asked the foreman to stand. As she'd predicted, Mr. Smith had been elected foreman."

"Has the jury reached a verdict?" the judge asked.

"Yes, Your Honor."

"To the charge of aggravated sexual assault of a minor child, what is the jury's verdict?"

"We find the defendant, Jose Gonzales, guilty of aggravated sexual abuse of a child."

CHAPTER 26

Alex's legs threatened to buckle, but she steadied herself on the table. Jose winced. The Reverend reached over the bar and Jose turned to embrace him. While the rest of the board members clung together in the row behind counsel table, Alex touched Jose's shoulder.

Alex saw Bryce shake Camilla Roe's hand and give her a half-hug. Alex recognized the woman beside her as the head of Houston CPS. She tried not to show her feelings of rage toward what she knew in her heart was a deep injustice, at least until the jury retired. After all, they still had to sentence Jose.

Judge Villareal called the Court to order. "Jury will retire again to determine punishment."

They all stood until the jurors left, then pandemonium broke out. CPS supporters and other district attorneys rallied on one side of the courtroom. Board members huddled around Jose and Alex until the bailiff returned to take Jose back to the holdover cell. "I'll be down to see you, Jose," Alex called.

She and Ruth left and headed for the ladies' room. Once outside the courtroom door, newspaper reporters surrounded

Alex. Cameras flashed and Christy Malone thrust a mike at her. "What do you think of this speedy verdict?"

"It's not over yet, Christy," she answered. "I can't comment until the jury decides punishment."

Alex entered the ladies' room lounge area and sat on the couch. She was numb; on automatic pilot. The quick verdict stung and there was nothing more she could do. She felt powerless, unable to form a reaction. The case was out of her control. She had to stay strong for Jose this afternoon. She wondered how long the jury would take to determine punishment ... or had they already decided? Alex's instinct about the jury had been correct. They didn't listen to a word she had said. Her efforts were in vain. She felt stuck in the middle of a bad dream. But she knew that this was reality, as cold and as barren as ever. And the worst, she feared, was yet to come.

★

While Alex felt the sting of defeat, Nick sprinted triumphantly to his truck to call Fred. "I've got the warrant!"

"Swing by," Fred said. "Let's go get him."

Realizing he couldn't approach the judge until she finished her morning docket, Nick sat impatiently beside Fred in the downtown municipal courtroom. Finally, the judge motioned them before the bench.

Fred handed over the warrant and the two men waited while she reviewed the request.

"I remember this fire ... on Thanksgiving." She looked at Nick. "You were the one who saved that boy's life, weren't you?"

Nick nodded.

"Where is Joshua Hamilton now?" she asked.

"I suspect he's in criminal court across the street watching the trial involving his nephew, a foster child at Shepherd's Cottages."

The judge raised an eyebrow. "I've seen the news."

Nick glanced at his watch.

"In a hurry?" the judge asked, with a slight grin.

"We'd like to nab him right there in front of the cameras," Nick answered.

The judge signed the warrant and gave it to Nick with a flourish. "What are you waiting for?"

★

After going through the quick sentencing phase, Alex waited with Jose in the small holdover room while the jury decided his fate. There was not much new evidence to put on and the judge would not let them rehash the whole trial. Her stomach had the same queasy feeling as the first day of trial. Something wasn't right. Punishment was taking longer than conviction!

Jose sat quietly.

Seated in an uncomfortable chair, she avoided Jose's haunting eyes by staring at the wall's ugly white paint, cracked and peeling. Without words to console him, she was afraid to offer hope.

Alex glanced at her watch. It was nearly five. Surely, rather than come back Monday, the jury would decide today. Even if it meant staying all night.

Jose broke the silence. "I shouldn't have followed Chris that day," he said ruefully.

"Don't beat yourself up. It won't change anything."

Lawyers don't determine case facts, but their expertise does affect the jury verdict. Trial lawyers know that you win cases you shouldn't win, and you lose cases you shouldn't lose. That's the price of admission when choosing a career as a trial lawyer. Adages aside, Alex didn't feel any better.

Jose being deprived of his liberty because of her ineptitude was heartbreaking. Not only was she unaccustomed to failure, she'd never lost a case!

Why this case?

She was perplexed because she'd put her heart and soul into it, had violated her own rule against getting personally involved with clients and her cases, and she had still come up empty-handed.

During trial, she'd resisted buckling under pressure and followed the dictates of her profession by hiding her true feelings behind a facade of strength and grace. It was a posture ingrained during law school and reinforced through life's hard knocks.

Alex desperately needed some air. The confines of the small room were closing in on her. "I need to check on the others. I'll be back," she told Jose before leaving the room and heading down the hall toward the courtroom.

Just as she reached the elevators, the doors opened and out stepped Nick and Fred.

Nick was all smiles. "Where's Voodoo?"

Alex shrugged. "Probably in the courtroom. I've been with Jose since the jury returned a guilty verdict this morning. They're deciding punishment now."

He saw strain on Alex's face and heard tension in her voice and regretted not asking first about the verdict. He'd gotten lost in the euphoria of finally putting the man behind the trouble at Shepherd's Cottages behind bars. "When did the verdict come in?"

"Before noon. Less than an hour after final arguments."

Nick wanted to pull her to him and comfort her, but knew it was not the time or place. "I'm sorry about the verdict, but I've got some good news." Nick pulled out the arrest warrant. "We've got him!"

"Good," she said with a wan smile.

The despair in Alex's eyes diluted Nick's sense of victory. All week he'd worked for this moment, hoping that Voodoo's arrest would make a difference in the verdict; but he was too late. Nick touched her arm. "Come with us."

TV reporters and cameramen sat on benches outside the courtroom. When Fred, in full uniform, approached with Nick and Alex, they rushed forward. "What's going on?" Christy Malone pressed.

Nick smiled and motioned them to follow. "You'll see."

Reporters and cameramen trailed them into the courtroom. Trial wasn't in session and events could be filmed without sanction from the judge.

Nick's adrenaline surged. At last, he would publicly humiliate the man at the root of all this trouble. Voodoo and Camilla stood behind prosecution's counsel table. "Joshua Hamilton?" Fred called.

Voodoo, in a boxy black suit, turned. "That's me," he answered. His eyes widened when he saw Nick, a uniformed policeman, and a battalion of press members.

Fred held out the warrant. "You're under arrest for the October 31 arson of Cottage Five at Shepherd's Cottages."

Voodoo's face was incredulous. "You've got to be kidding!"

Fred handcuffed Voodoo, gave him his Miranda warnings, then led him from the courtroom.

Pausing before Nick and Alex, his furious black eyes fastened on them and promised revenge.

"Let's get the others before the jury comes back," Alex whispered in Nick's ear. "I want everyone here for Jose."

Nick nodded and they headed out the door.

"What's the connection between the arrest and the trial?" one reporter asked.

Surrounded by media, Nick and Alex tried to push their way through the crowd.

"Didn't you rescue the boy from the burning building at the foster home on Thanksgiving Day?" another reporter quizzed.

Christy Malone blocked Nick's way. "You didn't answer my question."

Nick stopped, then chose his words carefully. "Joshua Hamilton is the uncle of the boy who accused the defendant of sexual abuse," Nick stated. "He's just a thug who exerts control in the Fifth Ward through drugs and crime. A year ago Reverend Morse replaced Joshua Hamilton's crack houses with Shepherd's Cottages and there's been a battle ever since. Reverend Morse wants to manage the community through faith and love and Joshua Hamilton will stop at nothing to keep the Fifth Ward full of drugs and crime."

With increasing admiration for Nick, Alex watched as reporters anxiously scribbled quotes as he spoke. His words held such conviction, one didn't doubt their truth. This tall, lanky man with sea-blue eyes had captivated the media, just as he'd penetrated her heart. For the first time, she realized how much she could learn from him. So far, the only life lessons she'd learned were through trial and error. Something told her it was time to listen to a voice other than her own.

"That's all I'm at liberty to say now," Nick calmly stated with a hand out, encouraging the press to let them pass. They ducked into the stairwell and left the media behind. Halfway down, Nick stopped and opened his arms for Alex.

"I'm sorry about the verdict," he murmured. "I should have been here."

"I'm glad you didn't see me fail," Alex said wistfully. Her eyes moistened, but she refused to give way to pent-up tears. Nuzzling her head deep into his neck, she hid from his gaze. Having a man like Nick comfort her after such an important loss was unfamiliar territory. Uncharted emotions made her feel vulnerable and weak, but until the jury returned, nothing would penetrate her armor.

Nick lifted her chin, forcing her to look at him. "You didn't fail. You did your best. It's not over yet."

Alex shook her head. "We can appeal on sufficiency of the evidence, but I honestly don't see grounds for reversal. His only shot might be a claim for ineffective assistance of counsel."

"Come on, Alex. It's not like you to think that way. Maybe Voodoo being in jail will change things. The tide still might turn yet. Don't give up."

At the thought of Voodoo in jail, Alex's spirit brightened.

"He isn't gloating now. Handcuffs were a new experience for him."

"He won't be released on bond anytime soon either. His paperwork will be 'mixed up' long enough for him to feel Jose's pain." Nick winked. "Who knows? Maybe he'll get Chris to come clean about his false charge against Jose."

Everyone waited, wondering whether the jury would deliberate long into the night. Alex sat at counsel table with Ruth, waiting for the verdict. She felt a touch on her shoulder and turned.

It was Mike Delany.

What is he doing here?

Alex wished she could have hidden the trial from him.

Is he here to tell me I'm out of the running for the judgeship?

She was out of options and she knew it.

"I'm sorry about the verdict, Alex," Mike said in a soft voice. "Good luck on punishment. I'm in your corner."

Alex gave Mike a hug and thanked him for being supportive. Now wasn't the time to talk about politics.

Delany turned and walked to the back of the courtroom, where he took a seat next to some reporters. Catching her lingering gaze, he gave her a thumbs-up. Alex was encouraged.

Maybe, like Nick said, it's not over yet.

At six, the Court's buzzer sounded.

"They have decided," the bailiff told the judge over the intercom. "I'll get the defendant."

Alex turned from counsel table and looked behind her. The Reverend's head was down; his eyes were shut. Alex knew he was praying. Nick and Miss May flanked him. Angelina, Mr. Samples and other board members sat behind her.

Straightening his tie, Bryce joined Marilyn at counsel table.

The jury entered the courtroom and sat in their seats in the jury box. None made eye contact with Jose or Alex.

Judge Villareal entered and sat at her bench. "Has the jury reached a verdict on punishment?"

Mr. Smith stood. "We have, Your Honor."

"And what is your decision?"

"We, the jury, having found the defendant guilty of aggravated sexual abuse of a child, find that punishment be set at a term of not less than twenty nor more than forty years."

Alex held her breath. Her chest tightened. Notice of appeal must be given immediately, but the words wouldn't come out of her mouth.

Forty years! How could the jury deliver such an outrageous sentence?

With a regal flair, Judge Villareal maintained order. "The Court accepts the verdict. The defendant is hereby remanded to custody."

The bailiff stood, walked over and handcuffed Jose.

Alex had to act fast. As a woman in a male-dominated profession, her choice of responses was narrowed. The law was no place for sissies, or the faint-hearted. Her only choice was to "take it like a man," or get out of the profession. She turned and looked at the Reverend, whose head was still down, and at the others, whose faces registered shock and dismay. Facing the Court and the jury, Alex stood. Finally, the words came out. "Your Honor, Notice of Appeal is hereby given on behalf of my client, Jose Gonzales."

"Accepted," Judge Villareal said, then banged her gavel for the last time. "Court is adjourned."

Once the judge and jury left the room, pandemonium erupted.

Nick watched Camilla squeal with delight and hug her obviously supportive supervisor. TV cameras and reporters surrounded Bryce, who seemed eager to exult himself for the evening news.

Then, looking out over the chaos, Nick saw Alex slip out the side door. He got up and began to follow her, but thought better of it.

She must be going to the restroom.

Nick pushed his way back through the throng of people to the front row where the Reverend sat slumped in his seat.

Nick touched his shoulder. "Reverend?"

The old man looked at him through glassy eyes and held a hand over his heart.

"Reverend, are you alright?" Nick asked.

The Reverend shook his head weakly.

Alarmed, Nick jumped up. "Someone call an ambulance."

The bailiff responded and dialed 911.

Suddenly, the courtroom grew quiet as all attention focused on the Reverend. The press quit fielding questions to the winners; court clerks stopped filing papers; court stenographers ceased rewinding their machines. Judge Villareal appeared from her chambers.

Nick looked at the man beside him. The Reverend's skin was ashen; his pulse faint.

With his arm around the Reverend, Nick motioned the crowd to back off. Judge Villareal leaned over the bar. "Does he need CPR?"

Nick shook his head.

"I'll call Dr. Kline, my cardiologist over at St. Luke's," she said, then disappeared to her chambers.

For decades, the Reverend had been an unfailing source of comfort to members of his community. He was strong in times of trouble. But battling Voodoo while protecting children had finally taken its toll. Nick sobered at the thought of the Reverend dying in this very courtroom. In that moment, everything else in life became insignificant.

Nick went into a silent rage at Voodoo and his henchmen. The minute he was released from jail, Voodoo would be right back to work. Even though the old saying *You can beat the rap, but you can't beat the ride* was true, Nick had to face the fact Voodoo might beat the charge altogether. And he'd most likely use his time in jail as a recruiting mission.

Nick couldn't think about that now. The Reverend, his mentor, needed his strength and faith. During the darkest hours of his life the Reverend had been strong for him. It was his turn to be strong.

"You're alright," Nick said, holding the Reverend close.

The paramedics arrived and carefully placed the Reverend on a stretcher. Nick feared he would lose this suddenly fragile man.

On his way out the door, Nick turned to look at the prosecution's table. Bryce, Camilla, her supervisor and Marilyn huddled together with self-satisfied expressions.

Do they think they've killed two birds with one stone?

Alex ignored the doves and barely patted Siva's head when she entered her townhome in darkness. She reluctantly lit a votive candle—she didn't want light, only darkness. The silence was deafening and the air was frigid, but she didn't want to turn on the heat. She wanted to freeze to death, dwelling on who might attend *her* funeral.

How many real friends do I have? Would judges mourn the talent lost by my early passing? Would Hal be relieved his judgeship faced no challenge?

Alex smiled wistfully at her tormented mind. Truth was, the world would go on as usual without her.

She walked over and scooped some food into Siva's bowl. The sensitive dog was not hungry. When Alex was upset, she was upset too.

Standing in the middle of her kitchen, Alex kicked off her heels and wiggled out of her suit. She opened the fridge and saw the bottle of wine from last night. It was still half-full. She looked at her wine rack and saw several good bottles in place. It was going to be a long night and she had all the company she needed.

She ignored her ringing phone. Before she could face anyone, she had to sort things out. A quick call with strict orders to the security guard ensured that no one, for any reason, would enter the gate. She couldn't explain the jury's sentence, nor could she think of what she could have done better. She was having a pity party with one special guest—herself.

She'd thought about Jose, sitting alone in his cell, wondering what was going to become of the rest of his life. Except for the Reverend, he'd had so few good breaks. Since Angelina's husband's death, Alex had secretly hoped she and Jose would reunite, maybe have a child. Those dreams were shattered by the conviction.

Now, with a glass of wine in hand, she sat in darkness on her living room floor before an unlit fire. Alex thought back over her career and couldn't remember feeling so responsible for a client's fate. Jose's case had prompted her to reach a new level of personal involvement. None before had ever consumed her mind, her will, or her emotions like Jose's. She had the specific feeling that her life would never be the same again. When she met the Reverend something had told her to help him. Even as bad as she felt, she still didn't regret taking Jose's case for free.

Since the beginning, she'd worked hard, had uncovered major flaws in the State's case, and yet the jury still rushed to judgment against Jose. What did they see that she'd missed?

Why, if taking the case still felt right, did things turn out so wrong?

The temperature finally got to Alex. She grabbed her wine glass and bottle, then climbed the stairs. She couldn't sleep yet, so she drew a bath. She didn't turn on soothing music; she wasn't ready to feel better.

Once in the tub, her mind went deeper and deeper into negative thoughts. She speculated how quickly the children of Shepherd's Cottages would be dispersed to different foster homes. Tears came to her eyes when she pictured Miss May no longer able to stand over them, hands on hips, all bark and no bite. It hurt Alex to know that, although the children were loved and Shepherd's Cottages was the closest thing to a loving home they'd ever had, it would be closed because she couldn't convince twelve people of Jose's innocence.

Because of her, the Reverend's dream was dead. She had let him down. She wondered if he regretted giving her the job. Probably not, knowing what a saint he was. She felt guilty for not telling the Reverend that the lead prosecutor had been her lover, and she didn't even want to think about what Nick would say once he found out. The courthouse grapevine couldn't have escaped his ear. She consoled herself. Even if she'd come clean with both of them, nothing would have changed. Bryce was still the better lawyer.

Finally, the noisy jets drowned out the cackling in her brain. She climbed out of the tub and rustled up an old muscle relaxer from her medicine cabinet. She swallowed it with her last sip of wine. She wanted to sleep ... a long time.

CHAPTER 27

Nick, along with Shepherd's Cottages board members, sat in St. Luke's Hospital's heart surgery waiting room. Three hours had passed since Reverend Morse was wheeled through the double doors into surgery.

Ironic that only weeks ago the Reverend sat in this hospital waiting for news of me. And Little Thomas.

Nick was reliving the past difficult hours of this fateful day when Dr. Kline emerged in his surgery gown. Nick and the others snapped to.

"He's stable," the doctor said. "You got him here in time. He'll need to take it easy for a while."

Nick stood. "We can't thank you enough."

"I was just leaving when Judge Villareal called. I'm glad I could help."

"Can he have visitors?"

Dr. Kline shook his head. "He's sedated. Wait until morning." The doctor glanced at the others. "Go on home and get some rest," he said.

Nick glanced at his watch. Visiting hours at the jail were

over. If he pulled some strings with old friends on the force, he might get in to see Voodoo and tell him what he'd done to the Reverend.

Half an hour later, Nick waited in an empty visiting chamber. Even though the Reverend loved this worthless man, Nick still doubted Voodoo had a redeeming bone in his body.

The heavy steel door clanged opened and a sleepy-eyed Voodoo in jailhouse skivvies appeared. Gone were the hip suit and the arrogant smile. "Yeah?" he drawled. "Did you come to tell me about the verdict? I already know."

Nick controlled his anger behind a thin veneer of calm. "That's not why I'm here." Nick peered at the man through the wire mesh. "Reverend Morse had a heart attack in court today. I thought you should know."

The announcement hung in the air for a long moment. Voodoo's face froze. Nick thought he saw pain, regret, and maybe a touch of sadness.

Running a hand through his hair, Voodoo leaned forward. "What happened?"

"Earlier this afternoon, we all thought he was praying. He was quiet, kind of slumped in his seat. After the verdict, I noticed he was having a hard time breathing."

Nick couldn't believe it when he saw perspiration on Voodoo's forehead. Was it possible the man the Rev had taken under his wing so many years ago was starting to break? Nick said a silent prayer for wisdom in this very important conversation.

"What happened then?"

"The judge called her cardiologist. He was rushed to St. Luke's Hospital and straight into surgery. The doctor said he was lucky to get there in time."

Voodoo was visibly shocked. "The old man's never been sick."

"He hasn't had time," Nick told him. "He's taken care of everyone else all these years."

Voodoo sat staring, lost in thought.

Nick waited.

"When I was a boy, he took me fishin' after church every Sunday."

"I know. He has the same picture in his office that you have on your desk."

"He had children, but both of them was killed early on," Voodoo said quietly.

Nick was surprised. He'd often wondered why the Rev had no children of his own, but never felt at liberty to ask.

"He's going to be alright." Nick was startled to find himself reassuring Voodoo. "He'll be in the hospital a few days, but the doctor says he'll be strong as an ox again."

Obviously pleased at the news, Voodoo gave a weak smile.

"This trial nearly killed him, Voodoo. When will you give up this battle and listen to the man who loves you?"

"Give up my lifestyle? Let someone else take over? This life is all I know."

"Why not follow him in the ministry?" Nick asked.

Something had changed in Voodoo's face, something almost imperceptible: a mild softening of lines; a knowing look in his eyes. Nick knew he'd planted a seed in Voodoo's hard heart.

"Oh yeah. I'm really qualified to take over for the Reverend."

Nick felt his palms begin to sweat. This was perhaps the most important conversation he'd ever have to help the Reverend.

"You know as well as I do that God takes the foolish things of the world to confound the wise. No one is prepared for ministry. You're called and God equips you. Period. Voodoo, you have a big investment in the Fifth Ward. Maybe it's time for a changing of the guard. This war hasn't placed either of you where you want to be. You're in jail; the Rev's in the hospital."

Voodoo gave no response. A long minute passed. "Better go, man," he said in a hoarse voice, then rose from his seat. He turned and left the room with the guard.

Nick's heart was flying high as he hit the elevator button to get back to the ground floor.

Maybe I hit a nerve?

Once outside, Nick called Alex. When he got no answer, he called Ruth, who said she had also been trying to reach Alex all evening.

Nick drove to Alex's townhome, worried. When he pulled in he was greeted by the familiar guard. "Sorry, sir. She's given me strict orders not to let anyone in tonight."

"Anyone includes me?"

"I'm afraid so," he said.

"She's there and she's alright?" Nick asked.

The guard nodded.

"Good. When you see or talk to her, please tell her to call. It's important."

"Sure will, sir."

With Voodoo in jail, Alex was safe. Nick drove the short distance to his home. He'd sleep in his own bed for the first time in several days.

In the middle of the night, Alex awoke with a start. She hopped up out of bed and headed to the bookcase in her study. She pulled out the Bible she had put the Post-it note in that the Reverend had given her several weeks ago. The one with the scripture references. She looked them up and turned to the second book of Daniel. Alex felt a chill as she read. Her dream earlier that evening was similar to that of King Nebuchadnezzar. The King, in an effort to interpret one of his dreams, went to prophets and soothsayers to no avail. He turned to Daniel, known as a prophet of God. Daniel's interpretation opened the King's heart and changed his life.

Stunned by the sudden sense of revelation, Alex realized she'd been looking elsewhere for answers that had been there all the time. She held the book close to her heart, went back to bed, and reread the story of Daniel.

In her dream, she and Nick were seated beneath a tall pine tree, waiting.

Why were we waiting?

Then she heard a clear commanding voice inside her head: "Ask God." And without hesitation, she did.

Please, God! Help me prove Jose's innocence.

She waited, then clear as a bell she heard her own voice say, "I need a witness."

Suddenly imbued with energy, she went to her bathroom mirror and took a long hard look. Beyond the smudged makeup and tired circles under her eyes, she saw a new woman. Trying to find justice on her own, she'd come to the end of herself.

Now, though she'd only gone to the Reverend's church a few times, she realized she hadn't applied any of his teachings to her life.

Her phone rang and she saw it was the security guard station. She answered.

"Everything alright?" the on-duty security guard asked.

Alex smiled to herself. "Everything's fine."

"Mr. Wright came by earlier. He says it's important you call."

It was after four a.m. and Alex was still awake and in bed, puzzling over her dream.

I'm supposed to go to Crosstown Park and wait. God will do the rest.

With that calming thought, she slept more deeply than she had in weeks.

She awoke Saturday morning and couldn't wait to tell Nick of her discovery. She dialed his number and he picked up on the first ring.

"Good morning. I'm glad you're alive."

His deep voice sent tingles through Alex's body. "I'm more than alive. Get over here. I have a plan."

"I'll be there in fifteen," he said, hanging up the phone. He wanted to tell her the news about the Reverend in person.

Alex jumped into the shower with more vigor than she'd felt in weeks. She was sure now, with God's help, she would find a way to vindicate Jose. The Reverend had shown her God's love in action and how to use His wisdom for problem solving. Jose's life was on the line and He would help save him.

Nick arrived in a sleeveless down jacket and flannel shirt. "Sure you don't need a jacket," he asked, looking at her sweater and blue jeans.

Alex nodded and grabbed one on the way out.

"Where are we going?" he asked as they climbed into his truck.

"To Crosstown Park. I had a dream last night that somehow we'd missed something."

Nick thought a moment. "Let's do it."

Alex began with an apology. "I'm sorry I took off yesterday. I was so depressed."

"I figured that." Nick's hand covered hers. "You needed to sort things out."

"Even fantasized about my funeral," she stated.

Nick frowned. "That would be one sad day in my book."

"I woke up at three-thirty and went and looked up some scriptures the Reverend gave me a few weeks ago. Then I tried this God thing you and the Reverend are so excited about. I prayed."

Nick tried to contain his joy at her words. Alex was finally getting it. He'd always marveled at her ability to accomplish so much without seeming to give God a thought. Even as he'd tried to tell her, he knew she'd have to learn on her own. Losing Jose's trial got her attention.

She was so excited about her revelation; he decided to wait a little while before telling her of the Reverend's heart attack.

They arrived at the park and, relying on trial testimony, they headed for the place Chris said he was attacked. They came to a clearing that fit the description. With trees hiding the street from view, a sexual offense could have occurred with no witnesses.

There was no one in sight when they sat beneath a tall pine tree. Realizing this spot was similar to her dream, she turned to tell Nick about it. But Nick was scanning the park with a wary stare.

"Do you have a gun?" she asked.

"You don't think I'd show up in drug land without a pistol?"

His presence was comforting and she was not afraid. She was on a mission and had more than a hunch that she was on the right track.

They sat in silence for the rest of the morning, observing the area. A couple of young boys rode by on their bikes; an adolescent thug strode through and gave them the peace sign.

Time went by and nothing happened. Alex fought doubt. She remembered the first time she went fishing with the Rev and Nick. Then, she could barely stay quiet for thirty minutes, much less two hours. She had changed.

Alex nudged Nick. "Look," she whispered, pointing to the other side of the clearing where a short, crooked woman shuffled into a makeshift hut next to the viaduct. In browns and beige, she blended into the background.

Alex rose to her feet. "This might be my witness."

CHAPTER 28

A moment later, the woman came back out of her lean-to and stared at them.

"Hello," Alex called. "Mind if we talk to you?"

Alex saw the old woman's eyes narrow. She sensed her hesitation.

"What is it?" she asked.

Alex and Nick approached. "I'm Alex Stockton. This is my friend, Nick Wright."

"I'm Grace Lee," she responded.

"I'm a lawyer and am investigating an important case. Maybe you can help."

"If it's about that boy from the Reverend's foster home, I already tried to report it."

Shocked, Alex remembered the missing page of the investigative CPS report. She'd known there had to be a reason.

"Who did you talk to?"

"I called CPS."

"I represent Jose Gonzales, the foster parent who chased the boy here to get him to finish his homework. Last night, a jury convicted him of aggravated sexual assault and gave him a forty-year sentence."

"That boy wasn't sexually assaulted."

"Are you talking about October 31st?"

Grace Lee nodded.

Alex had her witness.

She would prepare an unbeatable motion for new trial and file it Monday morning. If Judge Villareal heard Grace Lee's testimony and believed it, she would grant the motion. Then Bryce would either dismiss the case or there would be another trial. At best the case would be over and Jose would be free. At worst, he would get a second chance with a new jury.

"What did CPS say when you called?"

"I tried to tell them what happened, but before they'd listen, they wanted my address, phone number. When they found out I didn't have an address right now, they hung up."

"They didn't come out and question you about the incident?"

"No, they didn't. Seein's as I'm temporarily homeless, my word's no good."

"Miss Lee, with your help, I'm going to ask the judge for a new trial based on newly discovered evidence. I'll prepare an affidavit to file in the Court Monday. Would you come with me to Shepherd's Cottages? There are some folks there who'll be real happy to listen to you."

Grace Lee smiled and seemed to stand a bit taller. "Before I fell on bad times, I was a schoolteacher."

Nick and Alex exchanged a knowing glance. There was a room available at Shepherd's Cottages and the kids needed someone to help them learn. Miss Lee might just have found herself a new home.

"Why don't you get some of your things?" Alex suggested. "If you're willing, you could stay overnight at Shepherd's Cottages."

The woman smiled. "I'll be just a minute." She disappeared inside her humble dwelling. A few minutes later, she returned with a large cardboard box.

Nick quickly took it from her. He peeked inside and saw a Bible, a clock radio, a small jewelry box, a few articles of clothing, and some paperback books—romance novels no doubt.

On the short walk to Shepherd's Cottages, Alex was elated. She finally had her witness, and Jose was one step closer to being free. They entered the compound and walked down the driveway. "The Reverend's going to be so glad to meet you," Alex told Grace.

Nick cleared his throat. The time had come. "Alex, there's something I need to tell you," he began.

Before he could finish, Miss May appeared outside the administration building with Mr. Samples. "Where's the Rev?" Alex called.

Miss May and Mr. Samples exchanged puzzled glances. "Where you been girl?" Miss May asked. "He's still in the hospital."

Alex's eyes widened. "The hospital?"

"Don't you know about his heart attack yesterday after trial? He had heart surgery last night at St. Luke's."

Alex was shocked. She stamped her foot and gave Nick a look that could kill. "Why didn't you tell me?"

Nick shrugged. "We tried to call you all night. He's alright and will be back to normal in no time. You've been so happy this morning, I didn't want to spoil it."

Alex was angry, but she knew it was her own fault. She'd been selfish and engrossed in her pity party over Jose's trial. She wouldn't take her guilt out on Nick

"He's OK?" Alex asked Miss May.

"Yes, honey, he's fine and will be back home by midweek." Miss May turned to the woman standing next to Alex with an appreciative eye. "Who you got here?"

"This is Grace Lee, our answer to prayer," Alex said. "She was there that night in Crosstown Park and corroborates Jose's side of the story. Based on her testimony, I'm filing a motion for new trial Monday."

"Oh, Lordy!" Miss May exclaimed, clapping her hands. She hustled over to Grace and took her arm. "Can I get you some hot coffee or tea?"

Miss Lee grinned, obviously enjoying the attention.

Mr. Samples took the box from Nick. "Are these your things?" he asked Grace.

She nodded.

"Cottage Four is empty," he said kindly. "There's a bedroom where you can put your things. You all can talk in the kitchen."

Alex was elated. Mr. Samples had read her mind and said the magic words. Grace Lee had a new home.

"He's recently widowed," Alex whispered to Grace. "Why don't you get situated while we run over to the hospital and talk to the Reverend? I want to tell him the good news."

Grace Lee gave her a grateful smile. She wasn't likely to fuss about the new arrangements. "That'll be fine, dear. I'll be here when you get back."

Alex turned to Nick and gave him a hug. "You just might be right about things after all," she whispered.

★

Alex and Nick checked in at the cardiac unit for the Reverend's room number.

The attending nurse pointed at a slightly open door nearby. "He had a bad night. Needs rest. Doctor's orders."

Alex nodded and entered the Reverend's room, silent except for intermittent beeps from the panel behind him. Standing by his bed, she held back tears. There was so much she wanted to tell him about—her dream, her prayer and its answer in the form of Grace Lee. But communication was impossible. He was on oxygen, hooked to monitors and IVs. Despite his excellent prognosis for recovery, he looked alarmingly frail.

Across the bed, Nick's troubled eyes went from her to the Reverend. Then he gestured toward the door.

Back in Nick's truck, he put his arm around her and gave her a hug.

Alex returned the hug. She needed his comfort and support. "I can't wait to prepare that affidavit."

"I'll drop you off at Shepherd's Cottages, then run over to the jail and tell Jose the news."

Nick then filled her in on his visit with Voodoo.

She shook her head, too full of other emotions to respond.

Alex found Grace Lee in Cottage Six. Having showered and changed, she was sipping tea with Miss May and Mr. Samples.

Alex gave them the news on the Reverend.

"We decided since this cottage is empty," Miss May began, "Grace can stay here."

"That's great," Alex said, noting Grace Lee's bright smile.

From the beginning of Jose's case, she'd needed an eyewitness. But when her own efforts were exhausted, she'd asked God for help. Now the miracle was here.

Alex proceeded to interview Grace about that day in the park. After all Alex had been through, the truth now sounded surreal.

Within the hour, her notes formed the skeleton of a sound motion for new trial. She suppressed a smile at how Bryce would react.

Although rare, the judge must grant a motion for new trial if the defendant presents new evidence that he or she could not have "reasonably discovered" before trial. If the State withholds evidence favorable to the defendant, it's always grounds for a new trial. Alex was confident her new evidence was credible enough to overturn Jose's conviction. She had already proven the police investigation was flawed and that the CPS investigation report was missing a page. Since Jose's conviction rested solely on Chris Jackson's testimony, Alex knew the judge would look closely at her motion. After all, the judge knew what the jury didn't about Chris's background. Grace Lee's testimony would be direct evidence in a conviction that rested mostly on circumstantial evidence.

Alex looked closely at Grace Lee. The kindness in her eyes and the softness in her voice were authentic. Three months ago, she was evicted from her apartment and forced to move into the park near the bayou. Her only living son, a drug addict, had cleaned out her life savings. She didn't know of his addictions when she'd put him on her bank account. Toward the end, he'd taken her Social Security money that was deposited each month. Quickly, her bills had fallen behind. She'd taken her son off her account at the bank, but by then it was too late.

"Why didn't you go to a shelter?"

Grace Lee straightened her arthritic frame. "This is my neighborhood. I can take care of myself. I don't want handouts."

Miss May gave a snort. "They'll be no handouts here. We can't afford it. We'll have you working with the kids in no time."

Alex was happy to see Miss May so full of hope about Shepherd's Cottages again.

By the time Nick got back, it was dusk.

"Are you hungry?" he asked.

Alex realized she hadn't thought about food all day. "I'm starved."

"Let's go. I'll tell you about Jose on the way."

Alex hugged Grace, then put an arm around Miss May. "Take good care of my star witness. We waited so long to find her; we can't let her out of our sight."

Miss May winked. "Mr. Samples will keep her safe."

CHAPTER 29

On the way to dinner, Alex put her hand on Nick's arm. *Things are looking up.*

"Jose is afraid to get his hopes up," he began. "Says he'll celebrate after the judge grants the motion and Bryce dismisses his case."

They went to a casual barbecue restaurant. Decorated with saddles and cowboy memorabilia, the place smelled of mesquite and spices. Country music came over the sound system and Alex and Nick took a beer from the well-stocked ice bin. After ordering cafeteria style, they sat in a booth near a window.

"Is Angelina still with Ruth?" Nick asked.

"I think so, but let's call to be sure." Alex dialed Ruth on her cell phone.

While she listened, Nick watched her face.

Alex said goodbye, then looked at Nick. "Angelina is there and they were worried about me."

"You didn't answer their calls either?"

Alex shook her head. "Remember my pity party?"

★

On the way to the courthouse Monday morning, Alex realized she'd never worked so hard or so expeditiously on a motion. She'd pulled case law, copied the motion form, then dictated. Ruth typed and proofed. All during the preparation time, Alex felt someone or something other than herself was in control. Since her commitment in the wee hours of Saturday morning, she'd been on automatic pilot.

At eight-thirty a.m., half an hour before docket call, she entered the crowded courtroom. Marilyn Rivera looked startled to see her.

Pulling a copy of her motion for new trial from her slim file, Alex handed it to the prosecutor. "Let's approach the judge before docket to get an expedited hearing date. I want a Friday hearing at the latest."

Marilyn blinked and glanced at the motion. "Just a minute," she mumbled, then hurried into the court reporter's office.

Alex knew she was calling Bryce.

At the desk, the court reporter gave Alex the thumbs-up sign. Maybe Jose had more support in this court than she'd thought.

Alex approached Judge Villareal's chambers and knocked lightly.

"Come in."

She entered. "Good morning, judge. I don't mean to disturb you."

"How's the Reverend?"

"He's doing well. Dr. Kline was a wonderful referral. If all goes well, he'll be released by midweek."

"I know what he's going through. I've been there, but I'm happy to say I'm better. Cleaned up my diet and got on a steady exercise program. Cost of staying alive."

Just then a door slammed and angry footsteps approached the judge's chambers. Then an enraged Bryce, waving Alex's motion toward her, said, "Such a sore loser. You have as much a chance winning this motion as I do flying to Mars today."

Unperturbed, ready for battle, Alex replied, "Let's see what the judge has to say."

"What in the hell is going on here, counselor?" Judge Villareal barked at Bryce. "How dare you address a lady that way! Get in here."

"Your Honor," Alex said as she handed her the original, "My motion for new trial."

"Basis?"

"Newly discovered evidence."

While Bryce paced before her desk, the judge donned reading glasses and quickly reviewed the pleading.

The judge looked at Bryce. "Counselor, I suggest you find a place and light," she said sternly.

Bryce sat in an armchair a few feet away from Alex. He crossed his arms and frowned like a spoiled little boy.

When the judge finished, Alex began, "Your Honor, I request a Friday hearing."

"I have ten days to prepare my answer," Bryce stated angrily.

Alex shot a stern look at Bryce. "An innocent man has been sitting in jail for months. Friday gives you plenty of time."

"Why should I cut you slack?" Bryce asked. His neck and ears were bright red.

"Because, against office policy, the State refused to talk plea bargain; because you double-teamed me when you showed up here on trial day to pursue your vendetta against me. Don't forget, as prosecutor your public duty is to do justice."

The judge interrupted. "I have to call docket. Hearing on your motion is ten Friday morning." She looked at Bryce. "Mandamus me. I haven't been reversed in a long time."

Picking up her files, Judge Villareal marched into the courtroom and Alex followed.

★

Back at her office, Alex listened to her messages. Mike Delany left one he said was urgent. She hoped there was still time to salvage her chance at the judgeship, but just in case, she braced herself for bad news.

He picked up the phone on the second ring. "Delany."

"Hey, I'm back from the dead," Alex greeted. "More alive than ever."

"How so?"

"Saturday, I found an eyewitness that corroborates my client's version of what happened in the park. I filed my motion for new trial today and hearing is set for Friday morning." Alex paused. "The conviction will be overturned, Mike. Tell me I still have a chance for the judgeship."

Seconds seemed like hours while Delany formulated his response.

"The governor will be at Tony's tonight," he said at last. "Meet us for cocktails and make your pitch. He's followed the trial closely. He's obviously taken with your efforts."

"Look for me around six."

It was almost five o'clock when Alex left the office. She ran by her townhome to change for her meeting with the governor. An evening out, even if it was business, was exciting. So far this season, her holiday wardrobe hung dormant. Tonight, she would dress to the nines. She applied shimmery powder, curled her hair, then fluffed it up. She chose a long, A-line, black velvet skirt and halter. Then, covering her bare back with a reversible satin-velvet shawl, she slipped into classic black crepe pumps. Every bit of six feet, her inner confidence matched her outer appearance.

When she entered the exclusive restaurant, she was aware of men's admiring eyes. This was her night. She still thought she wanted the judgeship. Like a lion on the prowl, she smelled victory and was hungry to win. The governor was engaged in conversation at the end of the bar with a couple of hefty men who were obviously his bodyguards. Alex went to him and tapped his shoulder. "Do I know you?" she murmured in a low voice.

The governor turned and his eyes widened at the sight of her. "Good God! You look beautiful!"

His companions voiced agreement and Alex met the state attorney general and a couple of local bigwigs.

Taking her elbow, the governor excused himself to the obvious envy of his friends and steered her to an empty booth in a secluded alcove. Positioning himself close to her, his knees touched hers and she smelled the faint scent of his aftershave. Like before, she would resist his advances and beat him at his own game; and whether or not she slept with him, she would make him proud of her as a judge.

Arching her back to look beyond the fake palm tree hiding them, Alex told the waitress she would like a drink. Alex had always enjoyed her powers of seduction, but tonight she thought about her new commitment Saturday morning. Impulsively acting on her desires was no longer an option.

The waitress appeared with two strong Scotches and placed a delicious tray of appetizers before them. "Compliments of the chef."

Suddenly serious, the governor said, "I'm sorry about the verdict."

Alex held up her hand. "Hold on! You haven't heard the latest. I found an eyewitness—a homeless woman who saw everything. She tried to report it to CPS, but they ignored her. The hearing on my motion for new trial is Friday. If I win, Jose will get a new trial and the prosecution will most likely dismiss the case. Shepherd's Cottages will survive and your proposed CPS reforms will garner more public support."

The governor put an arm around her shoulders. "Hon, if you win that motion Friday, consider yourself judge of the new juvenile court."

His words rang in Alex's ears. Instead of elation and excitement, she felt empty. Determined men like the governor relish a challenge. Something inside told her this cat-and-mouse game would never end.

He downed his Scotch. "I better get back to my meeting— lobbyists on oilfield environmental issues. If it doesn't go long, maybe we could meet for a nightcap?"

Alex glanced at her watch, shook her head, then slid out of the booth. "I still have work to do, but you won't regret your decision."

On her way out of the restaurant, she bumped into Delany at the bar.

"How did it go?"

Alex smiled. "If I win the motion Friday, the appointment is mine."

Delany gave her an enthusiastic hug.

"Congratulations. I'll be there Friday to cheer you on. Today, we got wind that CPS has created a task force in anticipation of the governor's proposed reforms. Friday might be a good opportunity to build bridges."

Alex thought of the older woman she'd seen with Camilla during trial. "Who is the chairman of the task force?"

"Betty Harris," Delany said. "She's taken leave from the most active CPS division in the state."

"As with most bureaucracies, they protect their own. The governor wants to shake things up."

CHAPTER 30

Friday morning came quickly. Alex entered the courtroom early and found Jose seated at counsel table in his new suit. He looked rested and, for the first time in months, hopeful.

A few minutes later, Nick wheeled the Reverend into the aisle just behind counsel table. He was released Wednesday from the hospital and his doctor allowed him to attend the hearing. Board members, Angelina, and Ruth arrived and filled the front row. Miss May and Mr. Samples appeared with Grace Lee, and Alex motioned for her to sit close to counsel table.

Camilla arrived with Chris Jackson and the chairman of the task force, Betty Harris. Marilyn Rivera hovered near the prosecution's counsel table talking to what appeared to be curious coworkers.

Every local station had reporters and cameramen present. Christy Malone was determined to get the exclusive.

Mike Delany leaned across counsel table and whispered to Alex, "The governor is available by cell phone."

At ten sharp, Judge Villareal appeared from chambers and sat at the bench. "Court is called to order. Is counsel ready?"

Alex looked at the prosecution table. No Bryce. Would he force Marilyn to fade the heat?

No such luck. Just then, Bryce, looking uncharacteristically disheveled, entered the side courtroom door. "Sorry, judge," he said as he took his place at counsel table. "I had grand jury this morning on a capital case."

Judge Villareal looked at Alex. "Proceed with your motion, counsel.

Alex stood. She was prepared to move forward without notes. Her questions and arguments had been rehearsed into the wee hours of the morning. First, Alex made a record of the legal requirements for her motion and summarized the evidence. "Your Honor, I call my first witness, Grace Lee."

Alex watched her rise, walk gracefully to the witness box and take her seat. Dressed in a long, pleated gray skirt, a white blouse under a red cable knit sweater, she held her small handbag in her lap. Alex marveled at the transformation in her appearance since Saturday. Grace Lee looked like what she was, a retired schoolteacher, not the homeless woman she'd found in the park. "Could you please state your name for the Court?"

"Grace Lee."

"And where do you live, Miss Lee?"

"For the past three months I've lived in the park across the street from Shepherd's Cottages."

Alex asked questions about the circumstances leading to her homelessness. The testimony was flawless. She noticed how, without a jury to impress, Bryce was unusually quiet. Judge Villareal wasn't conned by flamboyant trial tactics. Her reputation as a fair trial judge mandated she follow the law and not allow an innocent man to be falsely convicted.

"On the early evening of October 31, were you at the park?"

"Yes, I was."

"Please tell the Court what you saw."

"I heard someone yelling and screaming and peeked my

head outside my lean-to. I saw that boy over there." Grace Lee pointed at Chris Jackson. "Then I saw him," she said, pointing at Jose, "run up behind him and grab his jacket."

Grace Lee's words were eerily similar to Jose's trial testimony. The court reporter hadn't prepared a trial transcript yet, nor had Grace been to see Jose in jail. "Have you ever spoken to Jose Gonzales?"

The witness shook her head. "No."

"Have you been paid for your testimony today?"

"No."

"Did you report the incident?"

Miss Lee nodded. "Yes, I called CPS that day, but they didn't listen."

Her statement caused a flurry of hushed conversation among the audience. Alex sensed Bryce's anger toward her and took delight in his newfound misery.

Alex didn't have to put on a show for Judge Villareal, but she took advantage of the opportunity to display her trial skills. Whereas during trial, she felt inept, now she had renewed confidence. "You called CPS and reported the incident, but they didn't listen?"

"No, the woman I spoke to said without a phone number or address, they couldn't use my information."

"Miss Lee, did you ever see my client, Jose Gonzales, threaten Chris Jackson with a knife?"

"No."

"Did my client force Chris Jackson to perform oral sex?"

"No."

"Do you remember who you talked to at CPS?"

Grace Lee nodded. "Camilla Roe."

"No further questions," Alex said.

It was Bryce's turn. In contrast to his trial demeanor, Bryce's "nice guy" veneer was thin today. "Miss Lee, if you were so worried about the defendant, why didn't you come out of your hovel to help him?"

Miss Grace stood up to the pressure. "I never said I was worried about him."

"Let me rephrase my question. Why didn't you help the defendant?"

"He was OK. The child was gone. The park isn't a bed of roses, mind you. But I did go to the convenience store and use their phone to call CPS."

"No further questions." Bryce sat down with a scowl on his face.

"Your Honor," Alex said. "I turn your attention to our pretrial hearing where I objected to a missing page of the CPS investigative report. I submit the missing page contained an entry relating to Miss Lee's call."

Before Bryce could respond, Judge Villareal stood. "I've heard enough. Counsel, Mr. Jackson, into my chambers."

As they made their way to her office, Alex turned and winked at Nick, the Reverend and the rest of her crew. Just then, the back door opened and Voodoo entered. His eyes had lost their viciousness. Something had changed. He took a seat on the back row.

In chambers, Judge Villareal addressed Chris Jackson. "Son, did you listen to the testimony?"

Slumped in his seat, Chris's eyes were lowered. "Yeah," he mumbled.

He'd gotten the judge's attention. "Sit up and look at me. Do you know what perjury is?"

Chris Jackson shook his head.

"The jury didn't see your juvenile history, but I did. It's time for you to tell me what happened that day."

Chris Jackson didn't respond.

"Now!"

Finally, the words came. "She's right. Jose wanted me to do my homework and I got mad. I was grounded from going trick-

or-treating."

Judge Villareal was furious. She stood and ordered the bailiff to hold Chris Jackson in juvenile detention until further notice. Then she turned a mean eye on Bryce. "The defense motion for new trial is granted. Will the State dismiss the case against Mr. Gonzales now, or should I go out in the courtroom and make an announcement to the press?"

The color drained from Bryce's face. He was obviously humiliated by the fact his own witness just gutted his entire case. Alex and Judge Villareal knew any rookie prosecutor would have questioned Chris more carefully before trial. But Bryce's case of revengitis had gotten the best of him.

"We'll dismiss our case," he said.

The judge stood. "Let's put it on the record."

The next few minutes were like a dream come true. When Bryce announced the dismissal, the judge ordered the bailiff to release Jose. He would still have paperwork to take care of, but he was a free man. Jose was speechless and Alex watched Angelina hug him as tears of joy streamed down his face. The judge ordered CPS to find a new foster home for Chris Jackson.

Mr. Samples stood close to Grace Lee, and Alex thought she saw a twinkle in both of their eyes.

Mike Delany appeared beside her. "I want to be the first person to call you judge," he said.

"Thanks, Mike. I appreciate your help, but tell the governor I've changed my mind. I want to try a few more good cases before I take the bench. I'll let you know when I'm ready."

Later, she'd fill him in on the governor's sexual advances and how, when she became judge, it would be on her merits alone, with no strings. But now she wanted to savor success with Jose, Nick, the Reverend, Ruth and the rest of the gang.

Alex watched an angry discourse between Betty Harris and Camilla Roe before Camilla grabbed her things and stormed out of the courtroom. Betty Harris approached the Reverend, who sat next to Nick with a big smile on his face.

"Reverend Morse, on behalf of the agency, I'm sorry for all your recent troubles. I'm personally taking over and looking into Camilla Roe's dealings. I hope you won't let what one case worker did spoil your opinion of the rest of us."

The Reverend took her hand gently and said, "Thank you, Miss Harris. I wouldn't do that."

Betty Harris continued. "This morning I heard that Thomas will be released from Shriners Hospital this afternoon. Shall we place him back at Shepherd's Cottages?"

The Reverend nodded. "And his sister?" he asked

"She'll be there too."

By now, TV reporters had gathered around them. "Reverend, would you consider working with me on the task force on foster home reform?"

The Reverend's eyes lit up. Although he'd threatened to throw in the towel with CPS after the trial, this was an opportunity to accomplish some of his goals.

"It would be an honor," the Reverend responded.

Nick took the handles of the Reverend's chair and, with Alex at his side, began to push him out of the courtroom. When they got to the back row, Voodoo stood and approached the Reverend. "Sir, I—"

Alex stepped in to protect the Reverend. "Haven't you done enough damage?" she asked.

The Reverend reached up and patted her arm. "Alex, this boy's my son. What is it Joshua?"

Voodoo leaned down and gave the old man a hug. "I'm sorry for what's happened. I want to try and make it up to you."

The Reverend eyes held a knowing twinkle. "Don't worry, son, you can."

CHAPTER 31

Church Sunday was a big celebration. Just like Thanksgiving Day, people arrived early, laden with sumptuous smelling dishes. Bertha was in charge of the kitchen, while the children were excited about singing a special welcome song to Jose. The two newest arrivals, Nikita and Thomas, were playing with old friends, obviously happy to be back home. Thomas's burns were still healing and he had to be watched carefully. It was a job Grace Lee took on without comment.

There was a peace about the place that was absent during trial. Jose tended to the barbecue pit with Angelina by his side, tending to her baby.

There hadn't been time for Alex to tell the Reverend about her newfound commitment to God. She decided to wait until the "Invitation" and surprise him by publicly responding. It would mean a lot to him. She was ready.

After the usual lively songs, the Reverend approached the pulpit. His steps were measured, but it was obvious he was on the road to recovery. He entered the pulpit and the room grew quiet.

"Greetings, Saints. I'm pleased to be back here this morning. Being in that hospital bed last week gave me time to think about life's many blessings. And to those of you who are concerned, my doctor reports I'm going to be fine. I've just got to change my diet and exercise more."

The audience voiced support audibly with "Amens."

The Reverend wiped his brow with his handkerchief. "Over the last couple of months this church has been through what we've talked about in the story of Peter. We've been broken, and now is the time for God to use us. It's restoration time!"

The choir exploded into song and the entire room joined in. Then the Reverend began the traditional "Invitation." The music grew softer, the choir hummed, and the Reverend called out to those who were ready to commit their lives.

Alex squeezed Nick's hand, slipped out of her seat, and walked to the front of the small sanctuary amid cries of joy from the audience. Her eyes stayed focused on the Reverend and the image of his apparent joy was imprinted on her memory forever. By the time she reached him, the noise of the crowd and the choir was deafening.

"Miss Stockton," he asked, "do you give your life to the Lord this day?"

"Yes," Alex answered, tears streaming down her face.

The Reverend said a few words to her and shook her hand. On her way back to her seat, she was elated. People held out their hands to her, hugged her, and gave congratulations. Alex had never felt so good.

The back door of the church opened. Voodoo and Chris Jackson entered. Chris sat in the back row, but Voodoo walked down the aisle toward the Reverend.

"Don't quit yet, Reverend. I want to answer that Invitation."

The choir got quiet, all eyes in the room riveted to Voodoo, and the Reverend's face shone with a brilliance from within.

By the time Voodoo arrived at the pulpit, the room was silent.

The Reverend spoke in a hushed tone to Voodoo—in the same way he did with Alex. Alex saw tears streaming down the Reverend's face. Miss May dabbed her eyes with Kleenex.

When Voodoo turned to walk back down the aisle, the Reverend called, "What name do you go by?"

Voodoo turned and stated, "Joshua Hamilton, sir."

"Good. Please join us for dinner in a few moments." The room exploded with cheers and claps as the choir picked back up with Holy, Holy, Holy.

Later, after everyone had their fill of down-home cooking in the activity center at Shepherd's Cottages, Nick pulled Alex aside. They found a table in the back of the room. He pulled a small box from his pocket and presented it to Alex.

Alex looked inside and saw a handcrafted silver pendant shaped like a dove along with a silver chain.

"Dove of Peace," he said.

Alex put on the necklace, then pulled a compact mirror from her purse. "It's beautiful!"

Alex thought a moment. "That day I met the Reverend, the white bird outside my plane window, it was the Holy Spirit."

Nick nodded.

Alex was incredulous. "God went to all this trouble just to find me?"

Nick nodded and took her into his arms.

"You're worth it, Alex."

Acknowledgements

A book is a labor of love and a journey for the author and her community. The first book is kind of like the first child, whose birth is filled with unknowing anticipation, fear and awe, and incredible joy. The author wishes to acknowledge the invaluable assistance of the following people: I owe a debt of gratitude to all of my friends and family who have been there in my quest to tell this story. There are too many to name, but a few stand out in the amounts of time and energy they have put into the book in a variety of ways: Rosalinda and Lee Villareal, for being the initial and continuing prayer warriors; Barbara Reid, an honest friend; Maria Valdez, for her strength; Susan Poag and Karen Mize, my life-long friends; my beautiful Dana Deangelis and Charme Gallini, my cuzzie wuzzies; Susan Sanders, my long time critique group partner; Debra & Donna Catlett & Vernon Smith; true friends are hard to find; Ann Bragg, for loving the book and for helping convince my father, Charles Bragg, that I wasn't going to give up my "day job;" to Jack Canfield for being the most selfless, authentic teacher and trainer I could ever meet and be proud to know; Rick Paszkiet, my ABA editor who has cheered me on endlessly; Kelly Keane, my ABA marketing director who has likewise been a constant beacon of light; to Lynn Allingham, my supportive roomie; Joan Burda, one of my best award-winning author friends, who reminded me that I needed to feed the dog;

the Carson's-Charles, Melissa & Megan, my Houston family; to Ivy Rosenberg, whose unfailing devotion to helping me with my books has been invaluable; and to Janet & Phil Butler, shining lights.

After *Crosstown Park* sat dormant for a season, waiting for events to unfold, I met and owe a debt of gratitude to the following people: to Rick & Robbi Frishman, who believed in me enough to put me on their stage at Author 101 University, which led directly to the publication of this book; to Terry Whalin, my fictions acquisition editor, for being the "angel" I have been waiting to meet for so long, who put me together with the perfect publisher, Koehler Books, who shares my values and understands my mission to communicate; to David Hancock, an innovative publisher and owner of Morgan James Publishing who truly cares about public service and helping authors reach their full potential; to John Koehler and Joe Coccaro, Koehler Books, my publisher and editor who rock 'n rolled me to the finish line with their insight, creativity and spirit-filled patience; to all the folks at Koehler Books and Morgan James Publishing who helped put the book together and get it out the door; to the MJ/Author 101 and Jack Canfield "families" for their never-ending worldwide network of love and support; to the Houston Writers Guild; to CK Brown, for her belief and enthusiasm; to Cynthia Sharp, a wise friend and coach; and to Larry Veitch, the Canadian who talked me through the homestretches.

The author also thanks and acknowledges the many judges (you know who you are), friends and supporters who helped make this book possible and the many prayers it took to bring it to fruition. And, to the readers, who I hope will connect with the characters and the story and that in some small way it might contribute to your quest for happiness. Books bring me happiness-they always have and they always will. It is my honor to share a story I love with you. And, I hope there are many more to come.

CPSIA information can be obtained at www.ICGtesting.com
Printed in the USA
LVOW05s1140180913

353017LV00002B/2/P

Three Secrets

to **HOLINESS** in

Marriage

"Dan and Amber have done something irresistible—making a holy marriage look like something not only possible but attractive as well. This book is easy to read, thought-provoking, and fun. Using great examples and plenty of wit, they help boil down timeless wisdom into practical insights. I heartily recommend this book!"

Rev. Nathan Cromly, C.S.J.
Founder of Eagle Eye Ministries and the St. John Institute

"We were challenged, humbled, and encouraged by Dan and Amber's insights as we embarked on this retreat, an experience that has been part of a pivotal healing in our sacrament."

Mark Ficocelli and Elizabeth Ficocelli
Catholic speakers

"Dan and Amber DeMatte have produced a book that has the potential to benefit many marriages. This self-guided retreat can help married couples grow together in holiness by helping them to appreciate how the evangelical counsels pertain to their vocation as Christian spouses."

Perry J. Cahall
Academic Dean of Theology
Pontifical College Josephinum

"This book is so important because it allows Catholic couples to enrich their marriage in the privacy of their own home. While we still need outside retreats, conferences, and date nights, resources such as *Three Secrets to Holiness in Marriage* are also must-have tools for any married couple wanting to get closer to God and each other."

Teresa Tomeo
Syndicated Catholic radio host and coauthor of *Intimate Graces*

"This book is a beautiful and deeply personal invitation to discover a deeper level in your marriage. Dan and Amber have done a marvelous job of being real and personal in a way that can help us all."

Dr. Allen Hunt
Senior Advisor
Dynamic Catholic Institute

Three Secrets to **HOLINESS** in Marriage

A 33-Day Self-Guided Retreat for Catholic Couples

DAN *AND* AMBER DEMATTE

AVE MARIA PRESS AVE Notre Dame, Indiana

Unless otherwise noted scripture texts in this work are taken from the *New American Bible, revised edition,* © 2010, 1991, 1986, 1970 Confraternity of Christian Doctrine, Washington, DC, and are used by permission of the copyright owner. All Rights Reserved. No part of the *New American Bible* may be reproduced in any form without permission in writing from the copyright owner.

© 2018 by Dan DeMatte and Amber DeMatte

All rights reserved. No part of this book may be used or reproduced in any manner whatsoever, except in the case of reprints in the context of reviews, without written permission from Ave Maria Press®, Inc., P.O. Box 428, Notre Dame, IN 46556, 1-800-282-1865.

Founded in 1865, Ave Maria Press is a ministry of the United States Province of Holy Cross.

www.avemariapress.com

Paperback: ISBN-13 978-1-59471-799-4

E-book: ISBN-13 978-1-59471-800-7

Cover image © Newton Daly/gettyimages.com.

Cover design by K. H. Bonelli.

Text design by Christopher D. Tobin.

Printed and bound in the United States of America

Library of Congress Cataloging-in-Publication Data is available.

Special thanks to:
Jesus, our fount of love, who has lavished his blessings
upon our marriage and family.
All our family and friends for always pushing us to be saints.
Fr. Oxley and Dr. Perry Cahall at the Pontifical College
Josephinum for inspiring and editing this work.

For this reason I kneel before the Father, from whom every family in heaven and on earth is named, that he may grant you in accord with the riches of his glory to be strengthened with power through his Spirit in the inner self, and that Christ may dwell in your hearts through faith; that you, rooted and grounded in love, may have strength to comprehend with all the holy ones what is the breadth and length and height and depth, and to know the love of Christ that surpasses knowledge, so that you may be filled with the fullness of God. Now to him who is able to accomplish far more than all we ask or imagine, by the power at work within us, to him be glory in the church and in Christ Jesus to all generations, forever and ever. Amen.

—Ephesians 3:14–21

CONTENTS

The First Three Days

PREPARATION FOR YOUR RETREAT

DAY 1

YOUR MARRIAGE MATTERS

We are head chefs, waitstaff, bussers, and dishwashers. We are chauffeurs, coaches, cheerleaders, and referees. We are wipers of countertops, poopy bottoms, snotty noses, and sticky fingers. We are teachers, principals, librarians, and janitors. We are doctors and boo-boo kissers. To our spouses, in addition to all the above, we are lover, friend, teammate, and advisor. Despite all the important roles we play as parents and spouses, how often do we find ourselves asking, "Does this matter? Do my marriage and all the sacrifices I make to raise a family really even matter?"

You will never receive the Nobel Peace Prize for raising toddlers or talking your teenage daughter through her emotional crisis, even though you deserve one. You won't be thanked enough, and you will probably place more blame upon yourself for difficulties than you deserve. But at the end of the day, we want you to know one thing: Your marriage matters. It really, really matters. And so does your yes. Day after day, your yes matters—your yes to love, your yes to your spouse, your yes to your children, your yes to Jesus. It matters so much. We want to start this retreat by letting you know the full impact of your yes.

Never before in human history have the stakes been so high. It's not hard to see that our culture has rejected God's plan for human sexuality and marriage. St. John Paul II said, "As the family goes, so goes the nation, and so goes the whole world."[1] If marriage and family crumble in America, so will America crumble. If we see a global collapse of marriage and family, we will also see a global collapse of human civilization as we know it. How can John Paul II say this? Simple. If you look back through human history, many great empires and nations have fallen apart and crumbled. Do you know what all these empires have in common? Before their collapse, they all exhibited two things: first, there was a general breakdown of respect for innocent human life; and second, there was a general breakdown of marriage and family within that civilization. When these breakdowns occur, nations crumble. In our modern world, we are witnessing these two things not just on a national level but also on a global scale like never before.

Never before in human history has the world seen such a massive massacre of innocent human life. Every day 125,000 children are killed through abortion. This amounts to forty-six million children every year. As a result, there is so much pain, so much suffering, so much hurt.

Why is this massacre taking place? There are many complicated and terribly sad reasons why a person would choose to have an abortion. But, for the most part, women in crisis don't have families they can turn to for support, encouragement, and love. We have been brought up by a secular culture that promotes relativism, materialism, and individualism instead of in a family of life and love.

Do you see it? Do you see the ever-increasing dictatorship of moral relativism where people have rejected objective moral truths and have bought into the lie that they can pick and choose for themselves what is right and wrong? Do you see the ever-increasing materialism where people live more and more for the treasures of this world and forget about the treasures of heaven? Do you see the ever-increasing individualism where the modern person acts and lives as if they are on an island and their choices don't impact the rest of human civilization?

As we mentioned earlier, St. John Paul II said, "As the family goes, so goes the nation, and so goes the whole world." Never before in human history has the world faced such a massive worldwide breakdown of marriage and family life. More and more we see broken homes, broken marriages, and broken hearts. This brokenness leads to more isolation, pain, and selfishness. The family is the classroom of love. The family teaches us that we are not islands, that life is meant to be interwoven in relationship with others, and those relationships make all of us better. But is this lesson still being taught?

These days many young couples have a tangible fear of getting married, or worse, they simply have no desire to get married. With divorce ever increasing in our culture, many young adults today don't want to relive the nightmare of divorce that they endured as children. Reflective of this, many young people postpone marriage and family life later and later. A recent NBC News poll estimates that 75 percent of women live with a man who isn't their spouse before the age of thirty. The poll concluded by suggesting, "The question becomes not who cohabits, but who doesn't?"[2]

We dare to say that if only we knew and embraced a proper understanding of marriage and family, none of this would be present, or at least a lot less of it. *Gaudium et Spes* at the Second Vatican Council remarked: "The well-being of the individual person and of human and Christian society is intimately linked with the healthy condition of that community produced by marriage and family" (*Gaudium et Spes*, 47).

We all find ourselves at a time in the Church when there is not only a desperate need to emphasize the importance and dignity of marriage and family life but also a desperate need for us to be a light in the darkness of American culture by displaying God's plan for the family. This is precisely why your marriage matters and why we have prepared this retreat for your marriage. The more our families can become what God has created them to be, the more we will be able to usher in the kingdom of God and overthrow the kingdom of darkness. The more we strengthen our own marriages and families, the more we will become a beacon of light for the world.

Your marriage matters. Your family matters. Not just for your good, but for the good of all. Today, Jesus needs your yes. The world needs your yes.

The fact that you chose to pick up this book shows that you see marriage and family life as important. But the reality is, for many of us, we are *surviving* instead of *thriving*. In simply trying to keep up with the speed of life, it's easy to let what is most important to us fall apart and for us to start seeking sanity instead of sanctity. This self-guided retreat is designed to energize you to continue on the path that your heart desires—the path of holiness and happiness, the path of a long and fruitful marriage.

Let's not become desensitized to just how high the stakes are right now in the twenty-first century. As the culture moves further and further away from God's plan for marriage and family life, it's easy for us to be deceived and slowly become complacent because maybe "we're doing better than most other couples we see." Well, Jesus says that the "thief comes only to steal and slaughter and destroy; I came so that they might have life and have it more abundantly" (Jn 10:10). The evil one desires to steal, slaughter, and destroy God's plan for your marriage, your family, and your children, but Jesus has come so you might have life and have it to the fullest. Jesus wants your family to be fully alive.

Is your family fully alive? Is your marriage dedicated to pursuing holiness and happiness? Are you raising your children in such a way that they are pursuing the treasures of heaven or the treasures of this world? Are you living the life Jesus wants you all to live?

We don't know about you, but we want to be fully alive. We want our marriage and our family to be everything God created it to be. We don't want to survive—we want to thrive. We don't want to settle for a counterfeit version of marriage and family. We want to live for everything God has in store for our family.

St. John Paul II talked about how important your role is as a married couple and how high the stakes really are when he said, "How indispensable is the witness of all families who live their vocation day by day" because "only if the truth about the communion of persons in marriage and the family can regain its splendor, will the building of the civilization of love truly begin."[3]

Everything we do impacts the world around us. Your vocation, your marriage, can have a tremendous impact. Your marriage matters. It matters not just to you and your spouse, not just to your kids; it matters to the good of human civilization. Your marriage matters to God. We are convinced that the restoration of culture doesn't rely on strong political leaders or governmental agencies but rather on strong marriages and families. Do you want to change the world? Then win marriage.

This is a thirty-three-day retreat. In that time period, many distractions will come up. There will be nights when you and your spouse don't want to go on because you are tired. Let this retreat be the beginning of a marriage in which you push through the tired, the beginning of a love that gives more when you feel you have nothing left to give, a romance of perseverance and dedication through difficulty. Pick up your crosses and let's head for the resurrection, together.

Today's Couple Discussion Questions

1. How are we living the full and abundant life right now? In what areas of our lives, marriage, and family do we want more?
2. In what areas of our marriage might we be surviving instead of thriving?
3. In what ways have we given Jesus all our lives? In what ways have we given Jesus just pockets of our lives?
4. How committed will we be to these thirty-three days? Have we selected a time and a place to take this retreat so as to set aside time each day for the glory of God and the good of our marriage?

Today's Couple Prayer

Holy Spirit, open our eyes to see. You have joined us together for a purpose. You have anointed us through the sacrament of Marriage to be on a mission for you in this world and to be happy with you forever in the next. The work of our marriage and family life is holy. We are anointed for this work, and this work matters to the world. We open our hearts to receive empowerment through the Holy Spirit to complete this work well and to complete it to the finish! Day by day let us see more and more how our love is transforming the culture, how necessary we are. Bless this love, Lord. Help us to be a light in the darkness, a hope for the nations. Amen.

DAY 2

YOU MAY KISS THE CROSS

There is a beautiful tradition among Croatian Catholics on their wedding day. In the Croatian town of Siroki Brijeg (about twenty-five miles from Medjugorje), not one single divorce has been recorded among its thirteen thousand Catholics in more than fifty years. That's right—not one single family has broken up in the living memory of anyone in the town. What? Is that really possible? How can an entire town be preserved from divorce?

Their "secret" to marital happiness is no secret at all. They simply have embraced the true meaning of marriage and rejected the lies of the culture. The secret is very simple: These Croatian Catholics know that authentic love comes through the Cross of Christ. When a couple is preparing for marriage, they go to the church and meet with their priest. They are not told that they have found their soul mate or the person of their dreams. What does the priest say? "You have found your lifelong cross. And it's a cross to be loved, to be carried, a cross not to be thrown away but to be cherished."

In Siroki Brijeg, the Cross represents the greatest love known to humankind, and thus the crucifix becomes the treasure of marriage and the heart of the home. When the bride and groom set off for the church to be wed, they bring a crucifix with them. The priest then blesses the crucifix, and during the exchange of vows the bride places her right hand on the crucifix and the groom places his hand over hers. The two hands are bound together on the cross. The priest covers their hands with his stole as they proclaim their vows. After their vows, the priest proclaims, "You may now kiss the cross." The bride and groom then kiss the crucified Lord as their first sign of marital love. They know that they are kissing the source of love, and that true love always entails death to self.

After their wedding ceremony, the newlyweds bring the crucifix to their new home together and give it a place of prominence and honor. It becomes the focal point of family prayer, for the family is born out of the self-giving and life-giving love of the couple just as the Church is born out of the self-giving and life-giving love of the Cross. When trouble arises or if a conflict breaks out, the couple seeks help before this cross. "For we do not have a high priest who is unable to sympathize with our weaknesses, but one who has similarly been tested in every way, yet without sin. So let us confidently approach the throne of grace to receive mercy and to find grace for timely help" (Heb 4:15–16). Before the cross, they find the strength to love just as he first loved us.

If you haven't figured it out already, marriage is messy. Along with all the incredible joy and beauty of marital love, we as married couples suffer through the difficulties and trials of everyday life, and we suffer through the messiness of selfishness and sin. Literally, just as Jesus did upon the Cross, we take upon ourselves the sins of our spouse. We suffer through their shortcomings, and they suffer through ours. Marriage is messy—and so was the Cross.

Often we fear that if our marriage isn't perfect, and if there is difficulty and struggle, then there must be something wrong with our marriage. But the opposite is true. It's through the Cross that redemption comes. It's precisely the difficulties and the struggles, the daily grind of life, that makes marriage so beautifully holy. Through marriage we are blessed to enter into the Paschal Mystery of Jesus—his own Passion, Death, and Resurrection. Not only is it normal if your marriage has brokenness, but it's also an opportunity for holiness, for it's in the brokenness of the Cross where we find life. If your marriage is a struggle, nothing is wrong with you or your marriage. These difficulties are the result of the wounds that Jesus brings to the surface so that he may sanctify and heal you. Remember, there is no Resurrection without the Cross.

In our own marriage, we have often asked ourselves, "How is it possible that two imperfect people could strive for perfect love?" That is the beauty of this retreat. This retreat will challenge you and call you to embrace the perfect love that Jesus calls all of us to in the sacrament of Marriage, but it does so coming from a strong understanding that we are imperfect people in desperate need of Jesus. We haven't written this retreat from the mountaintop of perfection, telling you to climb the mountain as we have. We have written this retreat as fellow climbers, striving to reach the summit of perfect love, knowing that the climb will be long and difficult but will come with great reward in the end. We want to climb with you. We hope you want to climb with us. In marriage we can't rely on our own human strength. Temptation and difficulty enter into every marriage in one way or another. In order to discover the fullness of the Father's plan, we must cling to the Cross; we must cling to Jesus. At the heart of the sacrament of Marriage lies the daily dose of marital grace that Jesus wants to pour out upon you.

Amber:

As a little girl growing up with fairy-tale ideals, I often viewed marriage as a destination instead of a journey. Marriage would be my happy ending. I thought I would simply find my prince; he provides a castle, and voila, I've made it!

Daniel and I were truly head over heels, in full ooey-gooey emotional love while we were dating and engaged. Both of us are very idealistic and romantic at heart, so we had our perfect life and our perfect love all figured out. After all, we both took Christian Marriage and Theology of the Body classes in college and aced them! Certainly we would ace marriage, too. You guessed it, I was going to be the perfect wife, and Dan was going to be the perfect husband—until we got married.

When I woke up and realized I was married with four children under the age of six and I wasn't living the idealistic, romanticized version of marriage that I believed I would, I found myself in deep despair. I cried myself to sleep many nights, so disappointed for failing at the only thing I'd ever wanted to do. I wanted to be perfect. I wanted to do this thing right. It took me almost a decade to realize I was chasing perfection for perfection's sake. Sure, it was laced with love for my babies and my husband. But the root of my drive was pride. I wanted to prove my worth to myself, to my family, to the world. Pride is funny; it tells you opposing lies, and you believe them. It simultaneously tells you that you are "better than" and "not enough." If I couldn't be perfect in every way, I told myself, if I wasn't the ideal mother, then I was a failure at motherhood. If I wasn't the picture-perfect bride, I was a failure at marriage.

Please listen to us, dear friends. Marriage is a journey, not a destination. As we sojourn together, we come as imperfect pilgrims. The struggle, the climb—we can't run from it, for it's precisely what is strengthening and perfecting us. You have found your cross, not your castle. Our castle, our happily-ever-after, is real and it awaits us. There will come a time when every tear is wiped from our eyes, and there is no more sorrow (Rv 21:4). But those tears and sorrows of yesterday and today are not trash that will be thrown away. If we allow them, those tears can cleanse our souls, washing away the selfishness, pride, and lies. Those sorrows can strengthen our faith and our shoulders to carry all that God has for us and to become the great saints he has created us to become. This journey isn't easy, but it's good. It's so, so good. When we set aside our desire to be perfect for perfection's sake, for pride's sake, for the sake of ease and comfort, we will find *true* joy and lasting love. Jesus calls imperfect people to strive for perfect love.

"The message of the cross is foolishness to those who are perishing, but to us who are being saved it is the power of God" (1 Cor 1:18).

You must stop running from the cross. You don't have to chase anything. The Lord himself has called you and given you the cross that will lead to your salvation—to joy and fulfillment not only in heaven but also here. Turn around and choose to pick up those crosses. Pick them up by your own choice and with love. As Fr. Jean C. J. d'Elbée writes in *I Believe in Love*, "Without love, everything is painful, everything is tiring, everything is burdensome. The cross, taken up hesitantly, is crushing. But, taken up smilingly, and by free will, and with love, the cross will carry you, much more than you will carry it."[4]

Trust the Cross. Trust our Jesus. He is the *only* way, the *only* truth, the *only* life. Together we will fall in love with the Cross over the next thirty-three days. We will fall more deeply in love with Jesus. We will fall deeper in love with our spouses, our children, and the world Christ has called us to serve together. Are you ready?

On our wedding day, we embraced the Croatian tradition. The crucifix has become the focal point of our house and in a world that has so many counterfeit portrayals of what love is. We use the crucifix to teach our children the real meaning of authentic love. Love isn't a fleeting emotion or an uncontrollable desire. Love is a sincere gift of self, a lesson taught upon the Cross. Just as we kissed the cross on the day we pledged our lives together, each night after family prayer our children kiss the cross, praying, "Jesus, I love you. Jesus, teach me how to love."

We invite you to take on this tradition in your family. Kiss the crucifix nightly with your family. If you don't have a crucifix, purchase one sometime this week. The words contained in this self-guided retreat are our simple reflections on perfect love from an imperfect married couple. In the classroom of this prayerful retreat, Christ the teacher will teach you more about love than could be contained in all the books of the world. Learn from him. Love like him. "Jesus, I love you. Jesus, teach me how to love."

Today's Couple Discussion Questions

1. What are the heaviest crosses we carry in our marriage? What are the heaviest crosses we carry in our family life?
2. Where is there beauty in the crosses in our family life?
3. What brings us the greatest joy in our marriage? What brings us the greatest joy in our family life?

Today's Couple Prayer

Lord Jesus, today we unite our cross with yours. As we journey through life on our own way of the cross, be our strength and our salvation. In the name of Jesus, we surrender the cross we carry. We abandon our lives into your hands. Amen.

With your spouse, find a crucifix and, placing your hands upon it, renew your vows in the quiet of your home:

Husband prays:

"I, _____, take you, _____, to be my wife, to have and to hold from this day forward, for better, for worse, for richer, for poorer, in sickness and in health, until death do us part."

Wife prays:

"I, _____, take you, _____, for my husband, to have and to hold from this day forward, for better, for worse, for richer, for poorer, in sickness and in health, until death do us part."

Now, having renewed your vows, you may kiss the cross.

"BEHOLD, I MAKE ALL THINGS NEW" (RV 21:5)

Yesterday we reflected on the Cross, and today we reflect on the Resurrection.

Marriage is filled with many, many crosses. Sometimes we feel as if our marriage and family life are the most difficult, demanding, and unpleasing things we could ever take part in. At the same time, there are moments when our lives are so full of joy and love that we feel as if our hearts could burst with joy. Through all the sufferings and "deaths to self" of marriage and family life come a life of resurrected joy and happiness. From death comes life—it seems like an unexplainable oxymoron, but for those of us who have experienced it, we know it's true.

While we all face difficulties in life, in our hearts we have an innate understanding that we were created for glorious freedom. How can we be called to accept and endure suffering, and simultaneously be made for greatness and glory? Jesus Christ wants to bring you freedom. He wants to heal you and your spouse from your brokenness and woundedness. Jesus wants you to walk in the freedom of his Resurrection. And he wants you to do so together.

Jesus Christ died for you. When we tell you that, if you are like most people, the news rolls right off your back because you have been blessed to hear it *so* many times before. But while you have heard it before, have you received it? Have you understood the depth and magnitude of these words? Perhaps in the past, when you have heard this Good News, you have heard it like this: "Jesus died for everyone." That's true. But we need to wrap our minds around the fact that Jesus didn't just die for everyone. He died for every single one. "Jesus died for me." Stop right now, close your eyes, and say that out loud: "Jesus died for me." Jesus died for you, a sinner. He didn't wait for you to ask, to be perfect, to be ready, or even to be wanting. No, "while we were *still* sinners, Christ died for us" (Rom 5:8, emphasis added).

In the midst of your hurt, lack of self-control, gluttony, laziness, selfishness, and all the rest, Jesus died for you. Why? Because scripture tells us, "All have sinned and are deprived of the glory of God" (Rom 3:23). However, Jesus, the Son of God, the Word made flesh, God made human, took up your cross and died your death. He paid your wage, and you are free indeed because of what he has already done for you.

Before our first parents sinned, there was no woundedness, broken-ness, sorrow, or sadness; no stain or wrinkle, fear or anxiety, depression or self-hatred. Before the Fall of man, there was no death. Jesus Christ came to restore a broken humanity, to give us a new life. "So whoever is in Christ is a new creation: the old things have passed away; behold, new things have come" (2 Cor 5:17).

When Jesus carried the weight of the Cross, he carried the weight of all our pain, suffering, hardship, feelings of rejection and inadequacies, fear, anxieties, depression, brokenness, burdens, and stress. He carried all of this. And when he died, all of this died with him. It was crucified with him upon the Cross of Calvary.

Jesus so desperately wants to set you free from all the death that is within you and to give you a share in his own divine life! He is a healer, a deliverer, a redeemer. He brings the dead to life. He brings freedom to the captive and recovery of sight to the blind. He heals the brokenhearted. Hear this Good News—you can stop beating yourself up, for he has already taken the blows for your sake. "By his wounds we were healed" (Is 53:5). It's time to rise and walk in the freedom and victory that Christ has won for us.

Jesus didn't just die for us; he rose for us. Do you believe that? He rose triumphant from the grave for us to know and believe that he has the power over sin and death, fear and anxiety, sadness and depression, self-hatred and our wounds of the past. Jesus rose victorious over our sins, addiction, and pain. Christ sets us free from slavery to sin and death and from all the strongholds that death has on us. Jesus Christ brings us *freedom*.

"Death is swallowed up in victory. Where, O death, is your victory? Where, O death, is your sting? The sting of death is sin, and the power of sin is the law. But thanks be to God who gives us the victory through our Lord Jesus Christ. Therefore, my beloved brothers [and sisters], be firm, steadfast, always fully devoted to the work of the Lord, knowing that in the Lord your labor is not in vain" (1 Cor 15:54–58).

In ministering to married couples, we have found that of the crosses we carry into marriage, our personal woundedness is the heaviest. Many of us enter into marriage with wounds from before we even met our spouse, wounds from our childhood that we have been carrying with us our entire lives. Many spouses carry wounds of insecurity, feeling as though they will never be enough and can't succeed, often blaming themselves for everything and turning within themselves instead of turning to a Father who loves them. Many more carry wounds from their own mothers or fathers, feeling as though their worthiness is found in what they do as opposed to who they are, often trying to prove themselves by getting the next promotion or buying the new car instead of seeing themselves as beloved children of God. The worst thing about wounds is that they usually are not something we have chosen but rather the result of something that someone did or said to us as children. Our wounds are often inflicted on us like the Cross was placed on Jesus' shoulders, and we carry them with us.

Today we want to bring our wounds to the surface and allow Jesus to heal them. "Behold, I make all things new" (Rv 21:5).

Jesus wants to heal your wounds. Many of us try to bury them and forget about them, but today Jesus wants to "open the tomb" so that you can be set free from these wounds and experience the freedom and joy of the Resurrection.

We invite you as a couple to enter into an examination of your own hearts. Spend time asking yourself and each other where there are wounds, and after opening the tomb and exposing the dead life within you, pray with each other for freedom and joy. As you read through this examination of wounds, write down or mark in your book which wounds afflict your heart. We have started a list below. Use our list, or if the Holy Spirit brings things to light that are not written here, add them. Add all of them and leave nothing in the tomb. It's resurrection time. We will be praying specifically into each area in the next step.

Before you begin, make the Sign of the Cross and take a deep breath. Allow your hearts to enter into Christ's peace. Invite the Holy Spirit to come and reveal what has been hidden. We can do nothing apart from the Holy Spirit. He is the comforter, the healer, and the power of God.

Come, Holy Spirit. Reveal to us the wounds of our hearts. Reveal the death that dwells within us. Expose the darkness, that it may be turned into light.

Lack of Forgiveness

Is there anyone in your life you have yet to forgive? Anyone from your childhood or adult life who has wounded you and still causes you to cling to resentment?

Is there any reason you need to forgive yourself?

Feeling Neglected or Ignored

Was there a time in your life when you felt neglected or ignored?
Are you feeling neglected or ignored right now in your life?

Conditional Love

Are there wounds from your past where you felt as if you had to earn love and that you were not enough?

Do you feel as if you are at risk of losing your spouse's love?

Abusive Past

Were you ever physically, sexually, or verbally abused?
Have you hidden this abuse and not allowed it to be healed?

Fears and Anxiety

Do you have fear or anxiety that negatively impacts your ability to love and invest in your family?

Do you have fear or anxiety that keeps you back from becoming the person God is asking you to be?

Sadness and Depression

Do you experience intense times of hopelessness and despair?

Does your sadness make it difficult to invest in your spouse or family?

Anger, Frustration, and Impatience

Often these can be generational wounds that are passed down through families. Was there anger in your family that was conditioned in you?

Do you hold your feelings in, causing resentment and outbursts of anger?

Perfectionistic Tendencies

Do you place unfair expectations upon yourself and refuse to have mercy on yourself for your shortcomings?

Do you place unfair expectations on your spouse and/or your children and refuse to have mercy on them for their shortcomings?

Escapism

Do you avoid conflict and difficult situations?

Are you afraid to let your spouse or others into your heart?

Do you escape from difficult situations by leaving the house, turning to media, or escaping into your phone?

Addictions

Escapism often leads to addictions. Are you forming an addiction or do you have an addiction to drinking, shopping, overeating, television, streaming, or pornography?

Today's Couple Discussion Questions

1. What are we each experiencing right now?

2. How can we support each other as we continue our journey through this retreat?

Today's Couple Prayer

Taking the hands of your spouse, each spouse should pray the renunciations below, praying for personal healing.

I n the name of Jesus, I forgive (*insert one name*) for (*insert the action done by this person*), and I call upon your love to flood my heart.

Repeat this simple prayer for as many people as you need to forgive.

In the name of Jesus, heal the wound of (*insert one wound*). Fill me with (*ask for whatever grace you want to be filled with to heal this wound in your life*).

Repeat this simple prayer for as many wounds you seek freedom from.

Week 1

THE MISSION AND THE CALL

DAY 4

THE MISSION OF MARRIAGE AND FAMILY LIFE

When we are speaking to large groups of adults at conferences or retreats, we will often ask this very simple question: "What is the mission of marriage and family life?" It's often amazing how few hands go up to answer the question. We often get vague answers such as "the mission is to be happy" or "the mission is to love each other."

In our mission we find our purpose and our goal. If we don't know the mission of marriage and family life, we don't know the purpose of marriage or the goal of marriage, and ultimately we don't know how to live as a married couple and as a family.

The mission of marriage is so important that the Church refers to marriage as one of the two sacraments of Mission. The first sacrament of Mission is Holy Orders, the ordination to the holy priesthood. It's easy to see how ordination would be a sacrament of Mission because the priesthood is directed toward service to others and leading them to salvation in and through Jesus. But the *Catechism of the Catholic Church* explains that marriage is a sacrament of Mission because it, too, is directed toward service to others and leading them to salvation in and through Jesus (see *CCC*, 1534).

Very simply put, the *Catechism* describes marriage as a vehicle for helping others get to heaven. To put it another way, the mission of marriage is that the married couple and all their children become saints.

We know what you are thinking: "Me, a saint? Ha! Yeah, right!"

Unfortunately that is what a lot of people think. When most people hear the word *saint*, they immediately think of Mother Teresa caring for those in leper colonies or dying in the streets covered with maggots. Or perhaps they think of St. Francis wearing rags and walking around the streets begging for food. Maybe they think of Padre Pio and his stigmata and his ability to read souls. When our view of sainthood is reduced to thinking of these godly superstars, we often end up with a misconception of sainthood. A saint is anyone who spends eternity with Jesus in heaven. Countless saints robed white in splendor lived simple, quiet lives of extraordinary holiness through the ordinary.

Often the world can distract us from our mission in marriage. We become wrapped up in building our own comfort kingdom. We set a standard of being nothing more than good, upstanding citizens raising nice, successful children and giving them a nice home in which to lay their heads at night. We spend all our time making ourselves comfortable and happy, and dealing with all the busy things on our to-do lists and our children's to-do lists. Our faith gets pushed to the corner. It's there . . . it's on the priority list, but it's not *the* priority. Then we find ourselves lost, without purpose, asking constantly, "Why do I feel empty?" or "What's the point?"

Every person has two choices: to live a saintly life, walking the "narrow path" of the Gospel and choosing heaven; or to live a distracted life of complacency, walking the "wide and easy" road and, as a result, finding that we have absentmindedly rejected God, his goodness, and his kingdom and finding ourselves in hell. Scripture speaks the words of the Lord during the last judgment: "I know your works; I know that you are neither cold nor hot. I wish you were either cold or hot. So, because you are lukewarm, neither cold or hot, I will spit you out of my mouth" (Rv 3:15–16). That isn't what any of us are going for, is it?

Yet far too many Christian married couples have become lukewarm and complacent. Sure, you are not called to live like Mother Teresa or Padre Pio, but you are called to be a saint and to raise a family of saints nonetheless. God the Father created you on purpose, with a purpose. As a Christian, you are not called merely to blend in with the culture. You are made to be the light of the world and the salt of the earth. You have been endowed with unique gifts and talents for this time and place. You have been created and sent. The two of you together have been called as a team.

Jesus calls all his disciples to live lives of radical holiness. In Matthew 7:13–14, Jesus says that we are to "enter through the narrow gate; for the gate is wide and the road broad that leads to destruction, and those who enter through it are many. How narrow the gate and constricted the road that leads to life. And those who find it are few."

Will you go in deep with us for just a moment? Trust Jesus, whose plan for our lives is freedom and joy. Listen close and really think about this. If few find the narrow road, wouldn't it seem that if we are the ones who are on the narrow road, our lives should look radically different from those of the rest of the world? People should be able to look at our marriages and family life and say, "Wow! These people are different. They live for heaven and not for this world." That is what this retreat is aimed to teach you. It will teach you how to live your mission, how to live for heaven and not for this world. We emphasize this because our measure for whether we are adequately living Christianity can no longer be contemporary culture or even other Christians. Our measure must be Christ himself.

So we are going to be up-front with you. This book, this thirty-three-day retreat, is going to challenge you. It's going to require that you honestly step back and examine whether your life together as a married couple is in line with the radical call to holiness that Christ proposes in the Gospel. Some of the things we present will make you uncomfortable, and that is okay because we don't desire your comfort. All we desire is your holiness. We desire that you and your family will be in heaven someday. We want to help you become saints. This book is meant to make you better, and in order to become better sometimes things in our lives need to change.

Today's Couple Discussion Questions

1. If eternity with God is the goal of our family, what are we doing as a family to approach this end?

2. What do we personally need to modify in our individual lives in order to reach the goal of heaven?

3. What do we as a team need to modify in our marriage or family life in order to reach the goal of heaven? Have work, sports, or hobbies become a priority over Christ?

Today's Couple Prayer

Lord Jesus Christ, have mercy on our sinful hearts. The call you have for us is great, but how often do we seek comfort over greatness? Wash us clean of complacent and lukewarm living, and fill us with the fire of the Holy Spirit. Today we declare that you are the Lord of our lives and the Lord of our marriage and family. We give our lives over to you, for the rest of our lives. Amen.

WHAT IS GOD'S WILL FOR MY LIFE?

We hear people ask this question often and, honestly, we think they over-complicate it. The answer is quite simple. What does God desire for your life and your marriage? As St. Paul tells the Thessalonians, "This is the will of God, your holiness" (1 Thes 4:3). God desires for you to be holy (see *Lumen Gentium*, 39).

Vatican II reaffirmed the words of St. Paul to the Thessalonians when the Council Fathers wrote, "All in the Church, whether they belong to the hierarchy or are cared for by it, are called to holiness" (*Lumen Gentium*, 39).

This universal call to holiness came in response to the prevailing public opinion that holiness was somehow a call only for priests who were consecrated to God through Holy Orders and for religious sisters or brothers who were consecrated to God through the vows of poverty, chastity, and obedience. But *all* are called to radical holiness according to their state in life because through the waters of Baptism all are con-secrated to God. So whether one is a priest or a husband, he is called to saintly holiness. Whether one is a mother or a spiritual sister, she is called to saintly holiness. "All of Christ's followers are invited and bound to pursue holiness and the perfect fulfillment of their own state of life" (*Lumen Genium*, 42).

We are all called to holiness. Radical Gospel living and apostolic holiness isn't something just for priests or the religious. Holiness is for everyone. Holiness is for married couples, families, children. And yes, holiness is even for teenagers! All in the Church are called to holiness. But we are also all called to holiness according to our state in life. Of course, holiness in marriage is different from holiness in the priesthood. It's different from holiness in religious life. Also, holiness for a mom and dad will look different from holiness for a son and daughter. It's different, but it's nonetheless a common call.

Before we got married we had a romanticized vision of what the perfect marriage would look like and how we would raise perfect little saints. Holiness would be easy for us because we knew and loved Jesus. How we pitied those who had let the fire of the Holy Spirit die within them as they busied themselves with carpools and PTA. Well, God blessed us immediately with a baby so that we would put *all* that holiness and perfection of ours to good use.

We were elated. Amber's womb held an eternal soul that God created and entrusted to *us*. We just knew that we were going to be *awesome* parents. Boy oh boy, was this kid lucky or what!

Then came the morning—actually, all-day, debilitating, can't-keep-a-sip-of-water-down—sickness. Our "holy hours" were kept by the toilet, and Amber was on bed rest with an IV attached to her arm. It was brutal. A grueling pregnancy with extreme sickness wasn't the opportunity for holiness we imagined, but there it was. And then the children came—the first baby, the second baby, the third baby, and yes, the fourth baby—all within about a six-year span. Our lives became consumed with changing diapers, wiping snotty noses, and, of course, enduring many sleepless nights. Then there was the hustle and bustle of married life—work, bills, in-laws, laundry, yard work, and house maintenance—that seemed unending.

Then there was the holy Mass on the "day of rest"—or should we say World War III? Keeping our "spirited" children quiet and peaceful during Mass was about as easy as taming wild boars. Mass went from an intimate time of prayer with Jesus to what often felt like one of the most difficult and trying parts of the week.

If parenthood for you has been a time of ease and comfort, and you are simply floating on a cloud of cotton-candy dreams, we applaud you! But for the rest of you, we hope you find comfort in knowing you are not alone. Please don't believe for one second that we don't adore our children and these precious "little years." But things *change* when you become parents, and change is difficult.

One of the biggest and most surprising changes for us was in how we carried out our relationship with Jesus. Our goal in marriage from the get-go was to be holy and serve God. But how could we be holy when our lives were so busy?

Dan

I wrestled with the Lord in prayer for years, asking him how holiness was possible in marriage when marriage seemed so worldly: filled with changing diapers, cooking dinners, cutting grass, going to work, and running errands. I discovered over the years that holiness in marriage is possible, and it's not a watered-down mediocre form of holiness but rather a radical, saintly holiness. I discovered something even deeper than this: holiness is possible not in spite of marriage and family life but precisely because of marriage and family life.

I struggled so much at the beginning of our marriage because I realized I had an improper view of holiness. I saw holiness as boxes to check off on a to-do list. If I went to daily Mass and I spent time in daily prayer, if I prayed enough Rosaries and attended enough holy hours, then I would be holy. I also confused holiness with the way I felt. I imagined peacefully passing through the distress that "other" people seemed to experience. We can do all things in Christ, right? Sure, but in my mind that was something that would just happen if I kept up with the prayers, the holy hours, and so on. But once the children came, I started to see how impossible this was. As a father, what was the "holier" thing to do: go to Eucharistic adoration after work and leave my wife alone with the babies for another hour, or go home and spend time with my family? I'm not suggesting that we shouldn't go to daily Mass or shouldn't pray a daily Rosary, but rather that holiness, especially within marriage, can't be reduced to a mere to-do list.

I remember an intense conversation Amber and I had one time when we were engaged. Before marriage, Amber and I were in the habit of going to Eucharistic adoration every day and making a holy hour. I asked Amber if she worried that after marriage and children we wouldn't have time for our daily holy hours. Her response amazed me: "When we're married I'll look at our babies and they'll be my monstrance, and I'll adore Jesus in and through them." Wow! These words gave me great pause—and still do. Holiness isn't always about what we do; it's about how we do it.

How are you doing the dishes? Are you doing this chore with love? How are you doing the laundry or cutting the grass? Are you doing these tasks with love? How are you going to work each day or helping your children advance further in their lives? Are you doing it with love? Holiness is so much more than a checklist. It's about taking the ordinary and doing it with extraordinary love. Tomorrow we will look even deeper at what holiness is and how we can live it in marriage, discovering that holiness isn't merely about doing but about becoming.

In one of his most popular books, *No Man Is an Island,* Thomas Merton accurately points out that "the ordinary way to holiness and to the fullness of Christian life is marriage. Most men and women will become saints in the married state."[1] We think there is a lack of formation on the practical implementation for how married couples can and should pursue holiness through their state of life. We hope throughout the course of this retreat and through these three secrets to holiness in marriage you will discover a very real and practical formation on how married couples are called to live radical holiness. Throughout this retreat, we hope to provide a spirituality for married couples who truly desire to be saints and who desire to raise saints.

On this journey we want to open your eyes to the depths of holiness we are called to and to a far deeper plunge into the personhood and humanity of Jesus. In him, and only in him, we will discover how to be holy.

Today's Couple Discussion Questions

1. If holiness isn't about what we do but how we do it, how well are we entering into the "daily grind" of life?

2. As a couple, how are we approaching daily tasks with great love? How can we do this more?

Today's Couple Prayer

Lord Jesus Christ, every word you spoke and every action you performed was spoken and performed with great love. Grant us hearts of incredible love. May we speak like you, live like you, and love like you. Jesus, you are a God of transformation. Transform our ordinary lives into an extraordinary mission. Amen.

WHAT IS HOLINESS ANYWAY?

Okay, so the mission in marriage is to be a saint—we are each called to radical holiness—but what the heck does that mean? What is "holiness" anyway? Embracing the call to holiness can be very difficult for many people to do because the word *holiness* itself seems vague and difficult to understand. Today let's see if we can make this term more concrete.

First and foremost, holiness is a *gift from God*. We can pray for holiness. We can ask God to make us holy, to make our spouse and our children holy, and to make our marriage holy. Fill us, O Lord, with your holiness! Scripture says, "Holy, holy, holy is the Lord God almighty" (Rv 4:8), and "Who will not fear you, Lord, or glorify your name? For you alone are holy" (Rv 15:4). God alone is perfectly holy, and God invites us to share in his perfect holiness. Thus any holiness we obtain is merely sharing in his divine holiness. Ultimately, Christianity is a share in the holiness of God. Sacramental marriage is a unique share in the holiness of God.

In the Old Testament holiness is set apart and separate from that which is profane.[2] Thus God alone is holy because he alone is totally separate from evil. Holiness is also understood to be something or someone that is set apart in order to be dedicated in a special way to God.[3] "Remember the sabbath day—keep it holy" (Ex 20:8). The Sabbath day is holy because it's a consecrated day; it's "set apart" from other days as a day dedicated to God. Throughout the Old Testament we see that objects, places, and people can be holy inasmuch as they are consecrated and dedicated to God. "In reverence I bow down toward your holy temple" (Ps 5:7). To be holy is to be set apart, to be dedicated to God for a particular purpose. So too we read, "You are to be my holy people" (Ex 22:30), and "For you are a people holy to the Lord, your God; the Lord, your God, has chosen you from all the peoples on the face of the earth to be a people specially his own" (Dt 7:6; 14:2). We see in the Old Testament that the Chosen People of God are holy; they are set apart and dedicated to the Lord for a particular purpose.

This basic understanding of holiness applies to us Christians today and must apply to holiness in marriage and family. You were made holy through the sacred waters of Baptism, which consecrates us, sets us apart, and makes each of us a new creation dedicated not to the world but to God. Your children have also been consecrated and set apart through Baptism. In fact, your married relationship has been consecrated and set apart through the sacrament of Marriage. Thus you personally, your marriage, and your family are all called to be set apart.

Please don't let this profound truth pass by you. Are you set apart, or do you conform with the rest of society? Is the way in which your family members live their lives different from the way of those who are not Christian or those who are lukewarm Christians? Is the way you love at work different from that of others? Is it set apart? Is the way you raise your children different from that of other parents? When we get to them, the three secrets to holiness in marriage provide a spirituality of consecration, of being set apart. These three secrets will seem like complete nonsense to some, but to those who desire holiness, to be set apart, and to give and receive love perfectly, these three secrets will become a beacon of life.

There is, however, a limited notion of holiness in the Old Testament. The Pharisees and the Sadducees saw holiness as conforming oneself to the Mosaic law, a list of 613 laws that were nearly impossible to fully conform to because they were so detailed and minute. Those who failed to live by the laws were considered unclean and faced serious alienation or punishment. Many Catholics still reduce our faith to nothing more than conforming to the laws of the Church. But if we do this, we run the risk of becoming Pharisees ourselves. Clearly no one would ever admit to being a Pharisee, but we suggest that the "cultural Catholicism" that we see in so many parishes is nothing more than modern-day Pharisees going to church. It's possible to go to Mass week after week and still not be a Christian. It's possible to follow the teachings of the Church, to pray devotion after devotion, and still not be a Christian. Pope Benedict XVI said, "Being Christian is not the result of an ethical choice or a lofty idea, but the encounter with an event, a person, which gives life a new horizon and a decisive direction."[4] This is what holiness in the New Testament is all about.

We are only Christian if we encounter Christ. When we encounter Jesus Christ, we are changed by him. He transforms our minds and our hearts. Our will becomes his will; our desires become his desires. If we simply go to Mass week after week as though it's nothing more than something we need to check off our to-do list; we have totally missed the mark on holiness. Holiness isn't about *doing*; it's about *becoming*. Holiness is ultimately about becoming the image of Jesus Christ.

We see in the gospels that the Pharisees and the Sadducees saw holiness as conforming oneself to the old law, but in the New Testament Jesus speaks of a transformation of the whole being that leads to a life of obedience. Holiness in the New Testament takes on a dimension of transformation. St. Paul explains this reality clearly to the Corinthians, saying, "So whoever is in Christ is a new creation: the old things have passed away; behold, new things have come" (2 Cor 5:17). The gift of holiness in the sacrament of Baptism brings us into an entirely new kind of life. It's not about actions that conform to a list of rules, but rather it's an altogether new life. In Christ, we are a new creation, entirely different from the old that has passed away. Jesus wants to make you a new creation. Why? So that we can say with St. Paul, "Yet I live, no longer I, but Christ lives in me; insofar as I now live in the flesh, I live by faith in the Son of God who has loved me and has given himself up for me" (Gal 2:20). It's no longer I who lives, but Christ who lives in me—this is holiness. As St. Augustine proclaims, "Let us rejoice and give thanks; we have not only become Christians, but Christ himself. . . . Stand in awe and rejoice, we have become Christ."[5] Amen! Amen! Amen! We want to become another

Christ. We don't want to live our lives; we want to live his life. We don't want to live a natural life; we want to live a supernatural life.

Why do we tell you this? Far too many of us get so bogged down in the worldliness of marriage and family life that we run the risk of not becoming everything that Jesus wants us to be. He wants you to receive new life. He wants you to be radically transformed in and through his love. He desires that you experience a transformation of your mind so that you think and reason as he thinks and reasons. He desires a transformation of your heart so that you love as he loves. He desires a transformation of your will so that your dreams and desires are his dreams and desires. He desires a transformation of your life so that you live as he lives. Holiness is the greatest gift because holiness is truly a radical transformation so that we think like Jesus, love like Jesus, will like Jesus, and live like Jesus.

In and through holiness we become another Christ. But holiness takes on a deeper dimension. In Matthew 5:48, Jesus commands us to "be perfect, just as your heavenly Father is perfect," or as some texts say, to "be holy, as your heavenly Father is holy." If you view holiness as a to-do list filled with human actions and human efforts, then the words of Jesus Christ—"be perfect, just as your heavenly Father is perfect"—may seem like an impossible task and an incredible burden because no one, not even the greatest of saints, can be holy as the heavenly Father is holy. But if one understands holiness as a gift from God, as an invitation to share in his divine life and love, then holiness takes upon itself a new dimension of relationality, of giving and receiving love.

Did you catch that? Jesus wants you to receive his love. He wants you personally to receive the gift of his love. That is why the greatest commandment is to "love the Lord, your God, with all your heart, with all your being, with all your strength, and with all your mind" (Lk 10:27). Receive his love by going to Mass and Confession. Receive his love by entering into daily periods of prayer and contemplation. Receive his love by feasting on the words of sacred scripture. Jesus pours his love out, saying, "This is my body, which will be given for you" (Lk 22:19).

Jesus wants us to receive his love, but he also wants us to give his love. That is why the second greatest commandment is that you shall love "your neighbor as yourself" (Lk 10:27). When our hearts have been transformed by love, we begin to see as Jesus sees, love as Jesus loves, and touch as Jesus touches. Comfort, power, prestige—these things are no longer what drive our wants and desires, "for the love of Christ impels us" (2 Cor 5:14).

The fullness of Christian holiness comes from a life of perfect love. Receive the perfect love of God, and give this perfect love to others. When Jesus calls his disciples to "be perfect, just as your heavenly Father is perfect," he is ultimately calling them to live a life of perfect love because "God is love" (1 Jn 4:16).

The new law is about *perfect love*. Thus all Christians, married and unmarried, are called to perfect love. Married couples are called to perfect love in and through marriage. It's not hard to make a list of the million ways married life can form you in perfect love. Whether it's the countless and unending list of household chores or the endless opportunities to make small sacrifices of love for your spouse or children, there is no shortage of ways to love the Lord your God and to love your neighbor. But this retreat is about more than just recognizing the opportunities to love. This retreat is about creating the framework by which perfect love will be exercised within your home and fostered in your children. Tomorrow we will discuss this framework for love.

Today's Couple Discussion Questions

1. What are the signs that our marriage and family life are set apart? When have we blended in with the rest of the world, and why?

2. How have we been transformed as individuals and as a couple? In what ways do we think like Jesus? Love like Jesus? Live like Jesus?

Today's Couple Prayer

(Tonight you are going to pray over your spouse. First, the husband should place his right hand upon his wife's shoulder and pray the prayer below. Next, the wife should place her right hand on her husband's shoulder and pray the prayer below.)

L ord Jesus Christ,
make my spouse holy as you are holy.
Fill him/her with your own divine holiness.
Increase in him/her a deeper capacity to give and receive love.
Consecrate him/her and set him/her apart for you.
Transform his/her eyes that he/she might see like you.
Transform his/her heart that he/she might love like you.
Transform his/her mind that he/she might reason like you.
Transform his/her will that he/she might will like you.
Transform his/her life that he/she might live like you.
Amen.

HOW IS PERFECT LOVE FORGED?

As we discovered yesterday, perfect holiness lies in perfect love, and the framework for perfect love is found in the three secrets to holiness in marriage. So what are the three secrets? The three secrets to holiness in marriage are chastity, poverty, and obedience.

Yes, you read that correctly. Let's just repeat them in case you haven't heard these words preached in a Sunday homily: the way in which all Christians become holy is through living chastity, poverty, and obedience. Known as the evangelical counsels, these three perfect virtues of Jesus—the virtues Jesus radically lived—allowed him to fulfill perfect love. Traditionally, religious brothers and sisters are known for taking vows of chastity, poverty, and obedience. We argue that this traditional attribution of the counsels only to the religious has done us married couples a major disservice. These three virtues of Jesus are what enabled him to live perfect love, and they are what will enable us to live perfect love in the married state. Careful study of Church documents and sacred scripture makes clear that the way in which *all* Christians become holy is through the evangelical counsels of chastity, poverty, and obedience.

The logic is pretty simple: the Church teaches that perfect holiness is achieved through perfect love, and that perfect love is achieved through living out the evangelical counsels of chastity, poverty, and obedience. Thus if a married couple desires to live holiness in marriage, this life of holiness comes from embracing the counsels. The *Catechism* explains just why these counsels are so incredible:

> Besides its precepts, the new law also includes the evangelical counsels. The traditional distinction between God's commandments and the evangelical counsels is drawn in relation to charity (perfect love), the perfection of the Christian life. The precepts are intended to remove whatever is incompatible with charity. *The aim of the counsels, however, is to remove whatever might hinder the development of charity. . . .*
>
> *The evangelical counsels manifest the living fullness of charity,* which is never satisfied with not giving more. They attest its vitality and call forth our spiritual readiness. The perfection of the new law consists essentially in the precepts of love of God and neighbor. *The counsels point out the more direct ways, the readier means, and are to be practiced in keeping with the vocation of each.* (CCC, 1973–74, emphasis added)

The *Catechism* explains that the new law, instituted by Jesus Christ, calls all Christians to perfect love, and the evangelical counsels remove whatever might get in the way of giving perfect love. Do you desire perfect love in your marriage and family life? Through this retreat you will discover a new dimension of holiness in marriage that will allow you to embrace the Gospel like never before. Chastity, poverty, and obedience lead to the perfect love that will make us and all our children the saints we were created to be.

We told you this book was going to be different from any others you have read and that this book was going to challenge you. This retreat is meant to lead you and your spouse down a path that may be an entirely new spirituality, but one that will bless you immensely and ultimately help you both progress toward perfect love and saintly holiness.

St. John Paul II says, "In fact, all those reborn in Christ are called to live out, with the strength which is the Spirit's gift, the chastity appropriate to their state of life, obedience to God and to the Church, and a reasonable detachment from material possessions: for all are called to holiness, which consists in the perfection of love."[6]

One of the most beautiful accounts in all of scripture is the story of the rich young man. When the rich young man approaches Jesus, he asks a very important question: "Teacher, what good must I do to gain eternal life?" (Mt 19:16). As married people, we should change this question a little bit: "Teacher, what good must I do, and what good must I lead my spouse and children in doing, so that we may all attain eternal life?"

Jesus answers that this man should keep the Commandments. Essentially Jesus is telling the young man to follow the old law. But the young man replies, "All of these I have observed. What do I still lack?" (Mt 19:20). Jesus replies, "If you wish to be perfect, go, sell what you have and give to [the] poor, and you will have treasure in heaven. Then come, follow me" (Mt 19:21). Jesus invites the young man to enter a totally new way of life that embraces the call to seek perfect love. This response challenges the rich young man to place love of God and love of neighbor above love of self and love of possessions. Just as he had done in the Sermon on the Mount when he told his followers to "be perfect, just as your heavenly Father is perfect," Jesus challenges the rich young man to go beyond the old law and to live the new law of perfect love. We know how the story ends. The rich young man "went away sad, for he had many possessions" (Mt 19:22). For the rich young man, love of self and love of possessions was more important than love of God and love of neighbor. The desire of his heart was to build up his own comfort kingdom, not the kingdom of God.

This text from Matthew 19 is often ignored by married couples because it suggests that we must sell all that we have and give it to the poor. The typical logic goes like this: "I'm married. I can't sell all that I have, because I have to care for a family, thus this passage isn't meant for me." Wrong. Nothing in this text tells us that this man himself was single. We know he was rich and that he was young. That's all. He could have had a family and children; after all, eleven of the twelve apostles were married.

Dan

I'm thirty-three and I have a full-time job in America, meaning I make more money than 80 percent of the world's population, so in reality I am a rich young man. This account is for me.

This text is also misinterpreted as Jesus inviting this young man to follow a higher calling through a more radical surrender of all that he has for the sake of others—the call to religious life. This is a poor understanding of the text. As theologian Fr. Francis Moloney says, "The rich young man was not called to the religious life, but to the Christian life, and Matthew calls that life, in both 5:48 and 19:21, a life of perfect love."[7]

St. John Paul II offers a similar interpretation in his encyclical *Veritatis Splendor*:

> This vocation to perfect love is not restricted to a small group of individuals. The invitation, "go, sell your possessions and give the money to the poor" and the promise, "you will have treasure in heaven" are meant for everyone, because they bring out the full meaning of the commandment of love of neighbor, just as the invitation which follows, "Come, follow me," is the new, specific form of the commandment of love of God. . . .
>
> As he calls the young man to follow him along the way of perfection, Jesus asks him to be perfect in the command of love, in "his" commandment: to become part of the unfolding of his complete giving, to imitate and rekindle the very love of the "Good" Teacher, the one who loved "to the end." This is what Jesus asks of everyone who wishes to follow him: "If any man would come after me, let him deny himself and take up his cross and follow me" (Mt 16:24, RSVCE). . . .
>
> Following Christ is not an outward imitation, since it touches man at the very depths of his being. Being a follower of Christ means becoming conformed to him who became a servant even to giving himself on the Cross (cf. Phil 2:5–8). (*Veritatis Splendor*, 18, 20, 21)

In this gospel account, Jesus extends to us an invitation to perfect love, to follow him and conform our lives to his own life of perfect love. When we embrace the counsels of chastity, poverty, and obedience, we imitate Christ. The invitation "follow me" is an invitation to imitate Christ's own chastity, poverty, and obedience. He places before us today the same invitation he placed before the rich young man. How will you respond?

Today's Couple Discussion Questions

1. What comes to mind when we hear the words *chastity*, *poverty*, and *obedience*? What are the positive associations? What are the negative associations?

2. If Jesus approached us as a married couple and asked us to do something we were uncomfortable doing, something that challenged our way of life, how would we react to his invitation?

3. In what ways are we each fulfilled in our life together? In what ways do we each feel lacking in our life together?

Today's Couple Prayer

Dear Jesus, you call us to be perfect in love, as our heavenly Father is perfect. Your bride the Church has shown to us these three secrets to perfect love: chastity, poverty, and obedience. Open our hearts, Lord, to receive a new way of loving, a fuller and more abundant way of loving you and loving one another. Open our ears to hear your call to venture into deeper waters. Open our arms to receive the gift of freedom that you have in store for us. Amen.

FOLLOW ME

We love the rich young man's question from yesterday's reflection, "What do I still lack?" Isn't this the question we ask all the time in our own marriage and family life? "Jesus, I'm trying to do everything right, but things just aren't working. What do I still lack?" or "Jesus, I'm giving you my time and placing you first in my life, but I'm always exhausted and burnt out. What do I still lack?"

Jesus replies by saying, "If you wish to be perfect, go, sell what you have and give to [the] poor, and you will have treasure in heaven. Then come, follow me" (Mt 19:21). Okay, Jesus, that sounds nice and all, but that isn't the answer we want. But it may be the answer we need. Throughout scripture we see two incredibly simple but scary words: *follow me*. To be a Christian is to be a follower of Jesus. To be Christian means to live like Jesus, love like Jesus, and act like Jesus.

A few years ago, there was a popular saying: "What would Jesus do?" At first it was great. We loved the concept of using this phrase. But before long this phrase became the means by which people justified whatever political or social agenda they personally had. There is one small problem with this phrase. It should focus not on what Jesus *would do* but rather on what Jesus *did*.

Jesus was a poor man who calls us to be poor. Jesus was a chaste man who calls us to be chaste. Jesus was an obedient man who calls us to be obedient.

During the Eucharistic Prayer at Mass, the priest proclaims, "All life, all holiness comes from you through your Son, Jesus Christ our Lord, by the working of the Holy Spirit." Jesus Christ reveals holiness to humanity and "fully reveals man to man himself" (*Gaudium et Spes*, 22).

The answer to the question "What do I still lack?" is "Follow me." The answer to the question is Jesus. The rich young man lacks Jesus. He is like the Christians who go to Mass and are basically good people. They follow the rules, but Jesus isn't radically alive in their hearts. They know about Jesus, but they will always lack something if they are not living like Jesus. Jesus reveals humankind to ourselves, which means that Jesus teaches us how to live. If we are not living like Jesus, we are not living the life we were created to live, and thus we are lacking something.

In Jesus we need not continue searching for fulfillment and satisfaction. We simply need to imitate and participate in Christ's perfect virtues. The evangelical counsels of poverty, chastity, and obedience are the perfect virtues of Jesus, and thus in them we discover how to follow Jesus perfectly.

Through Baptism all Christians have the same end: conforming ourselves to Jesus Christ. Jesus is the poor, the chaste, and the obedient Son of God. St. John Paul II tells us that those who embrace the counsels "make Christ the whole meaning of their lives," that they are "conforming one's whole existence to Christ," and that they "strive to reproduce in themselves, as far as possible, that form of life which he, as the Son of God, accepted and lived."[8]

Whether one is single, married, or a consecrated celibate, all Christians should strive to make Christ Jesus, and him crucified, the full measure of their lives. "The counsels," St. John Paul II tells us, "more than a simple renunciation, are a specific acceptance of the mystery of Christ."[9] The counsels of poverty, chastity, and obedience are how we as Christians can enter into the mystery of Christ's own life, death, and resurrection. The counsels of poverty, chastity, and obedience must ultimately be at the center of our lives because they were at the center of Christ's own life.

Holiness is found in living in imitation of Jesus Christ, and the evangelical counsels are the perfect means to imitate Christ. "The teaching and example of Christ provide the foundation of the evangelical counsels"

(*Lumen Gentium*, 43). Any Christian desiring to obtain holiness in imitation of Jesus Christ should see the counsels not as mere suggestions nor as scary threats upon our freedom but as a blueprint for holiness and a roadmap for authentic freedom and lasting joy. Christ himself and the Holy Family radically embraced these virtues in order to grow in perfect love, and they should be our virtues.

The *Catechism of the Catholic Church* says that "Christ proposes the evangelical counsels, in their great variety, to every disciple" (*CCC*, 915). How does Christ propose these counsels to his disciples? The call to every disciple is the same: "Come, follow me" (Mt 4:19, NIV). Christ calls us to follow him, to imitate him, and to live as he lives. Christ freely made himself poor, and so every disciple is called to follow him in his poverty. Christ was perfectly chaste, and so every disciple is called to walk in chastity. Christ was obedient to the Father, even unto death, and so every disciple is called to perfect obedience.

As this retreat continues, we are going to do something that we hope is deeply enriching for you—we are not going to focus on you. Yes, you read that correctly. There are so many marriage books out there, and most have this one thing in common: a focus on the married couple. We don't want to do that. You are not called to "follow your heart" or "follow your gut." Jesus calls you: "Follow me." So why wouldn't our book on marriage focus primarily on who Jesus is? As we journey deeper into these thirty-three days, if you seek nothing more, seek to discover more about who Jesus is and how you can follow him. In this you will discover everything you need.

Today's Couple Discussion Questions

1. What are some signs that Jesus is the whole meaning of our individual lives and our marriage and family life together? In what ways do we each conform our whole existence to him?

2. In what ways can we imitate and follow Christ in our marriage and family?

3. What do we each still lack?

Today's Couple Prayer

Lord Jesus Christ, mold us into the image of your own life. Help us make you the whole meaning of our lives, and please become the whole meaning of our children's lives. Lord, we freely choose to follow you throughout these thirty-three days, wherever you may lead us. Amen.

DAY 9

TRUE FREEDOM, AUTHENTIC LOVE, AND LASTING JOY

We presented the concept of this book to many people before writing this retreat, and we were laughed at more than once. "What are you talking about? Married people can't be called to poverty, chastity, and obedience. That doesn't make sense! How can a married person be called to poverty when they have kids?" We understand that this concept hasn't been the popular teaching of the Church, but that doesn't mean it's not biblical and rooted in Church doctrine. In today's reflection, we wish to provide you with the motivation behind embracing chastity, poverty, and obedience by demonstrating two simple truths:

1. All the major leading causes of divorce are the result of couples rejecting a spirit of poverty, chastity, and obedience in their marriage.

2. If married couples effectively embrace a spirituality of poverty, chastity, and obedience, not only will they be far less likely to divorce, but they also will find a life of true freedom, authentic love, and lasting joy.

Some argue that married couples shouldn't pursue the evangelical counsels, because such virtues as poverty, chastity, and obedience would wreak havoc on the very essence of married life. "How can we raise our children if we are poor?" "How will we experience intimacy as a couple if we're always worried we'll conceive another child?" "If a wife is obedient to her husband, won't that relationship become a relationship of dominance rather than love?" "If the husband is obedient to his wife, will he become weak and passive?" These questions make it seem as if poverty, chastity, and obedience are negative realities. However, they are positive realities that promote true freedom and authentic love.

The evangelical counsels of poverty, chastity, and obedience help married couples empty themselves of the vices that often get in the way of their love and joy as a couple. When the couple empties themselves of these vices, God can fill them with higher, eternal virtues.

Looking at the leading causes of divorce in America can help us better understand how conjugal poverty, chastity, and obedience can be the cure of division within marriage, instead of the cause of it. No one enters marriage with the desire to get divorced. However, nearly half of the marriages in America end that way. Why? What happens? Something always gets in the way of love.

If we look at statistics, many divorces arise out of the sins that a spirituality of poverty, chastity, and obedience helps to overcome.

A spirituality of poverty allows the couple to stay focused on the things that really matter and to maintain reasonable detachment from worldly possessions. How often do finances, possessions, and greed get in between couples? The study "Examining the Relationship between Financial Issues and Divorce," published in the journal *Family Relations*, determined after looking at data for 4,574 couples that financial disagreements were the strongest disagreements to predict divorce for both men and women.[10] In a poll conducted by *Divorce Magazine*, the leading cause of divorce was financial issues. According to Dan Couvrette, the magazine's publisher, "During the divorce, the two most contentious issues are usually finances and children—in that order."[11] Justin A. Reckers, a certified divorce financial analyst, reports, "I have long believed financial disagreements to be the most common cause of marital conflict and ultimately divorce. . . . Now we have empirical evidence proving this is the case across all socioeconomic classes. Disparate goals and values around money coupled with the power and control financial prosperity represents makes money a common battleground in marriages."[12]

Maybe Jesus knew what he was talking about when he called all his followers to embrace a spirit of poverty. Maybe more marriages would stay intact if finances were surrendered more fully to God. We bet you and your spouse have had one or two heated arguments over finances—we have. When we first got married, some of our biggest disagreements and arguments were over finances. But the more we grew in an understanding of a spirit of poverty, the more finances became a source of mutual blessing and agreement rather than difficulty and disagreement.

A spirituality of chastity orients husbands and wives to giving themselves to one another as a gift, and to each other alone. How often does the lack of chastity divide a couple? Much research shows that sexual infidelity and/or dissatisfaction with a couple's sexual life is second only to arguments about money. An article titled "Why Americans Divorce" claims that "22 percent of men cited sex as the reason for the divorce."[13] In another article, a law firm reports that "sex was a factor in 43 percent of divorce cases."[14] When a couple fails to have self-mastery and forms habits of taking instead of giving, it's only a matter of time before fidelity becomes a serious issue of concern.

Once again, maybe Jesus knew what he was talking about when he called all his followers to embrace a spirit of chastity. Maybe more marriages would stay intact if couples lived with self-mastery and self-giving love.

Finally, a spirituality of obedience trains our minds to "do nothing out of selfishness or out of vainglory; rather, humbly regard others as more important than yourselves" (Phil 2:3). How often do our pride and selfishness get in the way of love? A *Huffington Post* article suggests that communication problems could be the most common factor that leads to divorce (up to 65 percent), followed by couples' inability to resolve conflict (43 percent).[15] If husbands and wives regard each other as more important than themselves, they would carefully strive for a relationship that hears the other and validates and serves the other's desires. The survey also found that men and women have different communication complaints. Men cited nagging and complaining as the top communication problem in their marriage, whereas women most often felt that their husbands didn't validate their opinions or feelings enough. If spouses are focused on serving the needs of the other, and carefully listening to the other's needs, many communication problems would never arise.

And so it appears that the third major leading cause of divorce could be overcome through a spirituality of mutual obedience. Maybe Jesus knew what he was talking about when he called all his followers to embrace a spirit of obedience.

The consumerism of the American dream, the promised freedom of the sexual revolution, and the entitlement of individualism seemingly don't lead to marriages that possess true freedom, authentic love, and lasting joy. We need to look to Jesus who alone is the source of true freedom, authentic love, and lasting joy and learn from the life of poverty, chastity, and obedience that he himself lived.

Conjugal poverty will allow you as a couple to surrender your relationship in trust and dependence on God, calling you to prayer, not arguments, over finances. Conjugal poverty leads to true freedom over your finances.

Conjugal chastity will allow you as a couple to give and receive love according to God's design. In that, you won't fall prey to the world's false promises of love and passion but rather share in divine love itself. Conjugal chastity leads to authentic love in your marriage and trains your children how to seek authentic love in their lives.

Conjugal obedience will allow you as a couple to hear carefully the needs of your spouse and live a life in service to each other's needs. In this, everyone's needs are met because spouses are meeting one another's desires out of mutual love and affection. In a home where everyone's needs are heard and fulfilled, there is real peace and lasting joy.

True freedom. Authentic love. Real peace. Lasting joy. Isn't this what we all desire for our marriage and family life? It's what we desire, and because of that we desire the counsels.

Today's Couple Discussion Questions

1. In what ways do we individually embrace a spirit of simplicity toward belongings? When do we individually feel a freedom over finances, and when do we individually feel burdened by them?

2.   How are we oriented toward gift as a couple? In what ways are we giving to one another regularly? When do we feel authentic love between us?

3.   In what ways do we hear the needs of each other and live a life in service to each other's needs? How and when do we find joy in serving one another?

4.   When do we feel as if our spouse is not hearing our needs? What can we do to help communicate our needs more clearly?

Today's Couple Prayer

Lord Jesus Christ, bless our marriage with a spirit of poverty, chastity, and obedience that leads to true freedom, authentic love, and lasting joy. Remove from us anything that would enslave us, rob us of our joy, or cause us to settle for a counterfeit form of love. Protect us from consumerism, individualism, and a false notion of sexual freedom. Lord, preserve our marriage until death do us part. Let nothing divide us. Amen.

YOKED TOGETHER

Come to me, all you who labor and are burdened,
and I will give you rest.
Take my yoke upon you and learn from me, for I am meek and
humble of heart; and you will find rest for yourselves.
For my yoke is easy, and my burden light.
—Matthew 11:28–30

Yesterday we ended the reflection talking not about poverty, chastity, and obedience but rather about conjugal poverty, conjugal chastity, and conjugal obedience. It's important for each individual Christian to discover how they are called to embrace a spirit of poverty, chastity, and obedience. However, married couples are called to conjugal poverty, chastity, and obedience in a unique way. The word *conjugal* comes from the Latin roots *con*, meaning "together," and *jugum*, meaning "yoke," which suggests that married couples are "yoked together."

Since husbands and wives are yoked together, it's important for spouses during this retreat to ask not only, "How am I called to embrace poverty, chastity, and obedience?" but also, "How are we as a couple and a family called to embrace poverty, chastity, and obedience?"[16] Without this as a starting point—if spouses are not on the same page—a married couple runs the risk of the counsels leading to a collapse of love within the marriage instead of the perfection of love. Married couples should be careful to prayerfully discern and pursue these counsels as one flesh, yoked together, not as two individuals figuring things out on their own.

Picture the image of a yoke. People often have the idea that a yoke is a big wooden harness thrown over the shoulders of a poor ox forced to plow through a difficult field by himself. People often try to press through life this way, painfully trying to do it alone. But the *American Heritage Dictionary* defines *yoke* as a crossbar with *two* U-shaped pieces that encircle the necks of a pair of oxen working as a *team*. You could imagine the difficulty one ox would have trying to plow through a field of rough and rugged soil all by itself. The married couple has been "yoked together," not that they may take the easy way out and live a life of comfort and pleasure, but so that they need not respond alone to the call of the Gospel—the call to deny themselves, plow through the narrow path of Calvary, and suffer with Christ in his self-giving love. The Lord has yoked them together so that they may make this journey together. Alone, this journey is burdensome and perhaps even impossible. As with the oxen, the journey and the mission are made possible to fulfill when husband and wife are yoked side by side.

For married couples, being yoked together means we work in tandem, with each other and with Christ, in order to bear fruit for the kingdom of God. What then is the yoke of Christ that we have taken upon ourselves? The yoke of Christ is the incredible paradox of the Cross: when we die to ourselves, we bring life; when we give, we receive. Living the sacrament of Marriage, we have taken Jesus' yoke upon our shoulders in our vocation. Now Christ invites us to learn from [him] through living his perfect virtues: poverty, chastity, and obedience. In doing this, two incredible things will happen:

1. We will find rest because his yoke is easy and his burden is light.

2. We will bear abundant fruit.

It's easy to approach the challenges in the following days of this retreat as burdens placed upon your shoulders.

Dan

Honestly, when I first felt called to more radically embrace poverty, chastity, and obedience in my marriage, I felt they were a huge burden. I felt that if I wasn't "poor enough," I was letting Jesus down. I felt that it was impossible to give myself completely to my work, my spouse, and my family—that there simply wasn't enough of me to give. I felt as if I would never be able to establish enough discipline, order, and obedience in my home.

In prayer and with the guidance of an incredible priest, I discovered that the counsels are not a checklist of what I have to do and what I can't do. The counsels are supposed to set us free to live perfect love, not become a burden upon our shoulders. As the *Catechism* says (referenced on Day 7), the counsels help build the disposition within our hearts so that they are "never satisfied with not giving more" (*CCC*, 1974). That's the kind of hearts we desire for ourselves and for our children. When this is the motive of our hearts, giving more is a yoke that is easy and a burden that is light.

Jesus wants to bear abundant fruit in your marriage—fruit like you have never seen before. If you live a life that is never satisfied with not giving more, Jesus will bless you abundantly because he and his Father are truly never satisfied with not giving more. Since you are their children, the Father and the Son want to lavish good gifts upon you. They want abundant fruit in your life.

As we said earlier, we want to challenge you throughout the course of this retreat. As we enter into a prayerful look at each of the counsels, the Gospel may convict you to change certain aspects of your married lifestyle. At first you may be reluctant to make these changes, but we promise you that if you do, you will see abundant fruit in your marriage. You will experience more freedom with your finances, more love and intimacy as a couple, and a stronger, more prayerful home. The goal of the Gospel isn't ease and comfort but rather to bear fruit for the kingdom that lasts into eternity. Plowing through the fields isn't going to be an easy task, but we don't plow for the sake of plowing. We plow for the sake of the fruit it produces. Likewise, we don't embrace poverty, chastity, and obedience in the married life for the sake of poverty itself, chastity itself, or obedience itself, but rather for the fruit it produces—perfect love. Just imagine all the incredible fruit that would bless your family, your parish, your community, and your marriage if you oriented your whole life toward the disposition of perfect love.

Today's Couple Discussion Questions

1.   Spend some time meditating on John 15:

I am the true vine, and my Father is the vine grower. He takes away every branch in me that does not bear fruit, and every one that does he prunes so that it bears more fruit. . . . Remain in me, as I remain in you. Just as a branch cannot bear fruit on its own unless it remains on the vine, so neither can you unless you remain in me. I am the vine; you are the branches. Whoever remains in me and I in him will bear much fruit, because without me you can do nothing. Anyone who does not remain in me will be thrown out like a branch and wither; people will gather them and throw them into a fire and they will be burned. If you remain in me and my words remain in you, ask for whatever you want and it will be done for you. By this is my Father glorified, that you bear much fruit and become my disciples. As the Father loves me, so I also love you. Remain in my love. If you keep my commandments, you will remain in my love, just as I have kept my Father's commandments and remain in his love.

I have told you this so that my joy may be in you and your joy may be complete. This is my commandment: love one another as I love you. No one has greater love than this, to lay down one's life for one's friends. . . . It was not you who chose me, but I who chose you and appointed you to go and bear fruit that will remain, so that whatever you ask in the Father in my name he may give you. This I command you: love one another. (Jn 15:1–2, 4–13, 16–17)

2. What verses stuck out to us individually? How does this passage apply to our current state in marriage?

3. In what ways do we feel "yoked together" in our spiritual lives and in our daily lives?

4. In what ways can we depend on one another more fully?

Today's Couple Prayer

Lord Jesus Christ, yoke us together more and more, and yoked together, help us to remain in you in order to bear fruit that lasts. Whenever we are weary and heavily burdened, bring your rest. Allow us to take your yoke upon our shoulders every day of our lives and never be satisfied with not giving more. Amen.

Week 2

THE FIRST SECRET:
CONJUGAL CHASTITY

WHAT IS CHASTITY?

One of the most common misconceptions about chastity is that it's the same thing as celibacy. Let's clear that up right off that bat. Celibacy is the decision to remain unmarried so that a person is more readily able to serve the needs of the Lord and the people of God. Our priests and the religious embrace celibacy so that they may offer the good of undivided service to the kingdom of God. Chastity, on the other hand, is a virtue that can be embraced by all men and women, both married and unmarried. The Church affirms that all who are baptized are called to chastity "in keeping with their particular states in life" (*CCC*, 2348) and that "married people are called to live conjugal chastity" (*CCC*, 2349). That means that chastity looks different for the priest than for the married person. Chastity also looks different for the married couple than for their children.

This still doesn't really answer the question at hand: What is chastity? The *Catechism* puts it beautifully: "Chastity appears as a school of the gift of the person . . . ordered to the gift of self" (*CCC*, 2346). In simplest terms, chastity is the virtue of giving and receiving authentic love according to God's original plan before the Fall of man. The Fall deeply damaged God's plan for giving and receiving love, but Jesus came to restore the vision for giving and receiving love perfectly through the virtue of chastity.

In order to understand chastity, we must first understand original man and how original man's human sexuality was perfectly integrated toward the gift of self. And so let's go back to the beginning, before the Fall of man.

St. John Paul II spends a great deal of time reflecting on creation in his work that has come to be known as the theology of the body. He explains that creation itself is an overflowing act of self-giving love on the part of the Trinity. "Creation thus means not only calling from nothing to existence . . . but it also signifies gift; a fundamental and 'radical' gift, that is, an act of giving in which the gift comes into being precisely from nothing."[1] In creation, man is given life by the Creator, made in the likeness of the Creator, and is in turn capable of making a gift of his own life like the Creator. Humanity isn't only created in the image and likeness of God but also created "male" and "female." The reciprocal complementarity of "male" and "female" allows man and woman to discover and fully understand what it fundamentally means to be human. Being created as male and female allows the first man and first woman to form a "communion of persons in which they become a mutual gift for each other, through femininity and masculinity."[2]

St. John Paul II explains that first man and first woman viewed each other from a very different lens than through which we often see each other—through the lens of what he calls "original nakedness." In their original nakedness they come to understand that they are called not only to exist "with" someone but also to exist "for" someone.[3] Before the creation of woman, man was unable to give himself to another in an authentically human way. This is why "it is not good for the man to be alone" (Gn 2:18). And so God says, "I will make a helper suited to him" (Gn 2:18). When Eve is created, Adam bursts out in a song of praise, "This one, at last, is bone of my bones and flesh of my flesh" (Gn 2:23). Through the mystery of original nakedness Adam saw in Eve someone he could give himself to and that she would receive his love and return a mutual gift of self. The creation of woman helps man to understand who he is as a gift and helps him to be able to live as gift in an authentically human way.

"The gift reveals . . . the very essence of the person."[4] To be human means to exist in a communion of persons, which means to live in a lifestyle of reciprocal gift.

Man and woman are made for one another, quite literally, and they only can come to know themselves through each other. Giving the gift of one's self is how man and woman can truly come to know themselves. In existing "for another," each one discovers who they themselves truly are.

St. John Paul II describes a capacity within original man that is "the power to express love: precisely that love in which the human person becomes a gift and—through this gift—fulfills the very meaning of his being and existence."[5] He calls this capacity to be gift the "spousal meaning" of the body. Since "chastity appears as a school of the gift of the person . . . ordered to the gift of self" (CCC, 2346), then the virtue of chastity means living out the spousal meaning of the body, the capacity to be gift.

In chastity, we not only discover how to give and receive love but also what it means to be human at its most fundamental level. The spousal meaning of the body reveals the meaning of the person as gift. It's the capacity in the person, body and soul, to act in a way in which we freely give ourselves to the other. As stated above, through this gift the person is able to fulfill the very meaning of their human existence. So the spousal meaning of the body isn't only integral to our marriages but also to human existence itself.

In reference to the spousal meaning of the body, St. John Paul II, in speaking about how we are made in the image and likeness of God, consistently refers to *Gaudium et Spes*, section 24: "This likeness shows that man, who is the only creature on earth which God willed for itself, cannot fully find himself except through a sincere gift of himself." Without a clear understanding of the spousal meaning of the body and chastity, we will never fully understand ourselves. We will never fully *be* ourselves.

St. John Paul II is essentially teaching us that if we fail to be a total gift of self, then ultimately we run the risk of not fulfilling our purpose as humans. In a world that seeks happiness by existing for oneself, the spousal meaning of the body explains why those who exist for themselves are often so unhappy—they are in effect rejecting the very essence of who they are as people. Authentically realizing the spousal meaning of the body is what leads to human happiness.[6]

Dan

I have been blessed to be in ministry for many years now, and in that time I've been able to counsel a lot of people through hard times in their lives. I've met a lot of people who are filled with a whirlwind of loneliness and sadness. In talking to these people, do you know the one consistent quality I almost always discover? They think about themselves a lot! They are so concerned about what they're feeling, what others think about them, and why they're not happy. My advice? Pretty simple. I usually tell them to try to go an entire month without thinking about themselves. I encourage them to wake up and think about others. I encourage them, in social settings, to only think about how other people are feeling, not themselves. Essentially I encourage them to be gift and thus to live their lives as they were created to. Do you know what almost always happens? They come back a month later and they're not as lonely or sad or anxious. Of course, some people have true mental illnesses such as depression or anxiety that require treatment, but for the vast majority of people, when they feel as if life isn't living up to its potential, they realize it's almost always because they aren't living life as a sincere gift of self.

Have you ever been on a mission trip, maybe to help flood victims or hurricane survivors, to serve the poorest of the poor either here in America or in a developing country? I have done a lot of mission trips throughout my life and have probably taken well over two thousand youth on mission trips. One thing is consistent about these trips: people feel most fully alive while part of them. I hear the same testimonies every time we take a mission trip, both from youth and adults. They say, "It doesn't make sense. I haven't showered in days, I'm sleeping on a hard floor, my cell phone doesn't work here, and yet I'm happier than I've ever been before." Why? Because they're 100 percent focused on serving others, on being gift. So in a very real way, they're most fully human.

Ultimately love of God and love of neighbor are expressed in a total gift of self. When we embrace chastity, poverty, and obedience, we don't embrace these virtues as ends in themselves but as means to an end: perfect love. The evangelical counsels are three dispositions that prepare the soul to more readily and easily make a total gift of self and thus find authentic happiness. Marriage is our means to happiness because marriage provides an avenue to live our chastity, poverty, and obedience. "Marriage entails and requires a complete gift of self to the other: one's external goods (poverty), one's body, heart, and mind (chastity), and one's will (obedience)."[7]

Today's Couple Discussion Questions

1. How are we authentically living our lives as gifts?

2. How can we be a greater gift to each other, our children, our neighbors, and our coworkers?

Today's Couple Prayer

Lord Jesus Christ, you have created each of us to be a sincere gift to others. Make of us an outpouring gift to the world. Allow us to give ourselves more fully to our families, to our friends, and to the world. Help our hearts never to be satisfied with not giving more. Amen.

JESUS THE CHASTE

As stated on Day 8 of our retreat, St. John Paul II tells us that those who embrace the counsels "make Christ the whole meaning of their lives," that they are "conforming one's whole existence to Christ," and that they "strive to reproduce in themselves, as far as possible, that form of life which he, as the Son of God, accepted and lived."[8] So as we go through each counsel in these next three weeks, we are going to reflect on four different things:

1. How Jesus lived the counsels in his own life

2. How Jesus calls all the baptized to live the counsels

3. How the counsels are particularly embraced in married life

4. How the counsels can be fostered within the lives of our children

Today we look at how Jesus Christ embraced chastity in his own life. The Church affirms that Jesus Christ is "the model of chastity" (*CCC*, 2348), not just for celibates, but for us as married men and women, too.

"It is only in the mystery of the Word made flesh that the mystery of humanity truly becomes clear. . . . Christ, the new Adam, . . . fully reveals humanity to itself and brings to light its very high calling" (*Gaudium et Spes*, 22). Did you catch that? Jesus Christ reveals humanity to itself. When you look at Jesus, you learn what it means to be human and how to live your life as a human. Through perfectly living the virtue of chastity, Christ teaches humanity that "man cannot fully find himself except through a sincere gift of himself" (*Gaudium et Spes*, 24).

God the Father and Jesus Christ perfectly express self-giving love through the Incarnation. John 3:16 says, "For God so loved the world that he gave his only Son." The Incarnation was a total gift of self. The Father freely gave us his only-begotten Son, and the Son freely gave himself to us. Have you ever thought about just how radical this gift of self is?

Imagine that there is a criminal in your city who is on death row. Imagine that this criminal was born into an incredible family and was given everything he needed to thrive, and yet he made choice after choice that landed him in the position he is in now. Imagine the judge coming to your house and telling you that he will free this criminal, who by all measures of understanding had a just punishment, and spare his life under one condition: you willingly offer your only child in his place. There is probably not a chance in the world that you would go for a deal like that. After all, the criminal's choices placed him in that position, and your only child is completely innocent. Is this not what God the Father did for us? Were we not originally provided with the Garden of Eden, and did we not freely reject the goodwill that was upon us and freely choose a life of sin and pleasure instead? Yet God the Father "so loved the world that he gave his only Son" (Jn 3:16), who was totally innocent and not deserving of death. That is intense love!

Now look at the gift of God the Son who was lacking absolutely nothing in heaven but who freely chooses to give himself to us and take on the nature of humankind. The Incarnation is definitive proof of God's love for humanity because God the Son freely gives his life for us. The greatest classroom of Christ's self-giving love is found on Calvary, where "God proves his love for us in that while we were still sinners Christ died for us" (Rom 5:8). Christ models chastity and perfectly realizes the spousal meaning of the body in that he gives his entire self, body and soul, for all of humanity upon the Cross of Calvary. He doesn't just give a little bit of himself; he gives *all* of himself—every drop of his blood, every beat of his heart, every breath of his lungs, poured out for you and me. Christ is the exemplar of chastity, because chastity is about a complete and total self-gift, even when it hurts.

This total gift of self continues to be poured out week after week, day after day, through the gift of the Holy Eucharist, where Jesus gives us his own body, blood, soul, and divinity. "Take this all of you and eat of it": Jesus is essentially saying, "Here, take this gift of my very life; I give you everything that I have, not just once upon the Cross, but every time you consume this bread." The Eucharist is the gift of Jesus' life, poured out on the Cross, perpetuated through the ages.

In turn, we are called to give the gift of our lives for the sake of the other. But before we give the gift of our lives to the world, and even before we give the gift of our lives to our spouse and children, we are called to give the gift of our lives to the Father, through the Son, in the Holy Spirit.

The capacity within us to give and receive love is at its root a gift from God intended to call humans into union with God. It's a capacity to receive the love initiated by God and a capacity to give a total gift of self back to God. We are called to receive the love of God in our lives and to return the gift of God's own love back to God. Thus clearly understood, the deepest living of the virtue of chastity is receiving into one's own life the love of the Father in heaven and giving a total gift of oneself back to the Father, which is realized here on earth by obedience to the Father's will (Mt 7:21). Jesus, as the exemplar of chastity, perfectly does this because he and the Father are one (Jn 17:1ff.). He has received the Father's perfect love ("Behold, this is my beloved Son" [Mt 3:17]), and in receiving this love, he returns perfect love back to the Father ("Father, into your hands I commend my spirit" [Lk 23:46]). Christ models for humanity how to receive the Father's love and how to return this love back to the Father. We pray that you receive the Father's love and love him in return this day and all days.

Today's Couple Discussion Questions

1. How have we each received the love the Father has for us?

2. How have we each given a complete and total gift of ourselves to the Father?

Today's Couple Prayer

Lord Jesus Christ, you gave a complete and total gift of yourself upon the Cross of Calvary. You gave us every drop of your blood, every beat of your heart, every breath of your lungs—your whole being without reserve. Today, Lord, we give you our whole being without reserve. Take our lives and do with them whatever pleases you. Amen.

DAY 13

JESUS CALLS US TO BE CHASTE

Chastity is expressed in a person's life most notably through their vocation. In celibacy, a priest or religious person exists for the other in that they exist for the kingdom of God. Jesus explains this by saying, "Some renounce marriage *for* the sake of the kingdom of heaven" (Mt 19:12, emphasis added). In the vocation of marriage, man exists for his spouse and his children. St. Paul expresses this by saying, "Husbands, love your wives, even as Christ loved the church and handed himself over *for* her" (Eph 5:25, emphasis added). But even those who haven't entered their permanent vocation are called to live chastity, living *for* others according to God's original plan.

Just as Jesus lived his life for our sake, Christian disciples are called to live for the sake of others. Christians are called to lay down their lives for the sake of others. Baptism invites the death to self and the rise in new life in Christ, a life of grace in which chastity is lived in everyday circumstances and at every moment of our lives.

In John 21, Jesus asks Peter three times, "Peter, do you love me?" to which Peter responds, "Yes, Lord, you know that I love you" (Jn 21:15–17). Peter's response offering his love for Christ is simultaneously a call to give himself to others. Christ responds to Peter's profession of love by saying, "Feed my sheep" (Jn 21:17). If we love Christ, then we are called to give ourselves to others. It's as simple as that.

The most startling realization of the fact that we are fundamentally called to live our lives for the sake of others comes from Mathew 25:31–40 where we read the judgment of the nations:

> When the Son of Man comes in his glory, and all the angels with him, he will sit upon his glorious throne, and all the nations will be assembled before him. And he will separate them one from another, as a shepherd separates the sheep from the goats. He will place the sheep on his right and the goats on his left. Then the king will say to those on his right, "Come, you who are blessed by my Father. Inherit the kingdom prepared for you from the foundation of the world. For I was hungry and you gave me food, I was thirsty and you gave me drink, a stranger and you welcomed me, naked and you clothed me, ill and you cared for me, in prison and you visited me." Then the righteous will answer him and say, "Lord, when did we see you hungry and feed you, or thirsty and give you drink? When did we see you a stranger and welcome you, or naked and clothe you? When did we see you ill or in prison, and visit you?" And the king will say to them in reply, "Amen, I say to you, whatever you did for one of these least brothers of mine, you did for me."

In this passage, what is required for salvation? How well you treated your brothers and sisters, how well you lived as a self-gift for the sake of others.[9] According to Matthew 25, it appears that whether we each lived as a gift is the grounds for salvation. Humankind is called to live for the love of God and for the love of neighbor. Look at what Christ says to those who didn't live their lives as a gift:

> Then he will say to those on his left, "Depart from me, you accursed, into the eternal fire prepared for the devil and his angels. For I was hungry and you gave me no food, I was thirsty and you gave me no drink, a stranger and you gave me no welcome, naked and you gave me no clothing, ill and in prison, and you did not care for me." Then they will answer and say, "Lord, when did we see you hungry or thirsty or a stranger or naked or ill or in prison, and not minister to your needs?" He will reply, "Amen, I say to you, what you did not do for one of these least ones, you did not do for me." And these

will go off to eternal punishment, but the righteous to eternal life.
(Mt 25:41–46)

That's pretty intense, right? Those who lived as a gift for the sake of others went to heaven; those who didn't went to hell. What strikes us most about this passage is that they were surprised. They never meant to turn Christ away, to leave him naked, hungry, sick, and imprisoned. It seems that, had they *known*, they would have given Christ what he needed. These "goats" loved Jesus; they believed they knew Jesus. They were surprised to be cast aside, surprised to hear that they had not served Jesus. Similarly we read in Matthew 7:21, "Not everyone who says to me, 'Lord, Lord,' will enter the kingdom of heaven, but only the one who does the will of my Father in heaven." The way to heaven is not only about faith in Jesus but also about being a gift of self.

Most people believe they will go to heaven because they are "basically a good person." But Jesus calls us to more than this. He calls us to be a complete and total self-gift for the sake of others. We are not saying the whole world is going to hell, but a lot of people live life with the mentality of "me and my own" and that is about it.

Dan

I was once speaking at a men's conference in Canada and was challenging the attendees to give more of themselves for the sake of others. I spoke on the tragic problems facing the world such as human trafficking, world hunger, homelessness, foul and polluted water, and abortion, and I challenged the men to give more of themselves in order to bring an end to these worldwide problems. After the session was over a man came up to me and asked, "Why should I make their problem my problem?" Confused, I responded, "What do you mean?" He went on to explain how he works hard for his money, and he feels as if he should only look after "me and my own," as he put it. After a few minutes of conversing, the Spirit filled me with words to say, "Why should you make their problem your problem? What if Jesus had that mentality about the problem of our sin and death? You see,

Jesus made our problem his problem. So if you want to be a
Christian, you freely choose to make their problem your problem.
That is, after all, what Christianity is all about."

Humanity was created out of love and for love, and as a gift to be a
gift. Through this gift of self we are able to fulfill the very meaning of our
human existence. So it appears that the questions Jesus is going to ask us
at our final judgment are these:

"Did you give yourself away to those who needed you?"

"Did you live as the self-gift I created you to be?"

"Did you make others' problems your problems?"

Whether married, single, adult, or child, we are all called to this
same end—a life of giving ourselves to others as Jesus gave himself for us.

We need to spend a lot more time in prayer reflecting or how we are
called by God to give ourselves away to others. Answering this question
and living this reality will allow us to "fulfill the very meaning of [our]
being and existence."[10] Living this reality here on earth prepares the soul
to live this reality for all eternity with the Trinity, when we will perfectly
receive the love of God and love God in return through a total gift of self.

Today's Couple Discussion Questions

1. What gifts and talents do we individually have that could be more
    fully given for the sake of others?

2. What gifts and talents do our children have that we could help them
    more fully give for the sake of others?

3. If we were to die today, how would Jesus judge us?

Today's Couple Prayer

Lord Jesus Christ, thank you for making the problem of our sin and
eternal death your problem and freely coming to die for us so that we
might have life with you in heaven. Help us see the problems others face
and come to their aid as a sincere gift. Amen.

CONJUGAL CHASTITY (DAY 1)

What if we said that you and your spouse could bear witness to, and actually make present, Christ's love for his Church? Let's think about that for a minute. That is a bold statement, but it's true. When we embrace conjugal chastity in the sacrament of Marriage, we make Jesus' love for the Church present in the world. Husbands, when you love your wife, you make present in this world the mystical love that Christ has for the Church. Wives, when you love your husband, you make present the mystical love the Church has for Christ. That means the family can make the love of Christ present in every corner of humanity.

Why is the family so important to the revitalization of human culture? Because the family is the revelation of the love of God in this world. Your marriage proclaims the Gospel wherever you go. You reveal God's love at a Saturday morning ball game or in the grocery store or in your neighborhood. You are a revelation of life and love. This is why your marriage matters.

In Ephesians 5, we read, "Wives should be subordinate to their husbands as to the Lord. . . . Husbands, love your wives, even as Christ loved the church and handed himself over for her" (Eph 5:22, 25). St. Paul's words are the language of the gift. Wives, give yourselves to your husbands such that you are willing to be subject to them. Husbands, give yourselves to your wives such that you are willing to lay your lives down in sacrificial love for them. In doing this, it becomes a relationship where the reciprocal gift of self leads to a communion of persons, where the "two shall become one flesh" (Eph 5:31).

"The reciprocal relations of husband and wife must spring from their common relation with Christ,"[11] and thus the source of this reciprocal submission lies in first giving oneself to Christ. Here St. John Paul II links submission with self-gift and the reception of the gift. To be "subordinate to one another" (Eph 5:21) means to mutually give oneself to the other, each in different ways: the wife through submitting to the husband's headship, and the husband through a sacrificial love. This mutual gift of self is only able to take place because they have first received the love of God and returned love to God. If the husband has not yet submitted himself to the love of God, then he in a sense isn't deserving of his wife's submission. In this we learn that the mystery of Christ must first be present in a married couple's hearts, and from this comes their love for each other.

"He who loves his wife loves himself" (Eph 5:28). Even though they are equal, it's first and foremost the husband who loves his wife and the wife who receives the husband's love. Thus the primary role of husband is to initiate the gift of love, while the primary role of the wife is to receive the offering of love. The wife's "submission" is to "the receiving of love." It refers to the submission of the Church to Christ, which consists in experiencing his love. As St. John Paul II explains, "The Church, as Bride, being the object of the redemptive love of Christ, the Bridegroom, becomes his body. The wife, being the object of the spousal love of her husband, becomes 'one flesh' with him: in some sense, his 'own' flesh."[12]

Amber

Okay, let's take a break from theology for some "real talk." This is actually a situation that happens regularly in our house. I'll let you guess what time of the month. We're getting ready to go out for the evening, and I'm getting dressed. I try on one dress, hate it, throw it on the floor. I try on a second dress, hate it, throw it on the floor. I try on a third dress, hate it, throw it on the floor. No, I don't pick them up and hang them back in the closet. Instead I glare at them as they lay in the pile, as if to say, "You just sit there and think about what you've done." Then, cue loving, well-intentioned husband. "Sweetie, I think you look beautiful in all the dresses. I especially liked the first dress you put on." My gut reaction is to perceive him as anything but loving. *He just wants to leave. He doesn't want me to buy more clothes. He thinks I'm being stupid.* The worst-case scenario is that he actually does like that hideous thing, he's actually being honest, which means I can never trust his opinion again.

In this scenario, Dan is genuinely giving a gift of love, and I am allowing a wall of pride and self-doubt to block me from receiving his love. So his gift is rejected, and I turn further in on myself. Imagine how this scene would change, how both hearts would open and grow, if the gift had been received. I'm not suggesting that our dear husbands know more about fashion than we do. But I'm wondering, who are we getting dressed for anyway? Our husbands should be at the top of that list; their opinions used to be the only ones that mattered. Wives need to recall this and choose receptivity.

Dan

Now let's flip the coin. How difficult is it for a husband to allow his wife to love him in return? Imagine this familiar scene. It's been a rough week, and work is piling up. I'm stressed out over finances, household chores, and many other things. Completing my to-do list seems like an impossible feat. Amber starts being playful, trying to lessen the burden on my shoulders. But what do I do? I shrug her off. She tries again. I shrug her off again. She then asks if I want to talk and tries to be supportive, desiring to bear the burden with me. But I block her out. I don't want to talk. I don't want help. I just want to press through it on my own.

That's not chastity. Chastity is about giving *and* receiving love. Husbands, are you willing to receive love from your wife? You've been yoked together. When the stress of life comes, and surely it will, receive her love. In the times that I let my guard down and receive love from Amber, I feel the burden lessen. Love has the ability to lift the weight of the world off of your shoulders. In the end, I usually realize that everything that's burdening me isn't what is most important to me. It's her, my beautiful wife, and them, our four beloved children—they're all I want and need. Don't let the stress of the world consume the present. Leave work at work, and see your family, treasure them, receive them as a gift from the Father to you.

St. Paul goes on to say that "husbands should love their wives as their own bodies" (Eph 5:28), because we realize through the spousal meaning of the body that "love binds the bridegroom to be concerned for the good of the bride."[13] Love calls the husband to a selflessness in mind, heart, and action, where he genuinely cares for the other as he cares for himself—his thoughts and actions throughout the day are *for* the other. This draws us once again to the "one flesh" concept. The husband and wife are one flesh with an intentional character: the body of the wife isn't the husband's own body but should be loved as his own body.[14] It's a unity through love, through the mutual gift of self. If the husband loves his wife's body as his own body, he should love and respect her body and the beautiful dignity that she bears as a woman. Both the husband and the wife should seek to look at each other's bodies with the glance of love instead of the glance of lust. It is, after all, possible for a husband or a wife to lust over and objectify their spouse.

St. John Paul II demonstrates how Ephesians 5 allows us to see how marriage fits into the mystery of God's plan from the beginning. In God's saving plan, he unites marriage, the most ancient revelation, with the definitive revelation of Christ's self-giving love for the Church, showing that his redemptive love has a spousal nature and meaning.[15] God, in his salvific plan, establishes continuity between the ancient covenant of marriage and the new covenant so that the ancient covenant, through living and expressing conjugal chastity, allows us to better understand the mystery of the new covenant.[16] Marriage is thus a visible sign, a sacrament, pointing to Christ's love for the Church and to God's eternal love for man.[17] When a married couple lives conjugal chastity in their marriage, the whole world witnesses that the capacity within us to give and receive love is at its root a gift from God intended to call humankind into union with God—a capacity to receive the love initiated by God and a capacity to give a total gift of self back to God. Marriage draws humanity deeper into this mystery, becoming a visible sign to the world of our eternal call: loving union with the Father.

So here is the real question: How can your marriage point more people to God?

Today's Couple Discussion Questions

1. How well do we as a couple receive one another's love? How can we grow in this?

2. In what ways can our marriage point more people to God?

Today's Couple Prayer

Lord Jesus Christ, thank you for my spouse. Thank you for the moments in my life when this love is poured out upon me. Help me to receive this love with more humility and docility. Help me model your perfect love, since through your openness to receiving the Father's love, you were able to give love to others. May you make our marriage and family a revelation of your love to the world. Amen.

CONJUGAL CHASTITY (DAY 2)

It's no secret that infidelity is a major problem in the world today. What is behind this wrong understanding of marriage and sexual intimacy? Simply put, it's a failure to live chastely. The world has twisted sexual pleasure and even marriage to be "for you" instead of "for the other." Often relationships are sought for the sake of the personal fulfillment one receives from the relationship; once the individual fulfillment is no longer there, the person walks away from the relationship. We see this all too often within marriages that end in divorce after only a few years. What people fail to realize is that individual fulfillment only truly comes from a sincere gift of self.

Chastity is such a powerful virtue. It allows us to control our disordered sexual desires that would cause us to use another person, and it instead enables our sexual desires to be oriented toward gift of self. In our looks, our words, and our thoughts, chastity helps form the orientation to be gift given. Pray earnestly that Jesus pours out a deeper gift of chastity in your life and marriage.

In Matthew 19, the Pharisees come to Jesus, asking whether it's lawful for a man to divorce his wife for any reason. They ask this knowing that Mosaic law allows for a bill of divorce. Instead of addressing the Mosaic law, Jesus appeals to a higher source—the Creator. He says, "From the beginning it was not so" (Mt 19:8).

Do you see how brilliant Jesus is? He is backed into a corner with no right answer. So Jesus appeals to a higher authority, the "beginning." He appeals to rediscover God's original plan for humankind, for marriage, and for human sexuality. He appeals to rediscover chastity.

In the beginning we discover that "God himself is the author of marriage" (*CCC*, 1603; *Gaudium et Spes*, 48:1) and that "marriage has two fundamental ends or purposes toward which it is oriented, namely, the good of the spouses as well as the procreation of children. Thus, the Church teaches that marriage is both unitive and procreative, and that it is inseparably both."[18]

The unitive end of marriage, or the bonding of husband and wife, has already been spoken of at length through the reciprocal gift of self and the communion of persons that marriage produces. This end of marriage is seen clearly in the beginning wherein "man leaves his father and mother and clings to his wife, and the two of them become one body" (Gn 2:24). The key to this end of marriage is that there should be a mutual complete self-gift from both the husband and the wife. This union naturally and inseparably flows into the second end of marriage, the procreation and education of children (*CCC*, 1652). The Church even says that "children are the supreme gift of marriage" (*Gaudium et Spes*, 50:1) because children are the eternal bond of love between husband and wife.

Think about that phrase for one moment. We will never forget when we brought our first child, Sophia, home from the hospital. We adored Sophia. All we could do, night and day, was stare at her. She was everything. At the same time, Amber as a new mother was so scared and confused. One night, our little family sat on the couch watching a movie. Amber loved our new family but wondered: Would she ever be alone again? Would we ever be the same? We wouldn't. It would never be "the same." That kind of change is scary.

Dan

Amber looked to me with tear-filled eyes, and I knew. I tenderly reminded her and helped her more deeply understand, that for all of eternity, our love would be incarnate in this eternal soul lying sweetly on my lap. That even in heaven when the sacraments are no more, including marriage, our love for one another will exist eternally because of her. God created eternal life from our love. What a beautiful and mysterious reality.

These two ends of marriage, unitive and procreative, are inseparably linked to one another. The unitive dimension of love doesn't make sense if it's closed to the procreative end of marriage, for authentic unitive love desires this love to live forever through the procreative. "A child does not come from outside as something added on to the mutual love of the spouses, but springs from the very heart of that mutual giving, as its fruit and fulfillment" (*CCC*, 2366). Likewise, if the procreative end of marriage is pursued apart from the unitive end of marriage, the spouse is treated as a possession that is used to produce offspring for the other, not as a gift.

When speaking of conjugal chastity, it would be an injustice if we didn't speak of the offenses against chastity. As with all the evangelical counsels, chastity isn't merely a no to certain sins against the virtue but rather a yes to living the free, total, faithful, and fruitful love of Jesus Christ. Chastity is a yes to a love that binds husband and wife more closely together and allows their marriage to bear abundant fruit. Chastity is a virtue that leads to true freedom, but a freedom that necessarily entails self-possession and self-control. In understanding the offenses against chastity, couples are free to love in an authentic and Christlike manner. But let's be honest. If you want the joy and happiness that Jesus promises us, it will only come through the Cross. As married couples, we can't expect the joy of marriage without the sacrifice required through living chastity. Chastity requires sacrifice. Love requires sacrifice.

Any behavior, whether in action or within the heart, that isn't directed toward the unitive and procreative ends of marriage is an offense against conjugal chastity. The *Catechism of the Catholic Church* states that "among the sins gravely contrary to chastity are masturbation, fornication, pornography, and homosexual practices" (*CCC*, 2396). Additionally, "adultery, divorce, polygamy, and free unions are grave offenses against the dignity of marriage" (*CCC*, 2400).

As for the sins gravely contrary to conjugal chastity, it's easy to understand, through natural law, why these practices are opposed to one or both ends of marriage. But as Christians with the law on our hearts, it's important that we see not merely a list of deprivations. When Jesus addresses his followers in his Sermon on the Mount, he gives us a new law of love. As he does, he calls us deeper into love. For example, sexual intimacy with someone other than your spouse is sinful and harmful to a marriage, right? But what does Jesus say? He takes it further and says that to even look lustfully upon another person is like committing adultery in your heart. He wants more than actions; he wants our hearts to experience this radical freedom. So we are to guard our hearts and imaginations, our words and our thoughts, when we look on someone who isn't our spouse. It's also possible to look on our spouse in a way that reduces the other to an object instead of a person to whom we wish to give ourselves. While it's certainly good to be sexually attracted to your spouse, the look of desire should express that you desire to give all of yourself to your spouse and to receive all of your spouse. It shouldn't be a look that reduces the other to a mere object. Chaste love remains in that place of self-gift and avoids adultery in the heart.

Pornography and masturbation are not gifts of self and are neither unitive nor procreative. Masturbation engrains within the heart a love that takes from the other. If you fall prey to the habit of selfish pleasure, you have a harder time giving yourself as a gift to another, whether married or unmarried. Pornography, too, isn't a victimless sin. This kind of "entertainment" wounds everyone involved, degrading the dignity of both the viewer and the one being viewed. We can begin to see here how each and every one of these "rules" protects our love and allows it to remain oriented toward free and authentic self-giving, life-giving love.

If you struggle with these habits, don't allow the enemy to grab a foothold on you by filling you with lies that you are a failure and will never find victory. Jesus Christ is victorious over sin and death, and in Christ you already share in his victory. You simply need to take hold of the victory Christ has won for you. "So be imitators of God, as beloved children, and live in love, as Christ loved us and handed himself over for us as a sacrificial offering to God for a fragrant aroma. Immorality or any impurity . . . must not even be mentioned among you. . . . For you were once darkness, but now you are light in the Lord. Live as children of light.

. . . Everything exposed by the light becomes visible, for everything that becomes visible is light. Therefore, it says: 'Awake, O sleeper, and rise from the dead, and Christ will give you light'" (Eph 5:1–3, 8, 13–14). If you have impurity within you, find an accountability partner, preferably a brother or sister in the Lord at your parish, and seek prayer and fasting to move into the victory Christ has for you. If you want to move toward victory, visit www.integrityrestored.com for more resources.

Contraception is a grave wound against chastity that may not be readily perceived as contrary to both ends of marriage. Many couples believe that if they have at one point in their marriage already received children as a gift from the Father, and if their marriage in general is open to life, then nothing is wrong with using artificial forms of birth control to avoid future pregnancies, at least for a particular time period. The Church teaches that while "not every conjugal act is followed by a new life . . . each and every marriage act must remain open to the transmission of life" (*Humanae Vitae*, 11). In laymen's terms, you don't have to conceive a child every time you engage in the marital act, but the possibility has to be there. If you use artificial birth control to block fertility, you block that openness to life. Thus any form of artificial birth control is a grave offense against conjugal chastity, whether or not you already have children.

It may be easy to understand how contraception violates the procreative end of marriage but less obvious to see how it violates the unitive end of marriage. Contraceptives limit the ability for the couple to give a total gift of self to each other and to receive the totality of the one loved. Through an act of contraception, the spouses fail to give the part of themselves that shares in God's own creative power, and thus the spouses mutually fail to receive that aspect of each other.

St. John Paul II reflects on how the marital act communicates the "language of the body" or the "language of love." This language of the body is the same language of the couple's marital vows, promising to give all of themselves to one another in mutual self-gift in order to form a one-flesh union. Each and every marital act speaks the language that the couples professed on their wedding day, and thus each and every marital act must be a total mutual self-gift. You can see how an act of contraception would be considered a "lie with the body" wherein the body is trying to communicate the language of mutual self-gift and total self-gift but the heart is only giving a limited self-gift.[19] It's as if the spouses are saying to one another, "I give you all of myself, except my reproductive side." See how that is a lie with the body? You can't give someone a complete self-gift and at the same time block part of who you are from that gift.

Good intentions don't make a lie to your spouse with your body a good. The end can't justify the means. By using contraception, married couples may think that they are avoiding problems or easing tensions within marriage. They may think they are helping to heal the brokenness in their frail marriage. A spouse may use contraception to help meet the perceived sexual "needs" of their less chaste partner. No matter the circumstance, failure to follow God's design isn't only a grave offense against chastity but also has the potential to damage or destroy your marriage forever. Separating the unitive and procreative ends of marriage and violating chastity leads to a division in the "one-flesh" union. This division may not be realized at first, but after prolonged unchaste behavior, the inability for a couple to mutually give themselves to one another becomes manifest in other aspects of their lives. Selfishness, instead of selflessness, becomes the new standard in the marriage. And if it starts in the bedroom, it will leak out into every other room in the house.

What then is a couple to do? Today, married couples are blessed with different scientific methods known as natural family planning (NFP). NFP allows for married couples to understand God's plan for the fertility cycle and plan children around fertile periods and infertile periods. NFP calls the couple to embrace chastity. Honestly, NFP isn't easy. It requires sacrifice. We have realized that NFP safeguards us. It allows us to order our desires toward self-giving and life-giving love so that we are careful never to view each other as an object to fulfill our sexual desires but as a gift entrusted to us by God the Father. Is it hard? Of course! But it's worth it. To read more about natural family planning, please read appendix A.

When Christ freely chose to give himself as a ransom on the Cross, it required tremendous sacrifice and self-mastery. A sincere gift of self always requires sacrifice. Virtue, and thus love, is beautifully expressed in abstinence. While it may be difficult for the husband or the wife to abstain from the good of the marital act, the greater good is that husbands and wives are given the opportunity to express their love for one another in new and different ways, which in turn leads to deeper communication and deeper intimacy. They find that their love continues to be life-giving in new and exciting ways.

Remember, the heart of chastity, and all the evangelical counsels, is freedom. This is about being *free* to love as we were created to love—in a way of authentic gift of self. May self-giving and life-giving love drive your every word, your every thought, and your every action.

Today's Couple Discussion Questions

1.   In what ways have we experienced greater unity in physical intimacy? What are other things that we do together as a couple that bring deep unity?

2.   Chastity means living life as a gift. How can we give more of ourselves to each other through both emotional and physical intimacy?

3.   In what areas of our marriage do we violate God's plan for human sexuality and chastity, or the unitive and procreative end? How will we resolve to make necessary changes?

Individually, spend some time thinking about how your spouse makes a gift of self to you and thank him or her for that gift.

Today's Couple Prayer

Lord Jesus Christ, you have created man and woman for one another. You have created our human sexuality as a gift. May we treasure your original design for this gift and make the necessary sacrifices to walk according to your original plan for love and sexuality. Amen.

DAY 16

HABITS PROMOTING CONJUGAL CHASTITY

Chastity—giving and receiving love as Christ gives and receives love—should be seen as a virtue that is forged through the daily lives of married couples. Whenever the married couple gives completely of themselves to the other and to their children, they are promoting and living conjugal chastity.

Dan

Each night before bed I place a fresh glass of water on Amber's nightstand because I know she likes to have a drink of water throughout the night. For ten years of marriage I've been getting her that glass of water. It's a very simple way to serve her, to give myself to her. Believe it or not, if I forget to get her a glass of water at night, she immediately asks, "What's wrong?"

The author of Romans exhorts Christians to "love one another with mutual affection; anticipate one another in showing honor. Do not grow slack in zeal, be fervent in spirit, serve the Lord. Rejoice in hope, endure in affliction, persevere in prayer" (Rom 12:10–12). Stop. Read that passage again, nice and slow. Maybe even write down this anthem and place it in a prominent place in your house. This verse is a beautiful exhortation for married couples who desire to live conjugal chastity and for families who desire to foster the virtue of chastity within their children. Husbands and wives should love one another with mutual affection, wherein each spouse tries to understand carefully how the other spouse receives love and affection, and strives to love the other through that form of affection. Love between couples can be expressed in words, letters, notes, flowers, small gifts, date nights—simple means to show the other that you care for them and love them.[20] Then Romans tells us to anticipate one another in showing honor, which means husbands and wives should live not to be served "but to serve" (Mk 10:45). Every act of service within the home, if done with the language of love and with the desire to "lay down one's life" (Jn 15:13) for those you love, becomes a habit that promotes conjugal chastity.

We promote chastity when we engage in all different forms of self-giving service toward the other: doing the dishes, folding the laundry, making the bed, sweeping the floor, and cutting the grass. We are exhorted to outdo one another in showing this honor to each other and told not to "grow slack in zeal." The desire to serve our beloved—often tangibly present during the courtship and engagement periods of a relationship—should only be strengthened and enflamed throughout marriage, not allowed to fizzle out as though it's unnecessary. If you are not in love with your spouse anymore, it's probably because you have replaced selflessness with selfishness. Service to our spouse may not be the greatest joy of every moment, but for the married couple who climbs the mountain of Calvary with Christ and lovingly lays down their lives for each other and their children day after day, the joy of the Resurrection will become present in their marriage and family life. It's not enough just to do it; we must strive to do it with and in love. "Whatever you did for one of these least brothers of mine, you did for me" (Mt 25:40).

With love, even the most burdensome task can become a source of joy and consolation. In most cases, you have to do these tasks anyway. You have a choice: You can do them begrudgingly and pull your cross along through the dust. Or you can do them smilingly and by free will, as acts of love, service, and self-gift.

Amber

I have to give myself pep talks a lot. Yes, I talk to myself constantly. I answer myself, too, and I don't care who knows it. The
thing is, we naturally want to run from the cross, and so I need
help to take up my cross smilingly! "Love serves," I tell myself
as I pour the drinks. "It's my joy to give this gift of comfort," as
I prepare the table for dinner. "Thank you, Jesus, for providing
clothing for these babies of mine, who are never uncomfortable when so many are," as I fold the laundry. I remind myself
that my work matters, and I stay focused on the goal of joyful
self-gift. Many times love is a choice you make and the warm
fuzzies follow. Sometimes the warm fuzzies don't follow, and
that's okay too. How much more a gift is it when I receive
nothing in return?

Chastity is all about gift. Couples have the radical responsibly to
guard themselves against pride that desires to turn inward and ask,
"How is this marriage and family satisfying me?" Instead, they must
stay focused outward, asking, "How can I satisfy the needs of my spouse
and children?"

Here are three additional ways to foster conjugal chastity:

Eucharist: A very special mention should be made of the Eucharist. When we were preparing for marriage, the Franciscan priest who
was in charge of our marriage prep encouraged us to implement a little
habit that has served as a beautiful reminder to us to embrace chastity
and self-giving love all through our marriage. We still remember this
priest teaching us a very simple lesson: "The words of consecration that
you hear every weekend at Mass are the words of your marriage vows."
What did he mean by this? In the words of consecration, the priest
speaks Jesus' own words: "Take this, all of you, and eat it, for this is
my Body, which will be given up for you." This is the language of love
that Christ himself uses with his bride before he gives a complete gift
of himself to her. Jesus freely offers all of himself to his beloved. This
Franciscan priest encouraged us to hold each other's hands during the
words of consecration and to be reminded every time we hear these

words that marriage is about living the sacrifice of the Cross for the sake of your beloved. Ten years later, every time we go to Mass and hear the words of consecration, we are not only reminded of Jesus' incredible love for us, his beloveds, but we are also reminded of the kind of love we are called to have for each other, our beloveds. We still hold hands during the consecration. We encourage you to consider doing the same.

Confession: Never tire of asking Jesus for forgiveness. Jesus wants us to come to him with our sin and our shame, our weakness and our need. It pleases the Lord to forgive us. He doesn't look down upon those who struggle with chastity and other sins. He understands that the human heart is broken, and he has given us the gift of Confession to heal the brokenness of our hearts, to bind up our wounds, and to give us the strength necessary to overcome our weaknesses. Confession provides us not only with the grace of forgiveness but also with the special grace of supernatural strength to combat our temptations. If you struggle with difficult and shameful sins, never grow weary of going to Confession. Ask the Lord often for forgiveness. Ask the Lord to give you a selfless heart, to make your heart like his. So many men and women fail to receive sacramental forgiveness for their sins against chastity because they are embarrassed. If it helps you, go to Confession with a priest that you don't know. Whatever it takes. Just don't hide from Jesus. Jesus came in love and mercy so that we don't have to hide any longer. He loves you for who you are, not who you pretend to be.

As we make a habit of examining our conscience, we become men and women who are chasing perfect love. We are no longer settling and allowing things to remain stagnant. We become holiness chasers! By humbling ourselves to ask for forgiveness from the Lord, we get into the practice of recognizing our need for growth and to say, "I'm sorry." Every marriage needs more of this. Imagine this marriage of self-giving love, in which each spouse lives to serve the other's needs, to outdo them in love and kindness, all the while striving to perfect themselves and readily owning up to their shortcomings. Love, service, humility, and forgiveness—these are key ingredients to a thriving marriage.

Fasting: Jesus assumes fasting to be a regular part of his follow-ers' lives. In Matthew 6, he doesn't say "if you fast" but rather "when you fast" (Mt 6:16). In Matthew 9, he doesn't say that his followers might fast but rather "they will fast" (Mt 9:15). Fasting isn't meant to be relegated to just one season in the Church year but rather it is meant to be a regular part of our Christian life. Fasting fosters chastity because it breaks the power of the flesh and strongholds that lay hold of us. Many married men and women experience sexual temptation at some point within their married lives. Fasting teaches us to reject the desires of the flesh. Not all temptation toward the self is sexual, of course. Perhaps one spouse is tempted to spend like crazy while the other is tempted to save every single penny and spend nothing. We know a couple like that. Okay, we *are* a couple like that. As we foster the habit of fasting within ourselves, when temptations arise, the soul is predisposed to reject the desires of the flesh. When we freely choose to reject these desires of the flesh through fasting, we begin to live life in the Spirit with more ease and joy. The fruit of the Spirit is more readily manifest in our lives. "The fruit of the Spirit is love, joy, peace, patience, kindness, generosity, faithfulness, gentleness, self-control" (Gal 5:22–23). These sound like the qualities we want in our marriage! Fasting brings about these fruits.

Today's Couple Discussion Questions

For individual consideration:

> Love one another with mutual affection; anticipate one another in showing honor. Do not grow slack in zeal, be fervent in spirit, serve the Lord. Rejoice in hope, endure in affliction, persevere in prayer. (Rom 12:10–12)

1. Which part of this passage does your spouse live well? Honor them for that.

2. Which part of this passage would you like to grow in personally?

Together:

3. How can we incorporate fasting more into our lives?

Today's Couple Prayer

Lord Jesus Christ, help us to love one another with mutual affection and to outdo one another in showing honor. Fill us with your passion and zeal for one another and for the kingdom of God. Allow us always to rejoice in hope, endure in affliction, and persevere in prayer. Amen.

FOSTERING CHASTITY IN OUR CHILDREN

Fostering chastity within our children begins the moment they are born. Ultimately, training in chastity is training in authentic love. From the moment a child is born, mother and father can begin training that child in the self-giving and life-giving love they display to one another. Your authentic marital love is the best teaching on chastity that your children could ever receive.

Jesus grew up learning chastity from his parents. Their mutual affection and self-giving love that he witnessed growing up prepared him to give himself as a gift for all. Mary, who was full of grace, became for Christ the truest model of purity and chastity. Joseph forged the virtues of self-mastery, self-discipline, and self-denial in his son, which prepared Jesus for his moment of self-denial in the Garden (Lk 22:42). Like Mary and Joseph, parents become for their children educators of authentic love.

A family guided by chastity carefully trains their children to avoid a life of egocentrism and to seek a life dedicated to self-giving love. Mothers and fathers should raise their children knowing that their lives are not about state championship titles, college scholarships, prestige, and popularity. While all these things are fine and certainly could glorify the Lord, the goal of life is to be given in loving service to God and others. Parents should educate their children that love isn't about passions and unbridled desires but rather about giving, sacrificing, and laying down our lives for others, just as Christ laid his life down for us.

Jesus Christ crucified is the perfection of chastity and love. Our daughter, Gemma, just barely five, is learning much about this truth. During Lent we have a "sacrifice of love" jar full of dried lima beans on the dining room table. It's just a simple mason jar with a purple ribbon tied around it. When one offers a sacrifice of love for another, they are allowed to quietly move a bean from the jar to a second jar. As Lent goes on, we challenge ourselves to move all the beans to the new jar. On Easter, all the moved beans become jelly beans to show the sweetness of sacrifice. For Gemma, this challenge has been very motivating, so much so that when she kisses the crucifix each evening she replaces the words "Jesus, I love you. Jesus, teach me how to love" with "Jesus, I love you. Jesus, teach me how to sacrifice." Even little ones can understand self-sacrificial love.

As children grow older, parents should use authentic love as the backdrop for conversations on chaste behavior. Love is about giving, not taking. Love wills the good of the other. Love is self-giving and life-giving. One can see how these simple principles can be used to explain to a child why pornography is wrong or why they should dress with dignity and modesty. Pornography isn't an authentic expression of love, because you are taking from another person. Lovers don't take; they give. Immodesty isn't an authentic expression of love, because it's not willing the good of the other, but tempting the other to lust. Lovers will the good of the other, not the near occasion of sin.

We have been blessed to work in youth ministry for fifteen years now and have worked with thousands of young people each year. As a result, we have developed a few principles that parents should follow if they desire for their children to grow up living chaste lives. These principles are not always popular and they are not widely practiced, but we have seen what works and what doesn't work.

Principle 1: Media matters. The consumption of unchaste media is one area of behavior that often goes unnoticed by parents. It's not hard to think about the endless amounts of movies, television shows, magazines, books, and music that don't portray self-giving and life-giving love and authentic love according to God's design. We sometimes ask high school students to make a list of media (movies, television, and music) that portray love as self-giving and life-giving as well as a list that fails to portray love as self-giving and life-giving. Believe it or not, they can only make one list! High-schoolers have never been able to give us a movie or television show that actually portrays authentic love! But they are able to identify an endless list of shows that portray unauthentic love. Consumption of unchaste media, no matter how young or old one is, has a tremendously harmful effect on the custody of our eyes, mind, and heart. A married couple should be careful to make sure that all media within their home is chaste media. You can't expect your children to watch chaste movies if you don't. Do the books you and your children read portray love according to God's design? Do the television shows and movies you and your children watch show love as faithful sacrifice and service, or enslavement to passions and reductive desires? Are the magazines that come into your house upholding the dignity of the human body? Does the music you allow your children to listen to portray authentic love? If the answer is no, then it belongs in the trash. Be the parent. Be bold. Throw trash in the trash.

When you *do* see love portrayed as self-gift in media, take the time to point it out to your children. Make media consumption a family affair, and follow it with discussion. It's your responsibility as parents to monitor what goes in your children's minds, as it will most certainly effect what comes out of their hearts.

Principle 2: Modesty matters. St. Paul poses an important question and charge to all of us: "Do you not know that your body is a temple of the Holy Spirit within you, whom you have from God, and that you are not your own? For you have been purchased at a price. Therefore glorify God in your body" (1 Cor 6:19–20). Our culture seems to have forgotten that our bodies are not our own, that we are to glorify God with our bodies. We encourage you to engrain in your children's minds from the beginning that their value lies in the beauty of their hearts, and in their identity as children of God. As parents we need to help our children not settle for the counterfeit of true beauty. Fathers, fight for your daughters' dignity. Have a backbone. Be strong enough to say, "No, you can't wear that." Love your daughters. Mothers, be witnesses and examples of dignity and self-respect for your daughters. We speak of our daughters specifically here because the pressure on them to reveal everything is so great, and in turn they often hide what is of true worth.

Both men and women are created in the image and likeness of God, and our physical beauty is meant to point toward the beauty of God himself. The way we dress should lead others to discover the beauty of God within us. Let's strive to raise children who *know* their beauty and dignity. By filling their cup at home, reminding them of their value and how imperishable and unrepeatable it is, perhaps we can avoid the driving forces behind immodesty and indecency: the need for comparison and "keeping up," the need to find value in what we have or how we look. The way we dress reflects the way we feel. Modesty is not about the law; it's about the heart. Win them over to desire what is true, good, and beautiful.

Principle 3: Kids need to be monitored on social media. This is a pretty simple principle. Social media has become more and more dangerous over the years. Young people today are not afraid to share words and pictures via social media that they would never have the courage or the audacity to share in public. Here is our simple suggestion: let your child have one or perhaps two forms of social media, but you control the password, and you have the opportunity (and the obligation) to regularly monitor what they are posting and, sometimes more importantly, what others are posting.

Principle 4: Pornography is a drug. Recent studies show the similarities between pornography and heavy drugs. Here is a quick explanation: Drugs such as cocaine make the user feel high by triggering a reward pathway in the brain to release high levels of a chemical in the brain called dopamine without making the user do any work to earn it. Want to guess what else releases the same high levels of dopamine? Porn. That surge of dopamine causes more than just happy feelings. As it pulses through the brain, dopamine helps create new brain pathways that essentially lead the user back to the behavior that triggered the chemical release. Thus an addiction is formed. The more a drug user takes a hit or a porn user looks at porn, the more pathways get wired into the brain, making it easier and easier for the person to turn back to using, whether they want to or not.[21]

Parents, stay vigilant and protect your children, even at a young age. Research Internet blocks. Know who your kids are hanging out with.

Dan was first exposed to pornography in middle school while playing at a classmate's house. This friend was a good kid, from a good family. With smartphones and iPods, young people's access to pornography has never been easier. You need to decide as a couple how you are going to proactively protect your children.

One last point: Pornography isn't just something that impacts boys. More and more girls are being exposed to pornography at younger and younger ages, and it's ruining their lives. Pornography gives young people a distorted few of relationships, human sexuality, and self-worth. Protect your boys, yes, but also protect your girls.

Principle 5: Kids shouldn't have smartphones. We know this isn't a popular position. But smartphones are for adults, not for children. First, as mentioned above, media matters and pornography ruins lives. A smartphone is an unmonitored device where your child has unlimited access to unchaste media and, worse, unlimited access to free pornography. Second, it used to be that when a boy wanted to talk to your daughter, he would call the home phone on which the mother or father would answer, followed by the scariest question from a parent, "Who is this?" In order to talk to a girl, he had to pass through the parents. Now, any guy can call or text your daughter at any hour of the night. Any girl can call or text your son at any hour of the night. Provocative and suggestive texts can be sent without your knowledge. We have seen the best parents trust their sons or daughters with phones—great kids who deserved their parents' trust—only to have inappropriate conversations happen. Why? Simply because kids shouldn't have unlimited, unmonitored access to each other. It doesn't work. Help them avoid the near occasion of sin. If your child needs a phone to call for a ride, buy a track phone with prepaid minutes without a data plan that is only to be used for calling you.

Principle 6: Dating is for marriage. This may not be a popular principle, but we are firm believers that young people shouldn't enter into dating relationships until they are able to reasonably start discerning marriage. Often a person can't reasonably start discerning marriage until they have finished or nearly finished their education and have an income reliable enough for marriage and family. For this reason we find no good reason to date before one is eighteen years old. Why? We should date with a purpose. The purpose of dating is to discern whether someone will be a suitable spouse. If you are unable to realistically discern marriage because of your age or state in life, then dating becomes something else. Often it becomes about personal fulfillment as opposed to training ourselves to be selfless gifts to another. Don't believe us? Over the last fifty years dating has been separated from discerning marriage and family life. Likewise, over the last fifty years the divorce rate has continued to rise. The more dating is separated from discerning marriage and family, the more sexual promiscuity increases outside of marriage, the more cohabitation becomes normative, and the more marriages end in divorce.

Most parents wouldn't let their middle-school- or high-school-aged children enter the seminary or the convent until they are old enough to seriously discern priesthood and religious life, so why let them date?

Dating with a purpose helps us to discern by not just our heart but also our head. Is this person virtuous? Are they committed to things in their life? Do they live out their faith well? Would they be a good spouse and parent? Dating for discernment of marriage is really a matter of living with the virtue of prudence: doing the right thing, at the right time, in the right way. Scripture stresses that we do not awaken love until the right time. Song of Solomon 8:4 says, "I adjure you, Daughters of Jerusalem, do not awaken or stir up love until it is ready!" When your children are of age and start dating, talk with them about their relationships so that you are a part of the process of discerning their spouse.

So how should we approach dating and romance with our children? Well, we certainly advise against shaming them for feeling attracted to someone. Attractions and sexual desires are natural and normal. Already, our five-year-old daughter, Gemma, has certain young men on our college-aged camp staff whom she is drawn to pour her affection upon. We simply try not to make a huge deal of it. We teach her to respect them, to pray for their holiness, to thank God for all the goodness she sees in them, just as we do with any of her friends. We are careful not to poke fun at her or to toss around terms such as *boyfriend* or *crush*. We don't objectify the objects of her admiration. We ask her things such as, "Why do you like sitting with so-and-so?" We point out their godly qualities. And, of course, we encourage her to have lots of awesome girlfriends.

With the middle-school- and high-school-aged young people we serve, again, we tell them that if they feel attractions, that's awesome—everything is working correctly! And just as with our little girl, we encourage them to celebrate that person's godly character, thank God for them, pray for them, and continue to get to know them in group situations. *Have fun* together, but understand that there is no need to claim or possess that person as yours. We encourage them to trust in God's plan for their lives and to know that if this truly is the right person, they will be there at the right time.

Principle 7: Chastity involves the heart, not just the body. We have seen a number of different harmful effects of premature dating, such as young people neglecting healthy same-sex friendships and close relationships with family. Many parents are vigilant in trying to protect their children from unchaste behavior but neglect to see that chastity involves the heart, not just the body. So while young people may maintain sexual chastity through chaste actions, often children fall prey to unhealthy emotional intimacy. You don't want to train your children to just "save their bodies" for their future spouses. You also want to communicate that we should also preserve our heart for our spouse. Living emotional chastity means watching children's phone conversations and text messages, guarding their social media, and making sure they are not telling one another that they love each other too soon. If you do allow your children to date, they should date within group or family settings. The best way to raise our children in both sexual and emotional chastity is for mothers and fathers to show lots of love to their children. Parents should regularly compliment their children, honoring them and making them feel loved. Moms and dads should also give their children physical touch to communicate love, even though they may not always act like they desire it. Young people need words and touches of love from both of their parents.

Today's Couple Discussion Questions

1. After reading today's reflection, what changes should we make in the way we are raising our children with regard to modesty, media consumption, or any other area?

2. How can we continue to foster chastity in our children?

Today's Couple Prayer

Lord Jesus Christ, we are imperfect at raising our children, but you are perfect. We pray that you will make up for all our insufficiencies whatever they may be. We pray that you will safeguard and protect our children all the days of their lives. Give them the wisdom to know how to live chaste lives and the courage to avoid the near occasion of sin. Fill their lives with true freedom, authentic love, and lasting joy. Amen.

Week 3

THE SECOND SECRET: CONJUGAL POVERTY

JESUS THE POOR

For you know the gracious act of our
Lord Jesus Christ, that for your sake he became poor
although he was rich, so that by his poverty
you might become rich.
—2 Corinthians 8:9

The only-begotten Son of God, the second person of the most Holy Trinity, the maker of heaven and earth, of all things visible and invisible, he who is light from light, true God from true God, by whom all things were made—this one, for our sake, became poor. Jesus Christ, through the mystery of the Incarnation, freely undertook the greatest act of poverty ever seen. He, who while in heavenly union with the Father was lacking nothing and enjoying absolute perfection, "emptied himself, taking the form of a slave, coming in human likeness" (Phil 2:7). This rich God of ours entered our broken and impoverished humanity. Isn't this incredible love?

When the God of the universe decides to enter his own creation, where does he enter? The incarnate Son of God was "wrapped in swaddling clothes and lying in a manger" (Lk 2:12), a feed trough for animals, surrounded by the dirt, filth, mud, and, least of all, the manure of animals. Certainly this is no place fit for a king. But Jesus was no ordinary king. Jesus humbled himself and became totally poor, rejecting from the very moment of his birth a life of comfort and ease.

Jesus enters our world by way of the filth of the manger to communicate a profound reality—no place is too dirty for God. Thank you, Jesus. No heart is too broken, no soul too lost, no sin too despicable for the powerful love of Jesus. Jesus didn't come to dwell with the perfect but with the imperfect, those who are dirty, despised, and broken. No matter how far we have fallen or how broken we feel, Jesus is near. Your heart, be it muddied with sin and complacency, is Jesus' manger. Let him rest there. Jesus' love embraces poverty.

In Jesus' infancy, he not only enters the poverty of the world, but he takes upon himself another form of poverty, that of dependence. From the very start of Jesus' earthly life, he was entirely dependent on Mary and Joseph. Jesus became the poor man who was in need of food and drink, the naked man in need of being clothed, the stranger in need of a welcome, the child who needed to be cared for, the imprisoned in our fallen world who was visited by the Magi and the shepherds (cf. Mt 25:31–46). In Matthew 25, the only reason Jesus equates himself with the hungry, the naked, the homeless, the ill, and the imprisoned is because he actually is that man. Jesus, in God's divine plan, freely becomes the poor man presented in Matthew's account of the final judgment. Jesus becomes radically dependent on Mary and Joseph for everything.

Just a few days after his birth, "behold, the angel of the Lord appeared to Joseph in a dream and said, 'Rise, take the child and his mother, flee to Egypt, and stay there until I tell you'" (Mt 2:13). Jesus was born into a family of migrants, refugees, and exiles. The Holy Family of Nazareth most likely found themselves homeless, jobless, and poor while they struggled to settle in this new land. We see in the Holy Family a radical example of the evangelical counsel of poverty. Out of obedience to the will of God, they fled into Egypt with nothing and lived there for years in simplicity and poverty of spirit, trusting and depending entirely on divine providence. The richest of human families lived in the poorest of conditions. This was the divine plan of God.

Amber

Every Christmas I want to turn our home into a magical place. I spend October and November on Pinterest scheming how this year I'll make it more cozy, more shimmery, more rustic, or more whimsical. My motherly heart loves to provide beauty and warmth in my home for my family. But do you know what happens every single year? The reality falls short of my grand expectations. See, the poverty of the Holy Family should both amaze us and encourage us as parents. Imagine the expectations Mary must have had for her baby boy. Imagine Joseph's expectations for how he would provide for his family. He probably never expected to be the foster father of Mary's child when they were betrothed. Mary probably wouldn't have included a barn birth if she had written out her birth plan (although the way trends are headed, this may become a thing . . . barn weddings, barn births . . .). They spent those first months and years of their marriage sojourning. And yet we know there was love. We know that, through the difficulty, God's will was accomplished.

Little is known of the early years of Jesus from infancy until the start of his public ministry, but of this we can be certain: he faces poverty. The law of Leviticus 12:6–8 requires that a lamb as well as a turtledove be offered as a sacrifice at the Temple after childbirth, but the law allows for two turtledoves to be substituted for the normal sacrifice of a lamb when a person isn't able to afford the offering of the lamb. We see in Luke's account of the presentation in the Temple that the Holy Family makes a poor man's offering of two turtledoves (cf. Lk 2:24). The Holy Family offers the gifts they can with love and humility.

At the very beginning of his public ministry, Jesus chooses voluntary poverty.

> Then Jesus was led by the Spirit into the desert to be tempted by the devil. He fasted for forty days and forty nights, and afterwards he was hungry. The tempter approached and said to him, "If you are the Son of God, command that these stones become loaves of bread." He said in reply, "It is written: 'One does not live by bread alone, but by every word that comes forth from the mouth of God.' . . . Then the devil took him up to a very high mountain, and showed him all the kingdoms of the world in their magnificence, and he said to

him, "All these I shall give to you, if you will prostrate yourself and worship me" (Mt 4:1–4, 8–9).

In this temptation, Jesus enters the temptation that we all face. Surely the temptations of comfort and ease, luxury and riches, are a serious temptation for modern humans. Many Christians in developed countries have fallen prey to these temptations, choosing to live a perpetual feast instead of entering the fast of the desert, choosing the magnificence of the kingdom of this world instead of the treasure we have in heaven (cf. Mt 19:21). This isn't the case for Christ. He, too, is tempted with the temptation of a life filled with riches and comfort. Instead, he chooses voluntary poverty. In the midst of the temptation for a life of ease and comfort, power and fame, riches and vainglory, Jesus responds by saying, "Get away Satan! It is written: 'The Lord, your God, shall you worship and him alone shall you serve'" (Mt 4:10).

In his public ministry Jesus ministers to the poor as a poor rabbi himself. "Foxes have dens and birds of the sky have nests, but the Son of Man has nowhere to rest his head" (Lk 9:58). His preaching gives special attention to the poor. "The Spirit of the Lord is upon me, because he has anointed me to bring glad tidings to the poor" (Lk 4:18; see also Is 61:1). In a sense, if we reject the evangelical counsel of poverty, we reject the preacher who has come and the treasure he has for us. Plenty of evidence suggests that in rejecting evangelical poverty we reject the treasure of heaven. Jesus himself teaches us, "When you hold a banquet, invite the poor, the crippled, the lame, the blind" (Lk 14:13), and it's the poor, the crippled, the lame, and the blind that Christ will invite to the banquet of heaven.

Jesus not only embraces material poverty in his public ministry but also poverty in the spirit through the company he keeps. Jesus finds companionship with the undesirable, sinners, prostitutes, and tax collectors. Jesus enters the homes of those who are unclean and eats at their tables. His voluntary poverty includes rejecting desires to please others and to live according to the status quo of the culture. Why? Not for the sake of poverty itself but for the sake of love that is displayed, not through vague compassion, but rather in true solidarity by which Jesus actually enters into the poverty of the one suffering. All of us are called to imitate this kind of poverty.

Ultimately, the deepest expression of the poverty of Christ is found in his suffering and death upon the Cross of Calvary. Like all of Christ's poverty, his suffering and death are also acts of voluntary poverty, for he says, "No one takes [my life] from me, but I lay it down on my own" (Jn 10:18).

From the very start of his Passion, the King of kings clothes himself in poverty: "Jesus found an ass and sat upon it, as it is written: 'Fear no more, O daughter Zion; see, your king comes, seated upon an ass's colt'" (Jn 12:14–15). Upon his entry into Jerusalem, Jesus rejects the social status of humankind, riding not on a warhorse worthy of a king but upon a lowly donkey—riding not with power and prestige but in humility and simplicity. How often do we freely choose the donkey over the warhorse—in our clothing, our cars, our homes, our possessions?

In his suffering, like in his Incarnation, Jesus once more becomes the poor man from Matthew 25. He is the prisoner who is sentenced to death (Jn 19:16). He is the naked man who is stripped of his garments (Jn 19:23). He is the sick man visited in his suffering (Lk 23:27–28). He is the stranger who feels companionship neither in heaven nor on earth (Mt 27:46). He is the hungry and the thirsty man who cries out, "I thirst" (Jn 19:28).

Jesus becomes the poorest of the poor, giving everything he has to us, who are the poorest of the poor, for we are impoverished by sin and death that we ourselves had no means of overcoming. "For you know the gracious act of our Lord Jesus Christ, that for your sake he became poor although he was rich, so that by his poverty you might become rich" (2 Cor 8:9).

He becomes totally poor, giving us everything. He gives not some of his blood but every drop of blood for our sake. He gives us every breath of his lungs and every beat of his heart. For our sake, he enters the poverty of death, totally naked, hanging upon the Cross, exposed, beaten, and humiliated for all to see.

In this profound humiliation, there is also a deep emotional poverty. He gives up his worldly reputation, suffering the death of a criminal. He gives up using his divine power, willingly suffering even though he can come down off the Cross (Mt 27:42). Jesus gives an impoverished human-ity every treasure he possesses. Surely, as St. John looks upon Jesus on the Cross, he understands, "This is my body, which will be given for you; do this in memory of me" (Lk 22:19). This invitation to "do this in memory of me" isn't merely an invitation to celebrate the Eucharistic meal in memory of Christ but also a profound invitation to enter the voluntary poverty of the Cross with Christ, to suffer for the sake of others with Christ, and to make the suffering, death, and resurrection of Christ present in our own lives through our acts of voluntary material and spiritual poverty.

In a world of egotism, materialism, individualism, and consumer-ism, in a culture of waste and of comfort seekers, Christians are called to radically serve the other, to lay down their lives for the sake of the other, to suffer for the other. In a world that cares only about "what's in it for me," we are called to "humbly regard others as more important than [our] selves" (Phil 2:3). This is the poverty of Christ that Christ calls us to embrace.

Today's Couple Discussion Questions

1. What about Jesus' poverty touches our hearts the most?

2. When reading the reflection above, how does Jesus become more "real" to us? How does his love become more "real" to us?

3. Like Jesus' temptation, how have we bought into the temptation to live for the magnificence of the kingdom of this world instead of the treasure we have in heaven?

4. In what ways have we chosen the warhorse over the donkey?

Today's Couple Prayer

Lord Jesus Christ, you are absolutely amazing. Your radical love for your people is beyond words. Thank you for becoming poor for our sake, so that through your poverty, we might become rich. Fill us with the richness of your love and mercy. Allow us to discover comfort in your love and not in the things of this world. Amen.

DAY 19

JESUS CALLS US TO BE POOR (DAY 1)

Jesus clearly calls his followers to embrace poverty, expressing his intentions in the Sermon on the Mount through two of his most prominent poverty sayings: "Do not store up for yourselves treasures on earth, where moth and decay destroy, and thieves break in and steal. But store up treasures in heaven, where neither moth nor decay destroys, nor thieves break in and steal. For where your treasure is, there also will your heart be" (Mt 6:19–21). Jesus also teaches, "No one can serve two masters. He will either hate one and love the other or be devoted to one and despise the other" (Mt 6:24). Reread these words of Christ slowly with an honest examination of your heart.

Later in his public preaching, Jesus once again invites all his followers to embrace Gospel poverty, not just those called to follow him through the priesthood or religious life. Luke points out that "great crowds were traveling with him, and he turned and addressed them" (Lk 14:25). Here as he addresses the "great crowds" of people following him, not the select few, he proclaims, "Every one of you who does not renounce all his possessions cannot be my disciple" (Lk 14:33). Gospel poverty here isn't stated as an option for some but as an imperative to which all followers of Christ are called.

Suggesting that poverty is an imperative for all followers is confusing. Does this mean that all married couples are called by God to be poor in such a way that they are unable to provide the basic needs for their children or unable to provide their children with a healthy lifestyle and a proper education? Of course not. Maybe the best way to discover the kind of poverty Christ calls us to is first to discover what kind of poverty Christ doesn't call us to. In doing so, we draw a distinction between destitution and "Gospel poverty."

When people hear the word *poverty*, they immediately associate it with the economic connotations of poverty and falsely assume that Gospel poverty is equivalent with destitution or an outright rejection of wealth. Jesus doesn't call his disciples to embrace a life of destitution, meaning sacrificing the basic necessities and a dignified human life. Jesus also doesn't call his followers to refuse to make money or provide for their families. Christ came to heal those suffering from destitution and to bring them into a fulfilled and dignified life. He says, "I came so that they might have life and have it more abundantly" (Jn 10:10). It would be contrary to the Good News of the Gospel if Jesus called us to a life of destitution.[1] We also see that throughout the gospels, Jesus attends weddings, feasts, and celebrations. He isn't opposed to joyful celebration, so much so that his first miracle takes place at a wedding feast so that the feast can continue instead of ending early.

Furthermore, wealth isn't the problem. A faithful disciple of Jesus Christ can, and often should, pursue wealth. Hard work, strong leadership, and innovative ideas merit just reward and payment. The key difference between a disciple of the Lord and a disciple of the world is how they use the wealth they receive. A disciple of the world uses his wealth for the treasures of this world, building up his own kingdom of comfort. On the contrary, a disciple of the Lord, who is dedicated to living Gospel poverty, uses his wealth for the sake of the kingdom of God.

A proper use of wealth asks the question, "What portion of this income do I reasonably need to live my state in life with simplicity?" You can see how a CEO of a Fortune 500 company may need to own nicer clothes and possibly drive a nicer car than a small business owner in order to maintain their state in life. Yet each of these disciples is called to examine how much of their wealth is used on themselves and how much of their wealth is surrendered to the evangelization and charitable needs of the Church. Wealth and Gospel poverty aren't opposed to one another. Gospel poverty doesn't evaluate how much profit one makes, but rather how the one who profits uses their wealth.

So while Jesus doesn't call his followers to a life of undignified destitution and the avoidance of wealth, he also isn't merely calling his disciples to some vague spirit of "detachment," wherein a disciple of Jesus lives with all the luxuries and comforts of the world while the poor go unnoticed so long as the disciple isn't "attached" to his or her possessions. Often Christians fail to live Gospel poverty because they turn the sayings of Jesus on poverty into nothing more than metaphors dealing only with spiritual poverty and not material poverty. They justify that "as long as I'm not attached to my possessions, then I can continue to have all the possessions I want, live in the luxury I want, with all the comforts of life that I deserve." Often we push the Gospel aside by justifying that we are not "attached" to our possessions. But this isn't what Jesus calls us to. The Gospel calls us to more than a metaphorical poverty or even a mere spiritual detachment. Christ calls his followers to a life of material simplicity, to a sparing-sharing lifestyle, for the sake of others. He even goes as far as to say that our salvation is dependent upon the way we treat the poor and suffering (cf. Mt 25:31–36). What you discover in the gospels is that Jesus calls his followers to give up something for the sake of those who are suffering, to live a life of simplicity so that others might simply live, and in this to live in imitation of Christ who voluntarily became poor to make others rich.

Therefore Christ calls his followers to embrace Gospel poverty, which is neither a state of destitution nor merely a state of metaphorical detachment. To understand this better, let's examine the beatitude "Blessed are the poor in spirit, for theirs is the kingdom of heaven" (Mt 5:3). In this beatitude, we can better understand what Gospel poverty is and what Christ calls us to.

The Beatitudes should be understood as the fulfillment of the old law in the new and everlasting law of love (Mt 5:18–20). Another way of saying this is that the Beatitudes, like the counsels of chastity, poverty, and obedience, teach us how to live perfect love.

The new law of Christ challenges followers not merely to look at the external realities of a law. It asks us to understand the interior disposition of love of God and love of neighbor that a believer should cultivate that leads to actions. Jesus doesn't merely call his followers to embrace material external poverty. He challenges them to possess the interior disposition of being poor in spirit, so much so that he prioritizes the internal over the external. This interior disposition forms perfect love within us and compels us to live a life of simplicity of material possessions for the sake of love of God and love of neighbor. One who is poor in spirit will necessarily also be one who has embraced simplicity of possessions for the sake of others because the interior disposition of the heart is the motivation for the exterior actions.

When Christ proclaims, "Blessed are the poor in spirit, for theirs is the kingdom of heaven" (Mt 5:3), he challenges us to embrace a poverty that entails total dependence on God, not on self, and he tells us that this poverty is ultimately what is best for us. First and foremost, Gospel poverty entails a death to self and an acceptance that we are totally and completely dependent on God for everything. In his Passion and death, Jesus makes himself radically dependent on God the Father. We, too, are called to become radically dependent on the Father.

Christ calls all of us to be totally dependent on the Father for our earthly needs, our earthly comfort, and our earthly happiness. To obtain perfect love within our Christian life as well as within a vocation to marriage and family life, poverty of spirit is necessarily required. If you don't trust in the providence of God for all things, you will never be able to perfectly embrace love of God and love of neighbor. However, this poverty should be seen as a blessing, not a curse. Radically depending on the Father is an amazing gift because the Father is a good Father who desires our happiness more than we desire our own happiness.

Today's Couple Discussion Questions

1. How dependent are we on the Lord? How dependent are we on ourselves?

2. As stated above, a disciple of the world uses their wealth for the treasures of this world, building their own comfort kingdom, whereas a disciple of the Lord uses their wealth for the sake of the kingdom of God. How are we living as disciples of the world or of the Lord?

3. What portion of our income do we reasonably need in order to live the state in life we are called to with simplicity?

Today's Couple Prayer

Lord Jesus Christ, we give ourselves completely and totally to you, dependent on your love for us. We surrender our need for control. We surrender our need to be the "providers" of our family and declare that you are the true provider of our family. We love you and gratefully accept all the gifts you bestow upon our family. Amen.

JESUS CALLS US TO BE POOR (DAY 2)

Yesterday we reflected on the great beatitude found in the Gospel of Matthew, "Blessed are the poor in spirit, for theirs is the kingdom of heaven" (Mt 5:3). This beatitude points us to the inner disposition of Gospel poverty, a disposition of total dependence on God. But to understand the fullness of the poverty to which we are called, we should also look at the corresponding beatitude found in the Gospel of Luke. In doing so, we discover that Gospel poverty not only includes an interior disposition of dependence on God but also the exterior reality of a life of material simplicity.

Luke helps us understand that Jesus necessarily calls us to something more than dependence on him and mere detachment from earthly goods when he writes, "Blessed are you who are poor, for the kingdom of God is yours. . . . But woe to you who are rich, for you have received your consolation" (Lk 6:20, 25). Luke makes clear that wealth isn't the problem but rather the consolation, comfort, and luxury the wealthy enjoy while the poor go on suffering, unnoticed and ignored. Those who are blessed by wealth should use their abundance to aid those who are suffering.

Luke explains this concept further in his account of the rich man and the poor man named Lazarus:

There was a rich man who dressed in purple garments and fine linen and dined sumptuously each day. And lying at his door was a poor man named Lazarus, covered with sores, who would gladly have eaten his fill of the scraps that fell from the rich man's table. Dogs even used to come and lick his sores. When the poor man died, he was carried away by angels to the bosom of Abraham. The rich man also died and was buried, and from the netherworld, where he was in torment, he raised his eyes and saw Abraham far off and Lazarus at his side. And he cried out, "Father Abraham, have pity on me. Send Lazarus to dip the tip of his finger in water and cool my tongue, for I am suffering torment in these flames." Abraham replied, "My child, remember that you received what was good during your lifetime while Lazarus likewise received what was bad; but now he is comforted here, whereas you are tormented." (Lk 16:19–25)

We can see that it was not the rich man's wealth that caused him eternal torment but rather his lack of generosity with that wealth. The rich man chose to "dress in purple garments" and "dine sumptuously each day" instead of aiding in the relief of the poor man. Of course, when we hear this account, we are shocked that someone wouldn't care for the poor man at his doorstep, but let's be honest, many of us dress in fine clothes and dine sumptuously each day, ignoring the needs of the poor man. Granted, the poor man isn't at our doorstep, but only because we have pushed him away from our neighborhoods, not even allowing him near our doorstep. Luke's account reminds us that Christ calls us not only to embrace a poverty in spirit that entails total dependence on God but also a real simplicity of possessions for the sake of love of neighbor. In this account, Jesus suggests that even though the rich man could afford the nice clothes and afford to dine sumptuously each day, he should have used his wealth differently. Gospel poverty necessarily entails renouncing a life of self-comfort and dedicating oneself to a life that seeks to bring comfort to others.

One account that beautifully merges the full understanding of Gospel poverty, embracing a material simplicity accompanied by dependence on God, is that of the poor widow's gift. "When he looked up he saw some wealthy people putting their offerings into the treasury and he noticed a poor widow putting in two small coins. He said, 'I tell you truly, this poor widow put in more than all the rest; for those others have made offerings from their surplus of wealth, but she, from her poverty, has offered her whole livelihood'" (Lk 21:1–4).

Jesus calls all the lay faithful to embrace the counsel of poverty. This poverty is lived not when one gives from a surplus of wealth but when one gives truly from their want. Mother Teresa of Calcutta understood this clearly when she wrote, "I don't want you to give me what you have left over. I want you to give from your want until you really feel it!"[2]

Honestly, the entirety of the Gospel calls the Christian to be poor as Christ was poor, to depend entirely on the Father as Christ depended entirely on the Father, to give until it hurts. The poverty that Christ calls us to is the very paradox of Christianity:

- The rich are poor. The poor are rich (see Lk 6:20, 24).
- The first shall be last. The last shall be first (see Mt 19:30, 20:16).
- The exalted are humbled. The humble are exalted (see Lk 14:11).
- The one who would be greatest among us must be the servant of all (see Mt 23:11).
- The one who loves his life will lose it, while he who hates his life will live forever (see Jn 12:25).
- The one who is the least will be the greatest, and the greatest will be the least (see Lk 9:48).
- The one who loses his life will save it, and the one who saves his life will lose it (see Lk 9:24).
- If you wish to live, you must deny yourself and die to yourself (see Lk 9:23).
- The one who forgives is forgiven (see Mt 6:12).
- The one who mourns rejoices (see Mt 5:4).
- The one who is weak is strong (see 2 Cor 12:10).
- Give preference to one another in showing honor (see Rom 12:10).
- Regard others as more important than yourself (see Phil 2:3).

- Rejoice when you are persecuted (see Mt 5:11).

- Glory in your sufferings and tribulations (see Rom 5:3).

- Bless those who curse you (see Lk 6:28).

- Love those who hate you (see Mt 5:44).

- Pray for those who hurt you (see Lk 6:28).

Gospel poverty entails all the above. It's a life of complete paradox, a life of complete dependence on God.

We pray that you will live this paradox in your marriage and family life. We pray that you will embrace the paradox of the Gospel, because it's nothing more than the paradox of Jesus, the paradox of perfect love. We pray that you will raise your children to see this madness as greatness.

Today's Couple Discussion Questions

1. How do we care for Lazarus? Or, like the rich man, how do we ignore Lazarus's cry for help?

2. Which of the Christian paradoxes speak most deeply to our hearts? Which one or two would we like to live more radically?

Today's Couple Prayer

Lord Jesus Christ, we want to live the madness of the Cross. We want to live all for you and all for your kingdom. Help us embrace the radical call of the Christian life. Protect us from the trickery of the world that seeks to seduce us with comfort and pleasure. Make each of us another Christ in this world. Amen.

DAY 21

CONJUGAL POVERTY

Because of the great variety of socioeconomic and cultural situations of families, it becomes very difficult to draw definitive "rules" for conjugal poverty. Recall that Christ came to set us free from the law, not to place the burden of the law upon us. In calling your family to embrace conjugal poverty, we don't want this to be viewed as a burden or a law placed upon you but rather as an opportunity for greater, more perfect love and real freedom. The question shouldn't be "How much do we have to give?" but rather "How much can we give for the sake of others?"

Instead of focusing on definitive rules for conjugal poverty, it serves us better to reflect on the proper interior disposition of those who have embraced real Gospel poverty within their marriage. Couples can then prayerfully discern for themselves in what way God is calling them to live this virtue appropriately according to their own state in life, recalling the widow's mite and that they are called to give from their want and not merely their surplus.

For starters, let's just say that a married couple shouldn't embrace Gospel poverty for the sake of poverty itself but for the good it produces. Spiritual writer Fr. Thomas Dubay challenges married couples to embrace the "negative situation" of poverty for the sake of the four "positive values" it produces: "radical readiness for the divine word . . . a sparing lifestyle making sharing possible . . . apostolic credibility . . . pilgrim witness."[3] Today we look at how Gospel poverty leads to these four positive values.

Radical readiness for the divine Word: Gospel poverty allows the married couple to be radically ready for whatever Jesus calls them to as a couple. On a large scale, if a couple builds a kingdom for themselves and their family in this world, it would be difficult to respond to the Lord if he calls them to move or to serve as missionaries. Yet even on a smaller scale, this radical readiness is needed. Suppose a family structures its budget so tightly that there is little room for giving. If the Lord proposes to them particular needs in their community, such as a financial need in the parish, a young couple in need of hospitality, or a local soup kitchen with a sudden increased need of food for the poor, the couple may be unable to rise to answer God's call because their budget has no room for charity and almsgiving. Just because a married couple can afford a larger house or a nicer car doesn't always mean they should take on those financial commitments. Conjugal poverty entails that the couple budgets first and foremost for the freedom of giving so that when opportunities and needs arise, they are radically ready to respond to the divine Word and meet the needs of others. If your family has been blessed with an adequate income but your family budget is so tight that there isn't room for giving, that is a sign that serious conversations are in order about how God may be calling you to adjust your lifestyle for the sake of generosity. What can you and your children do without so that you can give more?

A sparing lifestyle making sharing possible: As Dubay suggests, conjugal poverty produces a sparing lifestyle that makes sharing possible. Married couples are not called to give all of their possessions to the poor, because their primary responsibility lies with their own children and fulfilling their children's needs and education. However, in our culture it's easy to be convinced that one's children "need" far more than they actually do. Instead of living Gospel poverty, many Christians almost accidently start spending money on what the rest of the culture spends money on. Conjugal poverty allows for a married couple to carefully discern what is needed for their family and what isn't. The more sparing the couple is, the more they have to share. This sharing can be exercised through the freedom of offering hospitality to guests and aiding in the corporal and spiritual works of mercy within the Church. Conjugal poverty produces the freedom to share, whereas couples who don't live a sparing lifestyle may not have the same freedom.

Apostolic credibility: Dubay places great importance on the responsibility of all Christians to provide apostolic credibility. How often we hear Christians say things such as, "I really wish we could help with that, but we just can't afford to right now." If these Christians spoke truthfully, many would say something closer to: "We could afford to help with that mission if we stopped drinking our cocktails, cut back on our expensive coffee habits, spent less on dining out, took simpler vacations, got rid of our cable, and bought a used car instead of a new one." Couples lose their apostolic credibility if they say they want to live a life of Christian solidarity but ultimately fail to stand with those who are suffering. Sometimes it's not enough to want to help. Sometimes we need to sacrifice bad or expensive habits in order to help. Consider what St. James says: "What good is it, my brothers, if someone says he has faith but does not have works? Can that faith save him? If a brother or sister has nothing to wear and has no food for the day, and one of you says to them, 'Go in peace, keep warm, and eat well,' but you do not give them the necessities of the body, what good is it? So also faith itself, if it does not have works, is dead" (Jas 2:14–17).

Simply put, many Christians just are not credible anymore. It's as though we are talking the talk but not walking the walk. You have probably heard it said that the single greatest cause of atheism in the world today is Christians themselves who often live more like pagans than the Christ they say they follow. We believe that! Here are the tough questions to ponder: Are you credible? When people look at your lifestyle, do they know that it's driven by the Gospel?

Pilgrim witness: Apostolic credibly naturally flows into a pilgrim witness. The Christian is called to live conjugal poverty not only for their own sake but also for the sake of the witness it provides. Many people falsely look to the world and its treasures as their source of hope, comfort, and consolation. But Fr. Dubay challenges us that "we need joyous, loving men and women to show in their lives that one can live a sparing-sharing lifestyle and still be happy and fulfilled. We need to induce conversion into the masses first of all by example, then by word."[4]

In the Gospel of John, shortly before Jesus is arrested and led to his death, he prays, "I do not ask that you take them out of the world but that you keep them from the evil one. They do not belong to the world any more than I belong to the world. . . . As you sent me into the world, so I sent them into the world" (Jn 17:15–16, 18). If you place water and oil in a bottle together, the two coexist but remain separate from one another. If you shake the bottle, the water and oil appear to become one, but after the bottle stands for just a little while, the water and oil separate again. This is how the Christian who has been baptized with the life-giving waters should exist in the world. Even though the Christian is mixed together in the daily affairs of the world, the Christian and the world are never one. For the Christian, the world isn't our home. The Christian is a pilgrim, a missionary, or as St. Peter says, an exile:

> But you are "a chosen race, a royal priesthood, a holy nation, a people for his own, so that you may announce the praises" of him who called you out of darkness into his wonderful light. Once you were "no people" but now you are God's people; you "had not received mercy" but now you have received mercy. Beloved, I urge you as aliens and sojourners to keep away from worldly desires that wage war against the soul. Maintain good conduct among the Gentiles, so if they speak of you as evildoers, they may observe your good works and glorify God. (1 Pt 2:9–12)

All the lay faithful, whether single or married, have passed through the waters of Baptism and have been made holy, not by our own accord, but by the workings of the Holy Spirit. As a holy people, we are set apart from this world and dedicated to God. St. Peter appropriately refers to us as "aliens and sojourners" who are no longer of this world but of the world to come until the day we see Christ in glory. We live in the world but not of the world. Thus married men and women exercise holiness in a way that is in the world but set apart from the world. This provides a powerful witness to all who see it.

When those living for the world see joyful Christians living a sparing-sharing lifestyle, with their eyes set on heaven, they are left questioning whether the treasure of heaven is the greater prize. Conjugal poverty is taken up for the sake of pilgrim witness. Imagine the powerful witness of a family that lives a sparing-sharing lifestyle—that witness will undoubtedly convert the hearts of other families. It will have an impact on culture in a big way. In fact, it will re-Christianize culture.

In the book of Joshua, we see something that readily applies to the Christian Church today. Joshua is on his deathbed, and before he dies, he calls together all the tribes of Israel, the elders, the leaders, the judges, and the officers. In his final speech to his people, he summarizes all the goodness of the Lord: how he made of them a people, how he led them out of slavery, how he provided for them in the desert, how he gave them the promised land, and how he destroyed all their enemies. But then comes the callout. Even though the Lord has done all of this for his people, his people are still worshiping false idols. They haven't stopped worshiping the God of Israel, but they are worshiping the God of Israel and the false idols of the world. It's an unhealthy mixture. The water and the oil are not separate anymore—they are mixed together.

Are we any different? The Lord has given us so much. He has freed us from sin and death, delivered us from the enemy, provided for our families, and cared for us in times of need. Yet how often do we turn to the false idols of our generation: money, possessions, comfort, entertainment, acceptance, success? Sure, we still worship the God of Israel, but we also worship idols. Our idols are anything that we serve, anything that consumes our time, mind, energy, and passions ahead of the living God.

Joshua boldly stands before his people and exhorts them, saying, "Fear the Lord and serve him completely and sincerely. Cast out the gods your ancestors served beyond the River" (Jos 24:14). He challenges them to "choose today whom you will serve" (Jos 24:15). With incredible boldness, Joshua proclaims, "As for me and my household, we will serve the Lord" (Jos 24:15).

You have a decision before you. Decide today whom you will serve, mammon or God. As God says, you can't serve two masters.

As for our house, we will serve the Lord.

As for our house, we will seek radical readiness for the divine Word.

As for our house, we will seek a sparing lifestyle, making sharing possible.

As for our house, we will seek apostolic credibility that leads to a pilgrim witness.

How about your house? What will you do?

Today's Couple Discussion Questions

1. In what ways are we tempted by the false idols of our modern day? How can we serve the Lord with a more undivided heart?

2. What does it mean to be a pilgrim witness? When we evaluate our spheres of influence (work, community, children), how are we pilgrim witnesses in these places?

3. In what ways do we exhibit radical readiness for the Word of God? If God asks us to do something, in what ways can we ensure that we are ready to do it?

Today's Couple Prayer

Lord Jesus Christ, we want to serve you, the Lord our God, with all our heart, mind, soul, and strength. Prepare in our hearts a radical readiness to serve you and your people. Help us desire and choose this day, and all days, that "as for me and my house, we will serve the Lord." Amen.

POVERTY AS A
DISPOSITION OF TRUST

Because each family's situation is unique, conjugal poverty can't become a definitive list of rules to be followed but is rather a set of interior dispositions of the heart. For the next two days, we will look at the two key dispositions of the heart that lead to a life of perfect love: a disposition of trust and a disposition of gift. Today we will focus on poverty as a disposition of trust.

Gospel poverty is ultimately about dependence on God, which is founded on the interior disposition of trust in God. Do you trust God? Do you have faith in him that he will provide for all your needs? Do you trust that he, not you, is the provider of your family? Jesus tells us in the Gospel of Matthew:

> Therefore I tell you, do not worry about your life, what you will eat [or drink], or about your body, what you will wear. Isn't life more than food and the body more than clothing? Look at the birds in the sky; they do not sow or reap, they gather nothing into barns, yet your heavenly Father feeds them. Are you not more important than they? Can any of you by worrying add a single moment to your life-span? Why are you anxious about clothes? Learn from the ways wildflowers grow. They do not work or spin. But I tell you that not even Solomon in all his splendor was clothed like one of them. If God so clothes the grass of the field, which grows today and is

thrown into the oven tomorrow, will he not much more provide for you, O you of little faith? So do not worry and say, "What are we to eat?" or "What are we to drink?" or "What are we to wear?" All these things the pagans seek. Your heavenly Father knows that you need them all. But seek first the kingdom [of God] and his righteousness, and all these things will be given you besides. Do not worry about tomorrow; tomorrow will take care of itself. Sufficient for a day is its own evil. (Mt 6:25–34)

Don't be deceived to think that you are the provider of your family. God alone provides all good things, and we can trust in him because he is a Father who loves his children. So many married couples live with such great anxiety and fear over finances. What if that wasn't the case? What if you had peace knowing God would care for you and your family? We testify that you can have this kind of peace and freedom.

How did we develop an interior disposition of trust in our marriage? For us, learning to tithe was the most effective means of placing our faith in God and thus fostering trust in our hearts. Scripture provides countless examples of how a tithe produces a disposition of trust. As early as Abel we see the generous gift of a tithe given to the Lord as witness to the trust he placed in God. In scripture, a tithe can include countless forms of offerings and gifts, but the faithful consistently give the "firstfruits" (cf. Gn 4:3–7, 14:18–20, 28:13–22; Lv 27:30–33; Nm 18:20–28; Dt 12:17–19, 14:22–29). Placing their trust in divine providence, the faithful don't give God their leftovers but rather the first portion, the best portion. Their tithe consists of giving God their best livestock or crops. Many Catholics have stopped giving God their firstfruits and simply give him their leftovers.

Jesus continues to call his followers to give the firstfruits of their treasure to God. In Matthew 6, after exhorting his followers to depend totally on God, he tells them to display this dependence and to "seek *first* the kingdom [of God] and his righteousness, and all these things will be given you besides" (Mt 6:33). The Christian faithful are called to aid in "helping the Church's mission with money, time, and personal resources of all kinds. This sharing is not an option for Catholics who understand what membership in the Church involves. It is a serious duty. It is a consequence of the faith which Catholics profess and celebrate."[5]

A healthy habit of a couple striving to embrace conjugal poverty includes giving the firstfruits of their income to God and the Church's mission of caring for the poor and evangelizing all nations. Prayerfully discern what percentage of your monthly income should be given as a tithe. We encourage couples to see the first 10 percent of their income at minimum as an offering to the Lord. Why 10 percent? Well, it's biblical. According to the Mosaic law, the Israelites were required to give 10 percent of their crops and livestock (cf. Lv 27:30; Nm 18:26; Dt 14:24; 2 Chr 31:5). Before this law was even given by the Lord, both Abraham and Jacob were inspired by their devotion to give a tenth of everything they received from the Lord (Gn 14:20; Heb 7:2, 4). Jacob makes a vow to the Lord, "Of everything you give me, I will return a tenth part to you without fail" (Gn 28:22). God provides your family with a means of income; it seems appropriate to make that same vow to the Lord: "Of everything you give me, Lord, I will faithfully return a tenth of everything back to you."

For many couples, and maybe for you, 10 percent seems like an outrageous amount to give. Most Catholics give less than 1 percent of their income to the poor and the missionary needs of the Church. According to recent studies through the Dynamic Catholic Institute, only 7 percent of Catholics contribute to 80 percent of the Church's resources, both volunteer and financial.[6] If 100 percent of Catholics gave generously, can you imagine how much good the Church could do in the world? Sometimes the reason Catholics give so little is because they lack trust. Other times it's because many of us have chosen to live for the treasures of this world rather than the treasures of heaven. Might God be challenging you to start giving 10 percent?

Some argue that the 10 percent tithe doesn't apply to us anymore because it was an Old Testament law, and Jesus has instituted the new law. But we see that Jesus calls the Christian to give everything, not just 10 percent. The new law of love calls us beyond legalistic giving. There is little value in giving 10 percent when one could easily give 20 percent. There is great value in giving 1 percent when one has very, very little to give. In writing to the Corinthians, St. Paul exhorts the people to give "whatever [they] can afford" (1 Cor 16:2). For some, that means giving more than 10 percent; for others, that means giving less than 10 percent in the circumstance of unemployment or serious medical bills. Every Christian should diligently pray and seek God's will on how much to give, based on a disposition of trust that God provides all things. Above all, tithes and offerings should be given with pure motives, an attitude of worship to God and service to the Body of Christ, and a joyful spirit of trust, for "God loves a cheerful giver" (2 Cor 9:7).

In our marriage, we discovered that at first we had a very hard time being disciplined in giving God our firstfruits. Then, a few years into our marriage, we made one very simple change that radically changed our lives and brought us so much freedom. We found ourselves as a young married couple with close to $75,000 of college debt, working on a parish youth minister's salary, and with our first baby on the way. We stumbled upon Dave Ramsey's book *The Total Money Makeover*. The simplicity of his biblical approach to finances was amazing and deeply convicting. Essentially he exhorts Christians to live debt-free and to seek wealth not to make a living but rather to make a giving. Within a few years we were not only able to overcome mountains of debt but also grew in a deep disposition of trust in God with our finances. We surrendered our finances over to the Lord, and before long we began giving him the first 10 percent of our income, whereas before we were giving less than 2 percent. Here was the simple but life-changing thing we did: in order to make sure that Jesus always received our firstfruits, we set up a secondary checking account wherein the first 10 percent of our paycheck went and we called that our "tithe account"; the other 90 percent went into our normal checking account. With automatic deposit, we never had a chance not to give God our firstfruits. This simple act led to so much financial freedom.

Quickly God began blessing us in tremendous ways, and we paid off 100 percent of our debt and were able to generously give to the needs of others. Because the separate checking account constantly has funds being added to it, paycheck after paycheck, there is almost always money to give when needs in the community or Church arise. This allows for the radical readiness we spoke of yesterday. We share this part of our lives with you not to exalt ourselves for giving but to testify to the freedom we have found. Finances used to be a huge cause of concern and anxiety. Now finances are a source of blessing and joy. And honestly, since making the decision to tithe, God has provided everything we could ever ask for and much, much more. God can't be outdone in generosity.

Today's Couple Discussion Questions

1.   On a scale of one to ten, how much trust (in general) do we have in the Lord? On a scale of one to ten, how much trust do we have in the Lord with regard to our finances?

2.   In what ways are we giving God the firstfruits of our time and treasure? How might we improve on that?

Today's Couple Prayer

Jesus, we trust in you. Jesus, we trust in you. Jesus, we trust in you. We trust that you will provide for all our needs. We trust that you love our family and desire their goodness more than we ever could. We trust that you will provide what is best for us. We abandon ourselves completely over to your divine will and will go wherever you lead us. Amen.

DAY 23

POVERTY AS A DISPOSITION OF GIFT

Yesterday we spoke of poverty as a disposition of trust. Today we will speak of poverty as a disposition of gift.

Psalm 23:6 says, "Indeed, goodness and mercy will pursue me all the days of my life." God's goodness and love are ever present in our lives, in every conversation and circumstance, but people are often blinded from this love and goodness by the "want" that consumes them. When wearing the blinders of want, people look ahead constantly, wanting what they don't have and failing to see what they already have. As the Psalmist tells us, "The Lord is my shepherd, there is nothing I lack" (Ps 23:1). There is nothing I shall want. He is our shepherd. He is our provider. And in him is goodness and love.[7]

People so often busy themselves striving to build their own king-doms of comfort instead of dwelling in the kingdom of God that is already at hand (Mk 1:15). In striving to build a kingdom of comfort, it's easy to be possessed by want. Married couples can easily fall prey to this temptation, wanting nicer cars or bigger houses, wanting more clothes or bigger tele-visions, wanting more entertainment for ourselves or for our children. It's easy for marriage and family life to be filled with endless lists of wants that consume our hearts and enslave us with ingratitude. We become blind to the countless gifts the Lord has showered upon us. A disposition of trust in the Lord naturally flows into a disposition of gift, wherein we see the

Lord, not ourselves, as the provider of all that we have. This fosters the disposition of gift that leads to praise and thanksgiving. Conjugal poverty always includes thanksgiving. "In all circumstances give thanks, for this is the will of God for you in Christ Jesus" (1 Thes 5:18).

Ultimately conjugal poverty results in a true disposition of gift, seeing all things as gifts from God and generously giving in return. Life is about making a giving, not making a living. Once the couple possesses these two interior dispositions of trust and gift, then external poverty begins to make sense. The couple begins to internalize the words of Christ, "Without cost you have received," and thus draw the same conclusion as Christ, "Without cost you are to give" (Mt 10:8). The couple begins to understand that Gospel poverty is less about the "giving up" and more about the "giving."

Within the context of this disposition of gift, we should remember that "children are the supreme gift of marriage" (*Gaudium et Spes*, 50). Children should be welcomed lovingly by the couple as a gift from the Lord. Being open to a larger family naturally allows the couple to live Gospel poverty and raise children in such because, as all parents know, raising children requires the generous giving of our own financial resources for the sake of the children. We understand raising children to be a fulfillment of the challenges Jesus imposes upon us in Matthew 25. After all, when we welcome the gift of children into our homes, we welcome Christ himself. When we feed our hungry children, give drink to our thirsty children, clothe our naked children, and care for them in their sicknesses and the struggles of life, we, in fact, do all of this for Jesus.

Couples should discern carefully when and how many children they will welcome into their families. We are not recommending you add to your family with reckless abandon, but welcoming another child into the world should be seen as more important than a larger house, nicer cars, and more vacations. The greatest gift you can give is the gift of life. Many parents feel as though they don't have the financial resources to welcome another child into the world when, in fact, they may have the resources but simply need to understand that children don't need to be raised in a consumerist mentality. Children, like adults, are more blessed by living lives of simplicity.

This disposition naturally overflows into a life of generosity. It should be repeated that the evangelical counsels are not ends in themselves, but rather they find their fulfillment in the greatest virtue, that of love (1 Cor 13:13). The virtue of poverty also enables married couples to focus on love of neighbor in a more radical way. For the vast majority of married men and women whose days are filled with work and family life, the ability for them to give their time generously to the needs of the poor becomes increasingly difficult. When we embrace poverty not only in finances but also in calendar planning, we find that we are able to be more generous with our time and talents.

St. Paul tells the Corinthians that the Church in Macedonia gave "in a wealth of generosity on their part" even while "their profound poverty overflowed" (2 Cor 8:2). The Christians in Macedonia understood that they weren't called to give from their excess but from their want. St. Paul follows this by exhorting the Corinthians to live lives of generosity: "Now as you excel in every respect . . . may you excel in this gracious act also. I say this not by way of command, but to test the genuineness of your love by your concern for others" (2 Cor 8:7–8).

When you have a genuine concern for others and when you see all that you have as a total gift from the Father, your heart is moved to deny yourself for the sake of others. Your heart is changed, and you freely choose simplicity in all things, so that instead of living at your means or beyond your means, you freely choose to live below your means so as to have more to give.

We encourage you as a couple to discern carefully how you can live a life of deeper simplicity for the sake of others. You can choose simplicity in the foods you eat, the hobbies and activities in which you participate, the entertainment you experience, the vacations you take, the cars you drive, the home in which you live, the clothes you wear, the cosmetic products you purchase, the electronics you choose to purchase or not purchase, the brands you support, and more. In the spirit of simplicity, you should carefully discern needs versus wants. Simple changes such as changing the brand of coffee you brew or the amount of times you eat out in a given month can really make the difference between having the ability to give 7 percent versus 10 percent of your income to the needs of others.

"Without cost you have received, without cost you are to give" (Mt 10:8).

Today's Couple Discussion Questions

1.   How do we express gratitude for everything the Lord has given us?

2.   In what areas in our lives could we cut back in order to give more?

Today's Couple Prayer

Lord Jesus Christ, you have given us more than we could ever ask for. Thank you, Jesus. Thank you for providing for our family and us. Thank you for your love and mercy. Make each of us another Christ so that we might be those who give "without cost," even when it is difficult. Amen.

FOSTERING POVERTY IN OUR CHILDREN

The title of today's reflection is probably one of the most countercultural phrases in this book. Yes, as Christians we want to foster Gospel poverty in our children's lives. But this smacks in the face of what the world would tell us. What does the world tell us to do for our children? We bet you already know. Here, we will prove it to you.

Fill in the blanks: Every morning Mom and Dad wake their children and send them off to _____. In school parents and teachers want kids to get good _____ so that they will get into a good _____. We want our children to get into good colleges so that they get good _____ and make a lot of _____. What was the last word you came up with? Was it *money*? Yep. That is what the world is teaching young people to live for. Nowadays, many pursuits in education are not for the sake of truth and understanding, nor for the sake of self-discovery and discovering how we can best serve others. Ultimately the modern education system for children boils down to getting a high enough grade point average so you can get a good scholarship, go to a good college, get a good job, and make a lot of money.

Remember, wealth isn't a bad thing, but often people don't raise their children to give their wealth away to others. Are you raising your children to make a living or make a giving?

Here is the issue: Often people worry more about their children's worldly happiness than they do about their eternal happiness. But those seeking perfect love don't want to raise their children to be nothing more than mules of the culture. They want to raise their children to be selfless givers.

We will be honest—this isn't easy. Consumerism is seductive. It pulls young people in, and they get swept away by hedonism and materialism. In our years of youth ministry, we have found that certain principles help form a spirit of simplicity within children:

Simplify gift giving: Children don't need as much as you think they need, and they definitely don't need as much as the world says they need. From the first moment a woman gets pregnant, the entire baby industry tries to convince parents that they need to buy all kinds of ridiculous things for their baby, and they must buy the best brands. Parents feel that if they don't buy this or that, they are bad parents. The best gift you can give your children is a simple and selfless heart. Be simple in gift giving for birthdays and holidays. Jesus received three gifts on his birthday, so why should our kids receive more than that on Christmas? Be simple in the clothes and electronics you buy for your children. Maybe they have a game console, but do they need three different game consoles? And do they need twenty-five different games? We repeat Psalm 23:1 in our hearts constantly: "The Lord is my shepherd; there is nothing I lack." Repeat this scripture often to your children. Teach them to replace a spirit of want with a spirit of gratitude.

Avoid waste and superfluities: Turn off the lights. Shut the door when you leave the house. Don't take more than you can eat. Teaching your children to avoid waste and superfluities is much more than simply telling them to close the door because it costs money to heat the house. You must teach them the motivation behind these actions. Everyone is called to be a good steward of the resources God has given us and to care for these resources in such a way that they are directed toward the service of others.

Humanize the poor: When we look at Christ's own poverty, we realize an earth-shattering reality: God didn't remain in the heavens and choose to help us from his lofty state but instead came to dwell within our mess. Jesus is the poor man. The poor are real people with real stories and real struggles. Conversations with the homeless are some of the best, most human conversations we have. You may not want to hand out cash to the homeless, but maybe you can carry nutrition bars and holy cards in your car so that when you see someone in need, you can roll down the window and talk to them and support them. It's important to let your children know that the poor are not statistics. People often are afraid of the poor, and so they intentionally avoid the "bad" neighborhoods, avert their eyes, or walk on the opposite side of the street. Instead, what if we intentionally drove through the poor neighborhoods and showed our children the boarded-up homes and talked to them about the hardships? What if, with our children, we intentionally engaged the homeless in conversation and let our kids see their humanity?

When we first got married, we intentionally moved into a lower-income neighborhood. We would often see the poor digging through the dumpsters in the alley behind our house. As a result, we would engage them in conversation, walk to the local grocery store with them, and buy them food. We would do this with our two- and four-year-old children. Never once was there a situation that was dangerous. Instead we experienced only grateful people ready and willing to share their stories and smile at our beautiful children. Sometimes, to humanize the poor for our children, we need to be intentional in our lives. We want to humanize the poor even in dangerous neighborhoods. We have spent time ministering to kids in the inner city and have found so much fear and brokenness in their own lives. Helping our children encounter that and learn from that is so powerful.

Take mission trips: We suggest that at some point in your children's lives you take a family mission trip to an impoverished country or even an impoverished county in America.

Dan

When I was in seventh grade, I went on a mission trip to the poorest county in the Appalachian Mountains. While I was there I encountered Jesus' face in the poor in such a radical way. It was a defining moment in my life. On that mission trip, Christ planted a flag on my heart that my heart would be claimed for others, not for myself. I'm positive that I wouldn't be the person I am today if not for that trip. Since that trip, I've made it a priority to take a mission in service to the poorest of the poor at least once a year. In the last fifteen years I've taken close to two thousand young people on different kinds of mission trips. If done well, the trips are always life-changing. I say "if done well" because I think there are a lot of mission trips where youth go and serve but never interact with the people. An effective mission trip isn't just about "doing" for the people but also "being" with the people.

Adopt a family apostolate: The family that embraces conjugal poverty should earnestly pray on how they can give more of their time, talent, and treasure in service to the poor and needy, as well as to the spiritually poor and needy. In this respect, it may be a wise practice for your family to adopt a family apostolate in service to the poor or spiritually poor so that you are generous through giving not only the firstfruits of your income to the Lord but also the firstfruits of your time. Serving regularly alongside your children will have a big impact on them. We have found that children and youth really get behind a mission. As a family, you should talk about different areas of need in our world and pick an apostolate that matters to you. Maybe it's an apostolate of service to the poor, increasing awareness of human trafficking, visiting the elderly, or praying at abortion clinics.

Seek nature: There is something profound about nature that proclaims the inexpressible grandeur of God. We find in nature a greater appreciation for simplicity. Sure, theme parks are really fun, but despite all the millions of dollars that go into theme parks and amusement parks, their pageantry will never compare to the beauty of nature. Allow your children to discover God's power and majesty in nature, be it through the mountains, oceans, canyons, or waterfalls. Visit national parks and take rustic camping trips for vacations.

Teach about work and finances: Work is good, especially if it's geared toward the service of others. Most human work is directed toward the service of humankind and the betterment of society. Teach your children that work isn't for selfish gain but for service. It's not about making a living but rather about making a giving. Help your children be entrepreneurs. Encourage them to ask, "What can I do to make others' lives better?" Most importantly, teach your children about tithing. If the Lord asks that you give 10 percent of your earnings, teach your children to give 10 percent of their earnings. Help them find a charity of their choosing that they want to donate to. And to the level possible, involve them in your own giving, allowing them to see that giving is a part of your life.

Fast regularly: Included in this simplicity of lifestyle could be a regular weekly habit of fasting for the poor and suffering. The practice might include not eating sweets unless it's a feast day, abstaining from meat on all Fridays throughout the year, or choosing to eat smaller portion sizes for lunch once or twice a week. Of course, these all depend on the ages and stages of your children, but no matter the age, everyone can give something. There is a beautiful quote attributed to Mother Teresa: "Live simply, so that others may simply live."

Parents should cultivate a home that lives simply and not in excess. In doing this, parents help cultivate the spirit of evangelical poverty in the lives of their children, raising them to be good Christians for the kingdom and not good consumers for the economy. Considerable prayer and discernment should be given on the part of parents as to what their children need and don't need, how they can cultivate a spirit of poverty in their children, and in what ways their children will learn responsible stewardship of belongings.

Today's Couple Discussion Questions

1. What are we raising our children for? What is the "end" that we desire for them?

2. How can we foster more simplicity in our children's lives?

3. Which of the categories above convicted our hearts the most? Why?

Today's Couple Prayer

Lord Jesus Christ, our children are the best treasure you have given us. Thank you for them. Help us raise them for you and for your people. Help us raise them with a heart that is selfless and focused on the needs of others. Protect them from the temptations to live an individualistic, hedonistic, materialistic lifestyle. Instead, give them a heart like yours so that they will love as you love. Amen.

Week 4

THE THIRD SECRET: CONJUGAL OBEDIENCE

WHAT IS OBEDIENCE?

Obedience is intimately linked with perfect love because it allows you to place the desires of the one you love before your own desires.

Obedience is often misunderstood to be something that it's not, and for this reason it's seen as a negative reality as opposed to a positive disposition. Obedience isn't a negative thing. It doesn't mean being forced to do something against your will. On the contrary, it's about discovering the will of the other and freely submitting to their will out of love for them. Obedience is motivated by love. One can easily see this within marriage and family life. As spouses, obedience to one another is driven by love. Obedience of children should flow forth from love and gratefulness for what their parents have given. Obedience to God or to the Church's teachings should be driven by love. You can even see how obedience to civil authority is ultimately driven by love for your fellow humans and by a desire for law and order to foster a peaceful civilization.

The word *obedience* is derived from the Latin word *audire* meaning "to listen, hear." Properly understood, obedience means to hear the other. Foundational to obedience is the ability to carefully hear the other's promptings, whether spoken or unspoken, and follow through on them. It's for this fundamental reason that authentic obedience is rooted in prayer. You can never be obedient to the will of God in your life if you don't hear his voice.

Jesus says, "My sheep hear my voice" (Jn 10:27). Do you hear his voice? Do you take time in prayer to carefully listen to the word of the Lord, allowing the Good Shepherd to speak to you so that you can humbly obey his words? The gospel writers are clear that Christ spent time in prayer listening to the Father. This life found in the silence of prayer, both for Christ and for us, is where obedience is discovered. In prayer we hear the Shepherd's voice and discover intimacy with him that transforms our hearts to desire the will of our Father in heaven above anything else.

Jesus instructs his disciples to pray, "Our Father in heaven, hallowed be your name, your kingdom come, your will be done, on earth as in heaven" (Mt 6:9–10). This is an incredibly profound prayer of surrender: Let your kingdom come. Let your will be done. When you pray these words, you surrender to the will of the Father. However, this incredible prayer of surrender begins with two key words: *Our Father*. It begins by acknowledging who he is and what kind of a relationship you are called to have with him. It starts with being able to call God "our Father." You can only pray "your will be done" if you first are able to pray "our Father."

This prayer calls us to experience intimacy with the Father as adopted sons and daughters. It challenges us to love the Father as Jesus loves the Father and to experience the Father's love as Jesus experiences the Father's love. Jesus experiences the Father's love so deeply and intimately that he refers to the Father as "Abba." Often this word *abba* is compared to the English word *daddy*, but this comparison leaves a lot lacking. The English expression *daddy* drops out of usage as the child matures. The expression in Aramaic reflects the quality and depth of the relationship, and thus doesn't fade as a son or daughter matures. Rather, it intensifies over time.[1] When Jesus challenges us to see God as our Father, or to seek God as our *Abba*, he is inviting us into a deep intimacy with the Father.

Our obedience to the will of God naturally flows through this relationship with the Father. Just as Jesus Christ was the beloved Son of the Father, and his obedience came forth from that experience of love, so too are we called to be the beloved children of God the Father and to experience Love himself (1 Jn 3:1–4). Without this intimacy, obedience to the will of God is nothing more than a rigid conformity to the law out of fear of punishment. The new law of love calls for a totally new kind of obedience that flows not from Church law or fear of punishment but rather from love.

Because we love the Father, we freely submit to his plan for our lives, knowing that he is a good Father and his will is always what is best for us. The universal call to obedience is a call to experience the Father's love and to become a beloved son or daughter of a Father in heaven who loves us. This love and obedience can only be found in prayerful intimacy with the Lord. Once we learn to heartfully pray, "Our Father," then and only then will we be able to pray, "Thy will be done."

So what is the Father's will? Most simply put, the will of the Father is intimacy and communion. Heaven is union with the heart of the Father through the Son in the Holy Spirit. It's allowing ourselves to become beloved children of the Father to the fullest extent possible. This obedience that flows forth from love is an obedience that leads to our own exaltation. It's an obedience that sets us free and gives us true joy.

Do you know him? Do you hear his voice? Prayerful intimacy with the Lord requires more than memorized prayers. It requires that we enter into the presence of a Father who loves us day after day, and in the stillness and silence of prayer, we begin to hear his voice and understand who he is calling us to be and what he is calling us to do. Having a regular time for individual prayer and silence has been the benchmark of our marriage. Without prayer, our love for each other as husband and wife is irritable and quick-tempered. With prayer, our love for each other is an overflow of the Father's love. Here are three simple ways to start an active prayer life:

Make time: You will never form a deep daily prayer life if you don't carve out time each day for prayer. Life is busy. Married life with children is even busier. Find a specific time each day that is your "go-to" time for prayer. For most parents, that is early in the morning before the children wake up or late at night after they have gone to bed. If you haven't done so already, choose a specific time each day to set aside for the Lord. Maybe it's twenty or thirty minutes. The important thing isn't how much time you give but simply that you give him designated time each day. We need to quiet ourselves and enter into the classroom of silence daily to discover our Father's whisper.

Designate a place: It's also extremely helpful to have a "go-to" place for prayer. Over and over again scripture states that Jesus "went away to pray." Mark 1:35 says, "Rising very early before dawn, he left and went off to a deserted place, where he prayed." Jesus had a time and a place for prayer. He removed himself from noise and distraction in order to focus on the voice of the Father.

Find a place free from distraction for prayer. Maybe that is the local church or an adoration chapel; maybe that is your basement or your back porch. It doesn't matter where you pray, just that you pray. It's helpful to find a place "set apart" from the ordinary. Some families make small chapels in their homes where all family members can go to pray in quiet.

Make a plan: You need a plan for prayer. A prayer plan that is easy to remember is ACTSS: Adoration, Contrition, Thanksgiving, Supplication, Silence.

Adoration: All prayer should begin with adoration that consists of worshiping the presence of an almighty God and simply loving him for who he is. Adoration is about acknowledging the power and majesty of God and falling on bended knee humbled by his presence. This God of the universe loves you enough to allow you to come into his holy presence. Enter into that presence with adoration and worship.

Contrition: After acknowledging how incredible God is, the heart is lead to acknowledge how little you have to give this almighty God. Contrition is recognizing your smallness before the almighty God and experiencing true sorrow and repentance from all the ways you have failed to live your life for him. Contrition is about the recognition that you are a sinner in need of mercy, for apart from God you can do nothing.

Thanksgiving: "Every joy and suffering, every event and need can become a matter for thanksgiving which . . . should fill one's life: 'Give thanks in all circumstances'" (*CCC*, 2648). Give thanks to the almighty God because he is deserving of our thanks and praise.

Supplication: Intercessory prayer is prayer on behalf of another person. It looks outside of yourself and looks toward the interests of others, especially those in need of healing and mercy. Beg God not only to work powerfully in the lives of others but also to work powerfully in your life. St. Augustine says, "In prayer, man is a beggar before God. Whether we realize it or not, prayer is the encounter of God's thirst with ours. God thirsts that we may thirst for Him" (*CCC*, 2559).

Silence: The ultimate goal of your time in prayer is to hear the voice of the Father, and so your prayer must include silence and listening to his voice. We suggest that you include scripture in your prayer. Catholic books and devotionals can be very helpful, but there is something unique about the Word of God. Spend time with the Lord's Word and allow him to speak to you. Read scripture and ask him, "Father, what do you want to say to me?" Listen to him. He will speak to you. He will instruct you and guide you. Have confidence that we worship a God who speaks to his children—all his children. Hearing the voice of the Lord isn't reserved only for the saints. If you ask him, he will speak. Listen.

Today's Couple Discussion Questions

1. In what ways are we intimate with the Lord?

2. How can we grow more deeply in our prayer life with the Lord?

3. How can we help each other be committed to daily time with the Lord in prayer?

Today's Couple Prayer

Lord Jesus Christ, we want to hear your voice. Speak to us in our inmost being. Help us make prayer a priority even in the midst of the busyness of daily life. Help us long for prayer and desire to be with you. Amen.

JESUS THE OBEDIENT

St. Paul says to the Romans, "For just as through the disobedience of one person the many were made sinners, so through the obedience of one the many will be made righteous" (Rom 5:19). Obedience has been part of the plan of salvation history from the moment of the Fall of man. St. Paul exhorts the Philippians to "have among yourselves the same attitude that is also yours in Christ Jesus, who, though he was in the form of God, did not regard equality with God something to be grasped. . . . He humbled himself, becoming obedient to death, even death on a cross" (Phil 2:5–6, 8). This attitude of obedience is imperative for those who wish to follow in the footsteps of Christ.

From the very moment of the Incarnation, the Son of God becomes obedient to human flesh. Think about how obedient we are to our flesh. We are hungry. We are thirsty. We are tired. We are sick. We experience pain. In all of this, to an extent, our will is obedient to our flesh. Jesus, who was lacking nothing, freely took upon himself human flesh, becoming obedient to flesh as well.

Jesus Christ entered into this world through the Incarnation as the obedient son of Mary and Joseph. Surely the Holy Family is a witness to the beauty of obedience, for from the moment the Incarnate Word was conceived in the womb of Mary, he was learning from her beautiful example of obedience to the will of the Father. "Hail, favored one. . . . Behold, you will conceive in your womb and bear a son, and you shall name him

Jesus. He will be great and will be called Son of the Most High, and the Lord God will give him the throne of David his father" (Lk 1:28, 31–32). The humble obedience of Mary is amazing. This simple young peasant girl is asked to risk shame and judgment among her people for becoming pregnant out of wedlock, and yet her response, with unwavering faithfulness to the plan of God, is, "Behold, I am the handmaid of the Lord. May it be done to me according to your word" (Lk 1:38).

Mary's obedience naturally flows forth from her knowledge of who she is. She sees herself as the handmaid, the servant, of the Lord. Her humble obedience was made possible through her faithfulness. She "put no trust in princes, in children of Adam powerless to save" (Ps 146:3). Instead, her soul "proclaims the greatness of the Lord," and her spirit places trust in God, her Savior (Lk 1:46–47). Mary remains perfectly obedient to the plan of her Savior even as a sword pierces her heart (Lk 2:35) as she watches her son suffer and die on Calvary. Because of the tremendous example of Mary's obedience, Jesus is able to proclaim, "My mother and my brothers are those who hear the word of God and act on it" (Lk 8:21), without offending his mother, for truly no one hears the Word of God and acts on it more perfectly than Mary.

Likewise, in the hidden home of Nazareth, Jesus learns the virtue of obedience from his foster father Joseph. Three times an angel appears to Joseph, each time instructing Joseph to carry out a command from God; three times Joseph does what the angel asks of him. Joseph is the man who foreshadows Jesus' words at the end of the Sermon on the Mount, "Not everyone who says to me, 'Lord, Lord,' will enter the kingdom of heaven, but only the one who does the will of my Father in heaven" (Mt 7:21).

Mary and Joseph demonstrate the two facets of obedience. At the annunciation and as she watches her only child suffer at the hands of men, Mary teaches us that often obedience comes in the form of yielding to the will of the Father. On the other hand, Joseph witnesses to that fact that obedience also entails acting upon the will of the Father.

The hidden life of Jesus is marked by perfect obedience to Mary and Joseph. When Jesus is twelve years old, he enters the Temple and begins teaching such that "all who heard him were astounded" (Lk 2:47). When his parents ask him to come home with them, scripture tells us that "he

went down with them and came to Nazareth, and was obedient to them"
(Lk 2:51). For the next eighteen years, Jesus continues in quiet obedience
to his earthly mother and father until finally, when he turns thirty years
old, he obediently listens to his mother when she tells him to start his
public ministry.

Jesus and Mary find themselves at the wedding feast in Cana, and
"when the wine ran short, the mother of Jesus said to him, 'They have no
wine.' [And] Jesus said to her, 'Woman, how does your concern affect me?
My hour has not yet come'" (Jn 2:3–4). Jesus refers to Mary as "woman"
in this passage, drawing a link to Eve. Through the *disobedience* of Eve sin
entered the world, but through the *obedience* of Mary, the new Eve, sin
has been defeated (cf. Rv 21:5). Jesus' words to Mary are not meant to be
rude, but rather are meant to show that Jesus is one who can do nothing
but that which his Father has directed him to do at the appropriate hour.
Mary seems to have no doubt that it's Jesus' time to intervene, but she is
uncertain about the means by which he will do so. Mary tells the servants
at the wedding to do whatever Jesus tells them (Jn 2:5).

As stated above, the idea of the "hour" comes not from what Jesus
thinks is best but rather from a time that is under the control of the Father.
One cannot assume that simply because Mary instructs the servants to
listen to Jesus, he decides not to listen to the Father. It's possible that Jesus
knows that his mother won't go against the Father's will, and so in hearing her confidence he realizes that the Father is speaking to him through
her. Ultimately what we see in this passage is that Jesus is portrayed as
being perfectly obedient to both his mother and his heavenly Father. One
could also suggest that in being obedient to his mother, he is obedient
to his heavenly Father. And thus Jesus' public ministry is launched with
perfect obedience, and in this, Mary teaches us that perfect discipleship
is embraced by those who "do whatever he tells [them]" (Jn 2:5).

Christ's public ministry is directed by obedience to his Father. He
can do nothing on his own: "I cannot do anything on my own . . . because
I do not seek my own will but the will of the one who sent me" (Jn 5:30;
see also Jn 5:19). He can speak nothing on his own: "I did not speak on my
own, but the Father who sent me commanded me what to say and speak"
(Jn 12:49; see also Jn 12:50, 14:10). He can save no one on his own: "No

one can come to me unless the Father who sent me draw him, and I will raise him on the last day" (Jn 6:44). Jesus is even obedient to the Father in that the Father through the Spirit performs the works of the Son and answers the prayers of the Son (cf. Jn 11:41, 15:16, 16:23).

In the Gospel of John, Jesus speaks tirelessly of his obedience to the Father because "the world must know that I love the Father and that I do just as the Father has commanded me" (Jn 14:31). For Jesus, love and obedience are connected. Jesus doesn't see obedience to the Father as a negative disposition as many falsely assume obedience to be. Jesus, who was beloved by the Father, experiences the Father's love and in this experience of love willingly and freely submits himself to the Father's plan and hour. First and foremost, the obedience of Christ is experiencing the Father's love. Christ's obedience lies in that he is "beloved" by the Father (Mt 3:17). It's this love, this obedience, that actually nourishes and strengthens the Son. "My food is to do the will of the one who sent me and to finish his work" (Jn 4:34).

Christ's obedience, while it was fundamentally the obedience of experiencing the Father's love, also required great sacrifice. Christ finds himself in the Garden of Gethsemane praying ardently, "My Father, if it is possible that this cup pass without my drinking it, your will be done" (Mt 26:42; see also Mk 14:36, Lk 22:42). Three times in the gospel Jesus petitions the Father to let this cup of suffering pass from him, but it's the will of the Father that, in order for all to have life, Jesus must freely offer himself in perfect obedience to the plan of the Father. Christ "humbled himself, becoming obedient to death, even death on a cross" (Phil 2:8). As a result of this obedience, "God greatly exalted him and bestowed on him the name that is above every name, that at the name of Jesus every knee should bend, of those in heaven and on earth and under the earth, and every tongue confess that Jesus Christ is Lord, to the glory of God the Father" (Phil 2:9–11). The paradox of obedience is that obedience leads to the Son's greatest glory and exaltation. Jesus even says himself, "If I glorify myself, my glory is worth nothing; but it is my Father who glorifies me" (Jn 8:54). Obedience leads to exaltation. Obedience leads to freedom. Obedience leads to life.

Today's Couple Discussion Questions

1. In what ways are we individually called to yield to the Father's will? In what ways are we as a couple called to yield to the Father's will?

2. How are we living a life where we are ready to "do whatever he tells [us]"? How can we ensure that we, like Christ, can say, "My food is to do the will of the one who sent me and to finish his work" (Jn 4:34)?

3. What might God be calling us to do?

Today's Couple Prayer

Lord Jesus Christ, you were obedient to the Father until the point of death. Prepare our hearts to exhibit this kind of radical obedience to your will. Help us see that obedience leads to freedom and that obedience leads to life. Speak clearly your desires for our marriage and our family. Amen.

JESUS CALLS US TO BE OBEDIENT

During the Sermon on the Mount, Jesus says something startling. He says, "Not everyone who says to me, 'Lord, Lord' will enter the kingdom of heaven, but only the one who does the will of my Father in heaven. Many will say to me on that day, Lord, Lord, did we not prophesy in your name? Did we not drive out demons in your name? Did we not do mighty deeds in your name? Then I will declare to them solemnly, 'I never knew you. Depart from me, you evildoers'" (Mt 7:21–23). This text appears confusing and abrasive. It seems that these people have a strong faith that prophesies, that drives out demons, that accomplishes mighty works. But at the same time, these mighty works are not what the kingdom of heaven is ultimately all about. The kingdom of heaven isn't about strict observance of the Mosaic law or mighty works in the name of Jesus, but rather about experiencing the Father's love in such a way that leads to obedience to his will.

Jesus instructs us that it's not enough to call him Lord. It's not enough to volunteer at church and perform service in his name. What is more important is that we do the will of the Father. It's not just important that we do things for him, but that we do what he asks us to do.

We are all called to obedience. On the broadest level, we are called to obedience to the Church's teachings, whether we find these teachings easy or difficult to follow. On an even deeper level, we are called to obedience to the whisper of the Spirit and the silent promptings of our hearts. Often we are prompted by the Spirit to say something in the middle of a tense conversation at work or to reach out to someone who is difficult to love. These promptings of the Holy Spirit are real, and the true test of holiness is how readily we "hear" these promptings and act on them. Doing the Father's will isn't always easy, especially when acting on the daily promptings of the heart.

As a matter of fact, obedience to the will of the Father naturally implies that in a fallen world we will suffer as Christ was called to suffer.

> "The Son of Man must suffer greatly and be rejected by the elders, the chief priests, and the scribes, and be killed and on the third day be raised." Then he said to all, "If anyone wishes to come after me, he must deny himself and take up his cross daily and follow me. For whoever wishes to save his life will lose it, but whoever loses his life for my sake will save it. What profit is there for one to gain the whole world yet lose or forfeit himself? Whoever is ashamed of me and of my words, the Son of Man will be ashamed of when he comes in his glory and in the glory of the Father." (Lk 9:22–26)

When Jesus spoke these words, it was a defining moment for the apostles. It was at this moment that they realized that Jesus wasn't going to bring about the kingdom of God in the way they had hoped. In other words, he wasn't sent to bring about God's kingdom by armed force and political power. He wasn't going to usher in a powerful military overthrow and reclaim Jerusalem as its own sovereign state. Instead, the Son of Man must suffer greatly. Historically, such a view was disturbing to the apostles, as we can see from the parallel passages in other gospels (cf. Mt 16:22–23), not just because it would be painful and seemingly disastrous, but also because the Messiah was supposed to be a glorious king and succeed in reestablishing the kingdom of Israel, making it greater than it had ever been before. He was supposed to be a great conquering king, but instead Jesus tells them that "the Son of Man must suffer." Even worse, he expects to be put to death by the Sanhedrin ("the elders, the chief priests, and the scribes"), the ruling body of Israel. In this moment, the personal wants, dreams, and ambitions of the apostles must have been shattered; the long-awaited

Messiah of Israel was different from what they expected. Some biblical scholars hypothesize that it's at this moment that Judas resolves in his heart to betray Jesus because he isn't the messiah he longed for. It's in this moment, when his followers are bewildered and confused by what he has just spoken, that Jesus gives them the core teaching on discipleship.

Scripture tells us this key teaching was given "to all," implying that this teaching of Jesus was not meant just for the apostles, but rather that this is an evangelical imperative for all disciples, just as poverty and chastity. First, Jesus instructs that if one is to be a follower of Christ, he must "deny himself." This is scriptural language that we don't immediately understand as his early listeners would have. The Greek word used here is *arnéomai*, meaning to "disown" oneself, to "repudiate" oneself, to refuse to accept or be associated with oneself.[2] To deny oneself in this sense means more than just giving up meat on Fridays during Lent or refraining from eating that second donut. Jesus isn't speaking about mere "self-denial." Rather, he calls his disciples to deny themselves in such a way that they deny that they belong to themselves. They are called to disown themselves as their own masters and see themselves as belonging to the Lord. To deny ourselves, then, is to give over our lives to the Lord and say that we are his without reserve, for whatever plans he has for us. Like Christ, we are now in the Father's service for the sake of his kingdom. Followers of Jesus disown themselves in a way that they no longer belong to themselves, but they now belong to the Father and are obedient to the Father as the Son is obedient. St. Paul understood this well, which is why he says, "I, then, a *prisoner* for the Lord, urge you to live in a manner worthy of the call you have received" (Eph 4:1, emphasis added).

Next, Jesus says that a disciple is to "take up his cross daily and follow me" (Lk 9:23). If you are not careful, you may miss the power of these words. Jesus isn't talking about carrying the little burdens of your daily life but rather about something much bigger. Due to centuries of metaphorical Christian preaching, the depth of this call could risk being lost. Imagine being in the position of the disciples. They weren't privy to our centuries of Christian metaphorical "cross carrying," and so they heard Jesus' words as he truly meant them to be understood. The first disciples of Jesus knew exactly what crucifixion was and, unlike any of

us, had probably all seen throughout their lives multiple prisoners crucified. Crucifixion was a punishment reserved for the worst criminals,
the vilest people. It involved nailing or tying someone to an upright post
and letting them die a slow, agonizing death by suffocation. To make this
punishment even more humiliating, this prisoner was stripped of their
garments so that they would hang from the cross exposed for the world to
see them suffer in shame (Jn 19:23). So when the followers of Jesus heard
him say that they were to take up their crosses and follow him, they heard
him calling them to a life of intense suffering, shame, and disgrace. This
was real for them—and it should be real for us. Jesus is calling us to live
radically for him, no matter the cost. Even if that means wounding our
reputations, losing friends, being despised and rejected, we are called to
this kind of obedience.

Jesus continues, "For whoever wishes to save his life will lose it,
but whoever loses his life for my sake will save it" (Lk 9:24). The virtue
of obedience is ultimately about losing your life to gain your life. You
surrender your life over to divine providence and the divine will of
God. You surrender your plans, dreams, agenda, and wants to his plan,
dreams, agenda, and wants. Obedience takes the form of living a life
dedicated to the advancement of the kingdom of God here on earth.
Everything a disciple does should be directed toward this end. "Whatever you do, do everything for the glory of God" (1 Cor 10:31). Your
family life, work life, and personal life are meant to advance the kingdom of God. "Whatever you do . . . be slaves of the Lord Christ" (Col
3:23–24). In truly accepting and living the Gospel, everything you do,
no matter who you are, is transformed so that you are now doing it for
the advancement of the Gospel. Can that be said about your life? Have
you placed everything on the altar?

Today's Couple Discussion Questions

1.   How have we denied ourselves? As individuals, do we view our lives
     as our own, or are we living life all for Jesus and his kingdom?

2.   How are we living for the sake of advancing the Gospel? In what
     ways can our lives better advance the kingdom of God?

3.   What evidence is there that we are willing to lay down our lives for
      Jesus?

Today's Couple Prayer

Lord Jesus Christ, help us understand the true cost of discipleship. Help us deny ourselves, take up our crosses daily, and follow you. Help us come to understand how we are called to advance the Gospel for your sake. Speak, Lord; your servants are listening. Amen.

DAY 28

OBEDIENCE TO GOD THE FATHER

Conjugal obedience necessarily entails obedience to God the Father. Since this obedience is "conjugal," the husband and wife should seek the Lord together, both desiring to hear his voice and follow his will for their lives together as a couple, because the decisions of the one impact the other. "The couple must give united obedience to what they have discerned to be their shared understanding of God's will."[3] Discernment of God's will for your marriage should include prayerful discernment about larger matters of importance: Should you open your home to another child? Should you purchase this home or this car? Where should you send your children to school, or should you homeschool? Should both of you work outside of the home, or should one stay home with the children? God's will should also be prayerfully discerned together in smaller matters as well: How will your family observe Advent or Lent this year? How many sports will your children be allowed to play? How many nights a week will you eat dinner together as a family? What kind of service will your family be involved in? How will your family approach media consumption, cell phones, and the Internet? Husbands and wives should act on the answers to these important questions based on a shared understanding of God's will for their family.

Couples should also carefully discern God's will for their young children. As children grow and mature, couples should carefully discern

God's will with their children, so as to teach children how to discover God's will for their lives. Helping to teach your children to pray through questions in life is very important. In youth ministry, young people often come to us seeking advice. We used to simply give them our advice and send them on their way. Now we spend time praying with them, teaching them how to hear the voice of the Father in prayer. We no longer need to give advice on what we think the Father's will is for them. Instead, we teach them to listen for and hear the Father's will for themselves. In doing so, they make better decisions and move more confidently in these decisions because they have heard the Father's voice in prayer.

This obedience from the couple must be pursued through a devout life of prayer. As mentioned above, obedience has to do with knowledge and intimacy with God in prayer. Jesus says that those who did the will of the Father were those he knew (Mt 7:21–23), and those who didn't do the will of the Father were those he didn't know. Obedience requires knowledge because knowledge of the other leads to obedience. A person can't do the will of the Father if they don't know the will of the Father. Knowledge brings trust, and trust leads to action. Intimacy and knowledge are only forged through prayer. Recall the root of the word *obedience*: "to listen" or "to hear." When making decisions about their family, husbands and wives should diligently cultivate a life of prayer by which they are able to hear the word of the Lord and act on it. "Blessed are those who hear the word of God and observe it" (Lk 11:28).

Married life poses many difficulties to a life of prayer. Between the many places children have to be because of academics and extracurricular activities, and because of work responsibilities, grocery shopping, and household chores, it's easy for prayer and silence to be pushed aside. When this happens, couples lose the ability to invite God into their daily lives, and ultimately their family's life becomes based more on their own will and their children's will than on the will of the Father. One healthy way to remedy the epidemic of busyness taking over our family lives is for couples, along with their children (if they are old enough), to form a "rule of life" that is fashioned around prayer and service.

If we look to the model of religious communities, the counsel of obedience is always lived and expressed through a rule of life. The vow of obedience for the religious often includes faithfully observing the "rule of life" of the community. This allows community members to clearly understand how to pursue the life they want to live. A family rule of life allows you to plan and execute the kind of life you desire to live as a family instead of allowing life to "just happen" without intentionality. Many times families end up compromising on things that are actually important to them—such as personal prayer, couple prayer, family prayer, family dinner, husband-wife date nights, family fun nights, and one-on-one time with the children—all because life starts moving too fast. Forming a family rule helps the family to live intentionally. If a couple creates a family rule of life and then strives to live according to that rule, they will find greater freedom to achieve the kind of marriage and family life that they desire.

The family rule should include things such as when and how you will accomplish personal prayer, couple prayer, and family prayer. For example, the rule could involve the couple saying personal prayers in the morning before the children awake, family prayers at the children's bedtime, and couple prayer before the husband and wife go to sleep. Resources such as *Shorter Christian Prayer* can be a great source of guidance if you and your spouse have a hard time praying together. The rule should also cover family mealtimes, family chores, family play, and family service to the parish and community. Of course, time for Mass and Confession, and possibly times for Eucharistic adoration, should be scheduled. This allows for these important aspects of family life to be deliberately planned and thus achieved.

Included in this as well should be a strategic plan for husband-wife meeting time as well as date nights and times when parents can spend one-on-one time with each of their children. We make sure that we have quality time together as a family in the evenings; we have been very careful not to commit our children to too many activities. We work hard to find activities that take place immediately after school so that they don't conflict with dinnertime and family time after dinner. The rule can and should be established as something based on the work and academic week, something scheduled and easily repeated day after day, week after week.

One thing we did early in our marriage was create a family mission statement. It was incredible for us as a couple to spend time talking about who we wanted to be as a family, how we wanted to pursue holiness, and how we were going to strive for sanctity as a family. Take time as a couple—include the children if they are old enough—to pray and think about who you are as a family and who you want to be. Ask God what he wants from your family. Live your family life intentionally. Don't let it just happen and pass by. Check out appendix B for more information on how to prepare a family mission statement.

It's important not to make the rule of life overly regimented. There will be times when the family won't be able to keep the rule due to illness or other unexpected family events. This shouldn't be cause for discouragement. The rule exists to serve the family, not the family to serve the rule. The rule allows the family to predetermine what is important in family life and then attempt to schedule extracurricular activities around the rule so that what is important doesn't get pushed aside. Couples—again, include the children if they are old enough—should prayerfully discern what their rule of life should look like so that their family can become saints. Then, after this rule is created, the couple strives to remain obedient to the rule and help the children see the value of remaining obedient to the rule according to their state in life.

Please don't see this as something overly complicated. It can be as simple as making a list of things that are important to you as a family and a list of things you believe that God wants from your family. Once you have created this list, simply put these items in a manageable schedule. The schedule may have to be adjusted during different seasons of life, but the unbendables on the list should never be removed.

Dan

As a father, I find that the biggest responsibility I have to fight for is quality time with my family. Work and ministry can easily take over if I don't have strong boundaries and work hard to maintain those boundaries.

Obedience to God's voice won't always be easy, but it will always work out for your good. If you are authentically praying and listening to the voice of God in your life, there will come times when the Father asks you to do something radical. He may call you to leave a high paying job to serve at a lesser paying one. He may call you to start a ministry or an apostolate that you don't think you are equipped to run. He may ask you to reach out to someone whom you think is unreachable. Don't be afraid. God has a plan for your life and your welfare, and not your harm. It's a plan for a future full of hope. His plan is for your eternal joy and fulfillment. His plan is for the good of all humankind and the fulfillment of the kingdom of heaven. "But what if God asks me to quit my job, sell everything, and move to *Africa*?" Would you believe we hear this question all the time? Friends, don't be afraid of God's will. He certainly isn't calling the whole world to up and run to Africa. Most likely he is calling you to greater holiness right where you are. But if he *is* calling you to a radical and challenging change, guess what? It's going to be okay.

As a couple, we got the chance to learn about making our relationship obedient to the will of God before we even started dating. It was a typical love story: Dan fell madly in love with Amber in a "love at first sight" kind of way, and Amber was mildly interested in Dan but enjoyed how much he liked her. There was only one problem: we were both serving as young eighteen-year-old missionaries, and the mission program had a rule for their missionaries—no dating! What? What kind of a rule is that! The first month we were serving on mission, we broke this rule time after time, sneaking off to be together and writing love letters to each other. But ultimately, after the threat of being kicked off the mission and a change of heart that was happening within both of us, we decided to lay our relationship on the altar. We agreed that it wasn't God's will that we date right now, because God had called us to a ministry that had a no-dating policy. We also knew that if it was God's will that we be together, then when it was his timing, we would be together. So for the entire mission year we were obedient. We served in different areas of the country, and so we spent the year apart and not talking to one another. We were obedient to God's timing.

At the end of the mission year, we sat down for a conversation. While we still loved each other and desired to be together, our hearts were now more consumed by love of Jesus than ever before. We willed not our own good but the good of the other. We knew it wasn't just about what we desired here and now. It was about the eternal salvation of the other. And so we felt God ask us to lay our relationship on the altar again. He had placed in both of our hearts a conviction to discern a vocation to religious life and priesthood.

For another two years we faithfully prayed for each other but kept our distance as we discerned our vocations. Finally, after a long and very emotional time of obedience, God spoke clearly and called us to pursue a relationship with one another. While the three-year process of being in love but being asked by the Father to patiently wait for his timing was difficult and often painful, following God's will for our relationship was ultimately the most beautiful and freeing process. If we had chosen our will over his will, there is a good chance we wouldn't be married today or as in love with Jesus as we are.

It's important for married couples to be always radically ready to respond to what God asks of you. Fear and doubt will try to creep in and keep you from following the Lord with obedience. Put on love, and walk in faith. We pray that God blesses you so richly with his call upon your life. We pray that he invites you on unexpected adventures. The Lord calls his people to live incredible adventures for him, but we often miss out on them because we don't respond. Respond! Don't be afraid. You have but one life to live—live all for Jesus and all for his kingdom.

True freedom and lasting joy lies in perfect uniformity with the will of God, when we not only conform to what God wills but also unite our own hearts to the will of God. May the prayer of Bl. Charles de Foucauld become our own prayer:

> Father, I abandon myself into your hands;
> do with me what you will.
> Whatever you may do, I thank you:
> I am ready for all, I accept all.
> Let only your will be done in me,
> and in all your creatures
> I wish no more than this, O Lord.
> Into your hands I commend my soul:
> I offer it to you with all the love of my heart,
> for I love you, Lord,

and so need to give myself,
to surrender myself into your hands without reserve,
and with boundless confidence,
for you are my Father.

Today's Couple Discussion Questions

1. How might our family be too busy? What do we need to get rid of or change?

2. What are our unbendables? *Make a list of the areas mentioned or not mentioned in today's reflection that you want to make sure are a part of your married and family life. Spend time making this list and putting it into a manageable schedule.*

3. Either as a couple or as individuals, is there anything that we feel God keeps asking us to do that we are afraid to do?

4. What line of Bl. Charles de Foucauld's prayer of abandonment speaks most to our hearts? Why?

Today's Couple Prayer

Lord Jesus Christ, help us be obedient to the simple discipline of living every day with passion and purpose. Help us execute life according to your will for us instead of letting life get away from us. Safeguard us from busyness that breaks our family and spiritual lives. Amen.

OBEDIENCE BETWEEN SPOUSES

St. Paul places a strong emphasis on spousal obedience. You have heard this reading before. It's one you hear at Mass on the Feast of the Holy Family. Husbands nudge their wives at the word *submissive*, and wives roll their eyes. Then they both have a good laugh and move on with life. But there is a beautiful and profound truth to be explored here that we don't want to miss. Let's read together—no eye rolling. In speaking to married couples, St. Paul exhorts:

> Be subordinate to one another out of reverence for Christ. Wives should be subordinate to their husbands as to the Lord. For the husband is the head of his wife just as Christ is head of the church, he himself the savior of the body. As the church is subordinate to Christ, so wives should be subordinate to their husbands in everything. Husbands, love your wives, even as Christ loved the church and handed himself over for her to sanctify her, cleansing her by the bath of water with the word, that he might present to himself the church in splendor, without spot or wrinkle or any such thing, that she might be holy and without blemish. So [also] husbands should love their wives as their own bodies. He who loves his wife loves himself. For no one hates his own flesh but rather nourishes and cherishes it. . . . "For this reason a man shall leave [his] father

and [his] mother and be joined to his wife and the two shall become one flesh." (Eph 5:21–29, 31)

One thing to note about this passage is that St. Paul takes the reader back to the beginning and God's original design for man and woman: "Man shall leave [his] father and [his] mother and be joined to his wife and the two shall become one flesh." St. Paul also draws a connection between spousal love and the relationship between Christ and the Church. The notion of conjugal obedience referenced in this text must be seen in light of these two realities: God's original plan for man and woman and the relationship of Christ and the Church.

St. Paul begins by challenging husbands and wives to "be subordinate to one another out of reverence for Christ." Husband and wife are called to a mutual obedience to one another that naturally flows from the husband and wife looking with reverence to Jesus Christ who was obedient to death for their sake. As the husband has reverence for Christ and sees in him the model of love, he freely becomes obedient to death for the one whom he loves, his wife. As the wife has reverence for Christ and sees in him the model of love, she freely becomes obedient to death for the one whom she loves, her husband. The fullness of God's plan for the domestic communion is realized through a reciprocal self-gift, which is also mutual subordination. St. Paul teaches the couple that Christ is the source and the model of this subordination. There should be no fear here because "there is no fear in love, but perfect love drives out fear" (1 Jn 4:18). As St. John Paul II explains, "When husband and wife are subject to one another 'in the fear of Christ' everything will find a just balance."[4] St. Paul suggests that it's in this mutual spousal obedience to one another that the true communion of persons is realized: "the two shall become one flesh."

"So [also] husbands should love their wives as their own bodies" (Eph 5:28). These words draw us once again to the "one flesh" concept and in a sense explain what is meant by husband and wife being "one flesh." St. John Paul II explains how the husband and wife are one flesh with an intentional character: the body of the wife isn't the husband's own body but should be loved as his own body. "Love binds the bridegroom to be concerned for the good of the bride."[5] Conjugal obedience means being concerned for the other's needs just as you are concerned for your own needs. Obedience takes the form of a selflessness in mind, heart, and action, where spouses genuinely care for the other as they care for themselves.

The best and simplest way to describe conjugal obedience is this: "Love makes the 'I' of another person one's own 'I': The wife's 'I' becomes through love the husband's 'I,' and the husband's 'I' becomes through love the wife's 'I.'"[6] This suggests that spouses practice conjugal obedience when, throughout the day and the week, they are driven to satisfy the needs, wants, and desires of each other. The husband fulfills the needs of his wife, and the wife fulfills the needs of her husband. The needs of each are satisfied through mutual giving and receiving instead of through selfishness. This forms the one-flesh union, where truly the needs of the other become one's own needs. This is the kind of love that Christ has for the Church and the Church has for Christ. This is the kind of love that the Father has for the Son and the Son has for the Father. This is authentic love.

However, St. Paul doesn't conclude with mutual obedience. Instead he explains that this mutual obedience also has an order to it. A company can't be run with two CEOs. A country can't be run with two presidents. A Church can't be run with two popes. All communities, big or small, need ordered obedience. As so St. Paul proclaims, "Wives should be subordinate to their husbands as to the Lord. For the husband is head of his wife just as Christ is the head of the church" (Eph 5:22–23). Hold on, wives! Stay with us. Avoid the eye rolling. Husbands, stop the elbowing.

Paul isn't proposing a contract of domination of the husband over the wife. It's not a one-sided submission, but rather a mutual submission with an order to it. In mutual submission to the Lord and to each other, "the wife can and should find the motivation for the relationship with her husband, which flows from the very essence of marriage and family."[7] "Husbands, love your wives" (Eph 5:25). With these words St. Paul takes away any fear the wife may have had of being "subordinate" to her husband, because true love doesn't allow for domination. A woman should never marry a man to whom she isn't willing to be subject, because that means fear exists within her that her husband doesn't desire what is best for her and her family. Rather, because a woman knows that her husband wills what is good for her out of love for her, she finds the motivation to be subordinate to him. Often, if the husband possesses true love, he himself might will and desire the good of the wife more than she desires it for herself. Likewise, the wife might will and desire the good of the husband more than he desires his own good. St. Paul is saying that a wife is only called to be subordinate in as much as the husband effectively loves.

St. John Paul II explains that "love makes the husband simultaneously subject to the wife, and subject to the Lord himself."[8] One could even interpret St. Paul to be saying that the husband is more subordinate to his wife than she is to him because of the challenge to lay down his life for her as Christ does so for the Church. Christ crucified becomes the model for how the husband is to love his wife. Christ's obedience unto death, holding nothing back for the sanctification and fulfillment of the beloved, becomes the obedience of the husband.

There are two ways in which we can look at the submission of the wife to the husband. The first way is similar to the obedience of God the Son to God the Father. For Christ, love and obedience are connected: "The world must know that I love the Father and that I do just as the Father has commanded me" (Jn 14:31). Christ's obedience to the Father lies in experiencing the Father's love, and in this experience of love he willingly and freely submits himself to the Father's plan and hour. Christ's obedience lies in that he is "beloved" by the Father (Mt 3:17). Thus St. Paul suggests that it's, above all, the role of the husband to love his wife and, above all, the role of the wife to be loved. The wife's submission in a sense is to the experience of being loved.[9] Often this submission is difficult for the wife. Women often struggle to allow themselves to be loved when they feel as if they are unlovable. The wife should allow herself to experience the husband's love and freely submit herself to his love. Receive his compliments and don't push him away. Listen to his words of affirmation. Receive his love for you. You are lovable.

St. Paul explains that the second kind of subordination that the wife should have toward her husband is likened to the kind of subordination the Church has to Christ. Christ is the head of the Church, and the Church is the Body of Christ. As the head, Christ leads the body, but in a way that is always best for the body. Also, the body helps the head perceive and understand what course of action the head should take. In a sense, the body informs the head, but the head leads. In matters of discussion, there is no division between the head and the body.

In the relationship between husband and wife, the wife should inform and advise the husband, but the husband should be the spiritual leader of the home. As the spiritual leader he has the responsibility to provide an environment in which his family can grow in holiness. He is the leader of loving his family as Christ loves the Church and lays down his life for her. What does this death to self look like for the husband? The husband must realize that his time is no longer his own; it belongs to his family. He has entered into a sacrament of Christian service. The husband must realize that his job isn't his only job. He should return from work ready to engage: in conversation with his wife, in love and play with the children, in household chores and cleaning up. Husbands should lead the family in prayer and spiritual formation. Wives should help set up husbands for success in this regard. Since this mutual obedience has an order to it, if ever the husband and wife disagree on minor decisions, the wife should humbly accept the will of her husband, trusting that God appointed him as head of the family, much in the same way we trust the will of the Holy Father, our pope, trusting that God has appointed him as head of the family of God. When there is disagreement in matters of great importance, husbands should carefully listen to their wives, and wives carefully listen to their husbands, until there is oneness of mind and heart. Remember, you are one body.

"St. John Chrysostom suggests that young husbands should say to their wives: I have taken you in my arms, and I love you, and I prefer you to my life itself. For the present life is nothing, and my most ardent dream is to spend it with you in such a way that we may be assured of not being separated in the life reserved for us. . . . I place your love above all things, and nothing would be more bitter or painful to me than to be of a different mind than you" (*CCC*, 2365). This is the language of conjugal obedience.

Today's Couple Discussion Questions

Husbands should ask themselves:

1. In what ways does my wife receive my love?

2. In what ways do I feel love and respected by my wife?

Wives should ask themselves:

3. In what ways does my husband receive my love?

4. In what ways do I feel love and respected by my husband?

5. How can I support my husband in effectively leading our family?

Together:

6. How can we give and receive better to one another?

Today's Couple Prayer

Lord Jesus Christ, help the two become one flesh. We pray that we will strive to love the other in such a way that makes the other's "I" our own "I." Grant unto us a mutual obedience to one another as to Christ. Amen.

DAY 30

LISTENING TO LOVE LANGUAGES

The word *obedience* is derived from the call to listen carefully to the other's needs, expressed and unexpressed. So often husbands and wives joke about the differences between sexes and the "mystery" of the other person. In his book *The 5 Love Languages*, Christian author Dr. Gary Chapman explains how people both give and receive love in different ways. We should be intentional to discover how our spouse (and our children) gives and receives love. In knowing how they receive love, we are able to be obedient to their unexpressed needs and desires and to be at service to those needs in and through love. Here is a brief description of Dr. Chapman's love languages:

Words of affirmation: One way to give and receive love is to use words that build up. Scripture says that "death and life are in the power of the tongue" (Prv 18:21). Many couples have yet to learn the tremendous power of verbally affirming each other. Verbal compliments or words of appreciation are powerful communicators of love. Some people can never get enough of them. Your spouse may give love through words of affirmation. If so, receive those words with a grateful heart. Rejecting or denying them makes your spouse feel rejected or denied. Your spouse may also feel more deeply loved when they receive words of affirmation. If this is the case, make sure you shower your spouse with sincere words of love and admiration. A simple thank-you for doing the laundry or cooking dinner can go a long, long way.

Acts of service: A second way to give and receive love is through acts of service. By acts of service we mean doing things you know your spouse would like you to do but may not have asked you to do. You seek to please them by serving them. Actions such as cooking a meal, setting the table, emptying the dishwasher, hanging a picture, and cleaning the car are all acts of service. They require thought, planning, time, effort, and energy. If your spouse receives love through acts of service, then actions speak louder than words. Make sure you carve time out of your busy schedule to show your spouse that you love them by accomplishing the tasks they want accomplished. If your spouse gives love through acts of service, make sure you acknowledge them and thank them for the love they are pouring out upon you.

Quality time: Another way to give and receive love is through quality time. This means giving your spouse your undivided, uninterrupted attention. This is more than sitting on the couch watching television together, where your attention is focused on the television. Quality time refers to time spent together talking, devices put away, giving each other your undivided attention. If your spouse primarily receives love through quality time, you need to make sure you carve out uninterrupted time to be with your spouse, to engage in conversation, and to listen sincerely. Often quality is much more valuable than quantity. It's not enough to be together if you are not actually together.

Physical touch: Humans have long known that physical touch is a way of giving and receiving love. Holding hands, kissing, cuddling, and sexual intercourse are all ways of communicating physical love to one's spouse. For some people, physical touch is the primary love language. Without it, they feel unloved and undesired. With it, they feel secure in the love of their spouse. If your spouse receives love through physical touch, make sure you are thoughtful in pouring that out upon them. Touching your spouse as you walk through the room takes only a moment but communicates love loudly. If you fail to give touch, your spouse may begin to feel undesired and unwanted. If your spouse gives love through physical touch, once again, be mindful to receive this love. Pushing them away may cause them to feel unwanted and unloved.

Receiving gifts: We have spoken a lot in this retreat about "being a gift" to your spouse. For some people, receiving gifts—visible, tangible gifts—speaks the loudest. For a person who receives love through receiving gifts, it's usually not the gift that they are excited about but merely being able to hold something and say to themselves, "Look, he was thinking of me," or "Wow, she remembered me." The gift itself is a symbol of the action of thoughtfulness. It doesn't matter whether it costs money or not. What is important is that you thought of your spouse. If your spouse's primary love language is receiving gifts, you should become a proficient gift giver.

Throughout this retreat, we have addressed giving and receiving love. These five love languages give us an understanding of how people give and receive love. Naturally, through obedience, you should seek to discover how your spouse best receives love and work diligently to love them through those means. Every person is unique. Many people receive love through multiple love languages. We crafted a fun "love language quiz" for you to take together as a couple. As you go through it, answer the questions honestly. At the end, you will see which love languages you exhibit most. Have fun! Before taking the quiz, see if you can guess your spouse's love language.

Love Language Quiz

1.   **I feel most loved when my spouse . . .**

    A.   tells me I'm valuable and/or attractive.

    B.   helps out around the house.

    C.   plans time for us to go out, just the two of us.

    D.   gives me a back rub or holds me close.

    E.   picks up a little gift for me, for no reason at all.

Wife: _____   Husband: _____

2.   **My ideal date night would include . . .**

A. my spouse taking the time to look me in the eyes and express their love for me.

B. a well thought-out surprise from my spouse.

C. anything, as long as we are *alone* together—no interruptions, just the two of us.

D. a hotel room, a bottle of wine, and some "conjugal chastity."

E. my spouse taking me out and buying me something I've been wanting.

Wife: _____ Husband: _____

3.   **We're going to watch a movie together. I'd be most honored if my spouse . . .**

A. tells me I'd earned the relaxation because of how important my work is to our family.

B. sets the movie up, pops the popcorn, and pours the drinks.

C. puts their phone and all other distractions away so we can be alone together.

D. sits very close to me and holds me.

E. buys a new movie I've been looking forward to seeing.

Wife: _____ Husband: _____

4.   **After the kids are in bed, I look forward to . . .**

A. being recognized for something I did well or hearing from my honey how important I am to our family.

B. my spouse changing the light bulbs that have gone out or emptying the dishwasher so I don't have to.

C. just the two of us taking the time to really talk to one another about how our days have gone, and just being together.

D. being physically intimate with my spouse, of course.

E. my spouse surprising me with some trinket they made for me that day.

Wife: _____ Husband: _____

5. **Darling, tell me you . . .**

A. love me.

B. cleaned the garage.

C. cleared your schedule to be with me.

D. want to kiss me.

E. have something for me.

Wife: _____ Husband: _____

6. **The best part about holidays is . . .**

A. the way everyone tells me how nice of a job I do with planning the details.

B. the way we work together to accomplish all the preparations.

C. being together as a family.

D. all the hugs.

E. the gifts—Easter baskets, Christmas presents, Valentine's flowers, I love it all.

Wife: _____ Husband: _____

7. **We're going on a weekend trip. If I had it my way . . .**

A. we will lead up to the trip sending little love notes to one another.

B. my spouse will do the work of planning it all for me.

C. who cares? We're going, just the two of us. I'm happy.

D. we will spend most of the time indoors cozied up near the fire.

E. my spouse will surprise me with the news by giving me a gift.

Wife: _____ Husband: _____

8.   **Hold . . .**

    A. that thought. I have to tell you how much you mean to me.

    B. my hammer while I hang this picture for you.

    C. the phone. I'm with my beloved and they're all that matters.

    D. me closer, darling.

    E. this beautifully wrapped package, and open it. It's just for you.

    Wife: _____ Husband: _____

How to Score Your Quiz:

> Primarily answered **A**? **Words of affirmation** are your primary love language.
>
> Primarily answered **B**? **Acts of service** are your primary love language.
>
> Primarily answered **C**? **Quality time** is your primary love language.
>
> Primarily answered **D**? **Physical touch** is your primary love language.
>
> Primarily answered **E**? **Gift giving** is your primary love language.

So how did you do? We hope you learned a little bit about yourself and your spouse. You may have been surprised to discover that you have been attempting to speak your love in a language your spouse doesn't comprehend. People often try to love others in the way that they desire to be loved. But when you strive to live obedience to your loved one, you learn to love them according to their desires, not just what makes you feel good. It benefits us in all our relationships, not just our marriages, to be aware of the ways people give and receive love. We want to recognize and appreciate the ways others are trying to love us, and be able to love others fully as well.

Today's Couple Discussion Questions

1. What did we discover about each other that we didn't know before today?

2. How do we each best receive love? *Take turns sharing with each other.*

3. What do we think are our children's love languages? How can we love them more knowing their primary love language?

Actions:
Spend some time thanking each other specifically for the unique ways you have loved each other (especially if your spouse loves words of affirmation).

On your own, spend some time thinking up three to five specific ways you will intentionally love your spouse in their love language.

Today's Couple Prayer

Lord Jesus Christ, you have heard and responded to our needs to be loved. Help us to love one another in obedience. Help us to love the other as they desire to be loved. May we never tire of learning about one another. Each day, allow us to love the other in deeper, more meaningful ways. Amen.

DAY 31

FOSTERING OBEDIENCE IN OUR CHILDREN

Before we address how to foster obedience within our children, we want to address the importance of husband and wife being obedient to their children. That sounds crazy, doesn't it? Why would we say that parents should be obedient to their children? At the root of the word *obedience* is the meaning "to listen" or "to hear." With regard to one's children, parents have an obligation to listen to and hear the needs of their children and to be of service to those needs. It's easy to "hear" the needs of young children because they communicate clearly and often: "I'm thirsty." "I'm hungry." "I don't like that." "I pooped." The list goes on.

But as children grow up, they don't always express their needs with words. Obedience to your children requires knowing your children. Parents should work to know in what ways their children need to be loved or need to be formed in virtue, in what ways they best take correction, and in what ways they best thrive. Many parents fall into the trap of imposing obedience on their children, which is domination, not true obedience. Of course, we are not suggesting that there shouldn't be law and order in your home, but rather that the law and order has the backdrop of deep communication and service to your children.

Imagine a home in which children and parents all listened carefully to each other's needs, spoken and unspoken, and worked to fulfill one another's needs. "Do nothing out of selfishness or out of vainglory; rather, humbly regard others as more important than yourselves, each looking out not for his own interests, but [also] everyone for those of others" (Phil 2:3–4). Herein lies the means by which the family fulfills its mission to be an "intimate community of life and love" (*Gaudium et Spes*, 48:1) that guards, reveals, and communicates love, "and this is a living reflection of and a real sharing in God's love for humanity and the love of Christ the Lord for the Church His bride."[10] Through carefully listening to each other's needs, the family fulfills the new law of love and obtains perfect love more quickly.

Of course, fostering obedience within our children is also of great importance. We are not going to address the many ways to discipline our children as we raise them, because there are already great resources out there on this topic from people who cover it much better than we would. Instead, let's look at the word *discipline*, which comes from the same root as *disciple*, meaning "to follow." A disciple of Jesus is a follower of Jesus, one who has learned from Jesus' way of life. Discipleship necessarily includes teaching people the art of living. Are you effectively disciple-ing your children? Are you teaching them to "be imitators of me, as I am of Christ" (1 Cor 11:1)? Ultimately discipline and obedience are about teaching our children to become everything God wants them to be, and teaching them about how to live a life of virtue and perfect love. If we demand obedience from our children, it should be directed so that they can imitate Christ and live perfect love.

Here are a few ways to foster obedience to God's will in our children's lives:

Enact daily prayer: Starting at a young age, children should be incorporated into family prayer. It may be challenging at first, and not all prayer needs to be standard memorized prayers. It's hard to teach a child to listen to the voice of God simply by reciting memorized prayers. We have found it helpful to read scripture with our children and ask them what they think Jesus is trying to teach them. We also like to teach them the value of spontaneous prayer and prayer from the heart, so that they pray whatever words are on their hearts or even sing "prayer songs," in which they sing whatever words Jesus places on their hearts. If you teach your children to sit in silence and ask Jesus questions, they can hear him speak to them. Give them leading and prompting questions. Have them ask, "Jesus, what do you want to say to me today?" Then ask them to listen and share if Jesus speaks something. As children reach middle-school years and older, they are more than capable of having a personal prayer life where they spend time daily with Jesus in silence. If you have a chapel or prayer space in the house, you can even make it part of your family rule of life that children spend fifteen minutes a day in the prayer chapel reading scripture or journaling.

Teach children how to discern: Vocational discernment starts at a very young age—from the moment children begin to dream about what they "could be." So often parents ask kids what they want instead of asking them what they think God wants. To help foster obedience, parents can change their language. Instead of asking children, "What do you want to be when you grow up?" parents could ask them, "What do you think Jesus wants you to be when you grow up?" Instead of asking children, "What college do you want to go to?" parents could ask them, "What college do you think Jesus wants you to go to?" You can apply this to anything. How much time do you think Jesus wants you to spend on social media? What kind of music does Jesus want you to listen to? Don't just ask the questions. Guide your children to ask Jesus the questions. When children are thinking about certain transitions and hobbies, send them to Jesus and encourage them to listen to him. When they are struggling with a certain situation, guide them to seek Jesus' counsel. Ultimately this prepares your children to turn to the Lord and listen to him.

Establish firm discipline and boundaries: Discipline is about teaching your children to become everything God wants them to be. You are blessing your children when you are involved in their lives and guiding the development of their moral character. Set firm boundaries for them, and be consistent. It's important for you to be strong for them. As they grow up, their moral character will struggle with weakness from time to time. You need to be strong, calling them to be who God wants them to be.

Encourage positive community and friendships: In our more than fifteen years of youth ministry, we have found that community and friendship are the make-it-or-break-it standards for youth and teenagers. If they hang around others who make good choices, they make good choices. If they start hanging out with friends who make poor choices, they start making poor choices. We have seen so many amazing kids get swept away by poor friendships. Get to know your children's friends, and offer your home as the place to hang out.

Today's Couple Discussion Questions

1.   How are we disciple-ing our children, helping them become every-thing God wants them to be?

2.   What are our children's unique and individual needs at this time in their lives? How can we serve them and love them?

3.   What would we like our time of family prayer to look like? How can we encourage our children to have personal prayer lives?

Today's Couple Prayer

Lord Jesus Christ, we desire to be saints. We desire our children and children's children to be saints. Take away from us anything that keeps us from fulfilling this desire. Wipe away from us all complacency and lukewarmness. Help us choose joyfully the radical life to which you have called us. Amen.

The Final Two Days

PREPARING FOR CONSECRATION

DAY 32

FINDING PERFECT LOVE IN MARRIAGE

The universal call to holiness is a call to faithfully live the new law of love given to us by Christ Jesus. This new law, this perfect love, is expressed in a sincere love for God and love for one's neighbor. We express the universal call to holiness when we embrace the evangelical counsels according to our state in life because embracing these counsels leads to perfect love.[1]

Dan

Why did you enter marriage? Before we married, I was discerning a vocation to the priesthood. I saw priests as superheroes, those incredible witnesses who were set apart to change the world in a radical way. I wanted to change the world so badly, and I thought the priesthood was the way to do it. But as I prayed about this more and more, I kept sensing that Jesus didn't want me to be a priest. I couldn't imagine myself consecrating the Eucharist or hearing Confession. I remember one day sitting in the pew at Mass and Jesus speaking to my heart, "You belong here in the pew. You are called to be a layperson in the Church." I still wasn't convinced. Like I said, I really wanted to be a priest. One day I was in adoration and was praying to Jesus in the Eucharist. "Jesus, I want to be everything you made me to be! I want to be perfectly holy," I cried out. Without expecting it, I heard Jesus say, "Then get married." "No, Jesus, you must have misheard me. I said that I want to be perfectly holy. I want to be set apart for you!" And then I heard it again, "Then get married." In this I discovered something that shocked me. As I continued praying and listening to our Lord, I discovered that the way I was called to obtain perfect love was through married life.

Looking back, if I had become a priest, I would have likely become a self-absorbed workaholic. I would have had shallow relationships and likely grown in pride. Jesus knew that my path toward perfect love would be discovered in the married life, the daily self-surrender to my wife and children. I can honestly say I have not even come close to obtaining perfect love, but I desire it with all that I am. We are so blessed to be given the gift of marriage, this gift by which Jesus is forming us in perfect love.

The law of love is fulfilled in marriage because "marriage entails and requires a complete gift of self to the other: one's external goods (poverty), one's body, heart, and mind (chastity), and one's will (obedience)."[2] The married couple who embraces poverty, chastity, and obedience does not embrace these virtues as ends in themselves but as means to an end: perfect love. Perfect love, love of God and love of neighbor, is expressed in a total gift of self. The evangelical counsels are three dispositions that prepare the soul to more readily and easily make a total gift of self, which is the perfection of charity. The evangelical counsels are thus the means to accomplishing the meaning of our human essence: a sincere gift of self.

What is the ultimate end of marriage? It's the salvation of the spouses and the children. The ultimate end of marriage is heaven. The call to holiness is ultimately a call to live a saintly life. A life of poverty, chastity, and obedience prepares the soul to live a radically saintly life because it allows the soul to follow in the footsteps of the poor, chaste, and obedient Son of God. We wrote this retreat to foster a spirituality for married men and women, for couples who want to be saints. There is no cookie-cutter approach to how married couples embrace these counsels or how they embrace holiness. The beautiful thing is that God the Father wants to speak to every married couple and form the spouses into the image of his Son. He wants to guide you in this journey of marriage and teach you to live radical holiness in our modern world. Through wrestling with the Lord in prayer, we pray that you will embrace these counsels to the fullest extent possible, in a way that harmonizes with your married life. "I, then, a prisoner for the Lord, urge you to live in a manner worthy of the call you have received" (Eph 4:1). You have been called to be saints. Live saintly lives!

In her autobiography *Story of a Soul*, St. Thérèse of Lisieux writes, "Perfection was set before me; I understood that to become a saint one has to suffer much, seek out always the most perfect thing to do, and forget self. I understood, too, there were many degrees of perfection and each soul was free to respond to the advances of Our Lord, to do little or much for Him, in a word, to choose among the sacrifices He was asking. Then, as in the days of my childhood, I cried out, 'My God, "I choose all!" I don't want to be a saint by halves, I'm not afraid to suffer for You, I fear only one thing: to keep my own will; so take it, for "I choose all" that You will!'"[3]

Following Jesus isn't a mandate—it's an invitation. This retreat isn't meant to place a burden upon your shoulders but rather to extend an invitation to you. How much do you want? Do you want a little bit of what God offers you, or do you want it all? Do you want a little bit of love, or do you want perfect love? The cry of our hearts as a married couple is the cry of St. Thérèse: "I choose all!" We want to live perfect love and radically surrender much for the kingdom. We don't want to be saints by halves. We don't want our children to be saints by halves. We will give him everything and hold nothing back—we choose all.

Today's Couple Discussion Questions

1. Have we chosen all? If not, what is holding us back?

2. In what areas of our personal lives are we still living in ways that are complacent and mediocre? In what areas in our marriage and family life are we still living in ways that are complacent and mediocre? What changes should we make?

Today's Couple Prayer

I n union with St. Thérèse, the Little Flower, we pray: "My God, 'I choose all!' I don't want to be a saint by halves, I'm not afraid to suffer for You, I fear only one thing: to keep my own will; so take it, for 'I choose all' that You will." Lord Jesus Christ, help us always to chose all, no matter how hard it may be. It is our greatest joy to follow you wherever you lead our family.

DAY 33

CONSECRATION DAY— A MARRIAGE SET APART FOR JESUS

Today we invite you into a fuller expression of your vocation to marriage. We invite you to make a consecration to set your marriage apart as distinct from the rest of the marriages in the world.

On the day you got married, you and your spouse entered a consecrated way of life. Through the sacrament of Marriage, Christ has already consecrated you to himself and himself to you. So we invite you not so much to take upon yourselves something new, but rather to renew the call that God has already given you through your sacramental marriage so that you can live it with greater vigor and more fervor.

A Christian marriage is meant to be "set apart" for Christ. When you enter into Christian marriage, you do so not for your own good but for the sake of the kingdom of God. We are not making this up. It may sound crazy because, over the years, our culture has made marriage all about the married couple. But Christian marriage is supposed to be all about the kingdom of God. You were married not for the sake of personal fulfillment, not because you really loved your spouse, but because God calls you to live radically for him and his people specifically through the married vocation.

Today we invite you to embrace this call. Couples often miss out on truly answering the call because of the fanfare associated with weddings. Today there is no fanfare—it's just you, your spouse, and your Creator. Today your Creator invites you to consider living your marriage anew, as a truly consecrated way of life set apart for the kingdom of God, by obediently living according to God's plan for your life.

In marriage you and your spouse are no longer living for yourselves. You are not simply living for your spouse and your children either. You are living for the advancement of the kingdom, and through your time, talent, and treasure, through the gift of not part of your life but all of your life, you are called to bring about God's kingdom here on earth: thy kingdom come, thy will be done, on earth as it is in heaven.

Before Consecration

It's customary before one makes a consecration to prepare your heart by going to Confession and receiving the Blessed Sacrament. There is no need to make the consecration today, so if you would like, prepare your heart for the consecration throughout the remainder of this week and go to Confession and Mass together as a couple as soon as you can, making the consecration afterward.

After Consecration

Celebrate! Take a nice date night together to mark the end of this incredible journey. Thank the Lord for the gift of one another and the gift of his everlasting love.

After your consecration, your marriage shouldn't continue to be lived as business as usual. The Lord invites you into a deeper call of radical readiness to respond to the needs of the Church, and he may have convicted your heart of changes that he wants you to make throughout the course of this retreat. Make those lifestyle changes.

We encourage you to pray the prayers of lordship and consecration often as a couple, even daily. It's hard to remain focused on the goal of our lives day after day. These prayers will remind you of the call you have received.

Lastly, we suggest that you give yourself a simple reminder that you are called to live poverty, chastity, and obedience. Religious brothers and sisters often wear a white cord tied around their waist with three knots tied upon it, one for each of the three counsels. Create a reminder for yourself of your special consecration to live these counsels. We recommend that you take a fine white thread, tie three knots in it, and wear it around your wrist. Over time, people will ask you what the knots represent, and you will be able to evangelize through your way of life.

Prayer of Consecration

The prayer of consecration is preceded first by an individual prayer of lordship from the husband, followed by a prayer of lordship from the wife. Then the consecration is prayed together as a couple.

Husband's Prayer of Lordship

Lord Jesus Christ,
Today I acknowledge my need for you
and proclaim you as my Lord, my Savior, and my Stronghold.
I repent of my past sins and resolve to turn away from them.
Today I invite you to take authority of my whole life.
Be the Lord of my thoughts, my desires, and my dreams.
Be the Lord of my time, my talent, and my treasure.
Be the Lord of my eyes, my ears, my mouth, my whole being.
I give you all my life for the rest of my life.
Today and all days, I will serve you and your people.
Make me more like you, Jesus, so that it is no longer I who lives, but You who lives in me.
Amen.

Wife's Prayer of Lordship

Lord Jesus Christ,
Today I acknowledge my need for you
and proclaim you as my Lord, my Savior, and my Stronghold.
I repent of my past sins and resolve to turn away from them.

Today I invite you to take authority of my whole life.
Be the Lord of my thoughts, my desires, and my dreams.
Be the Lord of my time, my talent, and my treasure.
Be the Lord of my eyes, my ears, my mouth, my whole being.
I give you all my life for the rest of my life.
Today and all days, I will serve you and your people.
Make me more like you, Jesus, so that it is no longer I who lives, but You
who lives in me.
Amen.

Couple's Prayer of Consecration

Lord Jesus Christ,
Today we consecrate our marriage to you.
We ask that you would set us apart for your glory.
Today we choose to live for you.
Today we choose to live for your kingdom.

We freely choose the call to embrace conjugal chastity.
We will live as a generous gift for others.
We will raise our children to be gifts.
We will love until it hurts.
With this gift, bring us authentic love.

We freely choose the call to embrace conjugal poverty.
We will love those you place before us.
We will seek out the lost, the lonely, the rejected, the forgotten.
We will use our wealth for the kingdom and not conceited self-interest.
With this gift, bring us true freedom.

We freely choose the call to embrace conjugal obedience.
We will follow you no matter where you lead us.
We will follow you no matter what the cost.
Our marriage is totally surrendered to your will.
Be the Lord of our marriage, our children, and our future.
With this gift, bring us lasting joy.

APPENDIX A
NATURAL FAMILY PLANNING

As was mentioned in the section on conjugal chastity, contraception is always a grave offense against chastity within the married state. However, avoiding contraception and living according to God's design for sexual intimacy doesn't mean that married couples can't plan the size of their families.

Part of the procreative end of marriage is the due and honorable education of the children conceived. This should include strong education in the virtues and life in Christ. This education should also take place within a home setting that is a healthy environment for those brought into the world, where children's basic human needs are met, both physically and emotionally. Thus a married couple has the responsibility to discern when they have the ability (financially, emotionally, and spiritually) to open their family to another child. If the family isn't in the position to welcome new life, they should be careful to abstain from the marital act during fertile periods so as not to conceive. Today, married couples are blessed with different scientific methods known as natural family planning (NFP). NFP allows for married couples to understand God's plan for the fertility cycle and plan children around fertile periods and infertile periods.

Couples should see NFP not only as a means to avoid pregnancy but also as a wonderful means to achieve pregnancy. Many married couples who have difficulty conceiving turn to forms of immoral behavior such as in vitro fertilization, which turns reproduction into a science experiment instead of a gift from God according to his designs. In vitro fertilization is another grave offense against the dignity of the human person and is always condemned by the Church. However, many couples who seek out artificial forms of conception could likely conceive naturally and according to God's design for procreation if they learn to chart the wife's fertility cycles, discovering the wife's fertility patterns more clearly.

A couple who is faithful to one another and who isn't using artificial means of birth control can still act in unchaste ways. Lack of chastity can lead to the irresponsible increase in family size. A couple should be careful to bring every child into a home that is stable and ready. There are many issues to consider: mental and physical health of all family members, financial stability, seasons of life, and stability of the marriage, just to name a few. We are not trying to suggest that a couple should wait until everything is "just so" or that they procreate with reckless abandon. Husband and wife should carefully discern a healthy and, yes, holy balance in conversation and surrender to God. If a married couple knows that they are unable to financially, emotionally, and spiritually welcome another child into this world, and they continue to embrace sexual intimacy during fertile time periods simply due to lack of self-control, this would be an offense against conjugal chastity.

Practicing natural family planning provides the couple with opportunities to practice and grow in the virtue of chastity, but doesn't guarantee that the virtue is actually being practiced. The reason that NFP is a beautiful expression of chaste love and not simply a "Catholic form of contraception" is because of the self-mastery and sacrifice it involves. If the couple discerns that they should avoid a pregnancy, practicing NFP requires that the couple abstain during fertile periods of the woman's cycle. For some couples, regulating these fertile and infertile periods can be difficult and requires more caution and thus more abstaining. Quite honestly, for us, when we are in the position of avoiding pregnancy, we find that we are met with prolonged periods of abstinence that are very difficult. So what are couples to do? Does God really want them to suffer through abstaining from sexual intercourse? Maybe. Why? Because abstaining (like any form of fasting) builds moral character and ultimately molds us more into the image of Jesus Christ. When Christ freely chose to give himself as a ransom on the Cross, it required tremendous sacrifice and self-mastery. A sincere gift of self always requires sacrifice. Chastity always requires sacrifice. Virtue, and thus love, is beautifully expressed in abstinence. While it may be difficult for husbands and wives to abstain from the good of the marital act, the greater good is that husbands and wives are given the opportunity to express their love for one another in new and different ways, which in turn will lead to deeper communication and deeper intimacy. We are not going to lie to you and say this is always easy. It's not. But that is just the thing. Love isn't always easy. That is why conjugal chastity molds us into the people God wants us to be.

APPENDIX B

CREATING A FAMILY MISSION STATEMENT

Steps to Preparing a Family Mission Statement

Husband and wife should spend quality time discussing the following:

1. Define a sense of purpose for your family, knowing where you want your family to go and how you are going to get there.

2. Begin with the end in mind: What kind of marriage do you want to have? What kind of children do you want to raise? What will define your family?

3. Identify key character traits and virtues you want your children to live and embrace throughout their lives.

4. Discuss how you will help your children become the kind of men and women who lay down their lives in service of God.

5. Identify scripture verses, prayers, and devotions that you would like to define your family life.

At the end of these conversations, you should already have a pretty clear vision for the mission that God has planned for your family. Meet with the whole family (if the children are old enough) in order to do the following:

- Determine as a family what the current state of your family life is (see below).

- Determine as a family how you as a family are going to grow in holiness and mission (see below).

Husband and wife can come together after the family meetings to write a draft of the family mission statement. Parents review their family mission statement with the children and make any final adjustments.

Questions to Ask While Planning
a Mission Statement

1.   *For each person:* Describe what you like most and least about your family.

2.   How do we offer love in the community around us?

3.   What are some ways our family can improve in holiness?

4.   What are some ways our relationships with one another can improve?

5.   Who are our family's favorite saints? Favorite devotions?

6.   What kind of family does God want us to be?

7.   How will we seek holiness as a family?

8.   What are the virtues or character traits we want to strive for?

9.   *For each person:* What are some key words that define the kind of person you want to be?

10. What are some key words that define the kind of family we want to be?

11. What qualities do we admire in our favorite saints?

12. How do we feel called to service within the home, the Church, and the world?

13. How can we witness to God's love in our home? In the Church? In the world?

14. Do we want to have a specific family mission given by God to help build the kingdom of God here on earth?

15. Complete the sentence: We will place a great importance on . . .

Signing Ritual

To emphasize the value of this family mission statement, have a signing ritual. We encourage you to print the family mission statement on quality paper and buy a decorative frame for it. In front of the family prayer space, spend some time in prayer together as a family, read the mission statement aloud, and have each member of the family sign it. After the signing, it can be framed and placed on the family altar.

Review Often

Determine how your family will come back to this mission statement often. Qualities of a good mission statement include these:

- The statement is the result of a collaborative and prayerful process of the parents in which the children are invited to participate.

- The statement briefly defines the family's desired vision, purpose, and way of life.

- The statement establishes a way of life that calls all family members (including the parents) to strive for holiness and mission.

- The statement is divided into short, memorable phrases that will stick in the children's minds.

- The statement has a prominent location within the home so that it can be discussed and read regularly.

Examples of Family Mission Statements

Example 1:

We are a family that believes in Catholic Christian values and the putting of these values into practice. We value education and strive to create a home environment of faith, hope, and love to provide each member of the family the opportunity to become holy in order for the family to enrich other people's lives through our own joys, works, and sufferings.

Example 2:

As a family, we . . .

1. place God first, family second, job or school or activities third.

2. practice regularly the sacraments of the Church.

3. treat each other with respect in the family.

4. respect Dad and Mom, especially Mom.

5. have fun with, laugh with, and love each other.

6. exhibit gratitude in all that we do.

7. live hospitality to others.

8.   live the Ten Commandments.

9.   serve the poor and suffering.

10.   solve issues with our siblings.

Example 3:

By the free gift of Christ Jesus our Lord, through the guidance of the Holy Spirit, and for the glory of God the Father, we the members of the _____ Family, and the eternal family of God, will strive to live by the following ideals, that the peace of Christ might reign within our hearts, in our home, and in the entire world.

We will dedicate ourselves to daily personal and family prayer, active participation in the sacraments, and the holy will of God, that the peace of Christ may reign in our hearts.

We will strive to build a community of life and love within the walls of our home, living at all times self-sacrificial love and striving to outdo one another in showing honor (Rom 12:10). In protection of this gift, we will allow nothing unsacred, be it speech, action, or media, to enter our walls, that the peace of Christ may reign within our home.

We will strive to see, love, and serve Christ in all whom we meet, in every situation, both common and extraordinary. We will humbly regard others as more important than ourselves (Phil 2:3). We shall live to serve and serve to build the kingdom of God, that the peace of Christ may reign in the whole world.

We affirm that we are a pilgrim people, and that we do not live for this world. We will keep our eyes fixed on heaven, our eternal home, "where he will wipe away every tear from our eyes, and death shall be no more, neither shall there be mourning, nor crying, nor pain anymore, for the former things will have passed away" (Rv 21:4). As a family we will strive therefore to help one another achieve heavenly glory, rather than worldly praise.

"We are all Thine, and all that we have is Thine, O most loving Jesus, through Mary, thy most loving Mother." St. Thérèse of Lisieux, pray for us.

APPENDIX C
A DEEPER LOOK AT CONSECRATED LIVING

The vows that most consecrated religious make are the expressed vows of poverty, chastity, and obedience. The religious make these vows, as we have already stressed, because they seek to live a life in conformity to Jesus Christ who is poor, chaste, and obedient. Likewise, married couples live a vowed life, making particular vows to one another and to the Church. If we break open these vows, we can easily see how married couples make the promise to one another and to the Church that they will pursue a life of Christian perfection through conjugal poverty, chastity, and obedience.

The typical understanding of the vow of poverty in religious life is that all things are held in common as a community; the individuals in the community hold nothing as their own. Because of the vow of the one-flesh union, marital consent can be seen as an implicit vow of poverty. The married couple vows to one another that there is no longer anything that is "mine" but that all things are "ours." The idea of a prenuptial agreement would violate the marriage vows and maybe even make the marriage invalid because the individuals getting married are trying to hold on to something that is their own before the marriage. This can't be the case. Sacramentally, marriage is a vow of poverty wherein all that you once had you now have together. In marriage you cling to nothing as your own. All property should be held in common between the husband and wife, as well as the children, just as in a religious order. In our consumer-driven, materialistic American culture, this seems difficult. We can picture how our children would want to have their "own" bedroom or their "own" clothes. Our culture frowns upon "hand-me-downs," and the idea of having common possessions is so foreign that many families own multiples of the same item, such as multiple televisions, so that each child can have their own television in their own rooms and watch their own shows. This multiple-possession mentality of our culture can lead to further division instead of deeper unity within marriage and family life. Married couples as well should be careful not to possess anything of their own such as trying to claim a particular place in the house as their own place. Nothing but division can result from this.

The notion of common possession should go beyond shared bank accounts and cars to a deeper form of common possession, such as having common goals, dreams, daily practices, and values. This vow of poverty also means that not even our own bodies are our own. In marriage, the couple doesn't exchange just their hearts but their bodies as well, given to the other as a gift. The language of the vows is a language that communicates, "I give everything to you: my heart, my soul, my body."

The religious vow of chastity usually entails total and complete faithfulness to the service of Christ and his Church through celibacy. Those who take a religious vow of chastity do so that they might have an undivided heart toward Christ. Likewise, the married couple vows to "be faithful" to each other no matter what and is called to have an undivided heart for the other. The vows of marriage are also directed toward total and complete faithfulness. As mentioned above about conjugal poverty, for the married couple this vow also entails an exchange. The husband gives his mind, his heart, and his body to his wife as a gift, and in turn, she gives her mind, her heart, and her body to him. They promise to love one another with an undivided heart that loves and pursues the desires and wants of no heart other than the heart of the beloved. It's a promise of total faithfulness. Married men and women should be careful to maintain this vow of having an undivided heart. The husband should maintain a physical and emotional distance from any other woman than his wife, and the same is true for the wife and any other man than her husband. Spouses should give precedence to the relationship with each other. Previous relationships, even relationships with one's own family members, take a back seat to the undivided heart for the beloved. Any couple who has been married for any amount of time knows the difficulty of joining two families together, two unique lifestyles and upbringings. Couples experience the tension and difficulty of navigating relationships with the in-laws. What is important here is that the heart remains undivided toward one's spouse.

This undivided heart is necessarily important not only when it comes to romantic relationships but also in all aspects of life. Often a desire for promotions and a successful career becomes a type of "affair" that steals the husband's time, thoughts, and desires from that of his wife. Spouses should remember that they make a pledge of faithfulness to each other—to love each other with an undivided heart. Nothing, no job or friendship, should get in the way of the undivided devotion husbands show to their wives and wives show to their husbands.

The religious vow of obedience usually entails promising obedience to the superior of the religious order in a similar way that Christ pledged obedience to his Father in heaven. For married couples, the vows expressed on their wedding day are truly vows of obedience to one other. They promise to be carefully attentive to the needs of their beloved no matter what. They vow to care for the other for better or for worse, in good times and in bad, in sickness and in health. In a sense, the couple vows obedience to one another no matter what life throws at them. The husband vows that even if the wife becomes too ill to dress herself or feed herself, he will be obedient to her needs and serve her as such. The wife vows that even if her husband tragically becomes an alcoholic, she will be obedient to his needs and stand by his side fighting this disease with and for him. They have vowed obedience to their love, a love that is greater than themselves. "Authentic married love is caught up into divine love and is directed and enriched by the redemptive power of Christ and the salvific action of the church" (*Gaudium et Spes*, 48).

The married couple as well, through their pledge to the openness of life, make a future pledge of obedience to the needs of their children. Anyone who has ever raised children knows well that once children enter your life, your life and time are not your own. Children have countless needs that must be fulfilled. Mothers and fathers are called to be carefully attentive to these needs and obedient to fulfilling them so that their children may live a dignified life.

Through the sacred vows of the one-flesh union, married couples are called to be faithful to a vowed way of living. They take a vow of poverty in that they are called to give themselves wholly and completely to one another, and thus they possess nothing as their own. They take a vow of chastity in that they promise to share their sexual intimacy with no one but their own spouse and to love their spouse with an undivided heart.

And they take a vow of obedience, promising to privilege the will of the other over their own will all the days of their lives. This gift of self on the altar in marriage is a gift made to the other for the sake of Christ and his holy Church—for the sake of imitating Christ's love for his Church in the world (cf. Eph 5:21ff.). This gift isn't made for personal self-fulfillment. It's as much a death to self as the religious life is a death to self. As was stated earlier, "The counsels, more than a simple renunciation, are a specific acceptance of the mystery of Christ, lived within the Church,"[1] and this mystery is made present in the consecrated life of the married couple (cf. Eph 5:32).

NOTES

The First Three Days

1. John Paul II, "Apostolic Pilgrimage to Bangladesh, Singapore, Fiji Islands, New Zealand, Australia And Seychelles," Libreria Editrice Vaticana, November 30, 1986, https://w2.vatican.va/content/john-paul-ii/en/homilies/1986/documents/hf_jp-ii_hom_19861130_perth-australia.html.

2. JoNel Aleccia, "'The New Normal': Cohabitation on the Rise, Study Finds," NBCNews.com, April 4, 2013, http://www.nbcnews.com/health/new-normal-cohabitation-rise-study-finds-1C9208429.

3. John Paul II, "Letter to Families," Libreria Editrice Vaticana, February 2, 1994, secs. 5, 13, https://w2.vatican.va/content/john-paul-ii/en/letters/1994/documents/hf_jp-ii_let_02021994_families.html.

4. Fr. Jean C. J. d'Elbée, *I Believe in Love: A Personal Retreat Based on the Teaching of St. Thérèse of Lisieux* (Bedford, NH: Sophia Institute Press, 2001), 18.

Week 1: The Mission and the Call

1. Thomas Merton, *No Man Is an Island* (New York: Sheed and Ward, 1965), 111.

2. Gerald O'Collins and Edward G. Farrugia, *A Concise Dictionary of Theology*, rev. and expanded ed. (New York: Paulist Press, 2000), 107.

3. John Hardon, *Modern Catholic Dictionary* (Bardstown, KY: Eternal Life, 2008), 251.

4. Benedict XVI, *Deus Caritas Est* [God Is Love], February 1, 2006 (Boston: Pauline Press, 2006), 1.

5. St. Augustine, *In Joannis Evangelium*, Tract. 21:8, CCL 36:216.

6. John Paul II, *Vita Consecrata* [On the Consecrated Life and Its Mission in the Church and in the World], March 25, 1996 (Boston: Pauline Press, 1996), 30.

7. Francis J. Moloney, *A Life of Promise: Poverty, Chastity, Obedience* (Eugene, OR: Wipf and Stock, 1984), 64.

8. John Paul II, *Vita Consecrata*, 16.

9. John Paul II, *Vita Consecrata*, 16.

10. Jeffrey Dew, Sonya Britt, and Sandra Huston, "Examining the Relationship between Financial Issues and Divorce," *Family Relations* 61, no. 4 (October 2012): 615–28, doi: 10.1111/j.1741-3729.2012.00715.x.

11. "Certified Divorce Financial Analyst Professionals Reveal the Leading Causes of Divorce," *Divorce Magazine*, accessed November 6, 2017, https://institutedfa.com/leading-causes-divorce.

12. "Leading Causes of Divorce."

13. Michelle Kimball, "Why Americans Divorce," accessed March 4, 2015, http://www. divorce360.com/divorce-articles/causes-of-divorce/information/why-americans-divorce.aspx?artid=169.

14. "Is Sex—or Lack of Sex—a Major Cause of Divorce?" *The Generous Husband*, May 21, 2011, http://www.the-generous-husband.com/2011/05/21/is-sex-or-lack-of-sex-a-major-cause-of-divorce.

15. "Poor Communication Is the #1 Reason Couples Split Up," *Huffington Post*, last modified November 30, 2013, http://www.huffingtonpost.com/ 2013/11/20/divorce-causes-_n_4304466.html.

16. Julie McCarty, "Marital Spirituality and the Quest for Poverty, Chastity, and Obedience," *Spiritual Life* 45, no. 2 (Summer 1999): 85.

Week 2: Conjugal Chastity

1. John Paul II, *Man and Woman He Created Them: A Theology of the Body*, trans. Michael Waldstein (Boston: Pauline Books and Media, 2006), 13:3.

2. John Paul II, *Man and Woman He Created Them*, 13:1.

3. John Paul II, *Man and Woman He Created Them*, 14:2.

4. John Paul II, *Man and Woman He Created Them*, 14:4.

5. John Paul II, *Man and Woman He Created Them*, 15:1.

6. John Paul II, *Man and Woman He Created Them*, 14:3.

7. Kent J. Lasnoski, *Vocation to Virtue: Christian Marriage as a Consecrated Life* (Washington, DC: Catholic University of America Press, 2014), 5.

8. John Paul II, *Vita Consecrata*, 16.

9. Michael Himes, *Doing the Truth in Love: Conversations about God, Relationships and Service* (Mahwah, NJ: Paulist Press, 1995), 51–59.

10. John Paul II, *Man and Woman He Created Them*, 15:1.

11. John Paul II, *Man and Woman He Created Them*, 89:1.

12. John Paul II, *Man and Woman He Created Them*, 92:6.

13. John Paul II, *Man and Woman He Created Them*, 92:4.

14. John Paul II, *Man and Woman He Created Them*, 92:5

15. John Paul II, *Man and Woman He Created Them*, 93:1.

16. John Paul II, *Man and Woman He Created Them*, 93:3.

17. John Paul II, *Man and Woman He Created Them*, 93:5.

18. United States Conference of Catholic Bishops, *Marriage: Love and Life in the Divine Plan* (Washington, DC: United States Conference of Catholic Bishops, 2009), 11.

19. See John Paul II, *Man and Woman He Created Them: A Theology of the Body,* general audiences, January 5–26, 1983, for more on the "language of the body."

20. We found it helpful to learn more about the way we give and receive love through Gary Chapman, *The 5 Love Languages: The Secret to Love That Lasts* (Chicago: Northfield Publishing, 2015), as well as personality tests such as the Myers-Briggs Type Indicator.

21. See Fight the New Drug, *How Porn Can Become Addictive*, accessed November 9, 2017; http://fightthenewdrug.org

Week 3: Conjugal Poverty

1. Thomas Dubay, *Happy Are You Poor: The Simple Life and Spiritual Freedom* (San Francisco: Ignatius Press, 2003), 17–25.

2. Mother Teresa, *No Greater Love* (Novato, CA: New World Library, 1989), 43.

3. Dubay, *Happy Are You Poor,* 117.

4. Dubay, *Happy Are You Poor,* 85.

5. United States Conference of Catholic Bishops, *Stewardship: A Disciple's Response* (Washington, DC: United States Conference of Catholic Bishops, 2002), 7.

6. "The Four Signs Research," accessed November 28, 2017, https://dynamiccatholic.com/learning/four=signs=research.

7. For a deeper appreciation of the disposition of gift, refer to Ann Morton Voskamp, *One Thousand Gifts: A Dare to Live Fully Right Where You Are* (Eugene, OR: Vondervan Press, 2010).

Week 4: Conjugal Obedience

1. Moloney, *A Life of Promise*, 132.

2. "arneomai," BibleHub, accessed March, 17, 2015, http://biblehub.com/greek/720.htm.

3. Lasnoski, *Vocation to Virtue*, 206.

4. John Paul II, *Man and Woman He Created Them*, 89:5.

5. John Paul II, *Man and Woman He Created Them*, 92:4.

6. John Paul II, *Man and Woman He Created Them*, 92:6.

7. John Paul II, *Man and Woman He Created Them*, 89:3.

8. John Paul II, *Man and Woman He Created Them*, 89:4.

9. John Paul II, *Man and Woman He Created Them*, 92:6.

10. John Paul II, *Familiaris Consortio*, 17.

The Final Two Days

1. John Paul II, *Vita Consecrata*, 30.

2. Lasnoski, *Vocation to Virtue*, 5.

3. Thérèse of Lisienx, *Story of a Soul*, trans. John Clarke (Washington, DC: ICS Publications, 1996), n.p.

Appendix C

1. John Paul II, *Vita Consecrata*, 16.

WORKS CONSULTED

Balthasar, Hans Urs von. *The Christian State of Life*. San Francisco: Ignatius Press, 1983.

———. *The Laity and the Life of the Counsels: The Church's Mission in the World*. Translated by Brian McNeil with D. C. Schindler. San Francisco: Ignatius Press, 2003.

The Catechism of the Catholic Church. New York: Doubleday, 1994.

Chapman, Gary. *The 5 Love Languages: The Secret to Love That Lasts*. Chicago: Northfield Publishing, 2015.

Dubay, Thomas. *Happy Are You Poor: The Simple Life and Spiritual Freedom*. San Francisco: Ignatius Press, 2003.

Erasmus, Desiderius. *The Praise of Folly*. Translated by Betty Radice. London: Penguin, 1971.

"Evangelical Counsels." In *The Catholic Encyclopedia*. New York: Robert Appleton Company. Accessed March, 2015, http:// www.newadvent. org/cathen/04435a.htm.

Hardon, John A. *Modern Catholic Dictionary*. Bardstown, KY: Eternal Life, 2008.

Hare, Douglas. *Interpretation: A Biblical Commentary for Teaching and Preaching—Matthew*. Louisville, KY: Westminster John Knox Press, 1993.

Himes, Michael J. *Doing the Truth in Love: Conversations about God, Relationships and Service*. Mahwah, NJ: Paulist Press, 1995.

John Paul II. *Encyclical Letter Veritatis Splendor*. Libreria Editrice Vaticana. Accessed February 6, 2015, http://w2.vatican.va/content/ john-paul-ii/en/encyclicals/documents/hf_jp-ii_enc_06081993_veritatis-splendor.html.

———. *Man and Woman He Created Them: A Theology of the Body*. Translated by Michael Waldstein. Boston: Pauline Books and Media, 2006.

———. *The Role of the Christian Family in the Modern World—Familiaris Consortio. Apostolic Exhortation of John Paul II*. Boston: Pauline Press, 1981.

———. *Vita Consecrata* [On the Consecrated Life and Its Mission in the Church and in the World]. Boston: Pauline Books and Media, 1996.

Lasnoski, Kent J. *Vocation to Virtue: Christian Marriage as a Consecrated Life*. Washington, DC: Catholic University of America Press, 2014.

McCarty, Julie. "Marital Spirituality and the Quest for Poverty, Chastity, and Obedience." *Spiritual Life* 45, no. 2 (Summer 1999): 84–93.

Merton, Thomas. *No Man Is an Island*. New York: Sheed and Ward, 1965.

Moloney, Francis J. *A Life of Promise: Poverty, Chastity, Obedience*. Eugene, OR: Wipf and Stock, 1984.

Mother Teresa. *No Greater Love*. Novato, CA: New World Library, 1989.

O'Collins, Gerald, and Edward G. Farrugia. *A Concise Dictionary of Theology*. Revised and expanded edition. New York: Paulist Press, 2000.

Paul VI. *Humanae Vitae: Encyclical Letter of Paul VI, Of Human Life*. Boston: Pauline Books and Media, 1968.

———. *Perfectae Caritatis* [Decree on the Adaptation and Renewal of Religious Life]. Libreria Editrice Vaticana. Accessed February 6, 2015, http://www.vatican.va/archive/hist_councils/ii_vatican_council/documents/vat-ii_decree_19651028_perfectae-caritatis_en.html.

Pinckaers, Servais. *The Pursuit of Happiness—God's Way: Living the Beatitudes*. Translated by Mary Thomas Noble. New York: St. Paul's Press, 1998.

Pius XI. *Casti Connubii* [Encyclical of Pope Pius XI on Christian Marriage]. Libreria Editrice Vaticana. December 31, 1930. Accessed February 6, 2015, https://w2.vatican.va/content/pius-xi/en/encyclicals/documents/hf_p-xi_enc_19301231_casti-connubii.html.

Second Vatican Council. "*Dei Verbum*: Dogmatic Constitution on Divine Revelation." In *Vatican Council II: Constitutions, Decrees, Declarations*, translated by Austin Flannery, 760–65. Northport, NY: Costello Publishing House, 1996.

———. "*Gaudium et Spes*: The Pastoral Constitution on the Church in the Modern World." In *Vatican Council II: Constitutions, Decrees, Declarations*, translated by Austin Flannery, 903–1001. Northport, NY: Costello Publishing House, 1996.

———. "*Lumen Gentium*: The Dogmatic Constitution on the Church." In *Vatican Council II: Constitutions, Decrees, Declarations*, translated by Austin Flannery, 350–425. Northport, NY: Costello Publishing House, 1996.

Stanton, Graham. *The Gospels and Jesus.* 2nd ed. New York: Oxford University Press, 2002.

United States Conference of Catholic Bishops. *Marriage: Love and Life in the Divine Plan.* Washington, DC: United States Conference of Catholic Bishops, 2009.

———. *Stewardship: A Disciple's Response.* Washington, DC: United States Conference of Catholic Bishops, 2002.

Dan and Amber DeMatte met while they served as missionaries for NET Ministries in 2004. Dan appeared on the A&E reality show *God or the Girl*, which followed his discernment to the priesthood or married life. The two married in 2007.

Dan is a Catholic speaker and youth minister who founded and serves as executive director of missions and advancement for Damascus Catholic Mission Campus. His book *Holiness Revolution* is part of Matthew Kelly's Dynamic Catholic program. Dan is the host of EWTN radio's *Encounter*.

Amber is a faith and fitness coach who volunteers in youth ministry, speaks at parish missions and women's conferences, and works at home raising the couple's four children.

The DeMattes live in Columbus, Ohio.

To bring Dan and Amber out to speak to your parish community, e-mail Dan DeMatte at Dan@HolinessRevolution.com.